About

Everything that happens in this story is completely fictitious as are all the characters and locations. However, the National treatment purchase fund is a very real entity that has had great success in helping to keep waiting lists under control. The fund is controlled and financed by offices within the Department of Health and not by International Insurance companies as is suggested in the story. There are no such hospitals as The Southwestern Clinic or the Holy Trinity University Hospital.

At the time of writing, there are ongoing negotiations between the Hospital Consultants and the Department of Health to complete and put in place a new contract for Hospital Consultants. These talks have taken over four years.

The plot is entirely a product of the author's imagination and has no basis in fact whatsoever. However, all of the Surgical and Perfusion techniques are scientifically correct as is any medical condition described, or at least to the best of the authors knowledge. Apologies are offered to anyone who finds any fact or technique to be scientifically inaccurate.

About the author

Noel Lynch has been working in the Irish Health Service for nearly twenty five years. Four years of that were in the Public Service in the Cardiology Department of a major University Hospital in Dublin, and the rest is in the Cardiac Surgery department of a large Private Hospital as a Perfusion Scientist. He studied in the Dublin Institute of Technology originally, graduating in 1990, and completed a Masters Degree in Primary Healthcare Management from the Royal College of Surgeons in Ireland, in 2003. He has written various scientific articles and papers for publication and presentation within the business of Cardiac Surgery and Perfusion. This is his first novel.

Noel Lives in Clontarf on the North side of Dublin with his Wife and two Daughters.

Glossary

Perfusion is the term used to describe the passage of fluid through tissue.

Perfusionists or Clinical Perfusion Scientists are members of the open-heart surgery team who are responsible for the operation of the heart-lung machine.

National Treatment Purchase Fund (NTPF): A fund set up in Ireland to take public patients waiting longest for procedures in public hospitals off waiting lists to have their treatment in a number of private hospitals.

Heart/Lung bypass machine: A machine which replaces the patient's heart and lungs during heart surgery.

Cardiopulmonary Bypass: The time that the patient is on the Heart/Lung machine

Oxygenator: an artificial lung used during heart surgery.

Priming: replacing all the room air in the oxygenators tubes and lines with a saline solution to ensure that the machine can be connected safely to a patient.

Cardioplegia: This is a mix of high doses of Potassium and Magnesium, in a very cold solution, used to paralyse a patient's heart.

Heparin: A drug which stops the blood clotting.

Intra Aortic Balloon Pump: It is a balloon that is threaded up the main artery in the leg and positioned outside the heart in the aorta. When the heart beats, the balloon inflates increasing the blood pressure

Coronary angiogram: A test where a dye had been injected into his coronary arteries and x-rayed.

Coronary Artery Disease: When the insides of the coronary arteries become coated with a substance known as plaque. The effect of this coating is to narrow and reduce the flow of blood down the artery. This reduces the supply of blood getting to the heart. This insufficient supply of blood to the heart muscle results in oxygen deprivation of the heart muscle and a pain across the chest known as "angina". If the supply is completely cut off, the section of heart muscle supplied by that artery will die, this is a Myocardial Infarction or a "heart attack".

Coronary Artery Bypass Grafts are when pieces of vein from the leg i.e. Saphenous veins or the Internal Mammary artery are implanted between the aorta and beyond the blocked or narrowed coronary arteries. The bypass grafts bridge the occluded or diseased coronary arteries and brings new blood to the heart.

Chest drains: These are tubes placed inside the chest during surgery of the chest coming out through the chest wall that drain any excess blood or fluids from around the heart and lungs.

Cardiac Tamponade: This is where blood fills the space surrounding the heart, restricting its movement and causing a dramatic drop in blood pressure.

Prologue

"MORE BLOOD PLEASE, quickly," the Anaesthetist called out, louder than usual.

"Four more units coming Doctor," answered one of the theatre nurses.

"Jesus, they made a right mess of this chap," the senior resident commented as he buried his hand, up to mid-forearm in the patient's chest to retrieve shotgun fragments. I had just arrived into the operating theatre, looking up at me, the Iranian surgeon with a grim look on his face said "I think we'll need to go on Bypass here Robbie, there's a large piece of shrapnel lodged in his right ventricle,"

"No problem, Khailid" I answered, "kit's all ready."

I ran out of the Operating theatre to fetch the Heart/Lung machine and passed two uniformed Gardai and a plain clothes detective with an Uzi sub-machine gun draped over his right shoulder standing outside the door of the theatre. The two uniformed police looked ridiculous with their neatly pressed uniforms and shiny black brogues covered by blue plastic overshoes and a blue shower cap. Theatre protocol had to be followed. The two uniforms helped me wheel the Machine from my equipment room to the double doors that opened into the operating theatre. As we manoeuvred the machine towards the theatre, curiosity overcame me and I asked: "What's with the reception committee and the hardware?" I nodded in the direction of the Uzi hanging over the detectives shoulder, "He a celebrity or something?"

The detective laughed. "Oh yes, celebrity all right," he answered in a thick Belfast accent, "do you not know who this fucker is?"

Curiosity now firmly aroused, I answered, "No, I was just called at home and told to get my arse into theatre double quick."

"You have the pleasure of patching up none other than Johnny McCullagh himself," the detective explained, "quartermaster general of the East-side boys. Shot by one of his own. Something to do with skimming off the top, I heard." He laughed with what appeared to be delight, "Wouldn't like to be in his shoes when Johnny boy gets out of hospital."

The thought of this stopped me in my tracks for an instant, and I began to wonder what would happen if I just walked away. The East Side boys were a notoriously vicious drug gang from a sprawling housing estate in the east of the city. They were renowned for their ruthless methods of cash collection from their customers. They modelled themselves on the West Side Boys, a gang of rebels in Sierra Leone, renowned for their drug and alcohol crazed killing sprees. Now, in Dublin, a well known drug dealer from this gang of animals, was on the operating table and would inevitably die if the team didn't pull out all the stops to save his life. What would letting him die do to the supply of drugs into the capital? My pondering was brought to an abrupt halt by the surgeon shouting for the defibrillator. "He's fibrillating, charge to 20, quick, shoot!"

I pushed the machine up to the operating table and joined the foray in doing what we were paid and morally bound to do. Khalid, the resident surgeon, was frantically trying to restart the heart which had been nearly ripped apart by the bullet fragments from a close range weapon. At the same time, he was also desperately trying to connect the patient to the Heart/ Lung machine, which would buy us some time. I switched into automatic mode, shaking off the remaining sleep that I had been prematurely snatched from, and joined the team in doing our job. The ink probably hadn't dried on my resignation yet. The main reason for my leaving was that I had had enough of this type of work. Midnight emergency calls were more and more coming a part of what used to be "routine" on-call stints. Over the past year or so, shootings, stabbings and general mayhem had become the staple diet of the midnight emergency calls to theatre.

I

"OK, GO ON BYPASS," the order was barked at me rather than given. This was the instruction to start the Heart/Lung bypass machine; in this case, it was the only chance to save this 52-year-old father of 4. He had suffered a massive Heart attack a week earlier. Thanks to his medical insurance, after a quick trip to the casualty of his local regional hospital he was transferred to the Southwestern clinic for investigation. He had undergone a battery of tests including a coronary angiogram, which revealed a heart condition affectionately known as "the widowmaker." Emergency Coronary Artery Bypass Graft surgery was recommended, and within 4 days of his condition being discovered he had been operated on, receiving 4 coronary artery bypass grafts, or in lay terms, a quadruple bypass.

The surgery had initially passed without incident and 16 hours after his return to the Intensive care unit he was doing well until a nurse noticed his chest drain bottle filling up rapidly. His blood pressure dropping rapidly led the Intensive care Nurse to conclude that he was suffering a Cardiac Tamponade. The patient was bleeding badly and something needed to be done quickly if he was to survive, so the nurse had started a cardiac emergency call that had brought the on-call operating team to his bedside. The surgical resident had decided to open his chest and find out what was going on.

And it wasn't pretty. One of the arteries that had been stitched on to his heart had torn off and blood was pouring out into the space around the heart. The heart was suffering from the restriction of the blood and also suffering because of the lack of blood flowing to where it was supposed to be going, down the artery to supply the muscle.

The situation had degenerated rapidly, and by the time I arrived, having been woken from a deep sleep by a phone call from the ITU nurse, the patient had suffered a cardiac arrest. The consultant surgeon had already arrived and was massaging the patient's heart to try to restore some blood supply to the patient's brain. The only option was to place the patient onto the Heart/Lung bypass machine. It would immediately restore circulation to the brain and allow the surgeon time to investigate further and repair whatever had caused the damage. He had already placed the tubes into the heart that would connect the patient to the Heart/Lung machine. My job was to set up, prime and operate the Heart/Lung machine. Normally night calls to the ITU involve a much less dramatic scene but tonight however we had a serious situation. In less dramatic circumstances, my presence at night calls was nearly always precautionary but 18 years experience had taught me to expect and be prepared for anything. Cardiac surgery was a sucker for Sod's law, so in this case, I decided to prepare for the worst and, sure enough within a few minutes of my arrival, I heard the Surgeon say to himself and the resident who was now standing on the left of the patient's bed "We'll have to get on bypass quickly here."

Finishing off the priming of the oxygenator, I pushed the Stokert SIII pump, about the size of a fridge on its side, alongside the bed. I connected the high-pressure air and oxygen hoses to a set of gas connections at a neighbouring bed. The occupant, a 48 year old man, 2 days after lung surgery was now wide awake and straining to see around the portable screen/curtains that the nurses had hastily placed around the next bed in an effort to try and block out the drama that was taking only metres away. Judging by the saucer eyes on the poor man, the screens were having little or no effect. Leaning over him to reach the gas connections, I smiled and assured him that the action was much less dramatic that it sounded and he could go back to sleep.

Before following the barked order, mentally I performed a quick system checklist. Normally I would have completed a full pre-bypass check list. This is modelled on the sorts of pre-flight checks that pilots carry out. But tonight so long as the basics were set up and functioning correctly, I intended to settle the patient onto the Heart/Lung system and then perform all the ancillary set-ups and check offs when the patient was stable. Initiating a cardiopulmonary bypass involves establishing a flow of Oxygen, ensuring full venous blood drainage from the patient and starting the main arterial pump, the artificial heart. Experience automatically took my eyes through a well-worn neural path. Starting with the large ½" tube, my eyes followed the tube leaving the gaping hole in the patient's chest, down the tube now full of saline, to the inlet of the reservoir. I was performing this visual check automatically as I was turning on the gas flow, set to 100% oxygen, as my right hand was moving down to the main control knob that would start the pump turning to start bringing badly needed oxygen-rich blood to the patients brain. My eyes followed the tubing circuit on through the pumphead, through the oxygenator, up the arterial side of the circuit, visually checking for breaks, leaks or air bubbles. My left hand was moving automatically towards the tubing clamp placed on the ½" line coming from the patients right Atrium. As soon as was appropriate, I would open this clamp, allowing blood to flow freely from the patient's heart to the Heart/Lung machine. My eyes were probably a millisecond ahead of my hands, and as I visually tracked the arterial line snaking up the side of the bed and disappearing back into the open chest, I was a hair's breath away from opening the clamp and turning the pump on when something came into my view. My peripheral vision caught something moving. I looked back a foot or so to where the aortic line was disappearing under a sterile green drape, an air bubble, about 1½ inches long, peeping out from under the sterile drape and dancing to the rhythm of the surgeon's hands massaging the heart. My right hand snapped back from the control knob of the pump as if I had received an electric shock. "There's a large bubble in the A-line, under the drape," I said, as calmly as I could. Turning the main control knob would have immediately driven the large bubble of air straight to the patient's brain. The result would undoubtedly be massive brain damage.

The surgeon, Peter Reddy, a 45 year old recently appointed consultant, responded by shouting the original order, only this time with a little embellishment, "Start the fucking pump, this man needs blood circulation, and he needs it now!"

I felt that starting a Heart/Lung bypass with a large air bubble in the arterial line whatever the circumstances was a career decision. I looked at the monitor above the patient's head noting the systolic blood pressure to be 65 millimetres of mercury, not bad considering that his heart was stopped and this pressure was being entirely generated by the hands of the surgeon. It was now decision time.

I explained as calmly as I could, "If he survives, but won't wake up, CT scan will show massive air embolus, my fault. If he doesn't make it, autopsy will show massive air embolus damage, again my fault so loose the air, please!" I was shaking with a combination of fear and anger as my voice started to rise.

Blue pyjama/scrub clothes equalise everyone on the operating team and a hat pulled low, coupled with a mask that hides the lower half of the face leaves only the eyes for non-verbal communication. At that moment his eyes said everything I needed to know.

He glared at me and, with venom in his voice having just had his authority challenged in front of the entire operating team and intensive care staff said, "I told you to go on bypass now!"

Now it really was decision time, "I'm too old for this shit" was the first thought through my head, the second was me standing in the Coroner's Court trying to explain away the fact that I pumped a large volume of air straight into a patient's brain. I there and then made a career decision. I stood up from the Heart/Lung machine, stepped away from the control consul, and trying to control the shake in my voice said "If you want to put this patient on bypass, do it yourself."

A hush had descended on the ITU at this stage and the tension was palpable, as was the knot in my stomach. He looked at me again, lowered his head and said nothing for a second. He mumbled something incomprehensible under his breath. I can only guess the content and it wasn't singing my praises. He instructed the assistant to take over the cardiac massage, tore the drape off the patient's lower chest and there in all its glory was the air bubble. He put a clamp on the tube, grabbed a scalpel from the sterile trolley, cut the arterial line at the point where it joined the cannula entering the patients aorta, bled out the air bubble re-connected the tube to the cannula and barked "Go!" Following the same procedure, I visually checked the circuit and this time, I started the pump.

Then came the long and difficult job of bringing all the blood parameters back onto an even keel. The patient had been without normal circulation for nearly 30 minutes and was hopefully surviving on the artificial cardiac massage that the surgeon was providing. Ninety minutes on the bypass pump had allowed the surgeon to stop the heart completely and allow him to reattach the artery that had torn off. Now came the difficult part, weaning the patient from the Heart/Lung machine. We anticipated great difficulty getting this patients heart to take up where it left off a few short hours ago.

With a drip stand resembling a Christmas tree, festooned with various coloured drug bottles and infusions, and a plethora of equipment such as artificial pacemakers, heart assist gadgets all throwing their tunes into the mix of beeps hisses and blips that was the midnight chorus of a busy intensive care unit, we set about trying to bring this heart back to life. Very slowly, we managed to cajole the heart into operating under its own steam again.

Other than an unintelligible grunt in my direction and a stream of instructions to the resident and intensive care staff, who now had the unenviable task of babysitting this poor patient for the rest of the night, Reddy didn't speak to me again as he noisily slapped his gloves off and marched in the direction of the waiting area where the patients family were, by now in a frantic state. I waited until the numbers on the monitor were of an acceptably high level, and until I saw Reddy leave the intensive care unit, I gave enough time for him to change and hopefully leave the building. Half an hour later I stood under the shower. Letting the scalding water pour over my back, I contemplated the night's events. The patient had made it through the emergency surgery. The question now remained whether the cardiac massage had been of sufficient quality to provide adequate circulation to the brain. I consoled myself with the fact that if the poor man didn't wake up, I had done what I thought was the right thing, and any amount of CT scans or post mortem tests couldn't point the finger at me for not doing my job properly. But still, that sickening feeling I always get from confrontations remained and I dreaded the river of shit that would probably follow when Reddy felt like sticking the knife in. He had powerful friends, he never tired of telling us and I imagined that they probably extended to the management of the hospital and whatever...I was totally drained, so I headed for the basement car park and home to try and sleep for the remaining hour or so left before I rose again to start my next shift. Having recently resigned from Holy Trinity University Hospital to work in the new Southwestern Private Clinic, falling for the promises of new equipment, research opportunities and mainly the prospect of mainly routine elective work and no more midnight battle zones. I began to wonder had I done the right thing.

2

FOR THE FIFTIETH TIME in the past hour Reddy craned his neck to check if his car was ok. From his position in the cramped office, he could, if he twisted slightly in the seat, see the boot and rear window of his new Mercedes CLK Kompressor. The gunmetal grey shone in the autumn sunshine. He hated this part of town and he hoped that his Merc would be in the same condition when this charade was over. The office was upstairs in a rundown building, on the periphery of the Financial Services district. It made him laugh that the address of this company required a lot of poetic licence to fool any clients into thinking that this low grade insurance company was part of the multi-million euro, glass and concrete jungle that was the beating heart of the Celtic Tiger. Some of the characters around the table looked like they had come straight from the unemployment office in Gardiner Street, or the methodone queue in Pearse street. He was attending a "Board Meeting" of Lighthouse Insurances Ltd.

"Board Meeting" that was a laugh. A bunch of lowlifes talking about the next deal that they could wrangle or con their way into.

He looked around the office. A pathetic attempt had been made to spruce up the office for the occasion. He wondered, as the only qualified professional on the "board," was the effort made to keep him sweet. It was amusing how the other men in the room tried to emulate the normal procedure of a real board meeting.

"Can I have a show of hands on dat ordur of de business" the chairman asked in his unmistakeable hoarse, north Dublin accent. "Doctor...Doctor, are you votin on dis eyerem?" The question was aimed directly at him and he was brought back from his dreaming.

"Oh...yes...of course...whatever," he stuttered with little enthusiasm. The chairman looked at him with disdain. He wasn't one of their own types, but they needed a professional on the board, it gave the company credibility.

"So, de motion is carried, dere will be an aggressive push to entur de car insurance business, and the good doctor here will help in the processing of any claims dat need medical reports." There was a ripple of low laughter.

He was staring back out at his Mercedes and the laughing made him turn his attention back into the room. He gave a quizzical look as he wondered if the laughing was directed at him. He smiled and joined in the chuckling. This seemed to make the others worse. He looked around at the other characters in the room, black leather, bald with a face full of scars, overweight and sweating profusely and smoking those sickening imported cigarettes. The room was full of smoke and sweat and stank like an All Blacks dressing room after a game. Also there was that sickening odour of Maple syrup that he got every time he came into this office. He felt that he could do with a shower as soon as he left here and went to the golf club in the sheltered cocoon of his Mercedes. He detested coming to these "meetings." They occurred every couple of months and pressure was always brought to bear to attend. He hated coming, he hated the characters, he hated the place but it was worth it. As a direct result of his involvement, his private practice was booming and he convinced himself that he was doing his bit to heal the poor of his native city. The chairman stood and this was the signal that the meeting was over.

"Lads, anyone going for a few scoops or some lunch?" the chairman announced. There were murmurs of approval all around. "You coming Doctor?" the chairman asked. "No, I'm due in surgery now," he lied, over his shoulder as he ran towards the door. He was teeing off in half an hour, followed by lunch in the clubhouse. Relieved, he hit the button on the key of his car. Climbing in, the smell of new leather and essence de showroom calmed him down.

"Thank Christ that's over," he said out loud as he slipped the car into drive and gently pulled away towards the city. The voice of Maria Callas singing Dom Epais from Lakme filled the cabin as he looked forward to celebrating a birdie in the clubhouse later with a large Dimple Scotch.

The chairman looked out the window at the Grey Mercedes spraying up stones and dust as it pulled away at speed. "We need to keep an eye on that prick," he said in a low voice.

The one in black leather and gold jewellery stood slightly behind his right shoulder. "No problem boss, I'll have one of the boys watch him, we need to keep him tight."

"Good lad," the chairman said, "he's a greedy bastard so there should be no problem, but watch him closely." He slapped his hands together loudly, "Right lads, lets get some lunch"

In a separate room, Patsy McGrane, a twenty two year old, recently released from a six month stretch for fraud worked feverously over the keys of a DELL Dimension 5150. Although he had left school at fifteen, with very little by way of formal education, a curious nature and a natural talent for computers had brought him to the attention of the management of Lighthouse Insurance services. Upon his release from prison, he had been offered a job as a researcher for the Insurance Company. He quickly set about reorganising their computer system and in a few weeks had set up an impressive database.

Today he had instructions to perform an internet search and find out as much about the make up of a standard Heart Surgery team, particularly the position of Perfusionist or

Clinical Perfusion Scientist. An Irish website told him that 'Perfusionists set up and control the equipment which enables a patient's heart and lungs to work during open heart surgery. During the operation, they monitor the heart and lungs and carry out procedures to keep the patient alive' Apparently, Perfusionists set up and control the heart-lung bypass equipment that takes over the functions of the heart and lungs during open-heart surgery. This equipment physically pumps blood around the body and oxygenates the blood, keeping a patient alive.' A few clicks later, he had a list of registered clinical Perfusion Scientists in the UK and Ireland and their email addresses. He printed this information off and handed it to his boss. Eamon Fitzpatrick, the "office manager" took the sheet of paper and closed the door on Patsy. Twenty minutes later, he approached the computer where Patsy was trying to look busy. "I want you to email this bloke here." He gave him the sheet of paper with one name highlighted. On the reverse of the sheet was a two line email. "Make sure that it can't be traced back to this office, OK?" Fitzpatrick dismissed Patsy with a wave. "Retard!" Patsy thought. In a few clicks, Patsy had created an anonymous email account and sent the message. He then quickly returned to his latest project, hacking into other peoples email accounts.

3

Crime Boss enjoys private medical treatment for free

The Irish Post has learned recently that the Crime boss Thomas "the Suit" Mulligan has been scheduled for Heart Surgery in the luxurious New South West Clinic in Dublin. According to a source inside the Department, this has been arranged under the Governments National Treatment Purchase fund within the next two weeks. This means that he will effectively skip the queue and enjoy the luxury of the €1000 a night Clinic at the taxpayer's expense. He was known to be suffering from a heart condition and was hospitalised recently. Sources within the Department of Health would not confirm or deny the report citing patient confidentiality. However a spokesman for the Department did state that if Mr. Mulligan qualified under the scheme, then he would be transferred to a participating hospital. In the Dail Chamber today, Labours spokeman on Health questioned the minister about the Gardai's interest in Mr Mulligan, and the fact that the Criminal Assets Bureau had been investigating him. The Minister would only say that these alleged facts had no bearing on a patient's right to qualify under the scheme. Mr O'Meara pressed the Minister, citing cases of honest taxpaying citizens having waited years for Heart Surgery and this known criminal enjoying the benefits of the Treatment Purchase fund when according to a Garda source, "the Criminal Assets Bureau had enough information on him to show that he probably

**had enough cash spirited away to build his own hospital."
A heated exchange followed during which Mr O'Meara
accused the Minister of Justice of being soft on crime
and The Minister of Health of having his eye seriously off
the ball with regard to the manner in which Department
funds were being squandered. Before being called to
order, the Minister of Health stated that he would have
officials controlling the National Treatment Purchase
fund investigate to ascertain that only appropriately
deserving cases were treated under the plan.**

I arrived at work at the South Western Clinic at 7.30, a state
of the art new private hospital built in a rundown part of
Dublin, in a tax incentive zone. The clinic was built by a
consortium of Medical Insurance companies with help from
the recent Department of Health's public/private partnership
agreements.

I lived about 8 miles from the Hospital, about a 30 minute
cycle. After changing into theatre scrubs, I switched on the
computer in my office, and then headed to the Secretary's
office to check for any last minute changes to the Operating
list. The list today showed three sets of coronary grafts and an
Aortic valve replacement.

Opening my e-mail, I found the standard information
bulletins from various different departments in the hospital.
The usual mix of inter departmental mumbo-jumbo filled
the email box. I noticed near the bottom of the list was an
e-mail with an address I didn't recognise. It looked like one
of those spam emails offering a million bucks, guaranteed.
It came between the offer for cheap last minute getaways to
Paris and how to obtain my PhD online. It was titled "use
your skills to earn easy money." It had come from a Hotmail
address, opportunity@hotmail.com. The message was that if I
was interested, then I was to reply to the e-mail. I hit "select
all" and "delete." I gathered the kit for the first case. This was

a standard Coronary bypass graft procedure. I primed the equipment and twenty minutes later I was sitting in the tea room enjoying a mug of coffee, with a couple of slices of toast. There was the gentle lull of conversation from the weekend, but the main topic of conversation seemed to be the article in the newspaper concerning the crime boss, who was scheduled for heart surgery here in the Southwestern Clinic. The NTPF had had an impressive effect on the Heart Surgery waiting list, but I wondered what would happen or how I would feel if after having paid expensive medical insurance for years, I ended up in a bed in a private hospital next to a criminal who had been granted free private treatment under the NTPF scheme.

By 9 o'clock the patient was in the operating theatre, having undergone a full anaesthetic procedure, which included strategically placed drips, an epidural injection and various blood pressure monitoring drips. Having been put asleep using a cocktail of narcotics and hypnotic agents, a tube was placed down his throat to connect him to the ventilator, the breathing machine.

After having been wheeled into the operating room, the patient was painted from head to toe in a sterile paint and then covered in sterile green drapes. There was a general air of quiet efficiency and friendly banter between the different members of the team. Consultant Anaesthetist, Dr. Jonathan Sapsford was conducting the Anaesthetics. The Surgical residents got underway with the start of the procedure; this involves the junior resident taking out the vein from the inside of the calf. The other more experienced resident opened the chest by splitting the breastbone down the centre. He then would dissect the internal mammary artery out from the inside of the chest wall. One end of this would be attached to one of the coronary artery's also providing a new flow of blood down the previously blocked artery. All this preparatory work takes place usually before the Consultant Surgeon arrives.

I set up my equipment to the table, handing the sterile tubes to the nurse. They were checked, clamped and positioned, ready to place in the heart and connect to the Heart/Lung machine. Having completed my set up, I retired to my office to catch up on the usual paperwork. I filled a coffee mug and opened my email again. I replied to the few internal emails that I hadn't deleted. I needed to send a request for some extra shelving to the technical services department and having just deleted an email from the secretary; I opened the "deleted items box." It was full of spam mail. Retrieving the deleted mail, I copied the address from the text of the mail, pasted it to the new mail I was writing and hit "send." The screen reverted back to the "deleted items" page and I noticed the email with the "opportunity" address. This type of spam mail normally offers degrees, masters and PhDs by submitting your credit card details to an unheard of university in Alabama or Mississippi. But this email was different. Something about the language didn't add up to the usual cheesy phraseology used in these types of emails. Although it didn't mention my name anywhere in the text, it seemed to be aimed directly at me. I stared at it for a few moments, and was interrupted by the floor nurse calling me, "The heparin has been given, Robert." This was the point where the resident or surgeon was ready to begin putting the tubes into the heart that would connect the patient to the Heart/Lung machine. I emptyied the contents of the computers trash can, closed my email and headed to theatre.

As I arrived, Dr. Sapsford the Anaesthetist was checking that the clotting time had increased enough to ensure that the patients' blood wouldn't clot when the Heart/Lung bypass machine was started. He had a worried look on his face. "Would somebody kindly fetch Niall?" he asked. The floor nurse left the room to call Professor O'Riada. "Ah, Robert," he looked at me.

"What's the problem Dr. Sapsford?" I inquired as I sat in the seat in front of the control consul. I immediately started my mental pre-bypass checklist. Part of this checklist was to check the patient monitor. This shows the patients vital signs including the electrocardiogram, the blood pressure, and various other readings. On checking the monitor, I immediately saw what was concerning Dr. Sapsford. The patient's heart was beginning to show signs of trouble.

"She's getting quite ischaemic," explained Dr. Sapsford.

"Yes, I see the ECG," I answered. Hopefully it would revert to normal soon, but this was showing that the patient wasn't tolerating the stress of the surgery very well so far. The surgeons hadn't even begun to operate on the heart yet.

"Her pressures haven't changed yet," he explained, "but I've increased the GTN to 20mls/hr and the ST segments are still abnormal. I think we need to get on bypass quickly here." This patient was beginning to get quite sick, and at any moment could have a major event. The calm and unflappable manner, in which Dr. Sapsford was conducting the anaesthetics, was helping the patient to stay on the right side of the Pearly Gates.

The clotting time counter was ticking away at 390 seconds. This showed that the drug to stop the blood clotting was working and the number was sufficiently high to allow us to use the Heart/Lung bypass system. Just then, Professor O'Riada walked into the room. "What's the problem guys?" he asked while leaning over the sterile barrier at the patient's head and looked into the gaping hole in the chest revealing the patient's heart and lungs. The heart had gotten progressively worse over the past few minutes and was now visibly struggling. Dr. Sapsford was busily adjusting drug rates, drips and injecting various different concoctions into the array of drips and lines disappearing under the drapes.

"She's gone very ischaemic Niall," Dr Sapsford explained without looking up from the syringe he was injecting. The senior resident had almost finished dissecting out the internal mammary artery. Professor O'Riada looked at the numbers on the monitor. "Stop where you are Hassan, and stick the tubes in, we need to get on bypass straight away here," he instructed the resident and walked quickly to the scrub area where he began to scrub up for the operation himself.

I was as prepared for the Heart/Lung bypass as I could possibly be, but again I walked myself through my mental checklist. This time I started my "what ifs." I always try to visualize as many problems as possible that could occur during a Bypass run. I will then run through what I would do about them if they occurred. This in my opinion gives you a headstart if a problem occurs. You have put yourself into problem solving mode and if you have mentally rehearsed a scenario that actually occurs, then you are more likely to be able to react correctly in the first vital few seconds and not act like a rabbit caught in headlights for the first minute of a critical situation. I looked up, just as Professor O'Riada was walking in from the scrub area, now dressed in a long green sterile gown and gloves. The blood pressure was approaching critically low levels by now and the Resident was furiously trying to stitch in the tubes. The junior resident was helping him.

"You OK, Hassan?" asked the Professor.

"Almost ready, Professor," he replied.

I looked up and laughed, Professor O'Riada was at that very moment positioned in the fully back position of his golf swing. He was studying the position of his hands. "Jonathon," he was asking Dr Sapsford, "are my wrists rotating too much on the backswing?"

Dr Sapsford looked up above his glasses perched on the end of his nose. "Niall," he replied with pity, "how many times have I told you to use the club professional, you're a great surgeon but a lousy golfer."

"Ready Professor" interjected Hassan, the resident. This scene was typical of Professor O'Riada, maintaining a sense of complete calm in a crisis. He stepped to the table and the work began in earnest, and with unnecessary politeness, ordered, "On bypass please Robert."

I released the clamps, started the oxygen flowing and turned the Heart/Lung pump on. Within five minutes the patient's paralysed heart was clamped out of the circulation. Once the heart was stopped, and the lungs switched off, Professor began to attach the pieces of the veins and mammary arteries to the diseased coronary arteries. Two hours later, the Patient was in the Intensive Care unit having had three difficult coronary artery grafts. The procedure had been quite difficult and although the atmosphere was quite tense throughout the surgery, Professor O'Riada's calm and controlled demeanour was infectious and the surgery passed off peacefully and sucessfully.

4

Minister announces expansion of National treatment Purchase Fund

The Minister of health today announced an increase in funding for the National Treatment Purchase fund. The fund was set up 5 years ago and to date, over 15000 patients have benefited from the fund, these varying from children's tonsillectomy up to major heart surgery. The fund was to be wound up this year as the original €34 million is set to run out at the end of the year. However, this expansion has received mixed reactions from both the Opposition and patient groups. While the chairman of the Patients support group welcomed the move, the leader of the Opposition called it a "blatant scam to buy votes," Edward Barry, leader of Fine Gael accused the minister of throwing money at the problem, while unchecked spending went on in the Hospital services. Mr Barry quoted figures of a 300% increase in funding of the Health service in the life of this administration resulting in a 20% increase in overall staff numbers in the health services only being accompanied by a 5% increase in the numbers of patients being treated. He was particularly scathing of some of the rules of the expanded scheme, these include patients without medical insurance part-funding their surgery and treatment in private hospitals. He called this "a new low in Tatcherite economics," and the "Americanisation of our health system." A spokesman for patient support groups, said that "anything that

reduced the waiting lists and took patients off trolleys in Accident & Emergency departments, was worth trying.

7.45PM FRIDAY:

The fourth and hopefully last patient of the day was being wheeled back to the Intensive care unit having undergone a successful combined heart operation of a Mitral valve replacement and two coronary artery bypass grafts. I was strolling alongside the bed listening to the Consultant Anaesthetist wax lyrical about how she was taken to the cleaners by a rogue builder on the construction of a conservatory. "It's because I'm a woman," she ranted.

The porter pushing the bed was hanging on her every word and nodding appropriately, adding comments, "definitely," "they are such a bunch of cowboys," and such gems as, "if they were only half as contentious about their jobs as you are Doctor." I knew he was taking the piss big style, but it was having the desired effect, as the story was getting more and more dramatic. I thought of telling her that there was a more than evens chance that the builder's company no longer existed. But I was tired and I just wanted to get out of here as fast as possible. Any contributions to this story would inevitably prolong the suffering. Mick, the porter, with the body of a silverback gorilla, and occasionally a brain to match, steered the bed skilfully into the bed space vacated for this patient.

Walking back from the Intensive Care Unit, Mick the Silverback caught up with me and started. "You know what she needs, don't you?" An image of a dominant male of the species leapt to mind, lazily crawling through the rainforest, servicing his harem of females. This brought a smile to my face but I didn't want to go down this particular boulevard of conversation.

"Hey Robbie," he shouted after me as I wandered back to my office, "fancy a pint?" This was normally the last thing I would think of after a day stuck with people who had the

23

conversational skills of iguanas, but a little lowbrow non-threatening conversation was as good as therapy after 12 hours stuck in a 20 x 20 room with no daylight. "Yeah, why not," I was almost surprised to hear myself say. "See you downstairs in 10." He gave me thumbs up and with a grin like a Chinaman who has just won the lotto, and disappeared into the porter's room.

Twenty minutes later, we walked into the bar of O'Learys pub. An old bar 5 minutes from the hospital that had up until recently retained the "no women in the bar" rule. It didn't look like much money was spent on décor, and the old fake leather seats, suffering from years of abuse as was the carpet that contrasted well with the huge 52" plasma screen television that dominated one corner of the room. I wondered if the bars on the windows were positioned to keep burglars out or to keep the poor buggers from escaping when they had broken in and were caught trying to lift the set off the wall. Judging by the state of some of the characters sitting at the bar, I didn't think that burglary was a concern in this particular establishment.

A lot of Dublin bars had started implementing the government's smoking ban, which made the occasional visit to a pub a comparatively pleasant experience. However this particular saloon wasn't having any of it. The air was thick with smoke. Rupert Murdoch was showing his world domination as one of the SKY sports channels was on announcing the statistics for the first half of a high profile Premiership showdown. Silverback gave a "oh shit, I forgot about this game," turning to me, giving me that male bonding look that suggested that I was now in for a real treat. Without consulting me, he called "two pints, Joe please" to a harassed looking barman about half his size who was wrestling with the dispenser of a monstrous catering size vodka bottle. He looked up from his vodka bottle, "Oh Mick, how's it going?" he asked in the thickest country accent I have ever heard. "Great, Joe," answered Silverback, then nodding in the direction of the TV asked "Any score?"

"Two fucking nil," was the disgusted update as Country Joe gave his total loving attention to putting two perfect creamy heads on the two pints of Guinness, I hadn't noticed the plethora of football memorabilia screaming the pubs undying support for the loosing team. We took our pints of black and found a quiet corner with a good view of the game and sat down.

I threw my black bomber jacket on the back of the seat. There were at least a dozen of them strewn across the backs of seats in this particular fashion Mecca, I looked like one of the locals, but perhaps that wasn't a bad thing in a place like this. I sat back in the seat and while trying to expose as little of my clothes as I could to the filthy upholstery, downed a third of the pint in one gulp. "Christ, that's good Mick," I said.

"Told you," replied Mick while he swallowed about half the pint in one long sup as he animatedly patted the pockets of his jacket looking for his cigarettes. He found them, lit up and relaxed back while studying the TV screen as the second half of the game got underway.

The game was revving up good style, and the half of the occupants of the bar that weren't playing dominoes or darts, were giving dog's abuse to the house team that appeared to be struggling to stay in touch. Mick was lifting his glass for the second sup, which undoubtedly would have emptied the glass. Leaving a man with an empty pint glass in a place like this was almost as bad as being a Garda. I caught country Joe's eye and gave him the victory sign. He nodded and 5 minutes later, two more creamy pints of stout arrived to the table carried by a skinny kid with a short top, belly button pierced, and an unrepeatable message printed on her tee shirt. Her greasy blonde hair was tied back in a ponytail. "Seven euro twenty," she said in a bored chant.

"Has your Da read that tee shirt, Chantal?" Mick asked laughing. I handed her a twenty-euro note, wondering what the standard tipping charge was in a place like this.

"He went bleedin mentel," she grinned at Mick revealing

teeth, which probably hadn't seen much of a toothbrush, never mind a dentist.

The match was now into extra time and it obviously didn't turn out the way the local supporters would have liked, as there was a general sense of disgust and dismay from the majority present. The final whistle sounded to general gloom and attentions shifted away from the cinema screen to lay siege to poor country Joe who now had the unenviable task of pulling thirty or forty consolation pints all at the same time. "Give me a fuckin minute," he barked at one bald, lanky young kid in a Nike tracksuit with two protruding front teeth, who called his order ignoring the large crowd that was waiting long before he had approached the bar. He reminded me of a Beano character.

Another pint was given the final treatment as Joe gave tracksuit a dressing down. "You're lucky to be served here at all," he went on, "after the behaviour of you and your mates last week, you'll wait your turn."

"Sorry Joe," tracksuit was trying to look suitably contrite, while trying to stop himself laughing. He looked the youngest of his mates, about nineteen or twenty, just old enough to drink, but probably considered middle aged around these parts. A group of about six had just walked in and were sitting at a table 12 feet or so from the bar and were giving him some stick as he took it like a man from Country Joe.

I turned to silverback as he was searching his pockets for something. He had a huge mischievous grin on his face. His smile was infectious, "I thought you were a United supporter," I remarked with a grin.

"I am...usually," he said slyly, "but 16 to 1 against them tonight was worth a tenner." He found the betting slip, kissed it, folded it neatly, and with reverence, placed it in the inside pocket of his jacket.

"Jammy fucker," I laughed. My amusement quickly evaporated when I remembered the 4 or 5 thousand that I still owed from my days of nonsensical and frequent gambling. With help from a therapist and a huge amount of support and patience from my wife, I had kicked that habit. However this one debt remained with a bookmaker who gave me a lot of latitude in paying back. He probably hoped that the longer I took to repay, the more likely I was to fall off the wagon. I nodded in the direction of tracksuit and his mates, "What's the story with Plug and the bash street kids?"

Mick exploded laughing, "Jaysus, you're spot on there, he's the ugliest fucker I've ever seen. Hey, Lanky," Mick shouted over, Plug looked up, "Robbie here's found you a new nickname." I nearly passed out with fright.

"Christ Mick," I whispered viciously, "shut up will you, I don't want to start a fight." Mick laughed, "Don't worry, he's as thick as horseshit, here come on over, they're a nice bunch of lads." "Oh shit," I thought, "this is the last thing I need." "Actually Mick, I think I'll head off, I've an early start," I started to get up, finishing my drink and grabbing my jacket.

"You're going nowhere," Mick stood up, and taking both jackets moved towards the group "You're going to help me spend some of this money I just won."

"OK, just one more for the road" I said resignedly, but he was already halfway across the floor with both our jackets, and I knew better than to try to reason with Mick, anyway, another one or two pints would make things bearable. We joined the group; Mick had already pulled up two stools, as the group moved their chairs back to allow us to join in. Mick obviously knew them well as greetings and insults were exchanged all around. I was astonished how he was getting away with these easy insults, but it quickly became obvious that they all held great respect for Mick.

He introduced me to the entire group and called the lovely Chantal over. "Drinks lads?" He looked around at everyone. Chantal looked mightily pissed off as she rummaged in her oversized jeans for something on which to write down the order. He continued the introductions and eventually she arrived with an overflowing tray, six pints of Guinness and Cider, and a couple of bottles of one of those designer American beers. One apparent red herring was a glass of mineral water. This was taken by a young quiet chap in the corner. He had the appearance of some with a chronic illness. I watched him for second, bloated features, under sized and weight. I guessed liver or kidney disease. Probably waiting for a transplant. His white Nike tee-shirt made a brave attempt to cover his bloated stomach. I realised I was staring and looked away quickly.

The round set Mick back over thirty Euro and he threw her two twentys saying "Keep the change luv."

"You win the fuckin lotto or something Mick?" asked Plug.

"Let's just say, I don't bet on losers," replied Mick, nodding in the direction of one of the group, who had made the fatal mistake of wearing a Man Utd tee-shirt, and was going to suffer for the rest of the night.

The conversation flowed for a while about all the standards, Man Utd, The Premiership, the horse racing results for the previous weekend and tips were exchanged for the upcoming weekend race meeting. I had no more than a passing interest in the Premiership and thanks to an Iraqi hypnotherapist, no longer an interest in horse racing. I threw in the occasional comment but generally kept quiet.

Suddenly one of the group with a pierced eyebrow looked up and half whispered to Plug sitting next to him, "Here's Macker."

There was instant silence as everyone in the group looked up at a tall thin bloke in his late thirties or early forties. Dressed all in black with an expensive looking leather jacket, he wore heavy gold chains round his neck hanging over a starched white tee-shirt. He half walked, half strutted across the floor. His extremely high forehead turned into jet black greased hair that fell loosely above his shoulders. He wore a pencil moustache and this immediately reminded me of Fredo Corleone from The Godfather. His eyebrows almost met which gave him a permanent scowl. Looking in our direction, his face broke into a huge grin as he caught sight of Mick who was getting to his feet with an equally devious grin.

"Macker," Mick said with a laugh, "I didn't know you were out."

Macker stretched his hand out to Mick, "How's the big man?" he asked with obvious fondness. "Still working in that dead end portering job, why don't you come and work for me?" he asked. I was intrigued by this exchange.

"It pays the mortgage and keeps me out of trouble, besides if I worked for you, I'd probably end up sharing that 8 by 8 in the Joy with you," Mick replied.

Macker called himself a drink and immediately retrieved a pack of cigarettes from his inside pocket. He lit up and added to the blue cloud hanging over our table. Given the circumstances, I was actually enjoying myself. And another pint of black cream appeared in front of me. I reminded myself to get a round in at the next opportunity and not commit the fatal offence of being shy with the bucks, particularly in a place like this. The three pints I had consumed so far were beginning to work their magic.

Mick and Fredo finished catching up and then Macker, turning to me asked Mick, "Who's your mate?"

"Oh sorry, lads," Mick explained, "Robbie Valentine, from work." I stuck my hand out to accept the tanned, bejewelled hand of Fredo. "Terry McCarthy," he introduced himself. "Call me Macker," he added giving me a look that for a second scared the shit out of me. It was as if he was looking directly into my mind. "What the hell!" I gave myself a mental slap; I definitely was working too hard.

"You from round here?" he asked.

"No," I answered, "but I went to school down the road."

"Really, where?" he asked with interest.

"St Finbars CBS," I replied.

"Get away!" he laughed. "I went there too, yeah. I was asked to leave in '78, know what I mean, yeah?" he replied laughing. I got the message and made no further queries.

He went on, "I went to South docks tech after Finbars."

"Tough school, I believe," I commented.

"Let's just say I learned more than the periodic table and Ovid selections, yeah?" he added. Surprised by this obtuse reference to science and Latin poetry, I started to make a few benign comments about the Latin and science teachers in Finbars. His references and comments about school gave me the distinct impression that he had received much more of an education than he revealed to his cronies. "You a porter too?" he asked.

"No, I wish," I answered, "I'm called a Perfusionist, I work in Heart Surgery. I run life support machines during heart surgery."

"No shit!" he replied, "are you a Doctor?"

"Actually I'm not," I launched off into the standard explanation of my job.

"Bet you must have had to do some serious studying for that job, yeah?" he asked with interest.

"Yeah" I suppose so," I answered. "I have a degree in Clinical Science and I've just finished some management stuff," I explained.

"Shit, you're a devil for punishment," Mick added.

Fredo was evidently quite interested in my line of work, "So are you there during the operation?" he inquired. I continued with my standard explanation, "During most Heart operations the heart needs to be stopped and paralysed. So an artificial heart is required." The rest of the group sat up and listened. As much as I hated talking about my job for any length, I was glad of the opportunity to contribute more than nods and uhuh's to the conversation. "My job is to set up, and manage the artificial heart during the operation." I had the complete interest of the group now and one or two of them started asking questions. Normally I changed the subject quickly but tonight they were having none of it.

"So where would you be in the operating theatre?" Baldilocks with the pierced eyebrow asked.

"The machine is about the size of a fridge and it's placed right next to the patient so the tubes can be as short as possible." Fuelled by Arthur Guinness, I continued, revelling in the alcohol induced attention. "The heart and lungs are switched off and I keep the patient alive for the duration of the operation."

"So you see everything that is going on?" asked one.

"Yeah, the patient is where you are," I indicated to where he was sitting, "and I am here," I pointed to my chair, about three feet from his position.

"Jaysus!" was one response, then Fredo piped up, "I couldn't do that, I can't stand the sight of blood, it makes me puke, yeah?" Two or three others burst out laughing. "Christ, Macker, it didn't bother you when you put that fucker from Cork in hospital," one brave soul offered. Macker shot him an icy glare that brought instant silence. "Don't open your mouth about that again," he said slowly with venom. "Sorry Macker, I was only sayin..." came the contrite response. "Well don't, yeah?" Macker closed down that avenue.

A short awkward silence was broken by Macker turning to me and continuing the interrogation about my line of work. "So you actually keep them alive during the operation, yeah?" he asked.

"Yeah, and when the patient is on the life support machine, I would look after the anaesthetics as well." The smallest of the group, the one I suspected was in some organ failure, asked in a strangely adult voice that was in total contrast to his childlike build, "Is that like a dialysis machine?"

"Yeah," I replied. "A dialysis machine does the work of the kidneys, a heart\lung machine replaces the heart and lungs."

In a strange way I was enjoying this. Normally any sort of detail about what I did for a living bored or sickened a lot of people, but I found this level of interest flattering.

"Sounds like quite a responsible sort of job, yeah?" Macker commented.

"Suppose so," I muttered into my drink as I drained another pint. Before I knew it, another tray of drink arrived. I struggled to pull my wallet from my jeans to pay, but Macker was having none of it. "No Macker," I tried to interject but he made a big deal about patting me on the back saying "It's great to meet one of the lads from the old school, yeah?" I resigned, sitting back, resolving to myself to catch Chantal by stealth at an opportune moment. I was by this stage getting quietly pissed. I tended to talk a lot and waffle myself into trouble.

"Does a job like that pay well?" Macker continued the inquiry. "Yeah, I suppose so" I answered, "we are paid as Medical Scientists, pretty good but nowhere near what the Doctors are."

"Those blokes are on big bucks I suppose, yeah?" Macker asked.

"Some of them drive cars that cost more than my house" I said. Mick perked up, "Yeah, most of the Surgeons drive top of the range Mercs, over 150 large." "So what do you do yourself Macker," I asked with a slightly slurred voice, the result of the five pints of Guinness. Two or three of the group stifled a laugh and I felt a tap on my ankle, and I moved my leg mumbling an apology to Mick. What I didn't realise was that it was a kick from Mick.

"Oh, I run a Security Company," Macker explained.

"There's a big demand for that nowadays," I went on.

"Who are you fuckin telling?" Macker replied, "especially with some of the knackers around here, yeah?" He nodded in the direction of the rest of the group. I had noticed on the keyring that Macker placed on the table was a new remote-key with the distinctive Jaguar logo emblazoned on it. I pressed on while I paid for another round, "Is it your own company Macker?" I asked.

"No, a mate owns it but I'm hoping to buy in to it soon, yeah? I'm fed up working for the bleedin taxman." "When did you starting paying tax Macker?" came a drunken remark from one of the group. Fredo shot him an icy glance.

"Doesn't it make you sick to see the difference between the gross salary and the number in the bottom right corner?" I rambled on.

"Thought you said that your job paid well?" Macker asked casually.

"Oh, it's not bad," I said, "but you know how difficult it is to put cash away for the rainy day, y'know the kids and stuff, and to clear off the bills."

"Yeah, I know what you mean," answered Macker with knowing nods from one or two of the lads.

"Imagine that one big win on the lotto," I mused.

"Yeah, that one big score," said a gangly young Rodney Trotter lookalike called Sully.

"Ah well," I said resignedly, "to sleep," Macker picked up and in his rough inner city accent, completed, "perchance to dream." I stood up to comments from both Fredo and Silverback, "You're not goin are ye Robbie?" "No, lads," I slurred, and headed a little unsteadily out to the toilet.

Standing in the toilet thinking, I could have sworn I got the faint whiff of maple syrup. "Strange" I thought to myself. I mused about how different this group were from my own circle of friends. Restaurants and concerts were the normal social outlet for Victoria and myself. My mind wandered and eventually came to rest on the stupid mistakes I had made some years ago. I had had a gambling problem owing €4500 to a sleazy bookie.

But the worst part of it was that I did all this without the knowledge of my wife. I was desperately trying to service it on the quiet. The usual sickening feeling came over me. I pushed it to one side and started thinking about Macker and the other colourful characters. I wondered what they really got up to and how Mick was so friendly and so casual with them. I looked at my watch and was shocked to see the time was 11.20. When I returned most of the group had dispersed leaving only Mick, Macker and one of his cohorts. There was a fresh pint on the table at my place. I sighed to myself, "I'm going to be in shit state in the morning."

Mick laughed as he took another quaff from his new pint, "Ah stop complaining Robbie," he said, "your problem is that you don't get out enough."

"I know Mick," I replied as I struggled to attack the new drink.

"That job of yours sounds like it has a lot of responsibility, yeah?" Macker piped up.

"Yeah, I suppose so," I mumbled.

"Can anything go wrong?" he inquired.

"Well if the system breaks down while the heart is paralysed, I've got to find the problem and fix it within a couple of minutes or else the patient will be left brain dead," I answered. We have safety and backup systems all designed to make the Heart/Lung machines safer. Also loads of check-off systems, and the equipment is so well maintained that failure is an extremely rare event.

Macker started making further inquiries, "So when the patient is on this bypass system, you are keeping them alive?"

"Yeah," I replied.

"Must be a very interesting job, yeah?" he went on.

"Yeah, but after a while it gets routine." Five pints of Guinness was making me feel a bit melancholic. I was nearly twenty years doing this and although I still enjoyed the fact of being at the very frontline of modern heart surgery, I was getting tired of the politics and all the bullshit that entailed, it began to show, it dawned on me a long time ago that as much as I thought of myself and my chosen profession, we were really only pawns. This was made clear to me on more than one occasion after near misses, or procedures that had less than favourable outcomes. I had been questioned by Surgeons, Anaesthetists and even on one occasion, Hospital lawyers. I realised that the object of the exercise of questioning me was more of looking for someone to blame and less of searching for the truth. "There's a lot of politics and power playing goes on in medicine and most of it is crap," I rambled.

"It sounds like you have a lot of power with what you do," Macker pressed on.

"Not really," I replied, "I'm really just a technician, I do what ever I'm told by the medics." I had fallen into the trap of a little flattery and I was off. "The Doctors and Surgeons have medical defence and insurance to protect themselves, but as a small cog in a very big wheel, I am on my own when the shit hits the fan."

Macker's demeanour had by now to me turned into something of a confessor. "Surely you have some sort of professional insurance cover?" He seemed surprised.

"Yeah, I am insured under the employer's professional liability cover, so by rights, they are legally obliged to defend me in case of me fucking up and killing someone." I was now seriously rambling, but Macker had a way of appearing interested in everything I had to say. "It pisses me off big time that when it suits the top cat medics I am an..." I mimed quotation marks in the air to emphasise my point, "important part of the team, a professional allied to surgery, a vital cog in the wheel, but when the shit hits fan, I'm really only a dispensable technician."

Macker shifted closer to me, and almost assumed the position of a priest in confession. Still gobbing off about the system, I went on, "As soon as there are any problems like a patient not waking up, the first person they look at is the Perfusionist, even if it's the surgeon or anaesthetist that has screwed up. What pisses me off big time also is that the top cats get big money for every operation, I get a day's wages, and you know how hard it is to stay on top moneywise, particularly when you have debts." My mind returned to my flirtation as a gambler

"You got money problems?" Macker asked.

"I ran up some gambling debts a couple of years ago and lost a few quid with that telecom debacle, I'm still trying to get on top of them," I replied. I was brought back to earth by my mobile phone beeping with a text message. "Don't wake the kids when you get in," was the short sharp message. It was Vickie, my wife's way of saying, "Where the hell are you?" I looked at my watch and was shocked to see that it was gone midnight. There seemed to be no let up in the service at the bar and there was no movement from Mick who was now in a heated debate about the new Ireland manager.

I stood up put my jacket on and stuck out my hand to Macker, "Sorry to hit you with all that crap Macker, the job's pissing me off big style lately and it's nice to talk to someone who gives a shit."

"Hey! No problem mate," he said with what seemed like genuine affection, "we all need to let off steam occasionally, yeah?"

I shouted "Seeya Monday Mick." He looked up, "Aah, you not coming to a club?"

"No way Mick!" I laughed, "I'm up at 7 in the morning, no mercy from the kids, they don't care that it's Saturday."

"Your loss," he grinned, nodding in the direction of a group of girls who were sitting next to him. "Enjoy yourself,"

I waved. Macker slapped me on the back and winked, "Talk to you again Robbie, no doubt, yeah?"

"Cheers Macker, nice to meet you," I said. For a second I thought, did I miss something here, is he gay or something. I laughed to myself, as I headed towards the door, Arthur could really make you paranoid. Macker was just a nice guy, who was a good listener and had a patient manner. After all he did come from a rough area and had done reasonably well for himself. He had gone to the same school and had showed camaraderie. I wandered out into the night. It had turned into a damp night with that drizzle that doesn't feel like rain but soaks you through. I had about a twenty minute walk before I caught a cab.

I arrived home at 1am. The more I tried to be quiet, the louder I became and when I eventually climbed into bed, after the regulation couple of glasses of water, I lay on my back staring into space. "Don't forget you're bringing Alice to ballet tomorrow," Victoria broke the silence, and it was obvious from the tone of her voice that she had been awake for some time.

"Oh, no problem," I lied. I had forgotten and now I knew that I was on a looser. I was now as well as facing a mighty hangover, facing a battle with Alice's hair and ballet costume.

"Ah shit!" I said to myself and turned over to try and sleep.

5

The Daily Post.

Crime Journalist's house attacked by arsonists

The Daily Post's own crime journalist, William Livingston's house was damaged on Tuesday night when a petrol bomb was thrown at his front door. Luckily a neighbor spotted the fire and called the emergency services and everybody was evacuated from the house, including William's wife, 18 month old baby boy and 76 year old mother who was staying with them at the time. NUJ spokesman, Eamon O'Leary was outspoken in his condemnation of "this blatant attack on free speech." William has been a crusader against organised crime for the past ten years and has been unrelenting in his writings, very often raising the public profile of criminals and making household names of some of the "godfathers." This is not the first attack on William. He narrowly escaped injury when shots were fired at his car last year and this was thought to be the work of Thomas "the suit" Mulligan, who was under investigation from the Criminal Assets Bureau and the Fraud Squad at the time. William was writing a major piece on Mulligan at the time and the attack was thought to be a scare tactic.

Thursday

"My mother was four days on a trolley in the Casualty, Joe." Her voice started to shake. "She's seventy four Joe, the poor soul was in a terrible state. We took it in turns to stay with her; we all did four or five hours with her. She even had to wash and use the toilet in the cubicle in the casualty, it was the most degrading thing I have ever had to witness." Her voice was beginning to tremble now.

I was on my way to work at 12.30 in the afternoon in the car with the radio on. I was listening to a talk show. The recent revelation that a major criminal was about to be the beneficiary of private Heart Surgery courtesy of the National Treatment Purchase fund had started a major debate. The phone lines on all of the afternoon talk shows were red hot with people telling there stories about the length of time waiting both in the casualty departments when they had their heart attacks and then having been placed on the waiting list and forgotten about. Although it was an old story, and had received more than its share of airtime, sob stories about people suffering due to the dreadful state of the health services always got listenership and sold papers.

This particular one concerned a seventy four year old lady who had taken a heart attack. She had spent four days on a trolley in casualty of a major hospital, along with twenty or thirty others. Having been diagnosed and treated for her condition, she was placed on the waiting list for heart surgery and remained on it ever since. She was already nine months on the list and had heard nothing. The National Treatment Purchase Fund stipulated that patients who were over a year on the waiting list were entitled to apply for treatment under the scheme, and would be guaranteed to be treated within 4 weeks of application.

"Joe," the lady was now pouring out her heart, "she can't walk up the stairs to the toilet, she has to sleep downstairs in the parlour."

Joe was making all the appropriate noises, and asking all the correct questions to get maximum listenership value for this call. "And does your mother live on her own, Mary?" he asked with sincerity.

"Yes Joe, but one of us goes up to her every day. We cook her dinner and clean her up," she explained, "how much longer does she have to wait, but that bastard, he gets his surgery in the Private hospital, how can that be fair Joe?" Her voice cracked.

"Here it comes," I said to myself. Then the tears started, Joe left just the right amount of time of poor Mary sobbing before he faded to advertisements.

I entered my office at 1.00 having parked my car and changed into scrubs. This shift incorporated being on-call and would deal with any emergencies that came in, or any follow up problems with any of the day's patients. Often this meant very late finishes and quite often call-backs to the theatre or Intensive Care Unit in the small hours of the morning. The computer in my office was switched on. This was normal as there were databases and files that my staff would normally use during the course of a normal working day. I opened the email program and entered my password. The usual plethora of spam greeted me. In amongst the medical journal updates and offers of "unlimited free DVDs" were a few internal emails concerning lectures and cardiopulmonary resuscitation training. Between an offer for "$5000 instant credit" and notification for the next Heads of Department meeting was a message from the "opportunity@hotmail.com address. Scanning down, I reached the "opportunity" message. Again there was something about the language that perked up my interest.

"Our records show that you have the required qualifications and skill to be very useful to us. Your qualifications and skill of running life support machines during heart surgery could earn you significant amounts of cash."

I received these types of mailings regularly. This latest offering on the face of it seemed the same as the rest but something was telling me that there was more to it. I thought about it for a couple of minutes and eventually gave up and continued on with some business stuff. They say that the subconscious never forgets and like an itch that I couldn't reach, something kept niggling at my memory. The more I thought about it, the more frustrated I became. I decided to abandon the computer work and go for coffee before preparing for the procedure that I was scheduled to manage the bypass run on. While supping a brew in the coffee room, I was browsing some notes that I had made for a series of lectures that I was giving to the staff nurses of one of the medical wards that look after patients who have just had their heart surgery. I was giving a lecture on a ward nurse's perspective on heart surgery. Something was tugging at my subconscious. I was reading some notes that I had downloaded from various medical websites explaining the procedures with diagrams. They were all followed with explanations of the various operations and various ways of explaining the workings of the Heart/Lung machine.

"To facilitate the surgery, the patient is connected to a Machine called the Heart/Lung machine. A tube is placed into the Right side of the Heart, which drains all of the patient's blood into a machine called an Oxygenator. This is an artificial lung. Here the blood is filled with oxygen, cleared of carbon dioxide. It is then sent back into the patients Aorta using a pump, an artificial heart. This is called Cardiopulmonary Bypass, the patient's heart and lungs are bypassed."

This and other variations on the same theme were the main content of my notes. I read them over and put a few changes to my lecture notes before closing up, finishing my coffee and heading to theatre to start the setup for the next procedure of the day. I strolled to my office, left the notes back into their folder and headed to theatre. My eyes caught a surgical text book that I had been using to prepare some lectures. I paused for a second, the book was written by an English Surgeon. His explanation of the operation of a Heart/Lung machine was quite simple but was quite different from my own. I paused and then a light slowly started coming on in my head. In all the research I had carried out while preparing lectures over the years, I had never heard or read anybody else use the description of Heart/ Lung bypass that I use, "running life support machines during heart surgery." This was a description that I had come up with myself and seemed to satisfy most people's curiosity. It wasn't a very scientific definition but it gave enough information to non-surgical staff an idea of what a Heart/Lung bypass machines was about. Whoever had written that email had either heard one of my lectures or read one of my articles. I had written one recently for the hospital's magazine giving an explanation of Coronary bypass surgery from a patient's point of view. I included a reference to Heart/Lung bypass machines using the life support machine description. As far as I had read or heard, no-one else described Heart/Lung bypass in these terms.

I went back to the email and read it again. *"If you are interested in obtaining some fast cash, reply YES to this email."* Partly it was the curiosity and flattery of who had sent the mail and partly the promise of fast cash following a couple of very difficult weeks which made me reply, but I typed a short note asking for the details to be forwarded on to me. I closed down the computer, left my office and headed towards the shouts of "Perfusionist in room 8, please."

Room 8 was the largest of the 10 operating theatres. It was a large square room, about 10 metres by 10 metres. It also was the only room with a window which made working in this particular room relatively pleasant. The hospital was recently constructed in the model of one of those high rise American Clinics. The operating theatres were on the ground floor. Rooms 6, 7 and 8 were exclusively for Cardiac Surgery. The whole hospital was designed ergonomically with the idea of keeping everything moving in the interest of "getting the patient through the system."

The case in room 8 was approaching the point where I was required and was way behind in my preparation for the procedure. The email had delayed me and I gave myself a mental slapping for falling so far behind. I now had to set up almost as if in an emergency. The scrub nurse at the table to the surgeon's right was looking for the sterile tubes from the Heart/Lung machine, and I hadn't set them up yet. As quick as I could, I rolled the Heart/Lung machine alongside the operating table and handed the sterile tubes to the nurse who was scrubbed up beside the surgeon. I let in enough sterile saline to the reservoir and started circulating the fluid around the tubes to remove all the air. The consultant Surgeon hadn't appeared yet. I was just finishing my hasty set up when Mr Reddy strolled into the operating room. "Afternoon all," he said to whoever was listening. He didn't get much of a response, apart from the senior resident who let him know that we were ready for him.

Mr Reddy placed his briefcase and Dictaphone on a small table in the corner, turned and headed for the door again. "Back in a minute, I just want to call my secretary," he announced over his shoulder as he disappeared out into the corridor.

The consultant Anaesthetist let out a loud sigh, looked at me and rolled his eyes. I responded by laughing. "Smile, you're on overtime," I said. Normally I would have chatted about nothing in particular, but today, I was grateful for the extra few minutes to catch up. Eventually I got myself organised and started my check-off before starting the Cardiopulmonary Bypass run. I also started my "what ifs?" and tried to put myself in a problem solving mood. This is the place where I wanted my brain to be before the start of a case, not wandering, trying to solve some email mystery. The case started as normal. The usual barked order, "go on bypass" was thrown in my direction.

I started the Heart/Lung machine and settled the patient onto the system. The heart was clamped and paralysed as normal and the surgeon proceeded to start the process of attaching the pieces of veins and arteries to the diseased coronary arteries. Having sent a couple of blood samples to the blood gas analyser, I made a few adjustments to the blood, oxygen and gas flows. All the numbers were within the normal limits expected of a patient on a Heart/Lung bypass system. I was sitting back and although my mind was wandering a little, I was regularly scanning the entire system.

The machine was effectively on autopilot with all the alarms and emergency cut-offs in place. Mr. Reddy was pontificating to the Anaesthetist about how much better his new Mercedes Kompressor was than the 7 Series BMW he had just got rid of.

One of my staff walked in "Wanna go for a brew Boss?" Bruce offered to take over the case to allow me out for a quick coffee and a pit-stop. This was like an answer to a prayer. I had neglected a lot of other work owing to my mind wandering over that strange email. I stood up, and gave my saviour a handover. Bruce was a tall, tanned New Zealander, who had joined the department on an exchange program from Auckland. I gave him a rundown of the vital information to the procedure. I gave him the flows, pressures and patient status. I let him know where the Surgeon was in the operation and when he had got the picture, I left the room, headed for the staff rest room, grabbed a quick mug of instant and sat in my office to finish a few reports that were due that evening. I was fully confident that Bruce could handle the case and wouldn't complain even if I didn't return before the bypass period was finished.

After about ten minutes, one of the Philippine floor nurses knocked gently on the door of my office, which was open and told me very politely that Bruce wanted me. I was slightly surprised as I had given him a comprehensive handover and didn't intend to be any more than a few minutes out of the operating room.

I walked back into the operating room and a very strange sight met my eyes. Normally, the Heart/Lung Machine is plugged into a UPS/Battery backup system in case of a power failure. If the power fails and the machine has no battery backup, the pump can be turned by hand. So normally the only reason that a Perfusionist would be turning the pump by hand is if there had been a power failure. What I saw was Bruce, turning the pump by hand. There are protocols to deal with all these types of situations and Bruce was handling the situation by the book in so much as he was hand-pumping perfectly, that is generating a perfectly normal blood pressure. However it took me a few seconds to realise that although the pump had stopped and hand cranking was required, the lights in the operating theatre had not gone out. There hadn't actually been a power failure.

"What's happening Bruce?" I asked with some urgency in my voice.

"Dunno mate," he answered rather calmer than I had. "The arterial pump just stopped," he explained without slowing down his manual operation of the pump.

At this stage, the heart was clamped and paralysed and the lungs were switched off and the Heart/Lung machine was completely supporting the patient and Reddy was beginning to take an interest in what was happening at the pump. "What's happening?" he asked with some irritation in his voice.

"Small problem with the pump sir," Bruce answered. This was understating it a little I thought to myself. My mind was racing through scenarios trying to get a handle on what was happening.

"Did you try all the overrides?" I asked Bruce. This was a very obvious question but I couldn't think of anything else and I was beginning to sweat a little, as was Bruce both from the stress of the situation and the physical effort of handcranking the pump. I was very impressed by Bruce's calmness in this situation. This was one I hadn't come across before. "What the fuck are we going to do here?" I asked, I thought, to myself, however Bruce's wide eyed look made me realise that I'd said it loud enough for him to hear.

I was still running through solutions in my head, and

Reddy was now getting concerned, "Can you fix this, lads?" he asked.

"Did you try a re-boot?" I asked Bruce.

"No," he replied with obvious relief that I had come up with a solution that might work. This involved stopping handcranking, and completely powering down the system and rebooting the Machine like a Computer powering back up. This would hopefully reset everything and start the system working again. I explained to Mr Reddy what I was going to try. Stopping the Heart/Lung machine completely while the patient's heart was paralysed was under normal circumstances very dangerous. If the circulation to the brain is stopped completely, irreversible brain damage occurs after 3–4 minutes. However a basic rule of thumb in physiology says that that for every one degree centigrade that the brain temperature is reduced, this gives approximately three minutes extra before brain damage occurs. This prolongs the amount of time it takes for brain damage to occur, so even after a considerable length of time submerged in icy water, drowned victims can return to normal. During heart surgery this theory is sometimes employed. Using the Heart/Lung Machine, the patient's temperature is reduced. Normally during a routine Bypass Grafts procedure, the temperature is reduced to around 30° Centigrade. This gives us significantly longer to diagnose and fix any technical problems that occur with the Heart/Lung machine. This safety net was just what we needed here in this situation. I performed a mental checklist of what I would need to do.

One by one I powered off the control modules and the main computer. "We're ready to try this now, Peter," I announced.

"Just get the damn thing working!" he hissed at me.

"OK Bruce, when I say so, stop hand cranking, and power down the main pump." Coordinating the movements was critical, so as to reduce the time that the patient was without blood circulation. "3...4...OK do it!"

Bruce stopped hand cranking, clamped the venous line

coming from the patient, reached under the consul and switched off the main power. The machine gave a low moan as all the electrics died.

I scanned the whole pump, in search of clues as well as to check that everything was off. There was a tense atmosphere in the room now. Word about incidents like these spreads like a bad smell and the number of staff in the room was increasing by the minute. Most of the new visitors genuinely were there to see if there was anything they could do to help. Unfortunately, a Perfusionist's job is so specialised, that it would be a rare treat when a theatre nurse could offer a solution. We were on our own here. I had already asked one of the floor nurses to page the Hospital's engineer. He would have been the only one who could come up with some intelligent suggestion. He hadn't arrived yet.

"Let's try this!" I muttered to Bruce. Having satisfied myself that the system was completely off, I then went through the boot-up procedure. This involves firing up the system in a particular order. Main power first, then Computer and finally the actual pumps. It would take just over a minute.

The system went through its internal checks as lights flicked on and off during the boot-up. Waiting for a minute in such difficult circumstances seemed like an eternity. I used the time to make a plan in case this didn't work and there wasn't mush else I could think of. The only thing I could come up with was to take a pump console from one of the other Heart/Lung machines and power it with an extension lead. Adjusting the tubing to fit into the replacement pump would be a nightmare, and dangerous.

My planning was interrupted by the final high pitched beep that signified the completion of the boot up procedure. I looked at the main pump console and was relieved to see the "ready" light glowing. "OK, Bruce switch it on." I looked up to the operating table and saw four pairs of eyes staring at me. I like to think they were willing me on and the pump to start turning, but I wasn't that naive.

"Bugger." The one word I didn't need to hear. This was

Bruce's one and only profanity. I looked down at Bruce and my stomach turned when I noticed that even though all the lights were back on and despite having rebooted the system, the pump was still not turning. "Start handcranking," I barked at Bruce, immediately regretting my tone.

Mr Reddy was now leaning over the table straining to see what was going on. His demeanour was beginning to change, "What the fuck is happening guys?" he asked, his voice beginning to get louder. "Can we get this sorted?"

I ignored him and started to tell Bruce what plan B was. My mind was racing now and I was working out where to get a spare pump console, and where the power extension cables were, when a strange thought entered my head. During an air show in France some years before, Airbus were showing off one of their new commercial jets. This was one of the first of the Jets with an almost completely computer controlled cockpit. While performing a flypast past the airshow, the aircraft passed over a heavily wooded area; it suddenly started to go into a landing position, and proceeded to crash land into the woods. It transpired after an investigation that the autopilot had decided that the aircraft was going to land. The pilot couldn't override the autopilot. This had lead to many discussions about how much control computers should have over systems like autopilots and in our case, Heart/Lung Machines.

I was turning to run and find a spare pump while Bruce was hand cranking and sweating profusely. Suddenly the pilot on the Airbus gave me an idea. I ran back towards the Heart/ Lung machine, paused for a second. "Stop cranking Bruce, I have an idea!" Bruce stopped, clamped the venous line again and looked at me questioningly.

Reddy was now decidedly nervous. "What are you at now?" he asked me with a shake in his voice.

I got down on my knees and opened the metal door at the bottom of the Heart/Lung machine. This was where access to the electronic workings of the pumps and computers were housed.

"What are you at Boss?" Bruce asked. "You're not an engineer and you're wasting time."

"Hold on a second," I said as I pulled out bits of dirt and plastic that had accumulated in the base of the machine. I was looking for one cable in particular. I craned my neck to see the underside of the main arterial pump and found the cable marked "remote control." I traced this cable to the back of the computer control system and prayed that this would work. I ran my hand along the cable until I came to an RS232 input. I checked that it read "Pump 1" and quickly disconnected it from the computer panel. "Now try it Bruce!" I almost shouted.

Bruce switched on the pump again and gingerly tried the control knob. The pump started to turn immediately. He brought the speed up to the normal flow rate, adjusted the gas flows and sat back and let out a huge sigh. I noticed that it had taken two minutes to restart the system. I estimated that the patient had been without circulation for just over two minutes.

Reddy had shrunk and asked "What happened?" Bruce also looked at me for the explanation.

"I think the computer received a message of some kind, probably an error, but it decided to stop the arterial pump, remember the Airbus air crash at the Toulouse Air Show. The computer in the Autopilot overrode the pilot and landed the plane in the forest. Apparently he couldn't get into the system to stop the plane landing. I just disconnected the control cable that connects the pump to the computer disabling it completely," I was nearly sick with relief, but I was trying to be cool and outwardly matter of fact about it.

"Shit, I would never have thought of that, thank Christ you were here," admitted Bruce.

"Go have a cuppa and change your scrubs," I told Bruce. I sat down in front of the console and tried to settle my nerves. Bruce disappeared out the door.

"Get that thing fixed before you use it again," Reddy piped up with a sneer.

"Damn right," I answered ignoring the sarcasm. Thanks, well done would have been nicer but I began to feel good that I had diagnosed and solved a very obscure problem. The case continued and finished without further incident and within a few hours, the patient was back in Intensive Care. I decided to keep a close eye on him and made a mental note to check in on him in a couple of hours when he should be awake. He had been without circulation for about a minute and a half. The patient's temperature at the time was 31° centigrade and that should have been enough to give about 15 minutes of protection from brain damage in the event of the problem taking longer to solve. We had taken two.

I checked in with the Intensive Care Nurse charged to look after him. I explained briefly that there had been a technical problem during the bypass period which had been dealt with quickly and I was being overcautious. I played down the details of the problem. There was no point in making too big a deal by explaining the gory details of the electronic failure. A misplaced word or sentence if the patient took longer than normal in recovering from the anaesthetics could result in blind panic by the family.

6

THOMAS "THE SUIT" MULLIGAN sat back in one of the cheap plastic chairs in the office at the back of one of his many warehouses. There were 7 or 8 of his trusted lieutenants with him as well as six or so 'soldiers' and the room was oppressively hot and full of smoke. The scene would easily fit into an episode of the Sopranos. There were ugly scars from previous encounters with rival gangs and the obligatory Nike track suit and Leather jackets.

Mulligan was holding a "business" meeting. Part of his business expansion scheme was into the rather complex game of scamming from automatic teller machines. This involved fitting external card readers over the standard cash card slots on Automatic teller machines. The extra reader could copy all the electronic details from the unsuspecting customers' cards. This, coupled with a tiny hidden camera, positioned to film the customer keying in their PIN number and transmitted to a receiver connected to a laptop, usually in a nearby van or car, gave the criminal gang enough electronic records to create replica cards and then came the simple task of emptying the accounts of as many cards as could be created before the extra kit was discovered attached to the ATM. This in any case was the theory. However things were not going as simply as the Nigerian engineer who modified the commercially available equipment had promised.

The engineer had obviously disappeared and the equipment wasn't functioning as it was designed or modified to. One of the lower ranking goons who, while inside on a 6–12 month stretch had taken computers in one of the many rehabilitation educational courses had discovered that the laptop that Mulligan's crew was using used Windows XP but the software that accompanied the equipment needed the latest version of Windows Millenium. He had nervously suggested to his boss, one of the more senior Captains in Mulligan's gang, that they should get hold of a newer, more powerful laptop.

Mulligan got wind of this simple omission and he was ranting and raving to his senior goon. He was threatening to have the junior member promoted at the expense of his second-in-command, and it wouldn't be a healthy retirement plan. The stress and hassle of this setback was taking its toll on Mulligan's ailing heart. Against all medical advice, he had had his usual chicken curry and chips earlier that evening. He followed up with a few pints. A couple of hours later he had started suffering from indigestion, and heartburn. Now three hours later, he was beginning to feel decidedly unwell. He had always dismissed as rubbish the advice given by the Cardiologist who diagnosed his coronary condition and continued with his normal diet. He had however almost given up or at least cut down on the fifty Benson & Hedges that he had smoked daily since his first Holy Communion forty odd years earlier.

Since his heart attack several months earlier, he had adopted the attitude that he would take it reasonably easy until the quacks could fix his heart. Then he could go back to his old ways. Now, he was beginning to sweat profusely. He felt cold and clammy even though the room where he was holding court was stuffy and hot. He had consumed 3 or 4 packets of Rennie, in a desperate attempt to quell what he hoped was a particularly nasty attack of indigestion. However he was beginning to come to the realisation that this heartburn wouldn't go away with the usual mix of antacids and cold milk and he was starting to worry. "Listen Bill Fuckin Gates," he shouted to his most trusted employee, "how can some snotty nosed kid from the flats tell me that the bleedin laptop uses some other XP or X fuckin YZ, and that mouthy rapper from woggawogga land who charged me a fuckin fortune couldn't?" He ranted on despite the discomfort in his chest now beginning to spread into his left arm. "I want this shaggin computer fixed or replaced bloody quick, and I want no more lame excuses."

Sweat was beginning to pour from his forehead and he felt like puking. The audience of his employees, a mixed bag of lowlife thugs all from the inner city who handled various aspects of his business held their collective breath. Mulligan's temper was legendary among the criminal fraternity and it was automatically understood that you kept your mouth shut when the "Suit" was on a roll. Dressed in his trademark dark navy suit, he looked like the drunken uncle at the family wedding. He had loosened his tie and opened the top button of his expensive shirt. This in itself was unprecedented as he had a rule never to be seen looking anything less than impeccable in front of his subordinates. The sight of Mulligan, shirt open at the neck, tie unkempt, black hair flying about and spit showering from his mouth as he gave serious grief to his henchmen, was a fearful sight to behold. Michael "Jap" Donnelly, called because of his perpetual squint was feeling either particularly brave or stupid, had watched his own father die of a heart attack, was beginning to become concerned. The world and his wife knew that Mulligan was due to go into hospital soon but Mulligan himself saw his heart problem as a sign of weakness.

He had deliberately played down the true nature of his illness. He had a Martin Scorsese style view of his own life and had the attitude that if his enemies knew of his heart problems, they would exploit this weakness. Jap began to recognise some of Mulligan's symptoms as being very similar to those of a heart attack. He made a career decision and nudged his mate leaning against the wall beside him smoking. This was a brave move as talking while Mulligan was ranting was a serious no-no if you wanted to progress in the "firm." Mulligan was really on form tonight and the entire room, to a man, didn't envy poor Spider Sheehan, Mulligan's "underboss." He was over 6 foot, built like a prop-forward with a nose that had been broken more than once, and not during the gentleman's game. He was head and shoulders over Mulligan and the sight of this giant, hanging his head as he took the full brunt of Mulligan's temper would have been comical had Mulligan not looked so sick.

"Colly," whispered Jap, nudging him in the ribs. Colly shot Jap a "shut the fuck up" glance. "The Suit is sick," Jap said in a loud whisper.

"Shut your face," Colly advised. Jap wasn't for turning as he noticed Mulligan's hand move to the centre of his chest. He was still raving on to the now firmly dressed down Sheehan.

"Colly, I think he's having a fuckin heart attack," Jap pressed on.

"Shut-the-fuck-up!" Colly spat out in through barred teeth. Some of the nearby members had heard the exchange and were torn between turning away from the inevitable rollicking that Jap was now guaranteed to receive and the by now quite obviously suffering Mulligan.

He had been standing, squaring up to Sheehan, when suddenly he stumbled backwards and collapsed into a chair. There was a collective lunge forward from the group to assist him. Mulligan looked up with a waxy grey appearance and, obviously quite breathless, managed to dismiss everyone in the room with a "what are you all staring at; get the fuck out of here."

He slumped back in the chair and started searching in his pockets for the Glyceril Trinitrate spray that his GP had given him to use whenever the pain got nasty.

The group slowly started leaving the room. Jap, in his oversized Nike tracksuit, pushed through the group. "You OK boss?" He was almost shouting. He approached Mulligan with something like panic. Most of the group looked over the shoulders and quickened their pace. Jap was now asking for trouble. They expected Mulligan to take out a gun or something from his pocket and silence the irritating little mouth. Sheehan moved towards Jap and being nearly twice his size, picked up Jap clean off the ground and made to physically eject him from the room. "Jaysus Spider, can't you see he's havin a fuckin heart attack?" Spider heaved Jap up into the air and lunged towards the door. This was the final insult, openly stating the unsaid, and he raised his massive right fist to silence the now panicking Jap. "Don't you know when to shut up, Doctor Fuckin Donnelly?"

Suddenly there was a loud exclamation from behind. Sheehan looked around and the remaining gang members were on their knees surrounding the now prone Mulligan. He dropped Jap like a hot potato and moved across the room with startling speed and agility. Mulligan had turned a horrible deathly grey colour and his lips were now a purpley blue. "What the fuck?" He touched Mulligan's face. It was cold and waxy. Immediately it reminded him of his dead grandfather when he was laid out in the coffin in the mortuary chapel where he had, as a child, been ushered in to say goodbye to his granddad. The memory sent shivers down his spine and a sense of pure panic engulfed him. He picked Mulligan up by the shoulders and shook him. "Mr. Mulligan, wake up!" Even now, protocol was still being observed. Mulligan slumped to the floor.

Suddenly Jap wriggled through. He opened Mulligan's jacket, ripped open his shirt revealing a large Celtic tattoo. He placed his left ear over Mulligan's mouth, stuck his middle finger into the side of his neck, searching for the carotid pulse and studied his chest for a few seconds. The other lads just stared incredulously.

"His heart has stopped!" Jap announced. "Spider, press on his chest as I count, and Jayo, call an ambulance and tell them it's a heart attack."

Jayo, another member of the goon squad, brushed the dust from the knees of his chinos and dug out his mobile. He walked outside to call 999.

Spider suddenly woke from his terror and tried to exert his authority. "What the fuck are you doing Jap?" he asked with obviously mock bravado. He didn't like a little scut like Jap telling him what to do. But the little fucker seemed to know what he was doing, and was taking control good style. He placed his hand flat on the centre of Mulligan's chest. "No, Spider, the heel of your hand in the centre of the tattoo, and interlock the fingers of your other hand and press to my count."

Jap leaned over, placed his mouth over Mulligan's, forming a seal. Despite the foul taste of curry, Guinness and cigarettes he blew twice while pinching Mulligan's nose shut. Mulligan's chest rose and fell perfectly. "Now, Spider!"

Taking a breath, Spider pushed down to Jap's count, "one and, two and three..." He counted up to five. Jap blew another two breaths, and then shouted more instructions, "Press harder Spider, and not so sharp."

Spider repeated the compressions and he was stunned to see a more normal colour return to Mulligan's face, "It's fucking workin!" he shouted.

Jap leaned over to give some more breaths and halfway through, Mulligan gave a loud half splutter, half cough. Jap ended up with a mouthful of foul tasting phlegm.

"Fuck me, he's come back" announced Spider.

Mulligan moaned and groaned and started to rub his chest. "Christ, I feel as if I've been hit by a truck, what the fuck happened?"

"I think you had a heart attack, Boss," Jap announced.

Spider interjected, "Sorry boss, I had to press on your chest, the Jap here told me what to do."

Mulligan shifted himself to see Jap's face. "So you're responsible for bringing me back, eh?"

"Sorry Mr. Mulligan sir" Jap stuttered, "Me Da died of

a heart attack and I nearly shit meself when I saw you keel over..." He expected a standard Mulligan dressing down, but nearly melted with relief when Mulligan smiled.

"Well done and thanks son," he reached up and shook Jap by the shoulder, "you obviously have more brains then all of these arseholes put together, I'll see you right." He winked and lay down closing his eyes appearing to go asleep. "Spider" he almost whispered, "will you call my own GP, I don't want to end up in one of those meat factories."

"No Problem Mr. Mulligan," Spider replied. Just then Jayo returned closing his mobile and smoking a cigarette. Spider grabbed the cigarette from him, "Gobshite! Gimme your mobile!"

Jayo looked suitable contrite but suddenly his face lit up, "Is the Suit ok? Where the fuck did you learn that stuff Jap?"

"Yeah Jap, who showed you that Doctor stuff, you were like one of those blokes off ER." Spider was coming down slowly.

Jap looked embarrassed as he explained "Last time I was inside, on a 3-6 month for aggravated assault, there was a course on First Aid. Me Da had only died from a heart attack and I was sick because there was nothing I could do. When the course came up, I jumped at it."

"Fair fuckin play to you sonny," Spider laughed, "Sorry for roughing you up, you know the way the boss is about his privacy."

"Yeah, good thing for you though, Spider," Jayo was looking out the window and picking his nose, "boss keeling over like that saved you a further bollicking." Spider looked at him in disgust; he started up towards Jayo who wasn't famous for his tact when the siren of a cardiac ambulance broke the cosy atmosphere.

"I'm not fuckin dead yet Jayo!" Mulligan made his presence felt again. Spider pulled the number of the unlucky GP from his notebook and stepped outside the door. He dialed the number and from the first 3 digits Spider noticed it was a Carrickmines number. The phone rang for 12 or 14 rings, not surprising considering it was nearly 3 o'clock in the morning. "Yes, hello?" came a sleepy voice with a clipped Dublin 4 accent. Spider wasn't one for long winded small talk, "Doctor O'Hara, me boss Mr. Mulligan told me to call you," he began, "we think he's had a heart attack and the ambulance is here…"

"Who the hell is this?" the GP's voice became louder and firm. "How did you get this number? Take your friend to the Accident and Emergency and call my secretary tomorrow…"

Spider let him rant on for a few seconds and then he moved in for the kill. He always enjoyed this bit, "Sorry Doctor for ringing you so late but…em…Mr. Mulligan…" he stressed the surname for effect "would really appreciate your help with his records?"

There was the expected pregnant pause at the other end of the line. "What did you say your friends name was?" the now very much awake GP inquired with a slight tremor to his voice.

"Mulligan, Thomas Mulligan."

"Is that Mr. Mulligan from St Helens Villas in Rathgar?" asked the GP slowly. Spider could almost hear the light coming on in the Doctor's head, "Yes Doctor."

After a muffled exchange with his wife, or at least Spider assumed it was, Doctor O'Hara came back, "Is the ambulance crew there?" he asked with new found authority and concern.

"Yes Doctor," Spider replied with a smile, "they've just arrived."

"Tell them to take him straight to the Southwestern Clinic, I'll call the Clinic and arrange the admission. If there are any problems, call me back on my mobile, 087 675…"

Spider interrupted him, "OK Doc, I have it already." O'Hara was about to ask how Spider had this number but he realised that he had just been called on a private, ex-directory number that he had changed recently, so he conceded. "Thanks Doc, talk to you tomorrow."

This was given by Spider and taken as an order rather than a parting greeting and immediately set O'Hara's agenda for the following day, as he now would be spending most of the day organizing Mulligan's records to be transferred from the University Hospital to the Southwestern Clinic, as well as cajoling the management staff of the Private Clinic to bear the cost of Mulligan's early admission as part of the National Treatment Purchase Fund's reimbursement for the pending surgery. The recent press that Mulligan's story had received had made this case even more difficult to deal with. The Private Clinic had accepted the transfer of Mulligan for the surgery under the terms of the NTPF, but the Press had made it into a bit of a poison chalice. Now the Management of the Clinic wanted to drop such a high profile lowlife. They felt, rightly or wrongly, that the presence of a known criminal, receiving treatment in their high class establishment, would affect business adversely.

O'Hara had treated Mulligan initially and arguably saved his life by a rapid diagnosis and emergency treatment. Mulligan was extremely grateful and showed his appreciation by "helping" the Doctor build an extension to his surgery. Firstly O'Hara was amused, then mildly grateful. But when he began to see the state of some of the builders who turned up to work on the extension, he began to get nervous. The crunch came when he was presented with a ridiculously low bill for a beautifully finished surgery at the side of his house. He tried unsuccessfully to bring the matter up with Mulligan. In return, Mulligan began to use him as his personal Physician. This stretched from arthritis medication for Mulligan's aging mother-in-law to methodone prescriptions for some of Mulligan's "employees."

Slowly and insidiously, his practice changed as his older, more "respectable" patients made their excuses and changed GPs and he had had more than his share of tut-tuts from the Residents' Association. He had made contact with some of

Mulligan's lieutenants and explained his case. The demeanor and attitude of these soldiers terrified him and by now he was officially fucked. He worked for Mulligan.

Like a scene from ER, a fully equipped Cardiac ambulance crew burst noisily into the room. One Emergency Medical Technician placed a clear green oxygen mask over Mulligan's face while the other quickly and confidently placed Electrocardiograph dots on his chest. He switched on the portable ECG machine and studied the paper ribbon that slowly poured from the side of the machine.

"Looks like a recent inferior MI," one said to the other.

"A whah?" Jayo asked.

"An MI, Myocardial Infarction, Heart attack," one of the crew explained.

"Jaysus, sounds serious," Jayo raised his eyebrows.

"Did he pass out at any stage?" one of the EMTs asked.

"Fuckin right he did, he keeled over," answered Micko, a scruffy looking character wearing a Leeds Utd jersey over dirty jeans who had stayed at the back of the room throughout the entire episode.

"Did anyone administer CPR?" the ambulance man asked removing the ECG dots from Mulligan's chest and replacing them with two large defibrillator sticky pads.

"No one gave him any drugs, if that's what you mean," Spider looked shocked.

"CPR, Cardiopulmonary resuscitation," clarified the technician.

"Yeah, I did," Jap piped up, "he had no pulse, so I gave him mouth-to-mouth and told Spider there to do the chest compressions."

"Well done, you most likely saved his life." He leaned over Mulligan and indicated towards Jap, "Your son here saved your life, better make sure you give him a decent Christmas present." The rest of the gang burst out laughing.

Spider took control again, "I just spoke to his GP, youse are to take him straight to the Southwest Clinic." He was relishing the authority that came when his boss was incapacitated.

The two ambulance crew looked at each other, "Sorry mister, he's going to The Mercy Hospital in town."

Spider stood up to his full height and held out the mobile phone, "Check with your control if you like, he's going to the Southwestern, OK?" he added with a little menace to his voice.

A slight tremor edged into the voice of the older of the two but he managed, "We'll radio control on the way and confirm the admission details, OK?" And, trying to be diplomatic, he explained, "We need to make sure that there is a bed available in the intensive care unit, no point in bringing him all over town if there are no beds in ITU, don't want to cause any more problems." This satisfied Spider and he walked alongside the trolley as it was wheeled towards the ambulance.

The entire gang started to climb into the back of the ambulance and was stopped by one of the crew. "Sorry Boys, only one or two." Spider pointed to Jayo and another large menacing animal to follow the Ambulance and told the rest of them to "fuck off home and forget that this ever happened."

The Ambulance crew were a little nervous and 5 minutes later they were speeding across the city towards the Southwestern Clinic having had it confirmed to them by a very pissed off radio dispatch operator that they had been given clearance from the ministers office to proceed straight to the Private Clinic. Within 20 minutes, the entourage had disgorged from the back of the ambulance and after a long and arduous admission procedure, Mulligan was tucked up in an Intensive Care bed with Spider and Jayo taking up sentry duty outside the main door of the ITU. The admissions clerk had been called out if bed at home to come straight to the hospital to admit a patient. This was a highly irregular procedure as emergency admissions were normally handled by the Medical Registrar on call. However the clerk was told that this patient was to be admitted as quickly and with as little "fuss" as possible. Fuss—that was a laugh. The admitting clerk had already received calls from the Director of Nursing, the Night Matron, the patients Cardiologist, GP and Surgeon. This sort of fuss was usually reserved for VIPs and Archbishops. Mulligan would have been quite charming had he not have been trying it on with the young clerk throughout the entire admission procedure. Obviously having recovered from his episode, he even managed to lean over from the gurney and pat her on the backside. "Thanks, Darlin," he said in a hoarse whisper, "sorry for getting you out of bed, didn't interrupt anything I hope," he leered at her. He disgusted her and she just about kept quiet until he had been taken to the lift and on to the Intensive Care Unit. When the Night Matron checked in with her after he had gone, she complained that he wasn't a particularly nice man and wondered what all the fuss was about. "Don't worry Dear, I'll see to it that the ITU girls are aware of his wandering hands," the old country Matron's concern was typically directed towards preserving the honour and morality of her "girls" in the big city.

7

I was in my mother's back garden trying to start the old beat up lawnmower. No matter how many times I tried, it wouldn't fire. My grandmother kept trying to pour water into the petrol tank. "No gran," I protested, "it takes petrol." I knew she was dead over 10 years, but I didn't want to tell her in case it upset her. Just then my older sister appeared in her school uniform. "Robbie," she called in a high immature childlike voice, "Mr. Cassin is here to see you, and he's at the front door." I looked at her. She was 46 but it didn't seem strange that she was wearing a primary school uniform.

Gran looked at me. She had suffered a stroke some years before she died and lost her speech. She looked at me and spoke clearly. But it was Victoria, my wife's voice that came out, "You shouldn't have gambled away that money, you know. Vicky will find out." A sickening feeling as I looked from my sister to gran and back. Just then the phone rang. I looked to see if my sister was going to answer it. She just stood there laughing. The phone kept ringing...

...Suddenly I woke up. The phone on the locker next to my bed was ringing. It took me a second to realize where I was. I snatched the phone up from the cradle. It was the nurse-in-charge of the Intensive care Unit. "Robbie," she said in that half whisper that only comes from years of experience of calling

63

staff in the dead of night with either emergency instructions to get their ass into the hospital double quick, or families, and that their relative had taken a turn for the worse and to get their ass into the hospital double quick. "It's Brigid in ITU, Mr Reddy is bringing in an emergency. I think you better come in."

Yawning, I sat up. "Is he going straight to theatre?" I asked as I started searching for my jeans.

"Sorry Robbie, I don't know. The patient's not here yet." Brigid sounded apologetic.

"Where's he coming from?" I enquired further. These snippets can give you a clue as to the condition of the patient and what may be facing you when you get to the hospital.

"How am I supposed to know?" she snapped back, "I only found out about this transfer 15 minutes ago, we're full here but I was basically told to create a bed."

I was shocked by Brigid's outburst. Then I thought about it, Reddy pulled these stunts regularly. It was no surprise really. Demands like these were commonplace. Don't sweat it, I told myself. I grabbed the first item of clothes that in the pitch dark felt like a pair of trousers and a jumper. Throwing on a pair of leather pumps I leaned over to Victoria, "No idea what's going on in here. I'll be back soon as I can, OK love?" She mumbled something sleepily and rolled over. I retrieved the keys of my Megane from the cutlery drawer in the kitchen, opened the hall door as quietly as I could and slipped off into the night.

Reddy arrived into the ITU wearing a high neck golf jumper over a pair of grey slacks. Even at this hour, he appeared to have made an effort to look cool. In contrast to my tracksuit bottoms and oversized woolly jumper. I was standing off to the side by the Nursing station waiting to see what treatment Reddy had in mind. He had already discussed the case with the Consultant Cardiologist and agreed that Mulligan probably hadn't in fact had another Heart attack, just a significant Ischaemic attack

His heart had slowed down considerably and mimicked a

cardiac arrest. Reddy and the Cardiologist had agreed that there most likely weren't any clots in the coronaries and further intervention wasn't warranted by the Cardiology team. My own feeling was that Reddy would take the conservative approach and not rush into surgery immediately, but probably insert an Intra Aortic Balloon Pump as a precaution. I guessed that this would be approach that Reddy would take and had already fetched the equipment from the store room. Turning to walk towards the sinks Reddy snapped "start an isoprenaline infusion and let's put in a balloon" to the surgical registrar who had made a mad dash to the Intensive Care Unit having been called from home by the ITU nurse manager.

I grabbed one of the ITU nurses standing at the foot of the bed. "Get a couple of sterile drapes and a kit for standard line insertion," I muttered to her, "oh and page the radiographer, he'll want a chest X-ray as soon as he's finished." The ITU was reasonably quiet and the Nurse slipped away to gather the bits and pieces needed.

I knew at this hour of the morning, Reddy could be an impatient prick, and true to his reputation he started his usual. "Would someone get me a gown and a pair of eights" he barked.

An Indian ITU nurse threw me a puzzled glance. "Pair of size 8 Biogel gloves" I translated for her. She thanked me a million times as she rummaged through one of the storage cupboards. "And an extra-large theatre hat as well" I whispered to her as she brushed past me. She sniggered and opened the gloves holding them out for Reddy to put on. He started to spread the green sterile drapes over Mulligan.

Between myself and two of the ITU nurses, we set up a sterile trolley and instrument set. Reddy began by palpating the femoral artery. He marked the spot with a sterile marker and painted the area with antiseptic paint. Mulligan gave a slight whimper as Reddy injected some Lignocaine into the area he had marked. This was to numb the insertion site. Using a large bore needle on a 10ml syringe, he poked and prodded until bright red blood filled the syringe. I wasn't sure if Reddy had noticed that Mulligan's heart rate had started to fall. It was down to fifty now and the blood pressure was struggling to stay at a reasonable level.

"Heart rate's down a bit." One of the ITU nurses slipped in behind and began to press buttons on the infusion pumps. Mulligan was snoring now, testament to the Valium that he had received when he was admitted to the ITU. He woke up and tried to raise himself up off the bed. Reddy almost shouted at him, "Lie down please Mr. Mulligan."

"Jaysus, Sorry Doctor," Mulligan lay back down, "not feeling the Mae West."

He seemed to be quite uncomfortable. It was getting difficult to insert the balloon and Reddy was starting to get frustrated. "Will you hold still please Mr. Mulligan," Reddy was as firm as he could without losing his temper. Mulligan shifted and lay still.

The blood pressure was holding at a systolic of 85, but the heart rate was beginning to concern me. Although it hadn't slowed, extra beats called ventricular ectopic beats had started to appear. On their own, these cause no problem, but when they appear with increasing regularity, and particularly when two or three appear together, then alarm bells should start to ring. I had the computerized pump set up and ready to go so I checked that the docs had everything they needed and I walked around to the head of the bed. Reddy had a bit to do yet before he inserted the balloon so I decided to use the time to try and help Mulligan stay calm and hopefully not slow down the procedure any further. "What do you think of this place, Sir?" I asked with a slightly exaggerated Dublin accent.

Mulligan looked up at me and then looked around at the nurses at the other beds. "Not bad, the scenery is better than some of the hounds in the other hospitals," he leered.

"You're from Rathgar I see, don't worry, this time next

month, you'll be in the Concorde Bar showing off your scar and telling your battle tales."

He looked at me grinning, "You know that place?"

"Yes," I replied, "went to college in The Institute of Technology and we drank there, nice pint." Sometimes making some simple connection with the patient, you could achieve a great deal of co-operation.

"I prefer the bars over this side of town," his voice had faded to a whisper.

I glanced at the monitor and then down at Reddy. He had started to thread the balloon over the guidewire. This meant that we were on the home stretch. The monitor showed that the Ventricular ectopic beats were coming hard and fast now. I nudged the Indian nurse. "Get a mini-jet of Lignocaine and Adrenaline ready," I whispered. She winked at me and revealed two of each already in the pocket of her uniform.

Looking up at the monitor, Reddy snapped "100mg push and start a Lignocaine infusion."

I headed to the computer console to connect the tubing to the balloon. Just as I turned to walk from my position at Mulligan's head, I heard him whisper, "feeling a bit dizzy." I threw a glance at the monitor to see a run of 15 or 20 ventricular ectopic beats. His heart had stopped its normal beating and just quivered. The nurse was running to fetch the defibrillator. Reddy hadn't noticed as he was concentrating on connecting the balloon to the tubing.

I looked at Mulligan. He had turned quite pale and his eyes were beginning to roll. I placed my hand on his shoulder. "Mr Mulligan," I said quite loud, "big cough now please." He half coughed, half grunted. Reddy stopped what he was doing and looked up.

"Come on Thomas, big cough!" I leaned over and spoke quite close to his face. The monitor showed ventricular tachycardia, a heart rate of over 200 beats per minute which produced very little output. He was slipping away fast. The nurse was struggling to manoeuvre the crash cart closer to the bed.

"Come on, come on," Reddy was moving towards Mulligan's head.

Just as I went to step away to make room for the crash cart, Mulligan gave a cough. I looked at the monitor and the heart rate had reverted to a more normal rhythm. Everyone stopped what they were doing and watched the monitor screen. I watched as the colour returned to Mulligan's face. The Indian nurse looked at me with a smile of congratulations. "Self defibrillation," I laughed. "Never saw that one before," she said, "must remember that."

Reddy resumed inserting the balloon catheter. I connected up the catheter to the computer console and adjusted the settings. Immediately, Mulligan's blood pressure started to rise as the rhythmic pumping of the console gave his heart a piggy-back ride. His heart rhythm stabilized and he looked decidedly a different man as he lay back on the pillow with his eyes closed. Reddy was over at the nurses station writing in Mulligan's chart. "Are you thinking of operating now or tomorrow?" I asked.

Although the urgency for Mulligan's surgery had gone up a notch or two, I didn't fancy going to surgery now, and the next day was a Friday and the operating list was already full. Any more additions would invariably spill over onto Saturday.

"No, don't think so," Reddy said without looking up, "We'll do an echo in the morning and see what his ventricle is like, he may be OK until next week when he's due." Music to my ears.

I checked with Sharia, the Indian nurse that the balloon pump was working well. Mulligan had woken up and was looking intently at the balloon pump parked at the side of the bed. I moved the machine slightly and gestured to it, "The noise might keep you awake, but you'll get used to it."

"No problem sonny," he laughed, "I'm used to noise, grew

up in a house with thirteen of us. Besides, if it helps me ticker, it's worth it." He lay back on the pillow.

I put my hand on his shoulder. "Have a good night sleep now sir," I added, "we'll see you tomorrow sometime." I headed for the door and hopefully to bed for an hour or so.

On the way out the door, I noticed two characters outside in the area usually reserved for patients' families. Two were over six feet tall, one had babyish features and the smallest of the three, dressed in chinos and a black leather jacket, despite the "no smoking" sign, had his head out a window and was blowing smoke out into the cool night air. I was tempted to say something but their menacing looks put me off. I skipped on down the stairs.

I passed the security desk and stopped. "Henry," I called into the security office.

A small, white haired figure emerged with mayonnaise stains on his mouth. "How'ya Robbie?" he asked, through a mouthful of sandwich.

"There's a couple of characters outside ITU, one of them was smoking out the window, look like a right bunch."

"Shit, yeah, they're with that Mulligan scumbag," Henry sighed, "looks like I'm gonna have a rough night."

Mulligan, Mulligan, shit! Mulligan. It came to me in a flash who it was. "There goes the neighborhood," I laughed. I headed for the car park and mused over the night's events. Thomas "The Suit" Mulligan, the criminal who was on the waiting list for heart surgery in the Private Clinic courtesy National Treatment Purchase Fund, in ITU on an Intra Aortic Balloon Pump. That explained Brigid's outburst on the phone earlier. Things were probably going to hot up. I had heard some of the radio debates, discussing the rights and wrongs of this case. Some of the print journalists were giving it loads if column inches. If anything, it put an interesting spin on the mission statement of the hospital. It certainly put it up to the management. Interesting days ahead, I chuckled as I hit the zapper to knock off the alarm on my car. I looked at my watch, two minutes to five, back to bed and with any luck, I would sleep for an hour or so. I wasn't due back to work till one in the afternoon.

8

MARTY SLOWLY PUSHED the gurney into the large service lift located in the back corridor of the hospital. He was the night porter on duty in and had just removed the remains of a 60-year-old Abdominal Aneurysm patient who had given up his fight two hours earlier. The patient had been given the Last Rights by the Hospital Chaplin and his family had been allowed an hour to say their goodbyes. Then after the standard RIP protocol that included washing the body, the placing of any religious artifacts requested by the family, wrapping in a clean white sheet and transferred to the hospital mortuary to await either post-mortem examination or removal by the undertakers. Marty sang quietly to himself. This type of duty would put the shivers up a lot of people, including some of the hospital porters, however it didn't bother Marty in the slightest. Death didn't bother him. He hadn't seen that many "stiffs" but in his five months in the position here, he had delivered at least one a week to the morgue. A major part of the RIP protocol was paperwork. There were a stack of papers to be filled out.

The Intensive Care nurse on duty was quietly pleased when she saw that it was Marty on duty. She laughed quietly, openly flirting with him, "I think all the paperwork is complete, Marty" throwing back her long blonde ponytail.

"Don't worry Karen, I'll be back," he grinned, putting on a stage Austrian Accent. He didn't hide the fact that he was looking her up and down. "Not bad," he thought to himself admiring her long legs and the way that the nurse's uniform hugged her slender waist, emphasising her chest.

"Hope so," she smiled.

Marty laughed to himself as he walked down the corridor, he still had it. He was over six feet tall, with the body of an athlete. This was the result of twenty lengths of the pool every morning without fail, and punishing circuit training and kickboxing classes almost every weekend. His maternal grandmother was Spanish and he had inherited her Latin good looks. Although educated to degree level and fit to almost Olympic standards, he was inherently lazy, and tended to hang around on the periphery of crime. He couldn't be bothered with hard work. He always looked for the quickest and easiest way to make a buck without getting his hands "dirty." A chance meeting in a bar in Ibiza with a failed jockey had proven very valuable. He had rescued the jockey from a fight outside the bar. The jockey worked in the weighing rooms of the major stadiums on the racing circuits. On a regular basis, he received tips, usually not the favorite. This name came apparently from the jockeys themselves, and was the real favorite. Marty had quickly learned the value of this information and within a few short years, was earning a very respectable living.

He also passed on tips regarding the security arrangements of some of his employers ranging from high street banks, to back-street warehouses. Marty liked to describe himself as an "information broker." This quickly gained him a reputation as a valuable contact in the criminal fraternity while remaining outside the circle. Cash started to make its way into his accounts, which he quickly laundered. Betting large sums of money on horses and games with very short odds gave resulting wins were "tax paid" and therefore fully legitimate. He always let his contacts know if he was going to change his legitimate employer. A recent call from one of his contacts had instructed him to have a closer look at the procedure for what happened when somebody died, what was the paperwork involved, who officially pronounced the patient dead and most importantly, what was the procedure when a post-mortem examination was required. Marty wondered if some of the big boys were moving into the undertaking business but had learned never to question the instructions he was given. This was one of the reasons he had become a trusted "player."

He wheeled the trolley with the recently deceased patient into one of the parking bays in the holding room beside the mortuary. A dim greenish glow from special lights gave the room an eerie feel. This coupled with the low temperature of the room made it positively spooky. There were two other remains already in the morgue. They had both died in the past day or so. At this hour of the night, there was no-one else about. Marty quickly checked the corridors leading to the morgue, checking that there were no security guards doing rounds. He was perfectly entitled to be there but he didn't want to be disturbed. He quickly lifted the charts from under the trolleys of the other two patients and checked the white form that was attached to the outside of each of them. These were two page check-off sheets for the procedure of dealing with a "RIP." Patient belongings, religious considerations, next-of-kin contact details were among the boxes to be checked. One was an eighty year old lady who had died of pneumonia the previous day, and the other was a fifty year old man who had underwent Cardiac Surgery but had suffered some major complication during the operation. Marty had taken the same journey to the mortuary twenty-eight hours earlier and now had noticed that this poor soul, having been brought to the morgue directly from Intensive Care in quite a sorry state with drips and tubes still left intact.

Marty had scanned the paperwork and noticed that a post-mortem examination had been ordered. This was normal procedure where there was any ambiguity about the cause of death. Near the end of the second page was a section pertaining to the main diagnosis and reason for admission to hospital and this contained the box marked, "Post-Mortem required?" Marty noticed on the way to the morgue that although it had been ticked, it hadn't been signed. Using a little creative photocopying, with some Tipp-ex, the form had remained virtually unchanged except a post-mortem was no longer requested.

Over twenty-four hours later, Marty noticed that the man had been cleaned up by one of the mortuary attendants, was dressed now in a suit, and when Marty opened the dead man's shirt button at about stomach level, he noticed straight away that there was no autopsy scar. If all went by the standard operating procedure, the remains would be collected by the undertakers first thing in the morning. The funeral arrangements would be carefully carried out and within thirty-six hours would be cremated in the central crematorium. By the time it was noticed that no post-mortem examination had been carried out, it would be too late to do anything about it. The blame would be laid squarely at the feet of the resident house doctor. No such examination had been ordered on the eighty year old, and comparing the forms had given Marty all the information he was after. He closed up the corpse's shirt, positioned the latest addition to the queue of RIPs, killed the lights and stepped outside into the corridor.

Ten minutes later he was in the service area at the back of the hospital. It was a cool, clear night and Marty spent a few minutes enjoying the stillness. The gentle hum of the generator and the distant sirens of fire engines and police cars gave a strange surreal backdrop to the night. Marty always enjoyed this time of the night, he did his best planning and thinking at this time of the night. He took out his cellphone which he changed regularly, sticking to either stolen models, or new pre-paid models. His caution was well served, as most of the people he communicated with were guaranteed to be monitored and Marty was happy with his position, firmly on the periphery of the underworld. Not ever wanting to be a cellmate of anyone of them.

Noting a full 5 bar signal he dialed his contact's number. Ringing at this time of the night didn't bother Marty. Most of his contacts operated in that shady space between dusk and the law and probably did all of their business after midnight. The call connected immediately. "It's me," Marty clipped.

He could hear the slow raunchy music in the background. His contact ran five or six lapdancing clubs and he was obviously in one now checking the takings for the night.

"I've checked out that procedure and it's a mess," he explained. "Just a bunch of paperwork that is rarely completed and no real checks, particularly at night. Piece of piss to change anything."

His contact grunted in a non-committal sort of way. "Yeah yeah great" he answered. "I need you check someone out," he went on in his flat Dublin accent.

"Sure, who?" Marty asked.

"Some bloke works in the operating theatre, Robbie, Bobby or something. Some sort of a doctor I think, heart surgery."

Marty suddenly got a little concerned, did they want him now to get his hands dirty by roughing up this chap. "What do you want me to do?" he asked with obvious concern in his voice.

"Don't worry," came the reply with a grunt of a laugh, "you don't need to touch him, just get to know him, find out who he his, where he goes, what he does, you know the usual stuff. Treat him like a bit of skirt, chat him up, I heard you're good at that." He laughed at his own joke and promptly broke down into a fit of smoking induced coughing.

"No problem," Marty replied, "I'll call you in a couple of…" But the line had already been disconnected.

Marty could picture the fat, overweight criminal, throwing the mobile phone to one of his entourage, surrounded by his goons and bimbos in the sleazy club. Marty scrolled down to the "call registry" menu, opened the recent calls dialled list and deleted the call history. Closing his phone, he switched it off, put it into his back trouser pocket and headed back into the hospital, checking his pager as he walked. "No calls, that was good, might even get my head down for an hour or so," he thought. He went to get himself a coffee from the machine in the hall, and then a wicked smile spread across his face. He pressed the button for a Latte on the coffee machine, night staff got to use the machine for free. He waited until the froth had settled on the top of the steaming liquid, pressed the button again and carried two cups up towards the ward where he had taken the stiff from an hour before. It was now 4.40 am, and most of the nightshift nurses were starting their meal breaks about now. He took the stairs two at a time hoping that Karen hadn't had her break yet and that she needed a cup of coffee. His luck might be in, and she had had that mischievous grin on her face that was a real come-on. So he was going to try and see if she would!

9

I STEPPED FROM THE TRAIN onto a deserted platform of Grand Canal Dock train station. The station was only a short walk to the Financial Services Centre, but was actually in an area which had been a very high unemployment, low socio-economic area. It was now a maze of boarded up tenements and burnt out cars.

I passed under a railway bridge and the smell was almost overpowering, urine and mould permeated the air. The sound of my own footsteps echoing gave the scene an eerie atmosphere. For a second, I thought I heard a second set of footsteps. Looking around, I hurried on out into the dismal evening. I didn't want to end up a victim to a mugging and spend the night on a trolley in casualty minus my watch, credit card and dignity.

The remaining houses that were occupied were guarded by iron grills over the windows. It was, in daylight, a scary place. Now at 7pm on a cold October evening, with a grey mist coming in from the river basin less than a mile away, a truly terrifying shithole. It could have been a million miles from the glass and chrome Financial Services Centre. Crossing the desolate street, I trotted towards the metal door of the bar. There wasn't much space left on the door that hadn't been redecorated by the locals. Just as I approached the door, a dark figure stepped from a doorway on the opposite side of the street. He raised a Digital Canon EOS fitted with a powerful zoom lens, let the lens focus and gently squeezed the shutter release. Four or five clicks, interspersed by the whirr of the motordrive, were barely audible. Once inside the bar the dark figure turned back into the doorway and set the camera to review. Result, three perfectly clear images of Robbie entering one of the most renowned criminal haunts in the city. Now the unenviable task of waiting until Robbie had left and trying to discover what he was doing there in the first place.

Ignoring the cloud of smoke that attacked me, I ordered a pint, and made my way to a corner table. I was making my monthly pilgrimage to pay off my gambling debt. I felt sick every time I had to do this but I consoled myself that the monthly visit here was sickening and scary enough to keep me from falling back off the wagon and betting again. Right on time at 7.30 a figure entered the bar. Probably in his mid fifties, he wore a suit that had seen better days, but was still sporting a red carnation in the lapel, probably from a recent wedding. An overweight, red faced typical Dublin "hard man," Joey "the Horse" Cassin wore his wealth with pride. A large cygnet ring sat alongside a gaudy gold sovereign ring on one hand while a gold watch was draped with three or four heavy chain bracelets. His thinning, "brillo pad" greasy hair was brylcreamed to his head and despite the autumn chills, he was sweating profusely. He ordered a large Irish and after adding a tiny drop of water from a jug placed on the bar, he turned to survey the evening's clientele. He placed his left heel on the brass foot rail, his right elbow on the bar and saluted on or two of the locals.

I caught his eye after a minute or two and he raised his glass to me. I returned his salute and started the usual ritual. I stood up, nodded to the barman, nodding to Joey's drink and stood up to join him at the bar. "Evening, Mr. Cassin," I said, "can I get you a drink?"

"Ah howaya son!" he retorted in a flat Dublin inner city accent. "Save many lives today?" he asked.

"Ya know," I forced a laugh, "healing the poor of Dublin."

He laughed out loud and broke into a fit of coughing. The barman slid a fresh whiskey over the bar towards the Horse. He took a gulp of the whiskey, licked his lips and sighed. "You're doing a great job in there son," he patted me on the back, "the brother's doing fine." He gave me a report. His brother had undergone heart surgery in the university hospital where I had worked for a number of years, and I had helped him and his family with a little advice and cups of tea here and there. They had made a big deal about it. After I had ended up in debt with Joey, I was struggling to keep up the payments to him; I bumped into him and his family in the hospital after an appointment. The family remembered me and I asked after the patient. Joey fussed a bit and when I made my next monthly pilgrimage to make my payment, he bought me a drink and told me that to return the favor of looking after his brother; he would waive the interest on the betting debt and I could take my time, within reason, in repaying it. This was obviously a huge thing to him and in reality it was. It meant I only owed him €4500. With typical inner city interest rates on such debts, this was about half what I could have expected to pay. I motioned to a table in the corner and handed him a small brown envelope with €650 in cash. I had pulled a few longer shifts than Victoria was happy with and even managed a little extra cash from some consultancy work with the Nursing College that I was paid for out of petty cash.

I was desperate to clear this debt and repeatedly cursed my own stupidity for incurring this millstone. I was starting to make headway. I had some more lectures lined up for the following month which would hopefully net me a couple of hundred and I could make another decent payment.

Horse glanced into the envelope and without seeming to count it said, "650, you must have been busy." The envelope disappeared into the inside pocket of his jacket.

"Thanks again for your kind let-off," I groveled as usual, "it's a great help."

"Looks like you're doing ok," he added, "if you fancy a flutter again, just let me know."

I laughed and trying not to make it sound like an insult to him and his business, added, "No thanks sir, I need to learn an awful lot more about the horses before I go down that road again."

"Ah, you're probably right son," he sighed, "only a mug's game." He stood up spotted what looked like another ex-dock worker, headed for the far side of the bar. That was that, the meeting was over for another month. I finished off the drink in front of me, and headed for the DART.

As I headed across the street, Marty slipped into the bar. Barely recognizable in with a baseball cap pulled over his dark hair and a pair of cheap over-the-counter reading glasses perched on the end of his nose, he stood at the door for a second looking decidedly confused. The barman looked up at him and raised his eyebrows in a "can I help you?" gesture.

"Excuse me sir," Marty went on in a fake financial sector accent. "I'm looking for a mate of mine Robbie, roight, tall, grey D&G jacket, supposed to meet him here at 7."

"Sorry son, not here," the barman looked away with obvious irritation. Just then Cassin strolled to the bar, "What's up with you sonny?" he asked in his thick Dublin accent.

"He's looking for his mate," the barman answered with a snort without looking up.

"Did I hear you say Robbie?" asked Cassin.

"Yeah, Robbie, tall, grey jacket, NYC baseball cap?" Marty answered.

"You just missed him," Cassin looked Marty up and down, "You work with Robbie or something?" he asked.

"No, just an old friend," Marty turned to leave.

"Robbie Valentine is a good lad, you better run if you want to catch him, this isn't a nice part of town," Cassin sounded like his father.

Marty was a little taken aback, "Cool, thanks!" He quickly left the bar and headed back to civilization to call a taxi. He had been surprised by Cassin's parting remarks. Marty hadn't mentioned Robbie's surname and he had recognised Cassin immediately as one of the biggest private bookies in the city. He had a reputation as a hard man and was apparently very wealthy with quite a large "client" base. Suddenly things were quite interesting.

Twenty-seven minutes later I opened the hall door of my house to be ambushed by a four year old dressed as Spiderman. I feigned injury from the web gun, then bundled Nicholas up in my arms and ran into Alice's bedroom. "Daddy, have you lost your mind?" asked Alice with a serious look on her face. This, coming from a six year old little girl in Barbie pyjamas with a green straw hat on her head and her lips thick with lipstick caused me to explode laughing. The tension from my last hour left me instantly and I picked up the two wriggling kids and gave them a huge hug. I was always humbled by their innocence and again swore to myself that I would never put myself in a position where I could jeopardise their future. Victoria appeared, looking super in tracksuit leggings and an expensive looking blouse. "Nice uniform," I joked slipping my arms around her and giving her a kiss. She pushed me away playfully and mouthed the word "later" winking. "You're home earlier that I expected." A pang of guilt stung my gut for a second, and for the millionth time I promised abstinence from all things gambling for the rest of my life.

IO

"...the blood then flows from the patient into the reservoir, is pumped across a membrane called an oxygenator where it is filled with oxygen, the carbon dioxide is removed...the Heart/ Lung machine is totally performing the function of the heart and lungs. The lungs are switched off by disconnecting them from the ventilator...when the surgeon has completed the repair and the clamp comes off, the heart will start again..."

THE SCRAPING OF CHAIRS and stretching and yawning marked the end of another lecture. I closed down the computer presentation, closed my folder and headed to theatre for the start of another fun day. Dropping off my briefcase in my office, I switched on the computer on the desk and, leaving it to boot up, I headed to the changing room to change. Five minutes later, I returned to the office carrying a cup of coffee. I was heading along the main corridor of the surgical department; here we had a surgical "suite" of the hospital towards the changing rooms reading the first few lines of a memo about some training schedules for CPR when I bumped into a tall muscular man in a porters' uniform. I wasn't looking where I was going and bumping into him was akin to walking into a tree. He was over six foot tall, dark with a decidedly Mediterranean look about him. I let out an "Oh Christ I'm sorry" and fully expecting a bollocking. I was surprised to hear nothing more than a

"Sugar" uttered without even a raised voice. He was carrying a bundle of patients' charts and they fell from his arms and scattered all over the floor. I dropped to my knees and began to gather them together. He joined me. I stood and stuck out my hand, "Robbie Valentine, Perfusion, Theatre." I looked at the nametag on his starched white shirt, Martin DeSouza.

"I'm only here a few months and I'm still trying to find my way around," he explained, "might see you around the house." He shifted the bundle in his arms and headed off up the corridor.

"Yeah, see you about." I headed for the back door of the operating theatre. This door was opposite the rear entrance to the Intensive Care Unit and close to the medical Cardiac ward where patients for Heart Surgery were usually kept during the work up for surgery. On the corner of the corridor leading from the ward and passing both Intensive care and my office stood a huge man. Looking a little lost, he shifted from foot to foot inspecting his shoes and looked up and down the corridor occasionally. I guessed he was in his late thirties. He had a silver military style haircut with boot cut jeans and a white shirt. A mustard check country style jacket stretched over his massive shoulders. He turned towards me. Immediately I noticed the bulge below his right armpit. This was obviously causing the wearer some discomfort. It was quite obviously a gun of some description in a shoulder holster. I was about to challenge him when it became clear to me that he could only be one thing, a plain clothes detective. Then a huge grin spread across his face and mine.

"Gorgeous McGovern," I laughed holding out my hand.

"Robby," he took my hand almost crushing it. George McGovern was an old schoolmate from the Christian Brothers. We kept in touch for a few years but had lost touch and only met again over ten years later at a recent 21st school reunion. He had told me that he was trying for the detectives' exam but didn't hold up much hope. "How's it going George?" I asked.

"Great Robbie," he grinned. "I passed the Detectives exam, God only knows how, and here I am."

"Cool," I said. I was genuinely pleased for him. "What are you doing here?" I asked, "Investigating one of our Docs, I hope."

"No such luck," he laughed, "no, babysitting, I'm afraid, your guest of honour inside here needs protection." He held his hands in the air and drew quotation marks. There was clear disgust in his voice which surprised me as George was normally completely unbiased when dealing with any criminal. He felt that everyone was innocent until proven otherwise. He obviously had made an exception in Mulligan's case. "I know the sort of protection I'd like to give him."

I laughed out loud. "Careful now DI McGovern," I said with a mock Kerry accent, "I'll have to report you to the police complaints authority."

We shot the breeze for a few minutes until his radio interrupted our ramblings. I headed for theatre and he headed to relieve some other detective probably to provide a fresh set of fists to encourage some scumbag to tell them where the loot was, I mused to myself. We gave the usual promises to keep in touch, but now as he was on protection duty here, we might just manage to get lunch. I entered my office, opened up the email program on the computer and put my lecture notes and discs into my locker. I returned to the computer and entered my password. The usual mix of spectacular offers of money, cheap Hi-fi and Viagra interspersed with standard hospital info greeted me.

In the middle was a mailing from the "opportunity@hotmail. com" address again. I had forgotten about the previous message I received with the phrase that I was sure only I used as a way to describe the job of a Perfusionist. Curiosity overcame me and I opened it immediately. There was an attachment and I ran a virus scan to make sure I wasn't going to be responsible for crashing the hospital system. The attachments passed the virus scan and the screen showed two attachments, a .jpg file and a .tif file. I opened the .tif file first. It was a scanned newspaper cutting from the Times from a week or ten days ago. It was an article that I had read outlining that Mr. Thomas "The Suit" Mulligan was due to undergo Cardiac Bypass surgery in the Southwestern Clinic, under the terms of the National Treatment Purchase Fund.

My curiosity was now firmly aroused and I opened the jpg file. With no idea what to expect, I took a few moments to realize what I was looking at. It was a photo of a row of bicycles and someone removing their cycling helmet and wearing a pair of wraparound Oakleys. It took me a couple of seconds to realize that I was looking at myself. I appeared to be staring directly at the camera but as I was still wearing the sunglasses, it was impossible to tell. I looked at the jacket, a blue golf windcheater and tried to figure out when this was taken. It was probably in the past few days but whatever, it scared the shit out of me. The picture had been taken in the basement of the hospital near the bicycle section. What the hell was this about?

I went back to the main body of the email and read it again, I had missed some text, "take a look at these and maybe you'd like to talk to us." There was a mobile phone number and that was it. I stood staring at the photo of myself with my heart pounding. The first thought that entered my head was "George, I'll talk to George."

I ran towards the door and then a thought struck me, I ran back to the computer, closed down the emails, and exited from Outlook. I ran back into the corridor. Where George had been standing, there now stood a uniformed Police officer. Trying to calm down, I asked the policeman as calmly as I could, "Will Detective McGovern be back today?"

"Sorry Doctor, I don't think so. He's gone back to the station," the policeman answered in a strong Cork accent.

"Thanks a million, I'll call him on his mobile." I didn't have his mobile number, but I thought I had it somewhere at home. I walked back to my office. I sat in front of the computer staring at a blank screen. Bruce walked in. "G'day, boss." He threw his daysack under the desk. As most Auzzie or Kiwi travelers, he carried a small rucksack everywhere. "You're very quiet this morning," he remarked as he opened his paper. I hardly noticed his presence. He leaned over towards the computer, "Mind if I check my email?"

I suddenly woke up from my trance and shot my hand towards the computer. "Hold on a minute," I snapped. I forgot that I had shut down my email and it wasn't on the screen. I didn't want anyone to see this strange email until I had had time to figure out what it was all about. "Sorry mate," I tried to backpedal, "feeling a bit under the weather this morning."

My mind was working overtime trying to make sense of the message and I knew that wherever my mind was, I certainly couldn't keep it focused on managing a cardiopulmonary bypass. "Bruce, could you run the first case, I can't concentrate on taking a piss today." I needed to free myself up for a couple of hours to try to find out what this was all about.

I decided the best way to deal with this was to find out what this was all about before making a song and dance about it. I threw on my white lab coat, changed my shoes and headed out to the service area of the hospital. I had printed the text from the email including the mobile phone number and I had it behind some notes on a clipboard. I walked out into the dull, dank morning. It was the sort of morning that looked like the sun hadn't bothered its arse rising. It matched the way I felt, and I was anxious to get some idea of what this was all about. I took my mobile from my lab coat pocket and dialed the number. I was just about to press the green connect button of my novelty Nokia picture phone. It was one of those that had a radio and a torch built in to it. My finger was on the dial button when a thought struck me. I cursed myself for my stupidity. Using my mobile would automatically send my number to whoever was pulling this stunt or practical joke or whatever the hell it was. I ran back to the department, taking the stairs two at a time. I walked into my office to where Mike, another of my staff, was drawing up doses of the drug, cardioplegia. "I've got to run out to the bank for a few minutes Mike," trying to sound as normal as possible, "Bruce OK inside?"

Without looking up, Mike answered "Yeah, no problem boss, take your time."

I changed quickly and headed out the back door of the hospital towards the group of shops. As I ran across the road towards the shops, a tall athletic figure in a long, expensive wax jacket and a baseball cap pulled low over his face appeared to be watching me. He stepped between a high sided transit van and a Guinness lorry unloading at a local bar, removed a mobile phone from the pocket of the wax jacket, stared in my direction and dialed the phone. Christ, I was getting paranoid now. Everybody was watching me. I shook off the feeling and headed into the first public telephone box. The first thing to greet me was the smell of urine. I rummaged in my jeans for some change and deposited 50 cents into the coin slot. Gripping the receiver between chin and shoulder, I removed the piece of paper with the phone number. I was concentrating on the number so much that I didn't notice that the receiver wasn't connected to the phone. It had been ripped out and placed back on the cradle. There was no chance of retrieving my 50 cent piece. Swearing, I moved to the next one. This time I was in luck. I found another couple of twenty cent pieces, and after firstly checking for a dial tone, inserted them. Not having used a public call box for years, I dialed the number. I hoped that there was enough in the eighty cents or so that I had inserted for what I hoped would be a quick "fuck off and leave me alone" type of conversation. I hit the last few digits and my stomach went into a knot as the ringing sounded in my ear.

My heart leapt when the call was answered, "Robbie, me old swiss, we've been expecting your call" said a rough voice with a flat inner city accent. The familiar greeting took me by surprise and it took me a couple of seconds to regain some composure.

"Who is this?" I demanded with as much authority as I could muster with a bone dry mouth.

"It's rude not to answer your emails" said the voice.

Again I looked for some clue as to what this was about, "Who the hell is this and what do you want?" My mouth felt like the inside of Ghandi's sandal and I looked longingly at a poster for Coke Cola outside. Some Brad Pitt lookalike was surfing on what appeared to be a fountain in the middle of a park.

"Now Robbie, a certain rather famous individual will be coming into your place of employment over the next few days" the voice started to get down to business.

"Who are you talking about?" I asked forgetting about the scanned news cutting.

"Did you read the fucking email?" the voice asked with thinly disguised irritation.

"Yeah, something about a Mr. Mulligan coming into the hospital for heart surgery" I answered with what I hoped sounded like the same irritation.

"We know that you'll be there when he goes under the knife, and we'd like you to do us a little favor, right!" said the spook.

"You can fuck off if you think that I am going to breach a patient's confidentiality," I raised my voice for effect, "now fuck off and don't contact me again or I will call the police." I made to slam the phone down but the sound of a throaty laugh that quickly became a fit of coughing stopped me for a second.

"Ah now Robbie, don't be like that" the spook regained his voice. "It's just a small favour, well within your capabilities, and let's just say, it'll be worth your while co-operating with us." The voice had become softer now and was obviously enjoying my discomfort.

I decided that this was it and tried to attack from another angle, "Listen, whoever you are, the police have a department of cyber crime and my next stop will be to contact them with these emails."

"Robbie, Robbie, Robbie, we know all about the Gardai and their little computer games experts, and fuck all use they are too. We also know that you were a little unlucky with the gee-gees and you are into a mutual acquaintance of ours for a tidy little sum, what is it now, four and a half grand?"

My blood froze and I began to feel sick. "Go to hell!" I shouted and slammed the phone down with such force that two passing women stopped and looked at me tut-tutting. I left the call box and headed back towards the hospital. I looked around to see if anyone standing about may have been the faceless spook. Whoever it was had known straight away it was me. An old man outside the post office was speaking on his mobile, but he was in his seventies. A young twentysomething in a dark top over near the bar, looked a bit young for the dark voice. I didn't notice the dark figure in a wax jacket slip down a side alley that led towards the mortuary entrance of the hospital.

II

I was in the back bedroom of my mother's house. Granny used to sleep there. She was asleep in bed and I was about 10. I heard it before I saw it. A low drone. It definitely wasn't a 737. We lived near the airport and were on the eastern approach. By 10 years of age, I could name most of the aircraft that flew overhead on their approach run to Dublin Airport. I looked up and saw a single engine Cesna or something small flying quite low. It appeared to be in trouble. I knew that it was going to crash. The Cesna spluttered and wobbled over the farm behind where we lived. I started calling to my dad. "Dad, dad, he's going to crash," I tried to shout without waking Granny. I watched as the plane got lower and lower and disappeared behind the trees. I tried to run downstairs to tell dad but I felt as if I was running through treacle. I could still hear the plane struggle to stay airborne. Dad was sitting in the armchair smoking. Funny, he never smokes in the living room. "Dad" I called, "did you see that plane, it's going to crash." I looked out the living room window just in time to see the plane disappear behind the trees and a large black cloud appeared. "That was that bastard Cassin" Dad said without looking up. "The guards will have a field day trawling through his records. I believe the world and his wife owed him money. They're all in for a visit now from the cops." A cold sweat came over me and I began to feel sick. The next door *neighbor's dog began to bark. Noisy little bugger, he barks all the time, keeping Dad awake when he works nights.*

THE DOG CONTINUED TO BARK. I woke up, still with the same sensation in my stomach. A nearby dog was giving it large to a milk or paper delivery merchant. I looked at my watch, it was still dark but the glowing hands of my watch said it was 6.20am. I was due in work at 8.00 and the alarm was set for 6.45. I had slept very little during the night. I crept downstairs and flicked on the kettle. Getting dressed in the bathroom, the kettle flicked off and I threw two spoonfuls of instant coffee and an equal amount of sugar into a mug. I reckoned I was going to need the caffeine and sugar shot as I felt as if I was had only fallen asleep when the dog barking woke me.

I sat for a few minutes in the silence of the kitchen. The rest of the house was still fast asleep and it was a rare moment of calm in a bustling madhouse. I mulled over the previous days events. Somebody obviously had been following me and knew my involvement with 'The Horse' Cassin. It was probably some lowlife scumbag's idea of blackmail and I tried to convince myself that I could deal with it. But something was niggling me that there may be more to this than I was trying to convince myself. I shook off the negative feelings, saw that it was close to 7am and decided to head to work. Cycling would help clear my head and I would be there early enough to have plenty of time to set up. I was going to need it given the state of my head this morning. Grabbing my mug of coffee, I tiptoed up the stairs and tentatively put my head round the door of our bedroom. "I'm off now love," I whispered. "See you later pet."

I felt that I could deal with the personalities involved in any scam, fake or otherwise. The one thing that was sickening me was that although Victoria knew about my unlucky history with the horses, I had convinced her that the outstanding debt was a lot lower and that I had paid it off a long time ago. So, as well as having to deal with whatever was the nub of this scam, I was going to have to tread very carefully with Victoria to avoid a river of shit that could threaten my marriage. I wheeled my bike out from the garage into the fresh late autumn morning.

Finishing my coffee, I closed the garage door as quietly as I could. To the west, the sky was a black-charcoal colour that looked ominous, but the sun was making a brave effort to break through the clouds in the eastern sky. It may turn into a reasonable day I thought. Strapping on my helmet and attaching the earpiece to my mobile phone, I switched on the radio. An early morning news talk show came on. The mood I was in wasn't conducive to early morning pontificating so I switched channels and found a music station. I pedalled down the road to REM, "pushing an elephant up the stairs." I pumped off towards work. My mind cleared and I felt better.

I was so engrossed in the music that I hardly noticed the dark tracksuited man, standing back, half hidden behind box-hedging 5 or 6 gates down from our own. He flashed past in an instant. He appeared to be staring at the screen of a mobile phone.

The memory was gone 5 seconds later as I pulled onto the sea front and headed towards the toll bridge and on into the city. I left Sandymount and headed left into Ringsend, an old area that was for a long time, the traditional home of the dock workers. I hit the Canal bike-lane at 7.10 and then took the extremely pleasant cycle towards the west of the city. I arrived at the back entrance of the hospital at 7.30 and immediately my stomach knotted up. I freewheeled towards the bike lock-up area, all the while my head turning like an owl, trying to spot any suspicious characters with cameras. Other than the cleaner, sweeping the tarmac, there was no-one else about. I began to think that it was all a figment of my imagination. I headed to the lift and with Oasis in my left ear, my spirits began to lift.

As the door of the lift began to close, a tanned hairy arm appeared and stalled the doors closing. A tall figure in a white shirt and dark tie jumped into the lift. White noise replaced Robbie as the signal was cut off so I removed the earpiece.

"Robbie, isn't it."

I looked up from switching the radio off on my phone. It took a second for the name to come back to me, "Marty, how are you?" Glad I recalled his name, not a great skill of mine, we shot the breeze for the 2 or 3 minutes.

"You cycle?" He nodded towards my helmet.

"As much as I can," I answered. "Makes you feel better after a long day in theatre, air conditioning an all that hot air," I laughed. The lift stopped and the doors opened one floor up.

"Tell you what really blows the cobwebs off," Marty hung back, holding the lift door by blocking the sensor with his leg, "Kickboxing Circuit Training."

"Really," I asked, with genuine interest, "You into kickboxing?" I inquired.

"At it a couple of years" he responded modestly "Why don't you come along to one of our open classes? You'd love it. You can work at your own pace."

My interest was now firmly aroused. "Where is your club?" I was genuinely interested in starting something like this.

"In the Southshore Gym in Merrion," he answered.

"That's only a few minutes cycle!" I was delighted.

"There's one on tonight at 6.30," he gave me the lowdown. "If you're interested, just wear loose tracksuit leggings and a tee shirt. We have everything else you'll need."

"Yeah, sounds brilliant, do I need to be a member or something?" I was animated now.

"No, just ask for me at reception," Marty replied.

"Super, I'll do my best to make it, see you there I hope." Suddenly the thought of something completely removed from all the politics and crap of what was going on was extremely inviting. I decided to make a big effort to attend.

As he headed away, Marty turned back, "Don't know if

you're into the horses, but there's one running in Goodwood today, Weatherman, eight to one shot."

I smiled, "No Marty, I gave that up a couple of years ago." Suddenly the old ghosts came out to haunt me. Two minutes of mental yoga and I pushed the urge to gamble back into the bowels of my brain. I headed on into the Theatre changing room.

Ten minutes later I headed into my office to check the schedule for the day. The list for the day showed three Cardiac procedures, two routine Coronary Artery Bypass Grafts and a re-operation to replace a previously repaired Mitral Valve and also two bypass grafts on a 48 year old woman. The re-op procedure was scheduled first. Today's surgeon, Kevin Graham, a 50 year old, abnormally high IQ, naturally gifted surgeon who was known to invent procedures on the spot. Mr. Graham had fixed ideas about how he liked the tubes arranged on the table. Any deviation from his standard would invite a bollocking in front of the entire team. However, during re-ops, I felt that the perfusionist had the final say on any changes to the bypass circuit. I checked in with Mike. He was almost finished and the patient was ready to be wheeled into the operating room. "You ready to go here?" I quickly scanned the pump and the circuit "I think you should add the supplementary lines now," I told Mike.

"Good idea, but you know what he's like," Mike responded.

"Why don't you cut them in and hide them under the drapes?" Mike's eyes widened, I went on, "If shit happens during the incision, the extra lines are ready to use, if it doesn't, and they are not needed, he never saw them, no harm done."

I headed back to my office. The computer on my desk was already switched on which wasn't unusual. The surgeons always watched the angiogram film before any cardiac procedure. The film came on a DVD disc and the program to view the films was loaded onto six or seven computers in the hospital.

Unfortunately, my computer was the most popular spot for three or four surgeons to gather discussing the findings.

I was in luck this morning, although the computer was on and opened on the viewing program, there were no surgeons in sight...yet. I quickly closed the viewing page and opened Outlook express, the email program. My guts were in a knot as the pages slowly opened, I let an audible sigh of relief as I realized that there were no emails from my new mates. Maybe it was a complete hoax after all and I had put the prospective blackmailer off.

I began to relax for the first time in a few days and my mind wandered to the kickboxing class that Marty had invited me to. I called Victoria in her office and was glad when she answered. I knew she was smiling as I told her about the kickboxing class. "What time will it be over at?" was her only comment. "I'll be home before 8," I answered, "and if I take it up, you'll have a lean mean fighting machine for a husband!" I joked.

She burst out laughing, "Will you be fighting with anyone?" she was still laughing.

"Don't know," I was laughing with her now, "I didn't ask."

"I'll be home by 5.30 and you can go," she finally said.

"Great, see you after work love," I was delighted. I was surprised to see that the patient had been put on Heart/Lung bypass through the main blood vessels in her groin. Normally there would be a drama if this happened but I hadn't heard a thing. "What's the story Mike?" I asked.

"Nicked an artery on the way in. Bled badly and he started shouting about going on femoral bypass," Mike explained with a grin.

"Did he mention the extra lines that were ready?" I inquired.
"No," Mike was laughing now, "he actually explained to the assistant that he always had them ready like this, nearly pissed myself laughing when he said it."

"I hope you blamed it on me, like you said you would."

"I can't get him tickets for the Game on Sunday so I'd better redeem myself with this." Mike was an ardent GAA player and he had contacts in his club that could sometimes get him tickets for games that were normally sold out. "Go on with you and do some chiefy stuff and quit bothering me," Mike dismissed me with mock distain.

After an hour or two of paper and other boring administration work I looked at my watch and was surprised to notice that it was well after 1pm. The last case was being wheeled into the operating theatre, so this meant that the operating list was heading for a nice early finish. I decided to head to the hospital restaurant for a quick sandwich and then if everything was ok with my team, head home.

One chicken balti sandwich and a coffee later, I changed back into civvies and made my way to the bike lock-up. I was leaving the service area when I met Marty carrying a cardboard box marked with the Blood Bank logo. He acknowledged me. "See you later?" he mouthed, pointing to his watch.

"Yeah, looking forward to it," I answered, "just booking a place in casualty for after the class," I grinned. He laughed and I climbed up on to my bike for the cycle home. I was feeling much better. The day's work had gone smoothly. There were no further emails from my new mates and I definitely thought that the whole thing was just a flash in the pan. I was looking forward to the class that night, although not knowing what to expect slightly unnerved me.

Arriving home, I fished out an old but clean tracksuit trousers from my wardrobe, found a towel and a clean tee-shirt and threw them into my sports bag. I left the bag ready in the hall. Checking the time, I realized that I had just enough time to collect Nicholas from Montessori school. Alice was finished an hour later, so I decided to give the kids a treat. I went to the back shed and took out the child seat that fitted on the back of my bike. It was a reasonable day. I knew that Nick would get a thrill when I arrived unannounced with his

Spiderman bike helmet. I arrived just as the teacher was opening the door. Twenty odd three and four year olds strained to see their mothers or pick ups. I spotted Nick through the window of the class comparing Action Men or something. He strolled out towards the door. His face broke into a huge grin when he saw me. I had hidden his helmet behind my back but left my own one on.

"Daddy," he shouted and ran towards me. Then he stopped when he didn't see his own helmet. "Are we going on your bike?" he asked with big pleading brown eyes.

"No, I don't think so, I think its going to rain." I tried to keep a straight face.

He looked up at the sky and scrunched up his face, "No, I don't think so." He had a very serious face on and I started laughing. I took his helmet from behind my back and he started jumping up and down.

"Yeah, cool" he said and ran over to one of his friends who was climbing into the back of a large 4x4 jeep. "Jonathon," he shouted, "I'm going home on my daddy's bike."

Jonathan looked suitably pissed off with his mum for arriving in a €50,000 jeep when his mate was going home on a bike. "Mum..." he started. Jonathan's mum, a striking looking blonde in her mid thirties, looked at me and rolled her eyes.

"It's the simple things that keep them happy," I called out, "and it's cheaper than the gym."

She laughed at me and promptly turned away to answer her mobile, "Yah, yah...yah, tennis for 11 and lunch for 1 at Roly's then." She snapped her phone shut and strapped Jonathan in. Great life, I thought to myself. I fastened Nick's helmet and lifted him into the child seat.

He was chattering a mile a minute and somewhere between Jonathan's painting accident and Micha falling off the slide at lunch I heard that there was to be a trip to the zoo with the class later that week. "Miss Barry gave us a note." He started rummaging in his bag.

"Leave it till we get home, soldier," I said, "you need to watch out for enemy snipers." That usually got his attention. He settled down for the fifteen minute cycle home.

An hour later, we left the house in my car to collect Alice from school. We stood outside the gates with the mothers and minders. Through the locked gates, I could see the classes starting to stand up and get their gear ready. The school janitor arrived to unlock the gates and the crowd surged forward to greet the hemorrhage of little red uniforms spilling out from the double doors. At the centre of the building. I hung back until I saw Alice's teacher appear. She looked in my direction and I waved. She gave me a smile and I recognised the first few girls from her class. I bent down on my hunkers, and spoke to Nick, "When you see Alice, tell her that you have been sent to pick her up instead of Mammy, pretend."

Nick grinned, nodded and charged forward and as soon as he saw her, he ran up to her and started speaking. I could see her face crease with a puzzled frown. She looked around, took his hand and walked towards the gate. As they approached the gate, I could hear Alice speak, "You will have to hold my hand crossing the road." She had put on her grown up hat now and adopted the role of big sister. She was very like her mother, very practical and responsible.

I stepped out from behind the pillar. "Hi, good looking," I sang.

Alice broke away from Nick and jumped into my arms. "Daddy, I thought mammy was coming today!" She buried her face into my shoulder. Then suddenly she lifted her face and put on her grown up voice, "Nicholas told me that he was here to collect me, but I knew that he is much too irrispondible for that."

"We were having a joke sweetie," I smiled.

"I knew, because Nicholas will have to be much more rispondible." Obviously the new word for the week. She chatted non-stop back to the car and ten minutes later we were back home. After having performed some domestic chores, including supervising Alice's homework, and making some dinner, I finally sat down for five minutes. I had called Victoria at work and left a message that all was well at home. Five minutes later I received a text message, "I'll be home in time for you to go out, Jean-Claude." It took a minute to realize that she was referring to Jean-Claude Van Damm. She probably had a good laugh with the girls, telling them that I was starting kickboxing. I replied to the text, "Do you have anything I could use as a headband!!"

At 5.30, I heard the car pull up in the garden and two minutes later the hall door opened. "I'm home!" Victoria called out.

"Mammy, do you know what Daddy and Nick did today?" Alice was off. I had the dinner ready but had decide not to eat as I had no idea how intense the training class was going to be and the last thing I wanted was to be struggling with a stomach full of spaghetti trying to keep up with the class.

At 6pm, I grabbed my sports bag and headed for my bike. "Where are you going Daddy?" Nick asked.

"Kickboxing," I replied.

"Coowell!" was Nick's response and he immediately struck a ninja turtle pose. "Like this?" he asked as he punched and kicked the air for all he was worth. "Can I come?" was the inevitable follow up.

"Sorry son, no can do," I lifted him up, "but I promise that I'll show everything I learn."

"Deal!" he gave me thumbs up. Alice just rolled her eyes and mouthed the word "boys" to Victoria. After the usual ten minute send off from the kids I was pumping up towards the Merrion road and on towards the state of the art building that was the Southshore sports and tennis club.

The lobby was a mix of glass and chrome; festooned with plenty of designer leotards and headbands on display alongside expensive tennis racquets and branded sportsbags. There was a small shop in the lobby selling designer tee-shirts, shorts and other expensive accoutrements that one just couldn't do without. I expected to see a canister of designer spray-on sweat among the vast array of liquids.

I spotted a shelf full of some isotonic yellow greeney drink in an impressive looking bottle. Trying to leave the house with as little fuss as possible from the kids, I had forgotten to throw a bottle of water into my bag. I strolled into the shop and browsed an impressive array of multi-colored rehydration therapy. I opted for a 750ml bottle of water with a sports cap. Ignoring the flashy looking prehydration fluid that would be absorbed 33% faster than water; I hoped that the extortionate price of my water would be justified by the "sports style, easy dispenser for the active life; filtered for thousands of years by Nature's purest volcanic rock."

Wondering why it had a best before date, I paid the equivalent of the price of a pint at my local to a tall blonde goddess in a Kappa tracksuit. She gave me a smile that alone probably justified the membership fee of the club that I had heard required a small mortgage to fund. Throwing my investment into my sportsbag, I headed towards the main reception.

"Yawh, yawh. So I, loike blanked him totally! Yawh, totally, by email, it was, oh my god!" Another airhead model was staffing the reception. There was a constant stream of members through the electronic turnstile. A membership card with a barcode on the back was scanned by a supermarket style scanner and the gate opened automatically. I felt like scanning the barcode on the back of my €4 bottle of Grand Cru water, just to see what would happen when I was greeted by a "Good evening sir, how can I help you?"

I looked into two china blue eyes. She was no more than twenty and had a body that most women would die, or at least pay vast amounts of money to a plastic surgeon for.

"I'm looking for Martin DeSouza," I said. "I think he's…"

I noticed a slight reddening of her cheeks as she immediately interrupted me, "No problem sir, I'll just page him."

I was expecting to have to give a long winded explanation but Marty obviously was well known to the female staff. She dialed a number and, turning slightly away from me half sang, half spoke, "Marty, como esta?" He was obviously flirting with her and her face went slightly pink as she gave a schoolgirl type giggle. "There's a gentleman here to see you," she just got out before bursting out laughing again and hanging up. "Sorry, he's loike, such a tease." She gave me an apologetic look.

I was admiring the futuristic reception area when Marty appeared from behind the reception area, a towel thrown loosely over his shoulder.

"Robbie," he stuck his hand out.

Shaking his hand I asked "Don't tell me you've started without me?"

"No don't worry, just taking a warm up class," he answered. "Katrina, be a pet and sign Robbie in." He leaned over to the Gwynett Paltrow lookalike.

"Only if you promise me an extra hour of Spanish," she gave him her best doe eyes.

"Sí señora," he crooned with his Spanish eyes half closed, "Mañana my sweetheart!"

Blondie blushed and we headed through the turnstile. Marty led me through the changing room. "By the way, that horse won today," he pointed towards the bench "You can leave your bag here."

Half of my brain, the part that had succumbed to the gambling in the first place wanted to shout out, "ah fuck." The other half completely ignored the comment.

The room was surprisingly sparse considering the luxurious surroundings of the reception area. I grabbed a towel and my expensive water from my bag and followed Marty. I had noticed that Marty was barefoot and I took his lead. Removing my shoes and socks, I followed him into a large rectangular room, about 25 metres by 15 metres. Kitted out with punchbags, an entire wall of mirrors and an oversize stereo in the corner, it resembled a dance studio with fighting equipment set up for good measure. With rubberised matting, it was quite comfortable underfoot.

There were about ten others in the room. Some were in various positions of stretching and bouncing on the balls of their feet. This looked serious. I started to perform some basic stretches. I didn't know if I was doing them correctly. I had cycled to the club so I reckoned that I was reasonably warmed up. On the dot of 6.30, an instructor entered the room and turned up the music. A fast thumping disco rhythm piped out and the class started jogging around the room. I parked in behind a short squat chap of about twenty-five and used his rhythm to pace myself. For the next forty minutes we performed a variety of different aerobic excercises. I managed to keep up with the class.

At last we stopped for five minutes. I immediately ran to retrieve my nectar. I swallowed over half the contents of the bottle in one gulp. I looked about, expecting to see the rest doing the same. However they were all busy tying on boxing gloves. I spotted Marty rummaging in a large green box. He looked up at me, "Try these on Robbie." He threw a pair of blue boxing gloves at me.

I pulled the gloves on, and tightening the Velcro straps I headed back to the business area. The class was broken up into three groups of different levels. It was then straight into left fighting stance and I began to learn a whole new set of skills. Left jab, right cross, right uppercut. Front kick, side kick, roundhouse kicks. Under the guidance of the instructor, I kicked, punched and bashed a punchbag for all I was worth. My technique was gently but firmly adjusted until I was surprised how effective a single punch, properly thrown could be.

Marty was with another group going through forms for their upcoming examination. The level and proficiency at which they worked was a sight to behold. With almost balletic grace they kicked almost twice their own height but hitting the punchbags with awesome power. Marty strolled over to me with a wide grin. "Enjoy that?" he asked me.

"Fantastic, really enjoyed that," I was animated, "same time next week?" I was already planning a trip to buy some cheap boxing gloves and a decent track suit for my next class. "Thanks a million for inviting me Marty," I stuck my hand out and he struck a left fighting stance with his fists ready.

"Sorry, force of habit," he laughed. He shook my hand, "Probably see you in work this week."

He saw me to the changing room door and then he disappeared into the instructor's office. I polished off the rest of my expensive water, grabbed a quick shower and 20 minutes later was pumping my bike back down the Merrion road towards Sandymount.

12

THERE FOLLOWED A WEEK of relatively normal work and family activity. I had no more emails from my new mates and with a few days of reasonably easy surgical lists, I began to think that it all had been a figment of my imagination. Our VIP patient in intensive care had caught a cold and developed a chest infection. He was transferred out to the Cardiac ward and despite holding up a valuable high dependency bed; his surgery had been postponed for a week or two at least.

This morning, I was woken thirty minutes earlier than my alarm by a hyper-excited Alice. She was going on her school trip to an open farm in County Meath, and she might as well have been going to Disneyland for the excitement. Having changed her mind eight times about which Wellingtons she would bring and packing her lunchbox herself, I made my escape to work just as a sleepy looking Victoria appeared on the landing. Blowing them both a kiss, I jumped on my bike and headed to work. I arrived at the office bright and early. After checking the operating list, I assigned the cases to the team, and headed to a meeting in the administration block. This morning's exciting feature was an overview of the hospitals new Patient Administration System. This was a computer system that managed the records of all aspects of patients'admission, treatment, drug prescription and final billing on discharge. Normally I would have had very little to do with the computer records of the administration side of a patients visit to the hospital, however, the management were making a big deal about it and were ensuring that all department heads were reasonably well versed in its operation. I signed in to the training room, grabbed a cup of coffee from a breakfast trolley and, never one to miss an opportunity, a Danish pastry. I headed to an empty chair halfway down the room and nodded to some familiar faces from other departments and settled down to tuck into my sticky pastry.

A freshfaced young man with prematurely receding hair took the podium and proceeded to give a demonstration of what the new system could do. I leaned back in the chair and paid just enough attention to his Daffy Duck tie to stop me falling asleep as I learned how to admit a patient on to the system, enter demographic information, insurance details. These all used drop down menus and the whole system appeared to be very user friendly. He then moved along to the "Theatre" section of the program. This again showed how operations could be booked onto the system, how operating space could be reserved by the Surgeon's secretaries and how the disposables used during the operation were billed to the patient's account. I was starting to doze off when Daffy showed an example of booking a patient for a Heart Operation. I sat up suddenly and had an idea. I waited until he was finished and asked if there were any questions. I waited for a moment before raising my hand and could hear the audible huff when Daffy pointed in my direction. "Yes Sir?" he prompted and judging by his expression, the last thing he wanted was a question from the audience.

"Is there a facility in the system to call up historical records for research?" I inquired.

A puzzled look came over his face, "Could you give me an example please?" he asked pleadingly.

I could hear the impatient shuffles and movements as the audience announced their disapproval as the talk would now go longer than the allotted forty minutes. "Could I for instance make an inquiry like how many males sixty years or older underwent Coronary Artery Bypass surgery in the last six months, operated on by...say...Professor O'Riada?" I was as clear as possible so as not to prolong the agony.

"Oh I see Sir," Daffy looked relieved, "yes, that would be possible, the only thing is that you would have to have a higher level of access, or come to the IT department and we could do it from there."

I was thrilled with the response as my department could now at last have an easy way to do some meaningful research without the normal camping out in the medical records department trawling through charts. The meeting broke up and I headed back towards theatre. I was scheduled to run the bypass on the second procedure. It was routine Coronary artery bypass grafts with the lovely Peter Reddy and I was delighted to see that one of my team had set up and primed the pump that I was going to use. The anesthetist and his assistant were still working on the last few fluid lines and then all that remained was to position the patient and wheel the operating table into the operating room. I had just enough time to gather the vital statistics that I needed so I grabbed a blank bypass data sheet and headed for the Anesthetic room. Scanning the chart, I found the numbers I needed, patients height, weight, blood group, hemoglobin, etc.

The meeting that I had been to earlier had shown the information that could be gleaned from the system. The roll out had started and the charts all had a new admissions page just inside the cover of the chart. This gave all the patients personal information as well as the insurance and financial details of the patient. I studied this with my idea for research in mind; I saw how useful it could be. Beside the "planned procedure" section, I noticed the insurance class details. On the old system, this would have shown as "A, B, C...etc," corresponding to the standard Voluntary Health Insurance details. "1, 2, 3..." corresponding to the two or three other insurers recently having entered the market. Then there were a variety of others that were self explanatory, G for the Garda plan, GU for Guinness employee plan and so on. This patient's new admission sheet showed EI-TP. Scanning the rest of the new admission sheet, I got some ideas about some simple research that we could use to test the new system. Something simple like the average age of female patients that were coming in for Cardiac Surgery or the geographic spread of the patients undergoing different procedures.

The doors of the operating theatre opened automatically and the massive frame of Mick, the senior theatre porter, skillfully wheeled the operating table from the anesthetic induction room and positioned the table perfectly in the centre of the operating room. He kicked the brakes on and turned to me. "Hey, Robbie," he said with a grin, "hear you're taking up Kung-fu."

I struck a pose, "Yeah, and you better watch yourself" I gave a scowl.

We were lucky this week to have a very skilled team of senior residents. We had two residents from Bahrain who were very experienced and skilled. Despite having completed their training and having been working in Oman for a number of years, they had rejoined the University training program for a year to gain experience in transplants. They were with us for a couple of weeks while their registration for the University transplant program was formalized. Their presence here meant that at least an hour would be knocked off the operating time.

Sure enough, Nasser and Habib appeared fully scrubbed and ready to go. Habib took up his position at the chest and Nasser started at the leg and within ten minutes, there was a buzz of industry as the operation got underway. With such skilled help and an anticipated shorter than normal operating time, I decided to get as ready as possible so as not to be chasing my tail when the call came to get the kit ready. I pushed the Heart/Lung machine up to its regular parking space beside the operating table and connected the oxygen and air hoses to their respective connections. One of the floor nurses passed me with an armful of sterile swab packs; I nudged her and asked, "Is Mr. Reddy here yet?"

"I don't think so," she replied with a quizzical look, "why, is there a problem?" She looked concerned.

"No," I explained, "the opposite, with Habib and Nasser scrubbed we'll be ready for him very quickly. Why don't you call him and gently remind him that we have expert help this morning."

Her eyes opened wide. "Good thinking!" she replied. She headed towards the corridor.

I continued with my preparations, and within ten minutes I heard Habib quietly ask the anesthetist to lower the table. This meant that he had finished harvesting the internal mammary artery from within the chest wall. This was at least twenty minutes faster than most other resident surgeons would take to prepare the artery. I upped the speed of my preparations, handing the sterile tubes to the scrub nurse.

"Heparin please," Habib asked with consummate politeness nearly thirty minutes earlier than would be normal.

We were ready now to give the drug that would stop the patient's blood clotting so we could safely use the Heart/Lung machine

With the tubes in position, I called over to the scrub nurse, "Will you let Mr. Reddy know that we have given the Heparin?" She nodded and headed towards the door to telephone him.

I finished setting up and moved to the head of the table to draw a blood sample to check that the clotting time was now sufficiently high to start using the machine. With the test tube slowly rotating in the clotting timer, I ran back through my office to grab my briefcase and headed. As I grabbed a handful of notes, I noticed that the computer was switched on. I paused for a second wondering if I had time to check my email. I stretched towards the mouse only to hear the dulcet tones of Mr. Reddy.

He sounded in good form and was shouting instructions from the changing room, "Tell Habib to go ahead and cannulate, I'll be with you in a minute."

I abandoned my idea of checking my email and headed back to the operating theatre just as the floor nurse opened the door and called, "Robbie, suckers on please!" This was my call to start the internal pump suckers that would recycle any blood that was sucked back to the Heart/Lung machine. Habib was motoring along at a rate and he was ready to put the tubes into the heart that would connect the patient to the Heart/Lung machine. We were nearly forty minutes ahead of schedule, and the fact that Reddy was in theatre meant an early finish.

He sauntered into the theatre and said brashly, "Habib, why can't you stay full time here, you'll save me a fortune, I'll be back in my rooms by 10."

Habib kept his head down and said shyly, "You couldn't afford me sir."

Reddy laughed and headed to the scrub area. Ten minutes later he had his head down over a paralysed empty heart, and was concentrating on attaching the pieces of veins and arteries to the patients' heart. The surgery passed off peacefully and the patient's heart recovered from the paralysis induced by the Cardioplegia drug and re-started easily. Fifty minutes after starting the grafting of the veins and mammary artery, Reddy completed the last of the suturing. Within a couple of minutes of placing the last suture, he surveyed his handiwork and noisily slapped off his gloves. "Finish up here Habib, please, there's a good chap," he ordered, stepping away from the operating table.

The rest of the team would be busy for the next couple of hours before he was summoned to join us again. Habib moved to the right side of the table, the traditional lead surgeons' position. He skillfully and with no fuss, attached a set of temporary pacemaker wires to the heart and began to prepare the heart for coming off the bypass machine. When everything was ready, he politely asked the anesthetist to re-start the lungs. They had been disconnected from the ventilator for the duration of the grafting as the Heart/Lung machine effectively was the replacement heart and lungs for this part of the operation.

The procedure for weaning a patient from the Heart/Lung bypass machine varies slightly with each operating team. The basic procedure is to firstly start the lungs inflating, then after ensuring that the heart has a normal rhythm, gradually filling the heart up until it produces a normal output. Then the machine is gradually turned down until the heart has completely taken over the circulation again. This is usually a tense moment during any heart operation as this is the time when many problems will come out to play.

The anesthetist inflated the lungs and when he was happy with their condition, he started the ventilator. The rhythmic hiss of the bellows joined the band, backing up the eighty beeps per minute that the pacemaker was sending to the heart. The most important thing during this part of the procedure is communication. It would spell disaster if the Perfusionist stopped the Heart/Lung machine and the lungs hadn't been reconnected to the ventilator. Equally if the surgeon decided to clamp the tubes coming out of the heart without telling the Perfusionist, there would be a major incident. Filling the heart by gradually occluding the large tube, the heart responded by starting to beat more and more vigorously.

As soon as a respectable blood, pressure was showing on the monitor, I asked out loud, "Lungs going?"

The anesthetist answered "Yes, ventilator is on."

I then started to reduce the flow rates on the Heart/Lung machine. As the flow rates on the pump started to approach zero, I called out the flow rates as I passed through each critical number, "Half flow, blood pressure's good, one quarter flow, happy to come off bypass?"

Habib looked at the heart and then looked at the monitor. "Fine Robert."

I checked one last time with the anesthetist that he was happy, and then stopped the pump. The heart was working well and the blood pressure was holding steady. Habib stood quietly as he always did at this point in the procedure, moving his gaze between the heart and the monitor for a couple of minutes. His calm demeanor was reassuring and added to the sense of relief and achievement that I always felt at this point in the operation.

After a couple of minutes, Habib and Nasser started the final bits and pieces, ensuring that the newly attached veins and arteries were all working and no leaks were obvious. Inserting chest drains, attaching pacemaker cables and the final closure, would all take at least forty minutes so I headed for a quick coffee. We were going to have this patient back to the Intensive Care unit before 11, which meant I was going to be free to perform all the other administration stuff that I needed to do, so I decided to leave it all until the patient was tucked up in bed before I started anything else.

Normally I would grab a few minutes between coming off bypass and cleaning up the disposables from the pump, to check email, write stock requisitions and the like. Today I looked forward to an hour or so uninterrupted productive work. Throwing down a quick instant coffee, I headed back to theatre and after having checked that Habib and the Anesthetist were happy with the patient's condition, I drained all the blood into a reinfusion bag. I handed this to the Anesthetist and started stripping back the tubes into a large yellow disposable bin. Habib and Nasser closed the chest in record time and by ten to eleven, the patient was being wheeled into the parking space for the bed in the Intensive Care unit.

I sat at my desk and opened Outlook. I was shuffling through some invoices as the program's pages opened. Looking up from the sheaf of papers, I glanced at the computer screen. There were about ten or so new emails awaiting my attention. I scanned down the list as I put the papers into a folder, staff briefing from HR, invoice clarification from purchasing and other items of earth shattering importance that demanded my attention. Reaching the bottom of the screen, I pressed the down arrow and two more messages appeared.

I stared at the screen and a nervous feeling came over me. There, above a notification for early booking for the staff Christmas party was a message from my friends at "opportunity@hotmail.com." I stared at the screen for a minute or two. I suddenly realized that I had been holding my breath. I exhaled slowly and looked around. There was no-one else in the office and the second operation was well under way so there wasn't likely to be anyone coming for the next few minutes. I kicked the external door closed and after checking that there was nobody about from theatre, I closed the door to the operating theatre.

My hands were shaking as I moved the cursor to the email notification. I noticed that there was the image of a paperclip beside the notification and this meant that there was an attachment with the message. Getting decidedly warm in the small stuffy office, I double-clicked on the message. It had been ten days since my last contact with my new mates and I had begun to relax, thinking that it had all evaporated and I had sent them packing.

The message opened with two short lines, "Take a look at this. Maybe you will speak to us now." Luckily I was sitting down as my legs began to feel weak as I saw that the attachment was a .jpg file, a photograph. I had been looking forward to my lunch, but now my appetite had all but vanished. Feeling sick, I moved the cursor over to the attachment file and double-clicked. It took about fifteen seconds to open. The image that opened was magnified many times and I had to transfer the file into a photo editor program in order to reduce it to normal viewing size. As soon as I had, I immediately regretted it. I took a few seconds to register what I was looking at, two grey single storey buildings with a gang of children, little girls running around.

"Oh sweet Jesus," I exclaimed, loud enough for anyone passing to hear. My stomach lurched, and I felt like I was going to throw up when I saw an image of my daughter and her classmates running around the schoolyard. It had obviously been taken from a distance away but nevertheless, the image and identity of young Alice was unmistakable. I quickly closed the picture and checked the email message; a second jpg file was part of the attachment. I was beginning to physically shake now. I opened the second image and again drew a sharp breath when I instantly recognized the red and black coat of my four year old son Nick. This one had been taken, probably from a passing car, as there was a small area of what looked like a rain splattered windscreen in the top left hand corner of the image. It was outside the front door of his Montessori school. I scanned the image as fast as I could to see if there were any indicators of when the pictures were taken. No luck on this one, so I closed it down and opened the first one again. I searched for clues. Nothing obvious, but then, in the corner of the picture, just out of the line of sight, was what looked like a tour bus. Zooming in on the image, I could just make out the logo on the side of the bus. I then remembered Alice early this morning, her school trip. The picture must have been taken some time after nine this morning before the buses were loaded with excited kids. A feeling of complete despair came over me. Had they been snatched, to make me comply with some ridiculous demand? I stopped for a minute and tried to take a few breaths.

"Ring Victoria quick!" was my first instinct. I picked up the phone, dialed an outside line and punched in the numbers of Victoria's mobile. Then I thought about it for a second. I hung up before the number connected. I tried to think this through. This was some tactic to scare me and to bring me round to someone's sick way of thinking. So far, the first part was working. I was scared out of my wits, and I couldn't think straight. I started to think about things. Ok, Alice was due to go on a school trip today and Victoria was off work. If anything had happened to Alice, then Victoria would already know about. I relaxed a little. What about Nick? His Montessori teacher was quite vigilant about people hanging about and had a very strict policy about unscheduled pickups. She had been known to piss off a grandparent big time by not allowing the child to be taken as a surprise from school by the poor grandparent until she had cleared it with the parents. I was confident that any suspicious movement would be noted by the teacher and that Nick was still safely in his desk in school. Still, to be sure, I would call Victoria. I tried to focus for a minute or so. Her mobile answered after a couple of rings. "Hi pet," I tried to sound as normal as possible. "How are you?" I inquired.

"Good, I'm in the village having coffee with the girls," she sounded bright and carefree. Hopefully this confirmed my hopes that all was well and that the kids were where they belonged at this moment in time, Alice scaring some chickens to death and Nick playing Spiderman with his mates in playschool.

"Alice get off OK on her trip?" I checked.

"Yes, there was mayhem in the yard before they headed off, comparing lunches and wellies."

I was relieved, "Great, I hope the weather stays good for them." I hung up after a minute or two and tried to gather my thoughts. There was nothing really to worry about at the moment, as nothing had happened, but definitely, I needed to make contact with these people again and see what all this was about. Checking around again to make sure that I wasn't going to have any visitors, I closed the picture file down and returned to the main email message.

There was a mobile number in the message. I jotted the number down onto a piece of paper and stuffed it into the pocket of my scrubs. Then a thought struck me. Quickly I closed the email message and opened the "deleted items" folder. I had deleted the original message, but I hoped that the Outlook program hadn't cleaned out the deleted items folder. Bingo! There it was the original email from ten days ago. I opened it and checked the mobile phone number on the message with the one I had just received. I had a vague hope that if the numbers matched, I could possibly use it to track down the sender if it came to approaching the police. Unfortunately, it was a different number. Whoever was trying to make contact with me was taking precautions by changing numbers regularly. I decided to finish in work and head home. On the way I would stop in a call box and see what this was about. In the meantime, I would try to track down George McGovern, my old schoolmate, now a detective, so I could have his contact details as a last resort if things got ugly. I knew I could rely on his discretion and he'd only give me advice. He wouldn't make any comment about the gambling debt.

After showering and changing, I left the hospital, heading the back of the hospital towards the bike park. I thought for a second, the police station where George was based years ago was located quite close to the hospital. I decided to leave my bike in the hospital and walk to the station first. I could possibly find out where he was stationed now and maybe get contact details. I strolled out the service entrance of the hospital and headed in the direction of the city. The station was positioned at the edge of a large inner-city housing project which was now in a state of disrepair with its fair share of drug and social problems. It was only about a five minute walk.

As I left the back gates of the hospital, I noticed three men leaning against a wall about fifty meters from the gates. They didn't look particularly threatening and I crossed the road in their direction to head towards the city. As I passed them, one of them wearing a brown leather jacket that was facing the other two dropped a cigarette onto the ground and stamped it out. As I approached them, he stepped out backwards and diagonally effectively blocking my path. I was in a world of my own thinking about the rogue emails and I didn't flag any danger. I drew level with them and stepped slightly sideways to avoid colliding. "Excuse me," I muttered, still daydreaming.

"Watch where you're fucking going!" the one in the middle of the pathway blurted out.

He was about my height but I could see that he worked out. He was wiry and wore a few scars on his face. I was momentarily taken aback, "Sorry mate!" I was woken from my trance and instantly apologized, "I was miles away."

"Relax Tommo," one of the other laughed. This one wore the standard uniform of a tracksuit, "You're still hung-over."

I smiled and started to walk away when the third, a small squat, bald character, wearing a golf jumper over a vest with the sleeves rolled up revealing a string of IRA and EIRE tattoos, stepped out. "Got a cigarette bud?" he asked.

I stopped and turned, "Sorry mate, don't smoke." I held out both my palms in an apologetic gesture.

I didn't see it coming, but Christ I felt it. First I saw stars, then I reeled and when I was wondering what had just happened; the pain hit me like a sledgehammer to the side of the head. I had been broadsided by a punch from Mr. Leather Jacket. I was still reeling from the blow when the smoker stepped in front of me and I received a kick in the groin that felt like it had been delivered by an All-Black. My two hands adopted the standard position, clutching my tackle and I bent over, only to receive another blow, but this time right to my nose. I thought my nose had just exploded. The pain was quickly replaced by an over whelming urge to vomit, standard after a swift kick to the nuts. It was compounded by the taste of blood running down the back of my throat. I fell to the ground and curled up into a fetal position. The thought of running away didn't enter my head when all I was aware of was the pain in my groin and what my nose was going to look like. Out of the corner of my eye I could see leather boy lining up for another penalty kick and scrambling to get up, I tried to make a break for it. I heard a bone crunching kick followed by a blood curdling choking sound. It took me a second to realize that I wasn't the recipient of these blows. I looked around and Leather Boy was limping away down the road clutching his face and there was no sign of the smoker. What I saw was Marty standing in classic left fighting stance, delivering punch after punch to the face of the last member of the trio. The swiftness and efficiency with which he was delivering them was breathtaking and the poor bastard's head was lolling from side to side like a rag doll.

At last, Marty stopped punishing the tracksuit and let him go. He wobbled for a second then staggered away down the street. Marty helped me to my feet and I half-fell, half-walked to a small wall and sat down to catch my breath. My head was pounding like I had been hit by a truck and my balls felt the size of grapefruits.

Marty handed me a handful of tissues. "Wipe your face Robbie and come on inside." We walked slowly back towards the hospital. "Let's get your face cleaned up, I don't think it's broken."

Marty gently touched the bridge, I pulled back sharply wincing in pain. "Feels like its three foot wide across my face," I moaned.

"Don't worry, I've seen enough broken noses in training and competition to know, you'll be ugly as fuck for a week but you'll stay a pretty boy."

Laughing and hurt, I began to seethe with anger as the shock wore off and fury began to set in. "What the fuck did they want, who do they think they are? Jesus, they need to be locked up!" I started to rant as the anger overcame me. Coupled with the fear put in by the emails, I nearly lost it.

"Don't worry, that's normal," Marty said gently as we entered the back of the hospital, "a friend of mine, 3rd Dan black belt, worked as a bouncer, was mugged in the park."

My eyes widened, "I'd hate to see the state of the poor mugger," I exclaimed.

"No, you see the trouble was that the guy was such an

athlete in competition, but he had never used his skills outside a ring. He stood there, frozen in fear while some scumbag took his wallet and mobile phone. So don't beat yourself up because some morons got the jump on you."

I was very surprised and it helped take away some of the anger. We headed to the theatre and I got one of the nurses to clean my face and nose up properly. "Thanks a million Marty," I shook his hand, "saved my bacon, big style, I owe you a million."

He slapped me on the back and laughed, pointing at my groin, he chuckled. "Get Victoria to nurse you down below," he winked at me as he headed away down the corridor. Holding the door open, he turned back towards me, "By the way, if you're interested, horse running in Ballinrobe tomorrow, *Two Fat Ladies,* ten to one and another in Utoxeter on Monday, twenty to one outsider, *Chinese take away.*" He pointed an index finger directly at me, "A double could clear your credit card bill."

I sat back in the chair and heaved a huge sigh, where the fuck was my luck at the moment. Anyway, this gave me a good excuse to go to the police station. That would be the first thing Victoria would say to me. I paused for a second, Marty knew Victoria's name. I didn't remember telling him any family details. Anyway it didn't matter; he was in the right place at the right time.

13

"WELL, SOMEONE GAVE YOU a right going over" said the giant Guard behind the front desk as I limped into the reception area of Fitzwilton place Garda station. I explained the events to the desk sergeant. He asked a few standard questions, "Did you recognise any of them, was there anything of value in your wallet?"

I hadn't thought of that. I felt the back pocket of my jeans, my wallet was still there and my mobile phone was still in my jacket pocket. "They didn't take anything, officer," I said with a little surprise in my voice.

He looked over the rims of his glasses, "Sounds like you owe your mate a few pints," he said in his Kerry accent. "I'll make this report and we'll be in touch if we come up with anything." He picked up the book and walked away dismissing me with his body language. Probably the twentieth mugging report this week.

"One more thing sir," I had to almost call out. He stopped and walked back, "I was wondering if you know a Detective George McGovern. He was stationed here a few years ago."

The sergeant eyed me suspiciously. "He won't be able to speed up anything," he said sternly.

"No, no sir," I explained, "we went to school together and lost touch but we met recently and I'd love to link up with him again." He lowered his eyes and nodded, I seized the opportunity, "If you could locate him would you please ask him to call Robert Valentine in theatre in the Southwestern Clinic, I'd really appreciate it," adding "Sir" for effect.

He softened, "I'll check with HQ and try to get a message to him."

I turned towards the door, "Thank you for your help sir" I threw in as I exited the station.

I felt like my luck had taken a kicking as well. Looking up, I noticed a bookies shop across the other side of the street. I thought of the names of the horses that Marty had called out to me. I had sworn never to gamble again, and my luck lately had been so bad, that putting money on a horse would be madness. Pulling my keys from my pocket, some crumpled up twenty euro notes fell on to the ground. Without thinking, I ran across the street. Five minutes later, I left the bookies shop with a docket for a twenty euro double and a wicked attack of conscience. I pushed the docket into the back of my wallet and the guilt to the back of my mind and concentrated on the difficult part, cycling home with what still felt like two oranges inside my boxers. Arriving back at the hospital, the thought of calling my "opportunity" mates made me feel sick. I grabbed my bag and took the back stairs down to the service exit and the bike park. Helmet on, bag on my back, I tentatively sat on the saddle. Adjusting myself slightly, I slowly pedaled out of the hospital and on towards home. I made reasonable progress considering the kicking I had received, but I cycled slower than normal for another reason. Headed along the canal towards Ringsend all the while looking out for a callbox in a quiet location, I never noticed the high powered BMW motorbike that managed to keep reasonably close to me, despite the lack of traffic at that time of the day. I spotted a call box just where the canal entered the final weir at the bridge at Grand Canal dock. An old lady was stepping out of the box when I came across it. I pulled the bike over to the side, and dismounted. Wheeling the bike towards the call box, I nodded at the old lady walking away from the call box. She gave me a polite nod, pulled her bag closer to her and almost ran away from me. I thought it a little strange until I got a jolt of pain as I rubbed my nose. It instantly reminded me of the experience earlier. I must have looked like I had just gone ten rounds with Mike Tyson and I suddenly understood why the old lady looked terrified. A shiver ran down my spine as I remembered the kicking I had received, immediately replaced by a sense of dread and nausea as the voice of that had answered the phone to me when I called, not ten days ago, returned to my memory.

I stepped into the relative calm of the callbox and closed the door. Thinking about things for a second, I had received a strange unsolicited email, a week and a half before that had been written by somebody who knew who I was and what I did for a living. This somebody knew that I could or would be present when a certain Mr. Mulligan, a high profile criminal was due to undergo heart surgery in the very near future, and wanted me to do something. This somebody also knew that I owed a substantial amount of money to a scumbag illegal bookie. This all added up to, Christ, what did it mean?

A wave of panic spread over me, and I began to sweat. I fished the number from my jeans pocket, along with a couple of fifty cent coins. Dialing the new mobile number, my mouth dried up again. My heart pounded as the number connected and a jolt of adrenaline shot through me as the call was answered. "Ah, Robbie me auld swiss," said the same throaty Dublin accent as before. "How've you been Son, how's the wife and kids?" was his pleasantry for the day.

The mention of the kids set me shaking with rage. "What the fuck do you want?" was all I could muster up.

"Robbie, you sound upset, having a bad day or something?" the laugh turned into a nasty cough again.

"Listen," I tried to sound in control and calm, "If you or any of your scum lays a finger on my family, I'll..."

The laugh appeared again. "You'll what Robbie?" he said

with menace. "You're in no position to be making threats, now are you son?" he added in a mocking tone. "We want a favour done, you are in a position to help us and we can make it worth your while." He got straight down to business, "We can help you with your account with Mr.Cassin. I'm sure that lovely wife of yours, what's her name, Vicky, would appreciate a reduction in outgoings."

The sound of Cassin's name, particularly from this bastard's mouth, sounded extremely horrifying and it really put the shits up me. The threat of Victoria finding out and the very mention of her name gave me a sense of despair and I physically collapsed against the wall of the call box. He must have sensed my despair because he seized the opportunity, "Relax, now Robbie, we just need a small favor done, and we'll be out of your hair for good, and we'll sort out your account with Mr. Cassin."

I was silent for a minute or so, and after weighing up my options, and in a cracked, defeated voice, I heard myself say "What do you want me to do?"

Spooky's mood brightened immediately, "Good lad Robbie, this'll all be over in no time." He turned into my best friend. "Why don't we meet for a pint, phones are very impersonal, don't you think?" He adopted an 'I'm your best mate' attitude.

"Where and when?" I tried to be as short as possible, both to psychologically maintain as much distance as possible and, I was concerned that I would lose it, I was still both seething with rage and shaking with fear, and I didn't want to say anything that would endanger Vicky and the Kids.

"How about Molloys, on Grand Canal street," said the voice, as if he was organizing a night's drinking with mates.

"Yeah, I know it," I said. It was actually just around the corner. A regular Provisional IRA haunt if I remembered correctly. The thought sent shivers down my spine as I realized the type of people that I was potentially dealing with. "When?" I asked.

"How about ten minutes?" was the answer. I paused for a second. Whoever I was talking to either was testing me, or they knew exactly where I was right now.

I looked around to see if anyone was following me. I saw nothing suspicious. "I'm on my way home, I can be there in twenty minutes" I tried to gain some control on the situation, and to give myself time to think.

I exited the call box, put back on my helmet and headed back down the canal away from Grand Canal Street. My plan was to circle the area for a few minutes to think, and to see if I could spot any tails. I lifted the bike up the access steps to the canal walkway back on to the road and headed off down Merrion road, towards Jurys hotel and Ballsbridge. I passed Jurys, and headed passed the impressive expanse of the American Embassy. I turned left down Shelbourne road past the AUDI garage and slowed down. As I did, a black, high powered BMW motorbike caught up on me and then accelerated past me. I wondered if that was a tail, I hadn't heard a bike engine as I cycled, but then again, my mind was so preoccupied that I probably wouldn't have heard a truck coming to run me down. I strained to get a glimpse of the bikes details, it was at least an 1100 cc and the only thing that I could make out was that it had a Wexford registration. I cycled on down Shelbourne Road, back towards the canal bridge and a date with God only knows who. As I approached Molloys bar, the knot in my stomach went up a notch or two. I parked and locked the bike in as open an area as I could find. Security, so as it wouldn't be stolen, or so as I wouldn't be jumped again like earlier, I didn't know. It just seemed the thing to do. It was 2.40 in the afternoon, and I wasn't expecting a crowded bar and I wasn't disappointed There were maybe five or six die-hards sitting at the bar, armed with the Racing pages and a pint, and staring like Meercats at some race meeting in some obscure part of the UK. Funny, in an ardently provisional IRA bar, they still pay homage to the Premiership and UK racing.

Seems sport is the only totally non-sectarian, international pastime. As my eyes adjusted to the semi-darkness, I looked around. These bars were all the same whatever part of town or whatever part of the world you found yourself in. An elderly, silver haired barman looked up at me and raised his eyebrows. As he was about to speak, obviously to inquire as to my health and how could he help me, a slightly built youngish chap in a tan check sports jacket stepped out from behind a pillar at the end of the bar. "Robert?" he held out his hand.

I didn't feel like shaking hands with the scum that were holding me by the balls, but as it wasn't the spook that I had endured on the telephone, I shook his hand. No point in making enemies. Christ, the last thing I needed was someone to take an instant dislike to me when they, to all intents and purposes, had me by the nuts. "Robert Valentine, pleased to meet you," I said. No sooner had I said it when I realized how ridiculous it sounded under the circumstances.

"Sorry to drag you in at such short notice," he apologized, leading me to a quiet corner. He looked at the barman, "Two pints please Padraig," he ordered politely.

"Not for me thanks," I held up my hand. My new mate looked insulted. "I'm on call," I explained, "I'll just have a glass of water." I felt stupid explaining myself to these blackmailers, but again I thought, no need for hostilities. Also, I needed to stay clear headed.

"OK so," he resigned. We sat down in a corner away from prying ears. "Sorry, I didn't introduce myself," my new friend looked crestfallen. He paused for a second. "Call me Tom" he announced. "I suppose you are wondering what we want from you?" he began. He had a slight northern accent, but he was definitely well educated.

"You could say that," I replied with as little sarcasm and hostility as I could manage.

"The thing is," he adopted the demeanor of an executive at a board meeting, "I work for a successful businessman here in

Dublin." He chose to ignore my look of surprise, and pressed on. "There is another, let's say, company, in this town that is making life quite difficult for my employer. Replacing the head of this company has become a matter of urgency. We know that the boss of this company is quite sick but is due to undergo major surgery in the near future." I was desperately trying to search for some clue as to where I fitted in to this. He seemed to read my thoughts, "That's where you come in." I tried not to show the tremor in my hands and I was sure that he could hear my heart thumping against the inside of my chest. "We see this upcoming heart surgery as an opportunity. We would like to have somebody on the inside to ensure that things go the way we want."

I was a little perplexed and it obviously showed on my face. "I'm still not sure where I come in," I tried to sound as naïve as possible, although it was beginning to dawn on me.

"We want you to help us by ensuring that the outcome of the surgery is, lets say, not as good as it should be," he lowered his voice, like a priest in confession.

"You want me to fucking sabotage the operation," I exclaimed, "you must be fucking joking!" I went to stand up.

I don't know whether I would have had the balls to walk out, but he didn't give me the chance. He grabbed me by the forearm, and with surprising strength, pulled me back down into the chair. "Sit down Robbie," he hissed, "and keep your voice down." He quickly switched back to best friend mode, "Robbie, there's a few things that you need to know." I was still shell shocked and sat down. "Firstly," he explained, "we know that you have quite a large outstanding debt with an illegal bookmaker, here in town. We can help you with that."

A feeling of complete helplessness came over me, but I tried to put on a brave face. "I don't need any help with my debts" I insisted.

He looked at me with a face that seemed to be showing pity, "Actually, I think you might need to check that."

"What do you mean?" I asked with a look of panic on my face.

He fished a mobile phone from his pocket and dialed a number ignoring my panic stricken face. "Boss," he said into the phone when it answered, "is our friend with you, good, could I talk to him for a second? Great."

He handed me the phone. With a quizzical look on my face, I took the phone and held it to my ear. "Hello?" I inquired, not knowing what or whom to expect.

"Ah Robbie son, howya," came a strangely familiar voice.

"Who is this?" I asked as politely as I could.

"Ah Jaysus son, don't insult me," replied the husky, inner-city Dublin accent, "It's Joey Cassin, some people call me the horse, and not because I'm a good runner." He laughed out loud at his own joke.

I was taken by surprise and tried to think of something to say, "I'll probably be up to you next week with another payment," was the only thing I could think of.

"Hang on son" Cassin butted in, "Johnny...here was telling me that you have done him a big favor, and he is very grateful." There was a pause and it sounded like he was being told not to mention somebody's name. Cassin went on, "Johnny is so grateful that he has paid off your debt...in full. Christ knows what you did for him but he is very impressed." He laughed again, "So you don't owe me anything. Drop in for a pint if you're in the area, good luck son."

I was a bit thrown and I didn't know what to say. A familiar voice then came on the phone which made my blood ran cold. "Robbie me auld swiss," the familiar throaty voice came on the line, "Robbie, how'ya, I heard you had a bit of trouble earlier. Look after yourself. Talk to Al Pacino there or whatever he's calling himself today, he'll explain the details."

I heard Cassin laugh loudly along with the spook. The phone went dead. I was left with a cold feeling of dread. "I'm well on top of my debts; I don't need any help, thanks," I was panicking now.

"I don't think you understand Robbie," Tom put his elbows on his knees and joined his hands. He lowered his voice, looked around and finally spoke, "We bought the debt from Cassin, you owe us now," he paused for effect. I felt like I had been hit by a truck. He decided to kick while I was down, "We will decide how and when you pay back. Get the picture?"

I nodded slowly. My brain was working overtime, trying to analyse the series of events. I was also desperately trying to think of a way to buy some time to think. "Let me get this straight," I said, "You want me basically to sabotage a heart operation to ensure that the patient doesn't wake up" I tried to put words onto what was fast becoming a nightmare option. "That's fucking insane; I'd be hung out to dry by the law. Besides, if you want rid of Mulligan, why don't you just have him whacked or whatever you guys call it nowadays."

I was talking a mile a minute but was quickly silenced by a hand on my arm. "Robbie, we've done our homework, we've looked into this and someone in your position is perfectly placed to help us get what we want. Besides, we don't want him dead, just...permanently incapacitated." Tom was as sincere as the situation would allow. "We don't want anyone to know that it was deliberate. I'm sure a man of your intelligence can come up with some way of helping us, what have you PhD, Masters? You're no fool."

I started to see their plan. Use a totally dispensable pawn that wasn't remotely connected to them. If it worked, they have effectively eliminated a major opponent in the business. Everybody, except me that is, is happy: if it doesn't, and he survives or I am caught, the buck stops with me. I buried my head in my hands and felt like crying, "Jesus, why me?" came out with more emotion than I wanted to show to bastards like these.

"Robbie, this can be over very quickly. This fucker Mulligan is a major drug supplier into this city. God only knows the misery and hardship that he and his cronies have inflicted on the most deprived parts of Dublin. You'd be doing the country a favor." He waffled on for a few more minutes. I missed most of it but what woke me from my trance was, "We can be very generous to those who help us, but by Christ, we are ruthless to anyone who doesn't." I stared at him for a couple of seconds and the cold stare that was returned to me was truly chilling.

"What if I refuse?" I asked quietly to the floor.

"Well, I don't think you really want to discuss that, do you now Robbie? We need this done, and it will be done. There isn't a lot of time left so the window of opportunity is getting smaller so let's just get on and get it over with and be on our way. Ok?" Tom started standing up to signal that the meeting was over.

"How will I..." I was scrambling for information.

"Don't worry, we'll contact you." He was clear. He stared at me with a look that clearly stated that despite what I thought, these people were anything but my best friends, and said, "I presume you're smart enough not to go to the cops?" It wasn't a question. He turned, straightened, his jacket and then he was gone.

In a daze, I went into the toilet, not to use the facilities, but just to make sure that Tom and his entourage were well gone. Five minutes later, I climbed onto my bike and headed home. My mind was completely consumed with the meeting and I hardly noticed the drizzle that started falling and soaked me to the bone.

14

I STOOD UNDER A SCALDING SHOWER for, I don't know how long. The bathroom door opened and in burst young Nick in his rain coat and wellies. The sight of him brought me back to my senses. The offer, if you could call it that, had consumed me so much that I had forgotten about the emails that preceded the afternoon's events. I jumped out of the shower, threw on my dressing gown and lifted up Nick in a giant bearhug. The thought of the danger that Vicky and the kids might be in came back to me in a flash.

"Dad, what happened your nose?" Nick asked pulling back from my assaulting hug.

"Oh, I was in a fight," I answered, trying to sound matter of fact about it.

"Did you kickbox them, Dad?" he asked wide eyed.

"No they were too quick for me," I disappointed him.

He wriggled free and proceeded to show me how he would have dealt with my assailants, "Like this, huh! And this hiyah!" he showed me his Spiderman moves as he headed off down the stairs, "Mom!" he shouted, "Dad was in a fight."

I dried myself quickly and headed into the bedroom to change. My nose had become a lovely shade of purple but at least it still had its normal shape. My nuts had recovered and I was checking them for bruising when Victoria walked into the room.

"What happened to you?" she asked incredulously, looking at my nose and the cuts on my face.

"I was mugged outside the hospital" I tried to play it down, "they got nothing, luckily that chap Marty appeared and gave them a hiding."

"Lucky you," she said sympathetically as she gently examined my nose. "You'll survive," she smiled. She started to slide her hand down my stomach, "Do we need to check these over?" she grinned mischievously.

I winced as a jolt of pain shot up through my groin and I pulled away. "Maybe later when the bruising has gone" I said. She laughed, "Your loss."

I slept very little that night, pawning off Victoria's attempts to comfort me. "You men are all the same," she said from under the duvet at about midnight, "you are all hung up about being macho, beating each other up, you're still like cavemen." She fell asleep, leaving me alone with my thoughts, at least cavemen didn't have gambling debts, I mused and for the millionth time, tried to find a way out of this mess.

At about 3.30 or 4.00, I was lying, still with my eyes wide open, when I heard the distinct sound of Nick's bed creaking. He was tossing and turning. Then came the expected, "Daddy," pause, "Daddy." I slipped out of bed quietly and tiptoed into his room, almost standing on a toy fire truck. "What's up soldier?" I asked in a gentle whisper.

"Can I have a drink Daddy? I have a sore throat," he asked in a sleepy voice.

I started with the usual responsible parent bit, "Now you know that mammy doesn't allow drinks during the night" but "pleeeeaseeee Daddy" was enough. I had enough on my mind without facing a battle of wits at 4 in the morning with a four year old so I said, "OK, but don't tell mommy."

I headed out on to the landing and down the stairs. The ceramic tiles in the hall were cold under my feet and I danced into the kitchen. I didn't flick the light switch, and when I opened the fridge door opened it threw a glow out into the whole kitchen. I half filled a spiderman cup, at least I hoped it wasn't a Barbie one, and turned and walked into the hall. Although it was dark, the moon outside bathed everything in an eerie ghoulish glow. I was walking as fast as I could while holding a cup of water and scanning the floor for minor obstacles that could be very sore if stood on when something caught my eye. I looked up towards the hall door and here, outside the porch, framed by the glass was the distinct figure of a man. My heart leapt into my mouth and I let out an "Oh Christ," and ducked immediately into the cloakroom, a small three foot square alcove that was built into the wall.

"Who the fuck is that?" I asked myself. My heart was pounding. I gingerly lifted a wax jacket that was hanging in the cloakroom and peered out towards the hall door. Whoever it was, still stood there. I couldn't tell if he was facing or had his back to the door. Slowly he raised a hand holding a cigarette to his face and the glow of the tip told me that he was facing the hall door and appeared to be staring in. I felt the surge of adrenaline through my body but with all the theory in the world about the "fight or flight" system, I was absolutely terrified. Maybe, I should have opened the door and challenged him, but all I could think of was getting back upstairs to where the kids were. Without taking my eyes off him, I rummaged about behind me hoping to find something that I could use as a weapon. I normally kept a baseball bat that I brought to the park with the kids occasionally. It wasn't there and the only thing I could find with any weight to it was one of Alice's rollerblades. I was trying to figure out the best and quickest way to go back up the stairs, all the while keeping a deathlike grip on my only available weapon, a pink, size 26 rollerblade. I weighed up my options, do I crawl along the floor, till I reach the stairs, or do I brazen it out, walking straight back up the stairs, pretending I didn't notice him. Anyway, he solved the problem for me. He turned and appeared to be scanning the road. Then he flicked his cigarette onto the ground. He stamped it out, turned and strode nonchalantly down the garden and out the gate. I stayed in the cloakroom for another few minutes and then, after a deep breath, I made a dash for the stairs, but not before checking that the perimeter alarm was on and hadn't been breached.

Reaching the landing, I paused for a moment, Nick appeared to have gone back to sleep, I had forgotten his drink of water which remained abandoned in the cloakroom. There was regular deep breathing from both Victoria and Alice. The thought of anyone doing anything to my family filled me with a blind fury that left me almost crying with helplessness. I slipped into the spare bedroom at the front of the house and peered out the window in the direction that I thought my midnight visitor had taken. Of course there wasn't a living soul about. I had no doubt that the visitor was sent by my new creditors. What was I going to do, call the cops? It had been made clear to me that that wasn't a healthy option. I wasn't going to get any more sleep tonight, so I grabbed a dressing gown and headed downstairs to think. I sat in the kitchen with a mug of tea in front of me holding my head in my hands. I was nearly crying with frustration. If I went along with the scheme and helped the operation go wrong, I was basically committing murder. If I refused, and contacted the police, I shuddered to think what would happen to Vicky and the kids. The gambling debt hung ever more precariously, like a sword of Damocles over my head. Something that the voice who came on the line after Cassin came back to me with startling clarity, "I heard you had a bit of trouble earlier."

"I was set up," I almost exclaimed out loud, probably to scare me into submission. What was I going to do? Apart from the doubt that I could plant in my own mind that Mulligan could probably die from a hundred and one other complications, or the fact that Mulligan was a known criminal with a large drug empire, I couldn't countenance the thought of my being deliberately directly involved with his death. A slight cough and the creaking of Alice's bed as she turned over in her sleep brought me back to reality. Then a thought struck me. As quietly as I could, I crept upstairs and grabbed my jeans. Back down in the kitchen, I fished in the pockets and after a few minutes of sifting through junk, I found the piece of scrap paper that I had written down the mobile number from the email with the attached pictures. Driven on by a determination to get on top of this, I decided to call them to try to regain some element of control. Our telephone at home was ex-directory, so there was no fear of my home number being transmitted to the recipient mobile. I dialed the number. Praying that it would answer quickly: any delay would allow time for doubt and fear to creep in and ruin what I wanted to sound controlled and logical.

After four rings, the familiar throathy Dublin accent came on the line. "Yeah?" he answered gruffly. I felt an immediate small victory, as the last two times I had called him; he knew who it was before I had opened my mouth, one nil to me.

Inspired by this small victory, I pressed on, "Robbie Valentine here," I started, trying to put as much authority into my voice, as much as to control the shake as to try to gain a slight psychological upper-hand.

"Listen, here, don't you dare fuckin call me..." He sounded irritated, I pressed on regardless. "No, you listen" I interrupted while on a roll, "I've just had some prowler wandering around my house, scaring the shit out of my kids. No doubt one of your monkeys, sent to keep an eye on me. And you seemed very sympathetic about my incident earlier, that I hadn't told anyone about, probably more of your monkeys sent to soften me up. So here's the deal."

He laughed in a mocking tone, "You're giving me orders now sonny, are you?"

Icy fingers of fear and doubt started crawling up my spine and neck as his chilling tone worked its charm. I tried to ignore it and pressed on, "If I or any of my family are hurt, or even scared, I'm going to have to take time off work, and that won't do you any good at all."

"What are you saying to me sonny?" he came back to me in a completely different tone.

"What I'm saying is that for very selfish reasons, I've decided to go along with your lunatic plan. Christ knows what it'll do to my career but I can't afford to take chances with the lives of my family, against a scumbag like Mulligan." I paused for breath. I had decided to try and buy as much time as I could.

"Now you're talking sense sonny," he replied in an upbeat manner.

I sensed the turn and pressed on to play the slight advantage, "If my kids or wife, or myself are hurt or scared unnecessarily, I'm gonna have to take a few days off work, and then you may have lost your 'man on the inside,' so call the goons off."

"I see where you're coming from, but remember, we don't have much time," he added.

"I know," seeing some chink in the defences made me press harder, "that's why I need to know that my family and I will be left alone. I need to do some proper research if I'm to pull this off. You may get what you want, but I'll be hung out to dry if there's any suspicion of foul play on my part, so give me the space to do this, OK?"

"Spoken like a true professional, son" he laughed. "Ok, I'll call the hounds off to let you do your job, but remember, we'll be watching, and any funny business and the gloves come off." He lost his friendliness as he landed the last threat, but for the first time today, I felt as if I had some semblance of control.

"Talk to you soon," I started to sign off, but the line had already gone dead. I needed to find out how much time I really had, and then use that time to find someone who could conceivably help me. A tall order, no doubt but I tried to cherish the small victory I felt I had scored. A sleepy voice behind me gave me a fright, "Daddy, who were you talking to?" It was Alice, in her pink nightdress clutching her fluffy bunny. The sight of her choked me up and I lifted her up, squeezing her body, burying my head into her shoulder. "Just work, sweetheart, let's get you back to bed." I carried her back to her bedroom, glancing out into the front garden as we passed the hall door. I shivered, thinking of the mindless animals that now had a grip on my life and swore that I would find a way out of this quagmire.

15

HISTORY: 54 year old male with previous history of angina. Background: ?MI August 04. Admitted to Cardiac Ward. Retrosternal chest pain radiating to left arm. ST elevation on ECG, Dyspnoea. Angiogram-severe 3-vessell disease. CABG strongly recommended. Placed on waiting list. Upgraded to NTPF waiting list 29th September, surgery scheduled for late October. Episode of severe chest pain with ?asystole. CPR administered at scene.

This was written and signed in the clear legible longhand of the admitting resident. Below it, in unintelligible hieroglyphics was:

Re-angio: 3 Vessel disease, no further deterioration. CABGX4 next Friday. Standard workup please.

This was signed in the illegible but instantly recognizable scrawl of Peter Reddy. I was grateful for one thing, Reddy was notoriously conservative when it came to operating. This explained the fact that Mulligan wasn't due for surgery until next Friday. This gave me a week, plenty of time, I tried to convince myself.

I had arrived for work at 7am having got very little sleep after the phone call to "Johnny." I decided to head to work early to start looking for information that I could use. After changing into theatre scrubs, I headed straight to the ward where Mulligan was. He was in a single-bedded fully private room. The single room was also useful for housing VIPs as the design incorporated a small ante-room that could be used for security or for VIPs assistants. In this case, the ante-room had been taken over by two of Mulligan's goons, who had effectively moved in. Someone high up in the police force had insisted on a police presence even though Mulligan was only under investigation and not under any type of arrest. Although they had been evicted from the ante-room where they would have normally camped in relative obscurity, and were now taking up space in the corridor. I had to show my hospital identity card to one of the detectives to approach the room. Thanks to the design of a drawer system, I could read the chart without having to take it from the room. I explained to the detective that I would be on the operating team and I needed to check if all the information I required was available.

A quick scan of the continuation sheets revealed the first piece of valuable information. This was the fact that I had a week's grace before the surgery. I had hoped to find some other snippet of information such as kidney or liver problems, diabetes, or any other complication that would greatly increase the risk of the surgery, would have been very welcome. This would have increased the chances of the procedure going wrong without intervention of any kind from me. Strange way to be thinking before a procedure. I still had no plan, so to speak but I felt that I needed to have some concrete information that I could talk confidently about should the need arise if Johnny or Tom, my new "business partners" should call again.

I wandered back to my office lost in thought. Waiting at the lift, I was joined by a jovial Marty. He was wheeling a trolley with three locked pharmacy boxes. "Robbie, how are you, nose OK?" he asked with concern.

"Fine, thanks Marty," I answered with little enthusiasm.

The mention of this had brought the whole ugly incident back to me.

"Why don't you come to another circuit training class, help you forget the whole thing, do you good," he suggested, "there's one tomorrow." Sounded good to me. Marty pushed his trolley out of the lift and headed off down the corridor. "Might see you tomorrow then?" he called over his shoulder.

As the lift doors closed, I began to think about the kickboxing class. I began to think that learning how to throw a decent punch or deliver an effective kick might prove to be useful over the next week or two. In my office, I logged on to the internet and sat staring at the Google search page for about five minutes. I didn't know what I was searching for and my brain was ticking over at a million miles an hour. The thought of the kickboxing circuit class drifted into my mind. I typed "kickboxing" into Google and got about eleven million hits. I hit a site from an "International Fitness Association." This gave a list of the basic moves and warm-ups. I scanned down the list of exercises while not really reading them. My mind was completely preoccupied. I was brought sharply back into focus by the exercises that appeared on the screen in front of me:

Nose Jab-Start Position: any, Description: A jab in the nose with the bottom of your palm. Sequence: bring arm back, launch forward with high force with bottom of palm, hit the front of nose. Targets: nose, chin, forehead.

My eyes opened like saucers. I read on:

Ogre Combo: Start Position: Preferable fighting stance. Description: Right punch, left punch, knee strike, elbow strike. Sequence: Right jab (to face) while stepping in closer. Left jab (to face) stepping closer still, follow through with L jab and grab head, pull head down and connect with a right elbow to head. Targets: Face, back of head.

I scanned back through the list. This was a list of moves put together and submitted to a discussion board on combinations and sequences to be used during competitions. Some of them by their description were downright ugly, and would, no doubt leave any opponent in no condition to continue in a competition. A lot of them were preceded with a warning; *this move is for street defence only. Use this move if there is one offender* (the idea is for it to buy you time to run). One that particularly tickled my fancy was the Serufu Dagger:

Start Position: Boxing offensive. Description: Sharp strike to throat. Sequence: draw back left shoulder, deliver a quick jab to offenders face as he is focusing, step forward with the right foot in an uppercut motion strike the offender's throat. Use fingertips not balled fist. Targets: First target anywhere in face. Second is either the Adam's apple or top of the throat.

The thought of how much damage one of these simple moves could inflict was inspiring and I made a mental note that if I made it to the circuit class, I would try out a few of these moves on the punchbag. I was dreaming about using some of these techniques on the three ratbags that jumped me the other day when my dreams were interrupted by the lovely Peter Reddy bursting into the room. He was followed by his entourage of junior Doctors and in ten seconds flat, my office resembled a bar at closing time, with eight or nine white coated interns with the regulation pockets full of medical Dictionaries, Drug formularies, tuning fork and of course the brand new stethoscope that Granny had bought as a graduation present, worn ostentatiously around the neck. And for good measure two or three patient information labels stuck to the sleeves of the starched white coat.

Not being in the mood to listen to Reddy lecturing, I pushed my chair back and headed out the door towards the coffee room. My arse had barely left the chair when there was an immediate jockeying for my vacated position. I headed to theatre to prepare for the procedure I was scheduled to run, an Aortic valve replacement with a possible aneurysm repair, a possibly long and difficult procedure. Ten minutes later I was sipping a mug of tea scanning the Daily Post. Between the obligatory page three boobs and the expanded sports section, there wasn't a whole lot of quality news reported. However I spotted an article by William Livingston about a recent "revenge killing" carried out by one of the major crime gangs in the city. It focussed on the latest in a spate of tit-for-tat killings that was spiralling out of control. The suggestions from the police were that it was a "turf war" involving drug territories. However, Livingston's analysis was that it was much simpler than that and it stemmed merely from a fight in a bar a year previous when somebody or other insulted someone else's wife or girlfriend and a fight ensued outside the bar resulting in someone ending up in intensive care from multiple stab wounds. The unfortunate victim died a month later from his injuries and his gang swore revenge. Five separate shootings and stabbings had followed, all reputedly a direct consequence of the row in the bar. Livingston outlined the connections between the gangs and the victims. What struck me about the details of the killings and the list of victims was the complete disregard for human life, and particularly the fact that the victims and alleged perpetrators were all related, cousins, in-laws. If Livingston was correct, six people had been killed because someone's wife had been called "lard-arse" after a night's drinking. A cold sickening feeling spread over me as I realised that if murder was the response to an insult to the shape of someone's behind, then the consequences of lack of co-operation with such a gang suddenly became startlingly clear.

I dumped the remains of my tea down the sink and headed to theatre mulling over my dilemma. Reddy and about half the juniors had changed into scrubs and were heading up the corridor towards me. Reddy gestured towards me and in an unusually pleasant tone, outlined his plan for the procedure. "Robert," he explained, "I will inspect the aorta after we go on bypass. It looks like the arch isn't involved, but I'd like to have the option to replace available just in case."

This was just as I had thought and set up accordingly. "No problem Peter, I have the kit all ready." I was pleasantly surprised with his demeanour.

Reddy turned to his flock and announced, "Having a skilled competent team that communicate well is a vital to ensure that a difficult procedure such as this runs smoothly."

Reddy's pleasant mood gave me an idea. I decided to approach him after the surgery and give him a very watered down version of the story so far and try to solicit some advice and hopefully some suggestions for a way out of this mire. The surgery went smoothly. Reddy was able to replace the aortic valve and damaged piece of aorta with an artificial valve attached to a ready made tube of Dacron wool. The damage stopped just below the arch and Reddy was able to fix the aorta quickly and simply.

Reddy was in his element with the students present. He was animated and happily explained every move as he made them. He was particularly pleasant to me and this reassured me that speaking to him was the correct thing to do. This made the surgery simpler and therefore a lot quicker. Within two and a half hours, the patient was off the bypass machine and functioning well on his own. Reddy left the operating table. He pulled his gloves off, and rolling them into a ball, he tossed them towards the bin in the corner. He made a scene of, "he shoots, he scores" as the rubber missile landed square in the middle of the "paper waste only" bin. Gathering up his Dictaphone and operating glasses, he dismissed his entourage. "Wednesday morning, bright and early, the joys of post-operative complications number 4 lecture room," he announced to the backs of the departing juniors, as Hassan and Habib started the job of closing up the patient. I waited until he had finished dictating his notes on the operation and nonchalantly followed him to the changing room.

He was on his mobile as I entered so I headed straight to the toilet to wait. "Terry, I swear, it was practically in the hole on the sixteenth when the bastard said to me, I saw you kick a stone from the bunker, that's a stroke where I come from. Well only that my registrar rang from ITU, I would have needed a colorectal surgeon to remove my putter from his orse." A burst of loud belly laughter was clearly audible from the phone. "What time are we teeing off on Saturday, ten? Great see you there." Terry signed off and Reddy snapped his phone shut. He was humming to himself, I flushed the toilet, took a few breaths to steady my nerves and walked back into the changing room.

"That was easier than expected," I tried to sound as casual as possible.

"Yes, He'll do fine," Reddy answered while studying a spot on his cheek in the mirror.

"Have you got a minute?" I asked cagily.

His brow furrowed a little, "Yes, what's the problem?" he asked shifting uncomfortably.

"Nothing probably, but It's just that I got a strange email concerning a patient that we are scheduled to operate on next week."

His look turned to that of a worried father. "Which patient?" he asked.

"That chap Mulligan," I answered. I was trying to be as economical with the information as possible.

"What did the email say?" he inquired, and for a second I could have sworn that he was acting. The way you would if you knew more than you were letting on.

"Something about using my skills to make the operation go the way they want." I was again trying to be economical with the information. I don't know why but it seemed the thing to do. Probably because I was frightened of my gambling skeletons coming out to play and the less people knew, the better.

Reddy paused for a second, as if contemplating his reply. "You know that man has lots of enemies if the reports in the papers are anything to go by, and I wouldn't be surprised if there are quite a few people in this town want someone like him dead." His tone changed to being my best mate. "Have you spoken to anyone else about this?" he asked.

"No, the email strongly suggested that I don't go to the police or anything and I thought it best to talk with you first, captain of the ship and all that?" I bullshitted a bit for effect.

"Listen," he said, "I will speak to a detective I know and find out the best way to handle this. We don't want to create an international incident if this is only a joke email, but we need to take this seriously. He can make discreet inquiries and get back to me. Don't worry about it, we'll look into it." He gave me the cheesy smile that he probably gave to patients when he announced that they had terminal lung cancer and he couldn't do anything but come back and see him in a month at 150 euro a pop. I felt a little relieved having partially shared my load, but not overwhelmingly confident that anything would be done about it.

16

Garda 'Sting' operation yields major drugs haul with link to Dublin Criminal.

Undercover Gardai today intercepted a major shipment of drugs. Heroin, Cocaine, Cannabis and Ecstasy Tablets with a street value of over €5 million. The drugs were found in specially converted compartments of a furniture removal van that had just disembarked from the Holyhead Ferry. The van had been tracked by Interpol from Amsterdam, and following a tip-off, Gardai from the Drugs Unit, posed as potential buyers and distributors for the drugs.

Four arrests were made in connection with the operation, three in Dublin and one in Amsterdam. One of the detainees in Dublin is unknown, but the other two are well known to the Gardai and are thought to be members of the Dublin based criminal gang led by a little known criminal John Brennan. This is the third major seizure this month and the Minister for Justice was full of praise for the Gardai, saying that they were making a major impact on the supply of drugs coming into the country.

The opposition's spokesman on Justice urged caution, saying that although this was a major coup for the Gardai, coming on the back of similar seizures, we shouldn't get complacent. He went on to say that follow through and legislation were required to ensure that the "Godfathers" of crime paid the ultimate price and ended up behind bars.

In a very pointed remark he referred to the fact that instead of being in jail where they should be, some of these criminals were "languishing in luxurious Private Hospitals courtesy of the taxpayer."

That night, I headed out for another kickboxing circuit class. Marty wasn't there. I kept up with the class and I was delighted to be given the opportunity to use the punchbags. I practised throwing punches, and with the help of one of the instructors, after half an hour, I was giving it large in both punches and kicks to Mr Spalding. I noticed immediately the increase in power that could be put into a punch by spinning from your hips and toes and by following through with your bodyweight, a kick could be massively more effective. The class finished but I stayed on for about another twenty minutes working the bag with kicks and punches. Eventually, I showered, changed and headed home. When I arrived home, Victoria was putting the kids to bed and the usual mayhem ensued. After an hour of stories, songs and cajoling, there was silence. Victoria was in great form and we enjoyed a glass of wine and some Van Morrison before retiring to bed at 11.30. I was feeling a little better having spoke to Reddy. I hoped my optimism wasn't misplaced, but, fuck it! I needed something to cling on to.

The alarm on my mobile phone woke me at 6.45. It was another dull dark October morning when the sun was struggling to make an appearance. I had promised to be home early today and so I decided to take the car to work instead of cycling. Grabbing a shower and a quick coffee, I threw my work folder into a black leather satchel that I brought to work whenever I wasn't cycling. It was one of those leatherette bags with a company name and crest printed on the side. I had received it years before at a conference. I disabled the house alarm, I had started putting it on again at night, and was encouraging Vicky to do likewise at night, especially when I wasn't at home. I strolled to my car, a seven year old Megane and hit the alarm remote. It blipped and the lights flashed three or four times, but there was no familiar chunk that signified that all the doors were now unlocked. The first thing that came to my head was that the central locking system was broken and I groaned to myself. However as I approached the driver's side if the car, I noticed that the locking buttons were up. The car was unlocked. Strange, I thought to myself, that means that the car was open already, and the remote reacted by just flashing the indicator lights. I was sure that I had locked it the previous evening after returning from the kickboxing class. I mentally scolded myself for not checking, particularly after the week's events. I opened the driver's door, threw my satchel onto the passenger seat and climbed in.

I immediately noticed something was off. There was a distinct smell of maple syrup in the car. It was a very strange smell to get, had someone had pancakes and syrup in the car during the night? It reminded me of something, I couldn't quite place it but the smell was vaguely familiar. However, there was something else inside the car that was a lot more sinister. In the middle of the steering wheel was a small yellow sticker with a smiley face. No bigger than a two euro coin, it beamed at me like a searchlight. I recognised it immediately. Some years ago there had been a number of reported incidents of date-rape in various colleges in the city. The culprit drug was thought to be Rohypnol, a very powerful sleeping drug, in liquid form. To draw attention to this phenomenon, the students had hundreds of these yellow stickers printed. Students union officers toured the college bars, when they saw an unattended drink on a table, they put a sticker on the glass. This was to show how easy a girls drink could be spiked. The campaign ran for a few weeks and the subject of date-rape seemed to go away. However the message here this morning was loud and clear, and it scared me to death, "we can get to you anywhere, anytime!" I don't remember driving to work, but the next conscious thought I remember was parking my car in the underground car park. I sat in the dark and in silence with the engine turned off staring at nothing in particular. Last night brought welcome relief, but it was short lived. I was wound up like a tight spring again. The roar of an engine snapped me back to reality and I lifted my head just in time to see a large black motorbike power up the slope and out onto the road. "Lucky fucker," I thought to myself as he sped away, "not a care in the world." Then I did a double take. As the bike roared up the passage towards the road, I noticed that it was a large black BMW, and I could have sworn that it had a WX registration. I nearly shit myself with fright. The bike that passed me in Ballsbridge was, as far as I could remember, very similar in size and I thought had a WX registration also. "Jesus, what the fuck is going on here?" I buried my head in my hands in despair. I needed to find out what was going on, and bloody quick as time was marching on and there was only a few days to the scheduled operating date.

After running the heart/lung machine on the first operation, I headed back to my office, debating whether to head home early or prepare my report for my monthly meeting with my clinical director. I decided to spend an hour starting my report and head home at 3.00. My report was a monthly check on the clinical and financial activity and status of my department. I called up the template of the monthly report and the previous months report. I ran down the standard sections giving updates with regards training and personnel reports. I reached the section on clinical and financial activity. I always gave an outline of the amount and types of activity, numbers and types of Cardiac procedures, broken down into valve, Coronary artery bypass procedures and any other types of operations performed that my department was involved in. Since the new computerised patient information system had been introduced, the finance department had been sending multiple reports concerning department expenditure and budgeting. Included in these reports was a breakdown of the numbers of the different insurance plans that patients were coming in under. I consulted the book which recorded all the cardiac procedures and started by counting them generally. I came up with a figure of seventy-two for the previous month. I recorded this. Next I broke them into different procedure groups. This was easy as valve procedures were easily identified by the implant sticker. I started to count the different insurance plan types. These were identified by a letter denoting which insurer and plan on the patient identification sticker. They ranged from A through to E in the case of VHI and similar lettering in the case of companies like BUPA, VIVAS and other such interested parties. There were also the large corporations such as Guinness, Aer Lingus and other semi-state companies who offered their employees private medical cover. Then there were four or five self payers and eight clearly identified NTPF patients who came from the public system. These had the letters TP, denoting "Treatment Purchase." I counted and logged all the different plans and this left me with ten cases that I couldn't identify fully. These had the annotation EI-TP. I noted these, and before typing the numbers into my report, I called the finance department to check the category of the outstanding EI-TP patients.

The call was answered by a bright bubbly woman's voice. "Patients's accounts, good afternoon."

I quickly identified myself and explained that I was writing my monthly report and could she explain what the financial code EI-TP meant.

"Well TP means that the patients are public from the National Treatment Purchase Fund" she explained.

"Yes I guessed that," I retorted. I glanced at the clock and was surprised to see that it was 3.30. I could hear her clicking away on the computer keyboard. I suddenly had the overwhelming urge to get home and I tried to hurry her up, "I just want to know if I include them with the rest of the NTPF or do I count them separately."

"I can't find any reference to the EI part," she said as

she continued to click away on her computer. I was getting impatient now, as it was well past the time that I wanted to leave. "Would it cause a problem if I lumped them in with the other NTPF numbers?" I asked hoping to get a straight answer that would finish the call and let me get home.

"Can't see why not," she responded.

"Would you look into it and let me know?" I asked, "I want to ensure that my figures are accurate."

"Yeah, sure," she promised without conviction.

I hung up quickly; closed up the document I was working on and headed towards the door. I spotted Mike leaving the operating theatre with a blood sample. "You still here Boss?" he grinned.

"Yeah, leaving now, all OK in there?" I nodded towards the operating room where the first patient had been returned to in a hurry.

"No big deal," he said over his shoulder, "see you tomorrow."

I changed quickly and left the hospital strolling towards the car-park. Having taken the car to work today instead of the bike and I felt a twinge of guilt as I crossed the grounds of the hospital in bright autumn sunshine. It would have been a nice day to cycle and the thought of the sticker I found in my car this morning gave me that familiar sense of dread and fear.

I mused over the whole sordid business and as I left the hospital to make the short walk along the side of the building towards the underground car-park up the road from the hospital, I didn't notice the scruffy looking character step out from behind a concrete pillar. He was wearing a Dublin GAA football jersey and oversize tracksuit bottoms with a pair or filthy trainers. "Story bud, got a fag?" he muttered without lifting his head. I was almost in a trance and I got an electric shock sensation when I realised that he was talking to me.

"Sorry mate, don't smoke" I gave an apologetic shrug and increased my step. He stepped out and moved alongside me. I got decidedly nervous and took my hands from my pockets. Since the little rumble on the streets the previous week, I had been mentally practicing some of the self defence moves that I discovered on the internet. I had tried out some of them in the gym and had, up to this moment felt that if I kept my head, I could use one or two of them to get out of trouble.

"Wallet and phone, now!" he said in a clear voice, his muttering had suddenly disappeared. I was terrified and kept up the pace, almost breaking into a trot. He put his hand on my shoulder and, as if a wall appeared in front of me, I stopped dead. The world seemed to slow down and events began to replay themselves in my head. "Ah howya Son...a large outstanding debt...ensure that things go the way we want..."

The faces of Tom, Joey the Horse Cassin and the image of Mulligan in Intensive Care all appeared and disappeared in front of my eyes. With startling clarity, the emails and photos of Alice and Nick outside their schools came into my mind and I was suddenly overwhelmed with anger.

"I-said-give-me-your-fuck-ing-wallet!" He was facing me directly now and with one hand in his pocket, the other hand was hidden up the sleeve of the dirty khaki coloured snorkel jacket that hung off his shoulders. I looked him in the eye and muttered something like "hold on a sec mate." I turned my head and shoulders to search in the back pocket of my jeans for my wallet.

"Turn from the hips, spinning on your heels to increase torque; hands in defensive position..." One of the self defense moves I had read came back to me in a flash. Something came over me. In the military, I think it's called the red mist, but whatever it was, all of a sudden my left hand came into boxing defensive position. I spun to the left, using my hips to gain power, I drove the heel of my right hand square into his face. My forearm moved like a battering ram and the heel of my hand caught him under his nose in an upward motion. He almost lifted off his feet. His head snapped backwards. It felt

like I had hit an egg inside a piece of cloth. I continued my right hand around the back of his neck and gripped his greasy hair. All the frustration and anger of the past few days, the mugging, the pictures of the kids, money trouble with Cassin came back to me in a flash and I was out of control. Pulling his head forward, I brought my knee up. His head came forward like a ragdoll's and collided with my knee which was moving upwards. His face and my knee met with a sickening thud. He hit the ground like a sack of shit. The sound of something plastic hitting the ground brought me back to my senses. He had dropped something. I looked down to see a five ml syringe half full of a dirty, bloody liquid. I shivered in horror at the thought of what was in it. I kicked it in the direction of a nearby drain. GAA man was curled up on the ground, moaning and cursing. As quickly as it had arrived, the mist of anger left me and was quickly replaced with a combination of terror and adrenaline. My instinct was to bend down and help the unfortunate on the ground but my logical brain started screaming at me, "This is one of the bastards who has you by the balls! Cop on man."

I looked around me to see if there were any witnesses. Other than the distant sound of cars, there wasn't a living soul about. I stood for a couple of minutes in a trance like state staring at the crumpled heap on the ground in front of me. I felt a mix of pity for the poor bastard, pride for having got the better of a potential mugger and also shame, never having been in any serious fights in my life. He started to wriggle about and turning his face up at me, I got a shock. His face looked like his nose had exploded. His eyes opened wide as he realized that I was still standing there. We probably both had the same thought, "get the fuck away from this madman." He started kicking his heels into the ground as if to try and get up. I was brought to my senses as I realized that he was getting up. I turned and ran as fast as I could towards my car. Thirty seconds later, I was climbing into my car. Hitting the central locking, I started the engine and gunned the car out into the lane towards the main road. Getting away from the area took on a sense of urgency and I had to check my speed. As I turned on to the main road leading back into the city, I didn't notice the character in jeans and a Chelsea football club strip standing on the corner staring at my car. As I passed, he removed a mobile phone from his pocket and dialed a number. I don't remember the journey home. My mind was racing between having, for the first time in my life, hit somebody really hard and won, and anger and frustration at the ruthless bastards who had me over a barrel. I made a clear cut decision. I would find some way of contacting the police. I decided to actively search and find George McGovern and find some way out of this mess. In the bathroom I scrubbed my hands until they hurt. They were covered in dried blood. I decided not to mention the incident to Victoria; I didn't fancy discussing what that scumbag might have done with the syringe. Victoria, as a nurse, would have insisted on me going to casualty, or at least to the GP, to ensure that I hadn't sustained any cuts, particularly when you think what GAA man was brandishing. Having made my decision to find some advocate among the police, with a renewed sense of purpose, I put on a happy face and got on with things.

18

At 8.02am, carrying my monthly report along with a cappuccino, I entered the office of my clinical manager. These monthly meetings were designed to give the brass at the top of the management chain, a clear picture of how the departments in their respective brief, were getting on. We normally discussed staffing issues, clinical and financial activity and occasional banter. Nathan Richards, an MBA graduate from the Smurfit business school, in his late forties was a relative newcomer to the hospital's management team. I kept as much of the irrelevant bullshit to a brief one or two liner and went straight for the numbers that I knew he would want to know.

"72 Cardiac procedures this month," I smiled, "another busy month, no bed problems here." I laughed.

"Now don't go comparing us with the public hospitals," he laughed. I went on to give the breakdown of the different types of cases and any ancillary work that my department had undertaken.

"We will have to be more and more competitive in our approach to new business," he gave his usual rant. "The flow of patients from the public service has slowed to a trickle now" he went on. I thought for a second, there was a time when half of our patients came through from public list, in the form of NTPF patients, but they had slowed down notably. Up until the new computer system was installed I hadn't taken much notice of the spread of the insurance details of the patients. However, by my calculations, this month there had been eighteen patients who I had placed in the NTPF column of my spreadsheet.

"Funny, I made eighteen NTPF patients in this count," I interrupted.

"No, only four, I think," he said while logging onto the computer system to check. He clicked a few keys, and then turned to me, "No, definitely four," he confirmed. I pointed out the EITP patients that I had come across on my count. "Probably some new shared cover program," he said dismissively. He promised he would look into it but not to worry about it. The hospital was being paid and that was all that mattered. We finished the meeting and I made my way back to theatre. The list was underway and under control by my team and I had time to grab a coffee and think.

Using the online golden pages, I looked up the phone number of the nearby police station where I had reported the mugging I had suffered, and where my old school friend, George McGovern had been stationed some time ago. I explained to a youthful sounding officer that I was trying to track down an old school mate for a reunion and that the last location that I had for him was there. The desk officer promised he would try to locate him and pass on my number to him I didn't mention that I had given the same information to another officer there the previous week. I hung up and thought for a moment. There had been another show of muscle with the sticker in my car, and although I had exacted some revenge with GAA man the previous day, I still felt extremely violated. I decided to visit a police station somewhere out of the way from the hospital and try to speak with someone and get some idea how to move forward.

I sat for a few minutes staring at the computer screen. Some thoughts came drifting into my brain. I had no idea of where I was going with this whole crazy business and I found myself browsing Google for information about "death by lethal injection." I don't know what brought me there but it only confirmed what I already knew and what I often used in my lectures about how anesthesia and cardiac arrest is induced during cardiac surgery. I was probably searching for something that I could tell my new mates, if I had to speak to them in the next day or two. I thought that if I could come up with some hair-brained scheme using some commonly used drugs that I had researched. I felt that I needed to come up with some credible system that anyone could look up on the net.

Sucsamethonium is a powerful muscle relaxant that is used routinely during surgery. A similar drug is also employed as an ingredient in the lethal cocktail used to execute poor unfortunates in various states around the world, including the good old US of A. My story was to be that I was thinking of using a combination of Sucsamethonium, morphine and Potassium to arrest the heart. All these are commonly used in an operating theatre and would be a normal finding in any toxicology screening at a post mortem examination. I was terrified of even thinking about such a regime, but I desperately tried to convince myself that speaking to the police on the quiet, would yield some miraculous way out of this.

I didn't hear Bruce walking into the office. I had a webpage open explaining the different techniques of execution. "Wow, boss, you thinking of knocking somebody off," he exclaimed.

I nearly leapt from my seat with fright. I scrambled to close down the web page. "I was asked two or three times at lectures, was the way we stopped the heart the same as death by lethal injection." I tried to put some logical spin on what he had seen on the screen. Inside I was shaking.

"Yeah, suppose it's strange to most folk, what we do here," he rationalized to himself.

The explanation seemed to satisfy him and he headed off for his breakfast. I completed all my reports and stock sheets and at the first available opportunity, having cleared it with my team, "I'm heading to the College library, OK guys?" I told a little white lie to my team. The Police station I was thinking of was near the College of Surgeons where I was studying recently and I was still entitled to use the library facilities. I could if need be, nip into the admissions office and pick up some forms to cover my visit.

I had cycled to work and I was glad of the bike, as it allowed me to beat the traffic and be across the city in a matter of minutes. I slipped between the lanes of traffic. Cars fought with trucks and vans to move another foot and the frustration showed on the faces of the drivers. It was a pleasure to be ahead of the traffic. I took a slightly roundabout route in the hope that anyone watching me, in case I went to the police would make the assumption that I would go to the local station. I threw my eyes about, keeping a wary eye out for large black BMW motorbikes. Not seeing any, I doubled back across town and arrived at the college thirty minutes later. The only business traffic that moved was the occasional cycle courier. One or two seemed to be taking the same route as me and we made the journey across the city in under twenty minutes. I still had the security code of the cycle park alongside the college and I pushed my bike into the cramped parking area. Throwing my bag over my shoulder, I left the college area and headed across the two or three streets to the police station. It was a large Georgian building in its own grounds. This was the place, ironically where all the bikes stolen in the city that happened to be recovered, ended up, for reclaim or auction. I entered the cavernous hall, and approached the front desk. A pretty young girl in a guard's uniform was on duty. Officer Mary Hanratty greeted me with a fresh Templemore smile, "How can I help you today sir?"

More like McDonalds than a cop shop, I thought to myself. My stomach was in a knot and my mouth dried up as I tried to think of the best way to phrase what I wanted. "I...I...need to talk to someone please," I stuttered along.

Officer Hanratty eyed me suspiciously. "What do you need to talk about?" she asked, staring hard at me.

"I have some information about a high profile criminal," I tried to sound as non-committal as possible.

She opened a large black ledger and took up a pen, "If you give me the information, I will pass it on to a senior officer."

I was expecting this sort of reception and took my hospital identity card from my wallet. "I'm a Medical Scientist from the Western Clinic, officer, and I think it would be more appropriate if I spoke to someone senior." I looked around the reception area, there was a large black lady sitting on a chair holding what looked like a letter from Foreign Affairs. She was crying. "In private if possible," I added.

Officer Mary was now intrigued and quite obviously pissed off. She took my ID card and left the desk. I was left alone with the coloured lady and her child. She was sniffling and occasionally sobbing. We made eye contact and she had a pleading look in her eye. She raised the document as if to show it to me. I was saved the experience by a Dublin accent coming from behind the desk, "How can I help you?" The voice came from a tall, well built man in his mid-fifties. He wore a dark suit and his graying hair was greased back in an Elvis style. He gave me a sneering look.

Trying to stay calm, I looked at him and explained myself again, "If possible, I'd like to speak to you in private...Officer... O'Gorman?"

He offered me my ID back, but not his hand to shake, "Come on through to my office." He disappeared for a second and reappeared through a door to the right of the desk. The first thing I noticed was his shoes. They were Raffaello handmade boots, and looked like they cost the better part of a policeman's monthly salary. I followed him on down a dark corridor. It looked like the building had been gutted and all the walls replaced with partition walls to create a warren of offices. Elvis led me into an eight by eight office. There were no windows and the only ventilation was a tall electric fan which served only to move the heavy, smoky air around and to continuously disturb the mound of papers that occupied every available space in the room. "Sorry bout the state of the place, fuckin snowed under." His Dublin accent was almost put-on, it was so pronounced, "Now, what's the problem?"

I began by briefly explaining what I did for a living. He looked at me quizzically. "This is important," I said. I then went on to mention Mulligan being in hospital and scheduled for surgery. "I was contacted by email and by phone," I got to the kernel of the situation, "whoever contacted me, knew exactly what I did and how I would be involved in the procedure."

His eyebrows furrowed and he kicked the door shut with one of his expensive shoes.

"Whoever contacted me, basically demanded that I sabotage the heart operation to ensure that Mulligan doesn't wake up," I blurted out. So far I hadn't mentioned my gambling debt but I could see that coming.

"Why didn't you contact the police immediately, and why don't you just tell them to fuck off?" he said with surprise after a pause.

I took a deep breath, gritted my teeth and confessed, "the problem is...I have a large gambling debt that they said that they cleared for me, and they sent photos of my kids to me. They obviously know all about me. I'm terrified what they might do to my family. I've already been beaten up and a message was left in my car the other night." I was shaking with both nerves and relief, having confessed to someone.

"How much are you into them for?" he asked. "Four and a half G's," I muttered.

He let a low whistle. "To who?" he asked.

"Joey Cassin."

His eyes opened wide. "You know what that means now, don't you son?" he asked in a patronizing tone. He wasn't much older than me but he adopted that wise, fatherly demeanor that he probably reserved for total scumbags.

"I guess I owe somebody a wad of cash. The problem is, I don't know who and they obviously know me." I sunk into the hard plastic chair.

"Sounds like you're in a spot of bother then...sorry son, what's your name again?" Elvis moved closer to me, sitting on the edge of the table, swinging his legs and admiring his expensive shoes.

"Robert...Robbie Valentine," I muttered.

"Here's what we're gonna do," he moved from the desk and sat in the remaining chair behind the desk. He fished among the papers on the desk and brought out a small black notebook. He waved it at me laughing, "My palmtop—never crashes, battery never fails." I gave a halfhearted laugh. "Give me your number and I'll make some discrete inquiries." A worried look spread over my face. "Don't worry," he reassured me, "I know a lot of these lowlifes and I'll be discrete. I'll try to find out how serious they are and we can hopefully move along from there, ok?" Smiling and trying to sound convincing, I shook his hand.

"Thanks a million...officer is it? I'm grateful for you help."

He raised himself to his full height and rolled his shoulders, "Denis will do, to serve and to protect."

I don't know if it was his accent, his manner or his ridiculous hair style, but I felt anything but served or protected and I couldn't shake the feeling that I was completely on my own in this mess.

I exited the police station, and headed back towards the college. For a minute I thought about heading into the centre of the city to while away an hour or so in a bookshop or music shop to try to forget the whole business but my mind was too preoccupied. I sauntered across the few blocks towards the college bike park. I had to pass alongside a block of city council flats, now rat-runs of drugs dealers and criminals. I looked at a bunch of kids, probably no more than eight or nine playing football in the central area of the complex. Linepoles served as goalposts and all of the kids wore different premiership football strips. Standing to the side, as if coaching them was a tall, shaven headed young man. He looked like he was on something illegal. Like three or four of the footballers, he wore a white football shirt with Emirates emblazoned across the chest.

I glanced at him momentarily. He looked away immediately. As I passed, he removed a mobile phone from his trouser pocket and started to text. I decided to head back to work to finish off some lecture work I was preparing. I arrived back in the hospital twenty minutes later and locked my bike in the basement. I headed to the theatre changing rooms. I pushed the door open and entered the room into the toilet area. This was separated from the main area by means of a set of saloon type doors. There were two or three people changing and I stopped for a second to use the toilet.

I pushed on through the saloon doors, grabbed a set of theatre scrubs and changed into them. Reddy was explaining the finer points of the satellite tracking system on his new Mercedes to an orthopedic surgeon with a spectacular accent, and an equally impressive double-barreled name. I entered my office, and sat down at the computer. I tentatively checked my email, nothing from my new creditors, thank God. There was just one new email, from the accounts department. It simply explained that they couldn't find any reference to the EI part of the patients' accounts that I had queried, and just to file them with the general NTPF patients. I opened my lecture folder and put the finishing touches to some PowerPoint presentations. There were some sets of notes from the last few days strewn about on the desk. They were the top copies of the bypass data sheets. The top copies were normally filed in the patient's chart. These ones looked like they had been misfiled and somebody had made a feeble attempt to gather them up for placing in the charts but was called away to do something more important, or just couldn't be arsed. Sometimes, particularly when I am stressed, I go on obsessive compulsive cleaning binges. I had been like that of late and so I gathered them all up, read the patient labels to identify which rooms the patients were in with a view to replacing them in their correct homes. Something struck me about them. They were from a couple of surgeons and insurance plans, but all but two of the sheets that had Reddy down as the attending surgeon were EI-TP plans. I went to the general filing cabinet to check all of the recent notes and sure enough, almost all of the patients that came in under this particular plan were in under the care of Mr. Peter Reddy. I thought about this for a few minutes. I gathered up the sheets and headed to the respective wards to drop them off. I spent a few brainless minutes wandering from ward to ward handing notes to various ward clerks. I passed the ward where Mulligan was still ensconced. After much debate and wrangling, the security presence had been reduced to just one plain clothes detective, outwardly unarmed but I'm sure he was packing some hardware. He was sitting on a chair, a couple of feet away from the room where Mulligan was, reading a paper looking completely uninterested in his task. I wasn't sure if the police presence was to protect Mulligan himself or the other patients. The sight of the room and the policeman brought back the familiar knot in my stomach. I spotted Marty on the same floor; he gave me a nod and a smile and disappeared around a corner. Two floors below, I ran into him again.

"Who's following who?" he laughed as we met again.

"Yeah, you can't scratch yourself in this place without someone spotting you" I replied. I looked at my watch and noticed that it was 4.30. It had started to get dusky so I decided to head for home.

Twenty minutes later I was changing into civvies, having switched off my computer and wrapped up my business. Dr. Sapsford was changing at the same time. "Any holidays planned Dr. Sapsford?" I inquired generally.

"Ah good evening Robert," he said looking up from

buttoning his cufflinks. "Yes, we hope to get down to the house in Connemara for a spell over the BankHoliday. A stroll on Forba beach followed by a glass of scotch by the fire," he dreamed for a minute or two.

"Sounds like heaven," I said. I decided to use the opportunity to inquire about the NTPF patients, and to see if there was any opinion among the Consultant staff about the extraneous Treatment Purchase patients that I came across. "What do you think of the National Treatment Purchase Fund situation?" I asked, "The radio seems to be getting plenty of mileage out of it."

"It's not a new idea," Dr. Sapsford began, "this has been used in many countries for years. It's a good short term plan to bring things under control, but it can't last."

"Yes, I agree, it'll only last so long as we have a Progressive Democrat presence in Health," I gave my tuppence worth. "Does it affect you much? There was a journalist on the radio the other day ranting."

"You know some of these journalists, they're always out to get us," he dropped his eyes back down to his cufflinks. I wasn't certain but it was as if he was deliberately avoiding eye contact.

"Do you see many of them?" I asked

"One or two a month," he answered, "my schedule doesn't allow me, suits me fine, they are usually quite sick and appear at the most inopportune times. A few disciplines or should I say specialists that have done particularly well out of it." He appeared uncomfortable talking about the subject and I decided not to push it. Dr. Sapsford straightened his tie and left the changing room having bid me good evening. I buttoned my jeans and pulled a shirt over my head. I looked about the room for my trainers. Not spotting them, I got down on my knees and looked under the bench that was placed against the wall. I saw my Nike trainers at the back and pulled them out. On the ground beside them was a brown calfskin wallet. I retrieved it and looked to see if it might have fallen from any of the remaining jackets. It was quite full, and without opening it up, I could see that there were quite a few Euros inside it. There were four or five credit cards and a bunch of business cards. I was looking for something that could identify the owner. I had a quick look in the section for drivers license and ID cards. I spotted a small identity card and I pulled it out. It was a membership card for the exclusive Glenross Golf & Country Club. Next to the club crest, was the smiling face of Mr. Peter Reddy. I went to push the membership card back into place and noticed that some business cards were now sticking out, having been dislodged as I pulled out the membership card. There were two or three business cards from an accountancy firm and one which had a striking colored logo of a lighthouse. I didn't pay much attention other than the fact that it was for some type of insurance company. I pushed it back, put my jacket on and headed home. I stopped by the theatre secretary's office to leave the wallet in. By 5.10, I was pumping my bicycle down the canal bank walk, listening to an old Rory Gallagher track on my MP3 player. Apparently, the common cold can kill you, but his baby drove him to drink!! I knew how he felt. I headed home and hoped that I would get a full night's sleep.

19

THE NEXT DAY PASSED UNEVENTFULLY, if you can call searching the internet for an untraceable, foolproof way to kill someone uneventful. I had decided to try to come up with something that would buy me some time for the call I was expecting from my new mates. Using Google, I performed a couple of searches, modifying them to target specific results. I was looking for some information that would satisfy any inquiries made of me from my new best mates. I came across a drug called Anectine. Its chemical name is Succinylcholine, and it is used during surgery. There was one instance reported, a nurse from Texas was tried on a charge of murder. She was believed to have been responsible for the deaths of over twelve children under her care. So Succinylcholine could definitely be used for homicide. Whatever I came across, I wanted to have credibility with anyone who called me. I was hoping that a convincing story like the use of this drug, could buy me time.

This type of plan would involve waiting until Mulligan was in the Intensive Care Unit after the operation. This at least meant that if I reached the surgery without any resolution, at least this would buy me a little time, the plan being to strike in ITU. Succinylcholine mimics a naturally occurring chemical acetylcholine whose job is to make muscles contract. When the acetylcholine has made the muscle contract, it must be removed from the junction. If it isn't, the muscle would remain contracted. If acetylcholine wasn't removed from, for instance, the heart muscle, the heart would remain contracted, and the person would die within minutes. These chemicals are broken down by naturally occurring enzymes in human blood. These are among the normal components of human tissues. This means that even at post-mortem, there would be no obvious signs of foul play. Also there would be a perfectly plausible explanation for the presence of a neuro-muscular blocker, the patient had had cardiac surgery within the past few days. Neuro-muscular blockers are a fundamental part of the cocktail of drugs used during this type of surgery.

My team handled the operating list for the day and I was free to deal with the other riveting tasks such as stock ordering and invoice control. I was filling out a pharmacy requisition form, ordering the standard fluids and other drugs that were the staple diet of my department. I had a notion to try a test order of Succinylcholine, or Sucsamethonium, as I thought the trade name was in Ireland, just to see what the reaction would be or if the drug was available. I disparched all the forms and notes to their respective homes and wandered back towards Theatre. As I passed the lift, it opened and a trolley, piled high with boxes of drip fluids exited, pushed by a red-faced Marty. "What's the news, Marty?" I called.

He looked up from trying to negotiate the trolley out of the lift, "Oh, hi Robbie!" he panted, "this trolley has a mind of its own." I helped him manoeuvre the load onto the corridor and he parked it against a wall and relaxed. "Anything strange with yourself?" he asked as he pushed his trolley towards the double doors leading to one of the wards.

I was sorely tempted to unburden myself of some of the shit that I was facing but stopped myself short. "Oh, the usual, same shit, different day," I said with no real enthusiasm, "spent a couple of hours in front of the computer, my eyes are killing me" I tried to lighten the mood a little.

"What're you doing, research?" Marty asked. I thought of

the stuff I had just downloaded and laughed to myself. "Yeah, some stuff about drugs for lectures, I'm giving a lecture now to a bunch of postgraduate nurses, exciting stuff," I answered.

"Gotta go," Marty turned a sharp left into the storeroom behind the nurses station of the ward.

"Cheers Marty." I headed towards theatre. Marty waved and disappeared behind the door.

20

SLOWLY BUT DELIBERATELY, the door of the office opened. The trick in a hospital is to act like you know exactly where you are going. That way nobody questions your whereabouts, and if challenged, never stutter or stumble your words and have a clear confident answer. He entered the Perfusion Services office, closed the door and locking the outer door from the inside. After firstly checking its exact position, he carefully manoeuvred one of the large Heart/Lung machines so as it was partially blocking the inner door that led to the main theatre corridor. Its exact position was important as it is very often a small change in the position of little things such as the placement of a pen, or the computer mouse that alerts somebody that there had been an intruder. Such small details are important.

Using his camera phone, he took two or three pictures of the layout of the desk. He would use these pictures as a check that everything was left exactly as he found it when he exited the office. The computer was in sleep mode but still switched on. One move of the mouse and the monitor sprang to life. A quick scan of the desktop screen showed that the internet window had only been minimised and not closed completely, again very typical in a big establishment like this. Checking to see if the window remained open was worthwhile and here he struck gold. There was no point in starting off on a long winded trial of passwords, only to find that the window had only been minimised, not closed. Windows XP Professional default page opened. Clicking on the minimised internet setting opened the main Google search page. Clicking the "Back" button in the top right hand corner of the screen, revealed a webpage containing what looked like a transcript of a post-mortem examination. Further reading showed it to be an investigation of someone who had died of some sort of poisoning. Succinylcholine was the drug responsible. The interesting thing was that the dialog on the screen explained that this drug would be untraceable at post-mortem as it is broken down by naturally occurring enzymes that would be present at post-mortem anyway so it is quite likely that there would be no suspicion of foul play if the drug was used to murder someone.

Clicking on the "history" icon showed about four or five other websites visited covering the same or related subjects. Quickly, he pulled a flash disk from his pocket and stuck it into the USB port in the front of the computer tower under the desk. Hitting the "start" button, he pulled up a new blank Word document. In less than a minute, he had copied the URL addresses of the sites visited that day. Racking his brains to think of the name of one of the junior Doctors, he titled the document RichardsonCV.doc. This meant that although no trace of the document remained on the computer, a scan of "recent documents" used would only show that someone named Richardson had probably used the computer to update their CV, a common occurrence in a place such as this. With the new Word document stored on the flash drive, now back in his trouser pocket, he returned to the main Google search page by clicking the "forward button." This ensured that when the user returned to continue their work, the order of the pages visited would be the same. He minimised the internet page and made sure that the default screen was as he had found it. Checking the pictures on his camera phone, he ensured that the desk was as it was when he arrived. He repositioned the mouse in the top left corner of the mouse mat. When he was ready to leave, he moved the Heart/Lung machine back into the position it occupied five minutes earlier. He had one quick last look around and unlocked the outer door. Checking for a few seconds, when the outside corridor was quiet, he slipped out and shut the door behind him. At that second his pager beeped. He moved quickly away from the door and around a corner before reading the number on the pager. He stopped at a nearby pantry and slipped inside. Despite the sign depicting a mobile phone in a circle with a line through it, he dialled a number on his Nokia.

"Whah?" the curt reply almost immediately.

"I've checked out his computer, and it looks like he's doing some research on some drugs that can kill you during surgery," he said quietly, "but I think he's been to the police,"

A silence followed for a couple of seconds, "Do nothing, but keep watching him, know what I mean? And send whatever you found on his computer to the office." Then the line went dead.

Slipping out of the pantry back onto the corridor, he lifted the phone from its cradle on the wall. He dialled an internal number. It rang for a few seconds, "Hello, Freeman ward," came a polite response.

"Hi, someone bleep a porter? Martin DeSouza here."

21

IRISH TIMES:

Minister under fire over Consultants Contract.

The Minister of Health came under fire yesterday from the Opposition's health spokesman about the stalled talks with Hospital Consultants concerning their proposed new contract. Michael O'Meara, accused the minister of cowing to a string of vested interest groups who he says are contributing to the condition of the Health service. Labour are calling for Consultants to have greater accountability of time and resources that have hitherto been absent from any contracts of employment. O'Meara asked how could a system let a Professional, employed by the Department of Health, on a 35hr week with a salary of €150,000 per year, have unhindered access to private patients, very often in the public hospitals. He blamed a succession of Ministers in the life of this administration on letting this situation develop, and effectively letting vested interest groups maintain the status quo of a two tiered system for the benefit of a small number of professionals. He also slammed GP's for their refusal to enter into negotiations on a contract that would see them become full employees of the Department of Health on contracts. He claimed that this would go a long way to solve the A&E crisis as it would allow 24hr GP clinics to operate and take the strain off the major casualty units. After a scathing attack on the health service unions, he accused the Minister of going soft on groups such as these and not looking after the interests of the taxpayer.

He likened the behaviour of some representative groups to Taxi drivers in the lead up to deregulation. He likened the behaviour of some of the union representatives to 'Jimmy Hoffa' style industrial relations. The minister dismissed these allegations and replied that he hoped that Mr. O'Meara or any of his family wouldn't be needing any hospital services in the near future. He went on to stress that accountability and transparency was the cornerstone of any funding of the Health service and that "significant progress" was being made in the negotiations with the various unions involved.

SKILFULLY REDDY TIED THE LAST STITCH, onto the last piece of vein that was now attached to the obtuse marginal branch of the left coronary artery of a sixty-two year old male. Peter Reddy, a forty-five year old College of Surgeons graduate, finished his fourth and final operation of the day. He was five years back in the Irish healthcare system and after firstly being appalled at the shambles that the system was in and ruffling more than a few feathers, trying to get patients into the public hospitals, he was an ardent supporter of the National Treatment Purchase fun as he felt it mimicked, to some degree, the American system where he had spent the previous seven years. He had been a surgical resident in the sprawling Beth Israel medical centre in San Francisco. The American system of mainly private medicine impressed him. It encouraged people to invest in their own healthcare. This meant that as well as paying for medical and dental insurance, it encouraged people to keep healthy. This, Reddy believed was the key to a successful health strategy. Invest in your own health. When the various plans under the National Treatment Purchase fund were launched, he embraced them with gusto. Within a short space of time, he had made a major impact on the infamous waiting list courtesy of the admitting privileges afforded him by the Southwestern Clinic. His bank balance grew accordingly, as did his ego. He had been contacted by an old classmate from college. The contact was made casually in a restaurant. He had been approached by a small wiry man in an expensive suit who appeared to know him, and after a few minutes searching the deeper files of his memory, Reddy remembered him from first year in medical school. He had left medical school to take up business studies and, if his clothes and bling were anything to go by, was doing quite well. The ex-classmate introduced himself as Eamonn Fitzpatrick. He was now in the insurance business, particularly in medical insurance. Over a bottle of Chateauneuf de Pape, they had discussed the crisis in the Health Service. Reddy was impressed with the ideas and forthrightness that Fitzpatrick expounded as they mimicked his own ideas and disillusionment with the system. After a few more bottles of good wine over a couple of weeks, Reddy was showing more than a passing interest in Fitzpatrick's insurance contacts. Within four months he had been roped in as an investor in a small insurance agency. The company handled two or three of the large insurance corporations with private medical insurance plans that had recently entered the newly deregulated market. It was right up Reddy's alley, especially when one of the lads in the company received a tip about a small tender document on the Government website. On the etenders.gov site, a small notice appeared seeking suppliers of a Healthcare Insurance Scheme. The provision of health insurance packages was invited from bidders to put forward various options to include cover for Heart, Hip and other major surgery. The bidders would be responsible for organisation of the payment of healthcare packages but would receive a percentage of the cost of the procedure paid to the relevant private hospitals.

Another facet to this arrangement was, thanks to a research officer who, as a result of a previous drug problem, owed the directors of Lighthouse more than a few months worth of Clerical officers' salary, a large amount of patients were recruited before they were confirmed with diagnosis of Heart disease. He would simply trawl through the letters from the GPs to the Cardiology Clinics requesting appointments and pick what he thought were the most likely to yield a positive result for heart disease. A large proportion of these patients were expected to be eligible for treatment under the National Treatment Purchase fund, and therefore were dead certs for payment. They were insured, courtesy of Lighthouse Ltd. The return from the NTPF fund resulted in a tidy profit as the Insurance Company's commission went straight to Lighthouse. The premiums were paid in full by Lighthouse, and when a definitive diagnosis of heart disease was made, the insurance companies paid out for major surgical procedures through Lighthouse. They took their commission and passed on the balance to the Private Hospitals. Of course the tender notice disappeared almost immediately from the etenders website, but not before the one and only applicant company had been awarded the contract.

The idea of national private medical cover had been floated by various politicians and received very little coverage. Some bright spark in the finance offices of the Department of Health had applied his accountancy brain to it and come up with some figures that could save the Department a fortune. By availing of a small loophole, a large number of patients on the waiting list could be insured by various insurance companies, paid for by the Department of Health and avail of the services of the Private Hospitals. The speed and efficiency of the Private Hospitals ensured that the patients were operated on in record time, and the resultant savings to the Department of Health were very well received by Government. Of course, this was kept very quiet. The opposition would have had a field day. But by the time the details of the Treatment Purchase Fund were analysed, a big enough impact on the waiting lists had been made so as not to receive major criticism from the bulk of the shadow government. Reddy was both a protagonist of the Treatment Purchase Fund, and a direct beneficiary of it, as the full fee for the Surgeons were paid because the Surgery was normally carried out outside of the Consultants normal contracted hours. What Reddy didn't know was that although the net profit to Lighthouse Ltd was quite small, every Euro put through the system was effectively being laundered. Lighthouse was the front company for Brennan's drug smuggling operation.

This evening, after a reasonably easy operating list in the University Hospital, as he finished the last coronary graft, he handed over to his senior residen to finish up and after a short ward round, headed to the changing room. He showered and changed. Tightening his silk tie, he pulled on the jacket of his Valentino suit and looked in the full-length mirror. He liked what he saw. Just turned forty eight, he had the physique of a man ten years his junior. His hair was dark with only slight greying at the temples, which, he thought, gave him an air of sophistication. Closing his locker, he spun the dials on the combination lock and headed for the car park. The hospital management kept an exclusive section of the car park free for Consultants. God knows what would happen if some of those bangers were allowed park near the rows of Mercs, BMWs and Jaguars. Heading for the underground section, he removed the plastic access card from his wallet to open the barrier. It was nearly nine and most of the day staff had gone home. Only one or two other Consultants cars remained. The sharp clip of his shoes echoed on the concrete. He approached his silver Kompressor Mercedes. One of the benefits of being involved with the insurance company was the company car. He had chosen the unadulterated status symbol of the top of the range Mercedes. He always got a shudder of pleasure whenever he saw it. It reminded him of one of those American fighter jets, cool, sophisticated and expensive. He raised the key and, pointing it at the car, pressed the switch. The car responded with a short, sharp, high pitched blip. As he approached the car from the back, he touched its sleek, aerodynamic shape. He ran his finger along the boot, up onto the roof, appreciating the smooth, cold skin. He felt the change in sensation from lacquered metal to the slightly rough vinyl texture of the retractable roof. The interior lights came on slowly, giving the impression that the car was coming to life. He had to stop himself talking to the car, it was so beautiful.

"Nice set of wheels Doctor," came a Dublin accent from over his right shoulder.

He turned sharply and was suddenly staring into the face of a slightly built young man with a head of red curls. He wore a tan check sports jacket over a pair of expensive looking jeans. "What the hell are you doing here?" Reddy snapped, "I thought I told you or your boys never to come near the Hospital."

Curly grinned. "Lovely car Doctor," he teased again, "terrible to see anything happen to it." He flicked the window wiper up and let it snap back against the window.

Reddy's jaw clenched and unclenched in frustration. "What do you want?" he asked quietly. Although he had bought into the insurance company and had prospered both directly and indirectly from involvement, he had kept a safe distance from the 'Business.' Nowadays, other than the occasional telephone conversation and the regular 'Board Meetings,' he had no direct involvement with the offices of Lighthouse Insurance Services Ltd. However, a recent phone conversation had put a new spin on things.

"Come on now Mr. Reddy," Curly switched from the respectful Doctor title, to a slow, "Mister," snarled, rather than said, it was given with undisguised menace and disrespect. "I'm here to remind you of our special patient and to make sure that you keep everything on track."

Reddy felt a cold gnawing of fear creep into his gut, and it was all he could do to keep control of his bowels. He had been contacted by one of the owners of Lighthouse Ltd. As a porter in the College of Surgeons John Brennan in reality ran the place. He had scams organized all over the college. After a short hospital placement, Reddy had discovered amphetamines as a way of helping him study and work extra shifts at the same time. Brennan very quickly found out about this and became a ready source. Even if Reddy had no money, the magic little pills would be forthcoming. He had made sure to settle any debts with Brennan before he finished final med and hadn't heard from him in years. He had forgotten about him until his return from the USA and had met him again on one or two occasions and frankly, he was terrified of him. Now, Brennan was owner and co-director of Lighthouse Insurance Ltd. It was probably the only legitimate business that he was ever involved in. He was one of the biggest criminal masterminds in the country. Reddy discovered this long after he had embraced the company, and by the time reality dawned on him, he was in too deep. A €150,000 car, and up to €20,000 per week in operating fees from patients generated directly by the insurance company took the sting out of the truth. As did the idealist approach that he personally was making a large impact on the Cardiac surgical waiting list. In his raspy inner city Dublin accent, Brennan had explained that a certain Mr. Mulligan would be scheduled for heart surgery over the next few weeks, and Reddy must ensure that the operation was carried out in the Southwestern Clinic before a certain date. "Peter, me owl swiss," Reddy remembered the throaty hoarse voice and shivered at the memory. He had managed to place Mulligan on the Treatment Purchase fund list which alone managed to stir up a hornet's nest of opinion. Other newspaper reports had revealed that the criminal underworld was engaged in a vicious war, resulting in regular shootings throughout the city. The names of both Mulligan and Brennan were mentioned in some of these reports, citing their various empires and assets. Lighthouse hadn't yet been mentioned, much to Reddys' relief, but he still intended to start distancing himself from the company and try to fill his operating lists from some other source.

Reddy stepped towards the driver's door of his car. Curly deftly blocked his way, "I want you to know how important this is to Mr. Brennan."

Reddy's bowels knotted again, and he stuttered, "Em... Mr.Mulligan is scheduled for surgery next Friday. That's organized. If he gets a cold or any other setback, it's not my fault, so back off!" He surprised himself with the outburst. He slid around Curly and climbed into the driver's seat. He reached out to close the door when suddenly Curly had a vice-like grip on his hand. The pain was excruciating.

"Doctor," Curly lowered his voice to barely a whisper, "you better see that he doesn't have any setbacks and is fit and ready for his surgery. After all, your hands are your livelihood, aren't they?" A huge grin replaced the bared teeth and, as quickly as he had appeared, he was gone.

Reddy slammed and locked the door. He sat there shaking both with fear and rage. He had to start winding up his involvement with this company. They were becoming too hot to handle He promised himself, and not for the first time that this would be the last round of patients he would accept from Lighthouse. He flicked on the stereo in his car and the eight concealed speakers filled the cabin with the sound of a duet from the Marriage of Figaro. The pure guttural rumble of a perfectly tuned 4.2 litre engine was a fitting backing to the two intertwining voices as they soared to the music of the Vienna State Opera as he pulled the Mercedes out into the damp November evening. Although there wasn't much traffic about, he didn't notice the red Kawasaki Z1000 pull out from a lane close to the entrance of the hospital and fall in two or three cars behind him. It stayed about one hundred metres or so back, tailing the Mercedes all the way to Howth, the affluent fishing village on the north coastline of the city. Reddy fished a remote control from his pocket, aimed at the large wooden gates which opened slowly and as Andrea Boccelli finished the last strains of a Puccini aria, he pulled the car into the gravel driveway of his large modern wood and glass, six bedroom bungalow. The view over the bay on a clear day was worth the 2.4 million euro that he had paid for this stunning piece of real estate and tonight, staring across the bay as far as Killiney and Dun Laoghaire, he began to relax.

The Kawasaki sped on past the gates, up the hill past the Summit bar and on into Howth village. The bike stopped briefly in the village opposite the Harbour and the rider pulled a mobile phone from inside his leather jumpsuit. He tapped out a short text message, sent it, kicked the bike into gear and sped off down the main street and out along the coast back towards the city.

22

THE RED KAWASAKI Z1000 roared back towards the city. On the coast road with a clear road ahead he was able to open the bike up to near its top speed. Although the machine was capable of over 150mph, as he spotted the Yacht bar ahead on the Clontarf road, he throttled back, bringing the speed down to less than 50mph. He knew that next to the plush bar, was the Clontarf Police station and the last thing he wanted was a high speed chase, not with the other business he had to attend to tonight. He kept his speed in check as he headed under the railway bridge at Fairview and on into the city centre. Gerry was a freelance security enforcement operative. This was the title he used in his own mind. He was the busiest and best "button" or "hitman" in the Dublin, and sometimes countrywide, criminal underworld. An IRA exile in London, following a botched raid on an RUC station he found himself outside the office of the French Foreign Legion after the Canary Warf bombing. He ended up in the training camp outside Marseille and after a punishing recruitment and selection; he passed and quickly settled into Legion life. He became a master of all types of handguns, and was given the opportunity to use these skills in situations such as the civil conflicts in far flung places such as Sierra Leone, Yemen, Bosnia, and Kosovo. He completed the requisite five years and then another two, and returned to Ireland just as the Celtic tiger was a squealing kitten. There were a lot of displaced, unemployed ex-gunmen for hire, thanks to the fledgling peace process up North. Gerry hooked up with some lads who specialised in armed robbery, particularly on security vans. However his skills acquired in the Legion meant that very quickly, he was the only one of his group not in prison or dead. On the grapevine, he heard of a "job" offering €5000. The job was to kill a known drug dealer. He took the job, and carried it out with the professionalism and style that was the mark of the French Foreign legion. Further offers of "work" followed and within a few short years and a dozen or so hits, he had a tidy sum in the bank and a reputation. He always stayed as anonymously as possible with a small circle of friends. He had landed a legitimate position working with the second love of his life, large motorbikes. He used motorbikes on all of his jobs, but not in the obvious way. Although he owned and rode a powerful Kawasaki Z1000, he never used anything like it on a job. He souped up an old Yamaha RD350 YPVS until it was capable of over 150mph. He made it look as old and battered as possible, even to the point of using a roll of brown plastic sticky tape to secure a storage box to the pillion seat. This immediately transformed him into one of those hundreds of motorbike couriers that buzz around the city all day. With his black leather jump suit, covered with a filthy jacket, and a courier's bag slung over his shoulder, he was virtually invisible in the city. Normally he would bribe some lowlife into stealing a large flashy motorbike, buzz about the general area for a bit, and then head off to one of the sprawling housing estates, have a bit of fun with the bike and then dispose of it. Gerry after having got to know the target's movements, would approach, and usually from close range, give him the classic military "double tap" to the head and one to the chest. Although he liked the power and versatility of the SIG-Sauer, he preferred the classic Walther PPK, as used by James Bond 007. His trusty RD 350, could carry him away at speeds up to 150mph, but to remain invisible, he would normally cut through the traffic in the normal speed and manner of a busy courier. He smiled when he heard reports of police searching for large, high powered motorbikes that were seen driving away at speed from the scene of a gangland shooting. Nobody notices another filthy traffic cutting courier, not even the mismatch between the apparently old beat up machine and the low gutsy, perfectly tuned purr of the modified Yamaha Power Valve System engine.

Tonight, he headed across the Liffey, left, out past Connolly station and on out through Sherriff Street and into East Wall. He pulled his bike up a lane behind a shop and manhandled the bike in through a gate that had been left unlocked thanks to a €50 note passed to a snotty nosed kid three days earlier. In the corner of a disused back yard, populated by old fridges and rusted washing machines, under a canvas tarpaulin was his RD350. He pulled the cover over the Kawasaki and pushed the Yamaha out into the lane. Pulling on his courier's outfit, he started the engine and rolled gently down the lane out onto East Wall road. He checked both ways for human traffic and more importantly, patrol cars and headed out on to the river front and stopped a couple of hundred metres from McRoarys bar on the opposite side of the road in the parking zone in front of the river As he positioned the bike behind the glass café bar in front of the river, the roar of a Kawasaki KLR650 broke the silence. The lime green off road bike roared past the old metal crane, bumped up onto the foot bridge and across the river where as loudly as possible, the rider cruised on down towards the old gasometer site. Gerry glanced at his watch, nine fifty, bang on time. He waited behind the café entrance for a minute or two, appearing to study a map, (of the Paris underground). He folded the map in half and placed it back inside his motorbike courier's jacket, his hand felt the rough grip of the PPK. Looking around, and seeing nobody, he quickly removed the pistol, checked chamber, and replaced it back inside his jacket. Pulling away from the cafe, he headed right back down towards McRoarys bar. He stopped on the opposite side of the street. There wasn't anybody about, he wasn't expecting there to be. At ten o'clock precisely a large heavy set figure exited the bar. The figure with a flattened nose stopped to light a cigarette. Slightly tipsy from a few pints, he wobbled a little as he rummaged in his pockets for his cigarettes. Gerry, took one last look around, pulled the bike out of the shadows, and removed the Walters PPK from inside his jacket with his left hand as he accelerated gently with his right. He pulled across the road, pausing beside the giant figure trying repeatedly to produce a flame from his lighter. The figure looked up from his battle with the lighter at the bike courier who had just pulled up beside him. "He can give me a fucking light if he wants directions," was the last thought that crossed his mind as a muffled thud announced the departure of a 7.65mm hollow point round from the silenced barrel of Gerrys Walters PPK. Two more followed rapid succession, and within thirty seconds of pulling across the road, Gerry drove away at a modest 40mph from the crumpled heap of Spider Sheehan, the underboss of Thomas "The Suit" Mulligan. Twenty minutes later, he was back on his Kawsaki heading out past Lansdowne Road, along Strand Road and into the Leafy suburb of Sandymount to check out an address. He had been given an address and a picture and told to check it out. He found the road easily in the dark, and keeping the speed and revs down, he cruised virtually unnoticed along the avenue until he saw the Renault Megane parked in the garden behind the wooden gates. Without stopping, he continued along the avenue and found an easy route back onto Strand road, from, when required, he had a number of distinct escape routes. Left back through Ringsend into the city, or Right over the level crossing and either right through Elm Park or left towards Blackrock and beyond.

23

"LUNGS ON. Fill the Heart Please, Robert," Reddy asked with uncharacteristic politeness. It took me a second or two to realise that he was talking to me. I confirmed with the anesthetist that the patient had been re-connected to the ventilator. As I slowly occluded the venous tube, the heart started to fill up and respond by contracting harder and harder until a normal blood pressure was being produced. Then I gradually turned down the main arterial pump until the heart itself was completely supporting the circulation and the pump was barely turning.

"Happy Michael? Happy Peter?" I asked both anesthetist and Surgeon at the last second before I finally stopped the pump. I always asked at least twice for confirmation before finally stopping the pump. I received two positive nods, and switched off the pump. Normally at this stage Reddy would slap off his gloves and hand over to the first assistant to finish up. Today however, Reddy started to remove the tubes and finish up the procedure himself. There were two or three surprised looks exchanged among the other members of the team. I pumped some of the remaining blood that was left in the Heart/Lung machine into a blood bag and handed it to the anesthetist. I then headed to my office to complete the notes for this operation. I checked the patient's chart, looking for sticky labels that I could use for my own log of procedures, and our departments register.

While rummaging through the chart, I came across some of the standard forms from the various departments within the hospital, completed request forms for blood tests, X-ray reports and various other tests. Among the standard admission documents was a form from the finance department outlining the insurance classification of the patient. I had seen this form before but what drew my attention to this one was the letter that was attached to it. There was a colourful logo of a lighthouse beside the header. Lighthouse Insurance Services Ltd. was the name of an insurance company that had brokered the underwriting of this patient. I checked the patient sticker and saw that it was another of the mysterious EI-TP patients. I read further down the finance form and it revealed that the patient was taken from the public waiting list and placed on the Treatment Purchase fund list two weeks ago, having been diagnosed with Ischaemic Heart disease three months earlier. It was the usual 'Dear Mr. Reddy, Thank you for accepting this patient under the Treatment Purchase Fund-External Insurer group...' I had never seen this type of letter included in the chart. The letter was signed with an unintelligible scrawl, as a PP to the financial director to Lighthouse Ltd, a Mr. E Fitzpatrick. This could explain the group of patients that I couldn't identify for my monthly report. I decided that I would look into it a little further when I had a minute, just to complete the circle, so to speak.

Before putting the notes back together, I looked at the Lighthouse headed notepaper. It gave a business address in the Financial Services Centre. What made me sit up was that among the small print at the bottom, in among the list of Directors of the company was the name P. Reddy, and followed by the initials FRCSI. Reddy's name was preceded by the name M. Brennan and T. McCarthy. Reddy was a director of this company! As far as the hospital was concerned, they were NTPF patients, coming in under a blanket insurer. The hospital got paid, bums on seats, no problems. I decided to file it away for my own interest but drop it from my monthly report.

Within thirty minutes of having stopped the Heart/Lung machine, the patient was ready to be taken back to the Intensive Care Unit. Just over three hours after the surgery commenced, the patient was tucked up in bed in the Intensive Care Unit and doing well. It was 11.30, and with the other lads on my team looking after the rest of the day's list, I was free to carry on with the other duties. Three mind numbing hours later, I changed and left the hospital. I decided to walk into the nearby shopping centre for an hour or so. Mulligan's surgery was four days away now, and other than the information from the net on Succinylcholine, I was no closer to having a way out of the train that was fast approaching. I strolled out of the main entrance of the Hospital, turned right and headed towards the shopping mall; about five minutes walk from the hospital. I crossed the street, dodging some delivery vans and headed past the Ambulance bays. As I turned onto the main road, I became conscious of someone walking behind and slightly to my right. After the last episode, I upped my pace slightly.

As I passed a lane, somebody in a low but clear voice said my name. I turned to see a skinny, bald chap with an earring and teeth like a crossword puzzle lope behind me. He wore an oversize tracksuit and a pair of expensive looking trainers. I froze in fear as the previous encounters came flooding back to me. I forced myself to calm down and think clearly. I stopped and gave him a puzzled look. "Yes, can I help you?" I asked.

He had one hand in the pocket of his tracksuit top, and the other, decorated with large rings and the tattoo, HATE, one letter per finger, hung by his side. "Johnny B. wants to see you," he snarled at me.

"Who the fuck is Johnny B?" was my reply.

This seemed to confuse him. "Mr.-Fuckin-Brennan!" he spelt it out for me.

The initial fear was now replaced with irritation and anger.

"I-don't-know-any-Mr-fuckin-Brennan," I spelt it back out to him.

His look of confusion turned to one of complete disbelief, and quickly was replaced with a look that I could only imagine he would give to someone that he was about to kick the living shit out of. His head was freshly shaved, he had very dark heavy eyebrows. They met through a scowl as he reached out and made to touch my arm, "Don't fuck about, you're coming to see the boss, now."

As he touched me, I began to almost shake with fear. I pulled away, but he moved closer to me and pulled his right hand partially out of his pocket, revealing what looked like the butt of a pistol. "Oh sweet Jesus!" I muttered to myself as my bowels almost opened. Images of Victoria, Alice and Nick flashed before my eyes. I pushed them out and tried to focus on some of the kickboxing training that I had taken up. I had no natural instincts at martial arts but I had been running over some basic self defense scenarios in my head ever since the previous episode. I was, like a frightened rabbit, staring into the headlights, seeing my life flash before me, when the busy lunchtime traffic noise was suddenly drowned out by the beating of a helicopter's rotor blade. I looked up and saw the police helicopter cruise overhead, unusually low and clear against the low dark grey October sky. I had seen it on occasions fly low like that after a bank raid or some other recent crime. As it passed overhead, I looked back to my new bodyguard. Baldy was staring up into the sky as if hypnotized. Looking up, his neck was stretched, and suddenly, there it was, like Kilimanjaro on its side, his Adam's apple was sticking out, like a beacon pointing to freedom. I suddenly saw the opportunity.

He was standing in front of me, slightly to my right, mouth open, still staring into the sky at the rapidly disappearing helicopter. I turned to my left as if to follow the path of the helicopter and without thinking any further than the next second, I spun on my right heel back towards Baldy. As I was spinning, I brought my right arm out and level with my shoulder. Using my hips and shoulders to gain torque, I put as much speed and power into the spin as I could, I stiffened my right hand. He began to lower his head from his plane spotting but there was still enough of Mount Kilimanjaro visible. As he slowly lowered his head, I targeted the area just below his Adam's apple. My hand collided with his neck with a sickening noise. It sounded like a cooked chickens leg being torn off. His head shot forward and he let out a sound that was half wretch, half choke. His two hands shot up to grip his throat as he fell to his knees. Through the sounds of him gasping for air, a loud clatter sounded.

"The gun!" I thought. Looking down expecting to see a pistol, I saw what looked like a black pistol handle with the rest cut off. In its place were two small protruding metal prongs, about a half inch long. Instinctively, I reached down and picked it up. Shoving it in my pocket, I ran like I'd never run before. I pounded along the pavement, down towards the shopping centre. I didn't know if he was up, still down or chasing me. I turned sharply left up a side street and continued running as fast as I could. As neared the end of the side street, I glanced behind me. Other than an old woman dumping a black plastic bag, there was no-one about. I kept trotting on down another lane which would bring me back in the direction of the Hospital. I stopped and checked behind again., nobody chasing me. I leaned against a wall and tried to catch my breath. I put my hand in my pocket to retrieve a tissue to wipe the sweat from my face and I hit the handle of whatever it was Baldy was threatening me with. It wasn't a gun. When I studied it for a minute or two and saw the manufacturer, Tazer, I realized what it was; a stun-gun. If you were at the business end of one of these, you would become partially paralyzed and temporarily incapacitated. I was intrigued by its simplicity. A stun gun steps the voltage from a 9-volt battery up to, in some versions, half a million volts. I was torn between throwing it into a builder's skip beside me, and holding on to it, after all I had now been beaten up and had two narrow escapes, and a little protection could prove useful.

I pushed it into my pocket and cautiously made my way back to the hospital, checking around for baldy, or anyone else who looked suspicious. I made it back to my office, which was thankfully empty. I fell into a chair, gulping three or four plastic cups of water from one of the water coolers. I thought about the incident, another scumbag had tried it on. I got my breath back and retrieved my bike bag and helmet. I thought about my new toy, and placed it in my backpack. I decided to leave it there until I decided what to do with it.

I put my bike jacket on and headed towards the basement to where the bikes were parked. I spotted Marty standing on a corner and I gave him a wave. He raised a hand to me but he had a look of total surprise on his face.

I was heading towards the bike rack when I felt my mobile phone buzz in my pocket. I'd forgotten that I had silenced it for the duration of the procedure. I fished it out of my jeans pocket. A number I didn't recognise was displayed. Pressing the call answer button, I answered, "Hello."...silence..."Hello?"

"I thought you were told to stay away from the fuckin police."

The hoarse unmistakable Dublin accent sent my guts into overdrive, and it was a physical effort to control the shaking, not to mention my bowels. "Wh...who is this?" I stuttered.

"No more fuckin games, Robbie. You were told not to go near the pigs, so youse are gonna have lo learn the hard way."

He had a wicked snarl to his voice. I ducked in behind a van and tried to control the shake in my voice. "I said nothing to the police..." I protested.

"I told you we were watching you. Youse were seen coming out of the station the other day," he ranted on, "Robbie, you were told that we would have to make sure that you didn't speak to the police. It's on your own fuckin head now. I'd hate to see something happen that lovely wife of yours…" He paused for effect.

I was certain that he could hear my heart hammering against my chest. The mention of Victoria was like an electric shock. I was thinking as fast as I could. "I was in the Central station the other day, but I was there to have a passport form signed."

He paused for a couple of seconds. In a low menacing voice he said, "Youse know that we can get to you or your family anytime."

"I know," I said, "I'm not fucking stupid." He stayed silent and I decided to play the only card I had, "That's why I've started researching this." I paused, wondering if I should continue.

"Go on," he growled.

I pressed on, "I've found a way of making sure that…Let's say, we get the result we want…and in a way that leaves no trace."

There was a palpable silence, until he spoke in a low voice, "What do you mean?"

I decided to play my only card. I guessed that it would be over his head anyway, so nothing ventured, "There's a drug available that I can get my hands on that, if given at the right time, will do the job. The beauty of it is that, he will have had a version of the drug anyway during the procedure so even if they do a toxicology screening, it will be a normal finding." I held my breath during the seemingly endless silence.

"What's this drug called?" he asked eventually.

"Succinylcholine, or Sucsamethonium," I answered.

"If you're bullshittin, there'll be trouble," he said with undisguised viciousness in his voice.

"I'm not, check it out for yourself, S-U-CC…" I started to spell it out, but I was interrupted.

"Don't worry, we will," he stated and suddenly the line was

dead. I almost collapsed except for a wooden box that was being kept for some storage or other. I sat on it and held my face in my hands for a few minutes. "Shit, Victoria," I quickly called home and melted with relief when Victoria answered. "Everything OK there?" I asked tentatively.

"Yes, kids are fine, Nick is at Josh's house, and Katie is over with Alice, we are baking cakes." I could hear the squeals of delight as Alice and her friend thrashed the kitchen with coloured icing and flour. I smiled to myself,

"I'll be home in about half an hour, need anything?" I asked with relief.

"Just an industrial vacuum cleaner," Victoria laughed.

"See you soon then."

I fastened my helmet, set my MP3 player to a Carlos Santana album, climbed up on my mountain bike and headed home. Eventually, after a glass of wine and some head time, we retired to bed at around 11.30. Sometime after midnight, I woke up with a start. I crept out of bed and down the stairs. I fished my backpack out from the cloakroom. I buried my hand down to the bottom and, after a minute, my hand found the rough grip of the Taser stun-gun. I retrieved it from the bag at last. I checked that there was silence from upstairs, and when I was happy, I headed into the utility room, closed the door and switched on the light. I studied the black, pistol grip shaped gadget, looking for a way to remove the battery. I could have hid it in the shed, but I felt that having it handy would be useful. I studied it for a moment and came across a wide slit in the side. I found a coin and it fitted into the slit. Twisting the coin slightly caused the handle to snap apart. The inside was simplicity itself. Two small transformers, a small circuit, a capacitor the size of a battery and a connection to a standard 9-volt square battery. I removed the battery and reassembled the handle. Placing it back in my bag, I pushed the bag back into the cloakroom. Heading back up to bed, I hoped that I would be able to sleep for a few hours. Sleep had become an elusive commodity since this whole mess began. I climbed into bed and lay awake staring at the shadows until either a magic solution came, I fell asleep or the alarm on my phone went off, whichever came first. The alarm had been winning hands down recently, and it was probably going to put in a good performance again tonight.

24

We were in the swimming pool of our local sports club. The kids were splashing about in the waves. There were lots of other people in the pool, and they were all fully dressed. I was naked. I tried to shepherd the children while trying to maintain my modesty. Nick ran straight up the steps of the waterslide. Alice followed him. Victoria didn't seem to see them. I followed them. At top of the slide there was a bald man with no face, dressed in an oversize tracksuit. He pointed slowly to the entrances to the slides. Normally, Nick wouldn't be allowed to use the slides but today he was. Alice jumped into the slide and disappeared into the black hole, Nick jumped into the other one. He looked over his shoulder and grinned and was swallowed up by the slide. I turned around and looked at the man in the tracksuit. In a rough Dublin accent, he snarled at me, "We have them now Robbie!" I started to panic. Looking down from the platform into the pool, I saw Victoria standing knee deep in water, she was alone, why hadn't she got the kids, they had only just gone down the slide. I started shouting, "Vicky, Vicky!" Tracksuit boy was laughing. I hit the emergency stop button for the water flow. Immediately a siren sounded. I was shouting, "Vicky, get the kids!!" The siren was still sounding. Tracksuit boy grabbed my arm, "Robbie, Robbie..."

"Robbie, Robbie, wake up." I woke up with a start, the

siren of the house alarm was sounding. Victoria was shaking me awake, "The alarm's going off, I heard glass smashing, I think there's someone downstairs." It took me a couple of seconds to wake up. I sat bolt upright. "The alarm's going off Robbie," Victoria had a look of fear on her face.

I leapt out of bed. I stuck my head into Alice's room. Despite the wailing of the siren, she was sleeping soundly. I closed the door securely and checked Nick's room. As I stepped into his room, he stirred, "Is it time for school Daddy?" he mumbled.

"No, soldier, go back to sleep." I pulled the duvet back over him and he wriggled down further under the cover. I also closed the door. I listened at the top of the stairs. Other than the siren still wailing, there didn't appear to be any other sound. I pulled a tee-shirt and jeans from the wooden wash basket and tiptoed down the stairs. It was a bit pointless, as the noise of the siren would have drowned out any sound. I rummaged in the cloakroom and my hand fell on the cold hard hickory of my baseball bat. I retrieved it and started towards the living room. The first thing I noticed was moonlight glistening off shards of glass scattered all over the ground. Standing still for a second, I felt a definite cold breeze. After disabling the siren, I slowly went from room to room. The silence was deafening, and straining to hear anything, I crept about the house. Within five minutes, I was happy that there was no-one in the house. I returned to the living room. In the silence and stillness, I noticed a smell of maple syrup again. I had definitely smelt it before, and the memory made my blood run cold. Someone had been in the house. I lifted the curtain and spotted that one of the windows was slightly open. It was quite windy and the curtain was moving about quite a bit. A glass vase had been knocked off the window ledge and shattered off the hard wooden floor. I pulled the window shut and locked it. I headed back up the stairs to where Victoria was sitting up in bed. She looked at me with two saucer eyes.

"One of the windows was open in the living room; the

curtain knocked the vase on to the floor." She looked relieved. "I'll clear it up now, and reset the alarm."

I headed back down the stairs, intending to check out the house a bit more carefully. I reset the alarm and swept up the broken glass, I began to think that if there was a visitor, there didn't seem to be anything taken, this was a clear message; they're watching me closely. I needed to be extremely careful. I desperately needed to get on top of things, as time was ticking away fast. I finished clearing up, put away the brush and pan and headed to bed to try to get some sleep before the alarm clock put paid to that idea.

25

Docks murder victim identified.

Gardai today confirmed today that the body found outside McRoarys pub near the Point Depot in the small hours of the morning was that of Stephen "Spider" Sheehan. He is thought to be a senior gang member and associate of Thomas "the Suit" Mulligan, who is currently in the exclusive Southwestern Clinic awaiting Heart surgery. Sheehan was thought to be the "underboss" and second in-command of Mulligan's Criminal Empire. He was well known to the Gardai and had a number of charges pending against him. The shooting resembled a professional hit. He was shot twice in the head and once in the chest. There were no witnesses to the shooting. Gardai are seeking information from anyone who was in the vicinity if McRoary's Bar or the Docks area around the new pedestrian bridge, between the hours of 9.pm and midnight last night. They are especially anxious to contact the driver of a green Kawasaki motorbike that was seen in the area. If anyone has any information, however irrelevant it may seem, please call the police confidential witness phone number.

I HEARD THE NEWS BULLETIN on my radio earpiece as I was back on my bike heading into work, a few short hours later. I would have to try to gather some information that I could use to gain some leverage in this mess. As I cycled along the canal, listening to this breaking news story, I realized that the stakes had gone up a notch or two. Someone was obviously making a move on Mulligan's business.

I freewheeled into the lockup area and locked my bike. I met Marty as I walked towards the service entrance. "Morning Robbie, you look tired," he said with concern.

"Haven't slept well the last week or two," I moaned.

"You still going to the kickboxing class, keep up the exercise, it'll help you sleep," he offered.

"Yeah, I'll go whenever I can." I waved and headed towards the door. I hit the intercom that was connected to security, to gain entrance to the service corridor of the basement. I still had my earpiece in that was connected to my mobile phone. I was listening to the morning talk show, although there was more white noise than chat as I was under the main structure of the building. As the security guard came on the intercom and I identified myself, my mobile phone rang in my ear. I jumped with fright; recently the sound of my mobile ringing had caused me more than a little anxiety. Before answering it, I fished it out of my pocket and looked at the screen to see if I could identify the caller. "Number Withheld" was the only message given. I let it ring for a second or two while trying to get my thoughts together in case it was one of my new best mates. I thought of Baldy, and the conquering of Kilimanjaro. I wondered how he was feeling now. I took a deep breath and pressed the answer button. "Hello," I said tentatively.

"Robbie mate, how are you? I heard you were looking for me," came an upbeat voice.

My caution lightened a little. "Who is this?" I asked.

"McGovern, George McGovern," came the response.

I felt an immediate sense of relief, both from the fact that the caller was genuine, and particularly that a call from George was extremely welcome. "George, great to hear from you. How are you?" I smiled.

"What's up?" He got straight to the point. Just like him.

I replied in kind, "George, I'm in a spot of bother, and it's a bit delicate." I was economical with the information.

"What's the problem?" he pried a bit further.

"I'd rather not talk about it over the phone, if you don't mind. Can we meet for coffee?" I was as cautious as I could be without pissing him off.

"Sounds intriguing are you free today?" he asked.

I was thrilled and jumped at the chance. "Yeah, anytime after two?" I suggested hopefully.

"How about coffee at three, I'm in the city, I could head straight to the hospital when I'm finished here," he offered.

I was delighted that he was going to see me so quick, but the warning rang in my ear, "we'll be watching you." "Fantastic," I said, "but there is another problem." I paused to find the best way of putting it, "This is something to do with…" I paused and looked around, "…that assignment that you were on when I met you last week."

There was a silence as he thought about this for a second. "Outside the ward in your hospital?" he asked slowly.

I could almost hear the wheels turning in his brain. To oil them a little further, I added a little more. Recent events in my life were making me paranoid. "Yes, and did you here the news report this morning?" There was a palpable silence.

"George, I'm in the shit big time, and I need your help. Also I think I'm being followed," I suddenly blurted out.

"OK, OK, calm down Robbie, here's the deal," he immediately changed to a serious business tone. "There's a coffee shop on Dawson Street, opposite the Mansion house, with a seating area outside it, you know it?"

"Yes," I said.

"How will you be getting there?" he asked.

"I'll probably cycle," I suggested.

"Leave your bike on the island opposite the Stephens Green centre, and walk down. I'll meet you at the café. If I'm not sitting outside the café, keep walking, circle the block and come back fifteen minutes later." I wondered what this arrangement was all about. "I want to see if you are being tailed," he read my mind, "if I'm not sitting waiting for you, it means you have a tail and I'll get rid of him for you."

It felt so good to have a professional looking out for me at last. "Sounds great, George. Listen I really appreciate this, I've been out of my mind with worry the past week…" I groveled a bit.

"Forget about it," he laughed. "By the way," he added, "if you spot a tail yourself, don't lead him to me. I'll wait till four, and then contact you by mobile, OK?"

"No problem, I'll do my best, see you at three then George."

I shut off my phone and headed up to the changing room. I was placing my helmet into my bag when a knocking of plastic reminded me of my new toy. I dug to the bottom of the bag and pulled the Tazer stun gun and battery from the bottom. I threw it into the back of my locker and covered it up with junk. I felt visibly lighter, having recruited some professional help. The problem was now to get to George, without bringing anyone along with me. The more I thought about it, the more I realized that every move I made was being watched, and it scared the shit out of me. I was too fired up to concentrate on anything, and I was delighted to see that the operating list comprised only of two patients, both having Coronary Artery Bypass Grafts. I quickly delegated these out and sat in my office with a cup of coffee, trying to recall as much of the detail of the previous few weeks events and information as I could remember. I tried to remember names that were mentioned. The only name I could remember clearly was Brennan, that baldy with the tracksuit was insistent on bringing me to see. He apparently was the boss of this motley crew, and responsible for the "plan" as it stood. I took out a small notebook, and jotted down a few notes, descriptions of "Tom Hagen" from Molloys bar, the rough hoarsy voice of the boss. I reckoned I could safely assume that this was the voice of Brennan, the brains of the operation. I wrote down the timeline, as far as I could remember. I contemplated printing off the pictures of the kids that I had received and the one of me in the bike park. I thought the better of it, but felt it would be prudent to have some record. I fished out a spare flash drive from the drawer in the filing cabinet. I retrieved the email messages from Outlook, I hadn't deleted them, and saved them to the flash drive. At least I had something solid to give George. On the desk was the chart from the second patient. Without really seeing, I stared at the open notes. The usual mix of laboratory, admission and financial forms stuck out. For no other reason than to pass time, I rummaged through the chart to see if I could find the finance form that I had come across a few days earlier which showed the EI-TP patient underwritten by the Lighthouse company, and that Reddy was a director. There was no sign of such a letter, and other than the EI-TP reference, there was no evidence to link this patient to any company called Lighthouse. I thought about this for a minute or two. The letter I had come across looked a little out of place in the patient's chart. I quickly forgot about it as I noticed that it was gone 12pm. I changed in the changing room. Thinking about George's instructions, I dumped my bike bag back in the office. It was a bright blue "Head" sports bag and anyone following me would have no problem spotting me in a crowd with this on my shoulder. I wasn't really hungry but using my logic of "eat now, you may not get another chance today" I headed to the hospital restaurant. Grabbing a tuna sandwich, a bag of crisps and a Coke, I found a seat near the door. I wasn't in the mood for general conversation so I kept my head down. At ten past two, I climbed onto my bicycle and freewheeled out of the service area of the hospital and on towards the centre of town.

I crossed between two delivery vans and had to be careful to avoid slipping in the LUAS tracks as I crossed the busy thoroughfare of St Stephens Green. I was turning my head like an owl, looking for anyone who might be tailing me. It was difficult on the bike. I saw no-one who might be following me. I dismounted and pushed my bike onto the traffic island. I found a small spot and managed to manhandle my bike in close enough to lock. My watch told me I had twenty minutes until I met George. I decided that I would use the time to see if I could spot any tails. I kept on my Oakleys, and looked around me as much as I could before setting off. A couple of tracksuits, one leather jacket over jeans, two separate bomber jackets with multiple piercings, all within spotting distance of me. I sauntered over towards the main entrance of the Stephens Green Centre, trying to see if any of my suspects followed me. Shit, the bomber jackets had disappeared from my line of sight, but wait, leather jacket was moving towards the entrance. Was he my tail?

I joined the throng entering the centre and headed straight for the escalator. I used the mirrored wall to see if leather jacket was following me. I spotted him entering the centre, look around and move beyond the stairs. I turned and looked over the moving rail. Leather boy was looking around, yes, he was definitely looking for someone. I felt a surge of victory until I saw his face break into a grin. A tall dark woman approached him. They embraced and left, arm in arm back out onto Grafton Street. I scanned the crowd around me, and wandered the first floor of the centre for another five or six minutes. Seeing no-one suspicious, I left the centre by the side door onto South King Street and walked quickly back towards the corner of Grafton and the Green and moved cautiously towards Dawson Street. From a clock over a shop, I noted that it was five minutes to three. I strolled on down past the Mansion House. I spotted the coffee shop, and crossed the street between the cars. There were four or five tables in an enclosed area outside the café. At one, a group of girls enjoying a late lunch, a bearded man in a tourist type anorak occupied the second, and apart from a waiter clearing the third, there was no sign of George.

A surge of panic rose in my stomach. I fought the urge to stop and search the café for any sign of my new ally. I made a pass of the café, trying to look inside without turning my head. I saw one or two people inside the door but no George. I kept on walking to the end of the block and turned left on to South Anne Street. It was quite busy with lots of shoppers about. George had said that if he wasn't sitting outside the café, then I had a tail. Shit, I thought my spotting efforts in the Stephens Green Centre had lost any tails, but obviously, I had a lot to learn.

As I passed an antique shop, I became aware of a commotion behind me. I looked behind and saw two uniformed police manhandling a skinny, scruffy looking teenager up against the wall. A silver BMX bicycle was thrown on the ground beside the patrol car which was parked with one wheel up on the footpath. The kid was giving it large to the two policemen. But the guards were taking none of it and were physically body searching him. "Probably some shoplifter," I thought to myself as I continued on past the restaurants and shops. As I turned back on to Grafton Street, I passed the bank on the corner. The flower sellers were shouting their bargains. There were the usual colourful mix of characters, a puppeteer and a man in a gold suit, in classic statue pose. Anytime somebody dropped a coin into his hat, he changed his pose. This had the effect of sending children scurrying for cover while sending gangs of schoolgirls into fits of uncontrollable giggles. Ten metres further on, I saw two more Gardai in yellow jackets hold a teenager in a Man. Utd. football strip over black combat trousers up against a shop window. He was turning out his pockets while giving dog's abuse to the police, As I looked across, he caught my eye and glared at me. I looked away quickly. I reached the top of Grafton Street, turned left onto the green and made my way back down towards the Mansion House and my rendezvous.

A look at my watch showed it to be twelve minutes past, and so I upped my pace slightly. As I approached the café this time, I was met by a huge grinning George. Catching my eye, he stood up and, with an inclination of his head, we left the café area and he led me on down Dawson Street. He was silent for a few minutes and walked quite fast. I almost had to trot to keep up with him. After a hundred metres or so, he finally slowed down and turned to me. "Robbie," he grinned, "what's going on?" he asked.

"Missed you at three," I said.

He looked at me wide-eyed, "don't tell me you didn't see your tail."

I looked at him. "Where?" I asked.

"Two teenagers, one on a silver bike, one in a Man Utd. top"

I looked at him incredulously. "I saw both of them being lifted, five minutes ago."

He grinned, "Yeah, I picked them up just after you locked your bike. I recognised the kid in the football top. He has a bench warrant out for his arrest, and a form sheet the length of your arm. I called in a favour."

I listened in awe. "What about football head?" I asked, anxious to hear more.

"When I noticed him, I twigged the uniforms and let them know that he was casing some potential pickpocket victims. I pointed you out to them and when they saw him tailing you, they stepped in and did the rest."

I was gobsmacked. As we walked, he glanced about at regular intervals. We seemed to take a roundabout way but after ten or twelve minutes walking we ended up in a small coffee shop behind the National Gallery, off Merrion Square. We found an empty booth and sat down with a coffee. "Now, Robbie my man, what's the trouble?" he asked in the voice of a priest in confession.

For the next hour and a half, I opened up and spilled out all of the shit that was bottled up. I had given Detective Elvis as much of a full picture as I dared, but I felt nowhere near as relieved after as I did now with my old school pal. Apart from stopping me occasionally to repeat or clarify something, he said very little. I told him about visiting Detective Elvis. He rolled his eyes and laughed, "I know of that joker," he laughed, "useful as a one legged man at an arse kicking contest. You won't be getting much help from him, I'm afraid." I burst out laughing. He asked me if I could remember talking to anyone outside my normal social circle, any occasions where I explained what I did for a living where the company was a bit suspect. "Cassin would have an idea what I do, but that was a long time ago," I explained. George nodded, deep in thought. Then a thought struck me, "I was out for a few beers with a porter from the hospital a month or so ago." George looked at me hopefully. I continued, "We were in a bar, not far from the hospital."

"Do you remember any of their names?" he asked.

I blushed slightly, "I had quite a few beers, McCaffery, McCartney, something like that." Then I remembered that he was very friendly with Mick, our hospital porter. I could follow that up and get his name. When I finally finished talking, he was silent for a minute or two and then got down to business. "Have you any copies of the emails that you received?"

I fished out the flash drive from my pocket. "The emails and pictures are on this," I said handing it to him.

"Right," he said, "the first thing to do is to find out who and how serious these scumbags are."

"I think they're serious all right" I suggested. "One of Mulligan's goons was killed the other night; I think they mean business."

George looked at me square in the eye and lowered his voice, "Robbie, we'll get on top of this, don't worry."

I looked back at him and for the first time in a month, I felt reassured that a professional was on my side, and Christ, it felt great. Maybe I would get a few hours sleep tonight. George promised to get back to me and before we left, he gave me a few very simple tips on how to spot a tail, and how to shake one off if I was being followed. I left the coffee shop feeling physically lighter in spirit and with a genuine sense of hope. As I strolled back towards my bike, my phone beeped and buzzed in my pocket. It was a text message from George, he had forgotten to give me his mobile number. Quickly I saved it. Now I felt protected.

26

PEARSE O'CEALLAIGH, a junior civil servant in the Department of Health and Children, posted to the Ministers office, sat quietly on the buttoned leather couch with a manila folder on his knee. He had been summoned by the Permanent Under-Secretary of the Department to gather some statistics to show the extent of the spending on the National Treatment Purchase Fund. Although he had not been asked, he had included all disciplines of Surgery. He knew that Cardiac Surgery was the main area of interest to the Minister, as there was a University Hospital in his constituency of West Limerick that was actively lobbying for the green light from the Department to commence a Cardiac Surgery Program. Fergus Fitzpatrick, the youngest Ministerial appointee to the Health Portfolio was torn between awarding the program to the Hospital at a cost of tens of millions, and the money and votes that were being saved by increasing funding to the Treatment Purchase Fund. The TPF was well on the way to wiping out the waiting list, although there was quite a ways to go yet, he had reaped the benefits by way of votes and credibility. A closet Progressive Democrat, he supported what they stood for in terms of Public/Private partnership and had come up with the idea over a few brandies in the Dail bar with some of the newer faces in the House. But from strict Republican stock, he won his grandfather's seat in a by-election six years earlier, he had progressed quickly through the ranks, ending up with the Health portfolio at the tender age of thirty eight. "Bobby," he turned to his Permanent Under-Secretary, "I'm having my balls squeezed by the whingers in Limerick, you know that, don't you?"

Bobby O'Shea, looked with sympathetic eyes, "Yes Minister, I know the lobbying that's been going on." O'Shea took a mouthful of Earl Grey from his bone china cup and stared out the window. "The question is, Minister, who will squeeze harder, Biffo up in Finance, or the whingers in Limerick." O'Shea reveled in the power. A career civil servant, he had climbed to the top of the heap in Health and felt he was ultimately responsible for the reductions in waiting lists. He was constantly annoyed by what he saw as the spineless vote-catching that the politicians passed off as decision-making. "Ministers come and go, but Permanent Under-Secretaries do exactly as the title suggests, we run the shagging departments," was his usual rant after a night on the Famous Grouse.

He had suggested the idea of the NTPF to the Minister, particularly the idea of bringing in large multinational insurance companies for the high-cost surgical procedures. After a few months of the Fund's operation, he was contacted by an old work colleague from a hospital where he had worked as a junior Clerical Officer. John Brennan had been a Porter while O'Shea worked in the Finance Section of Holy Trinity University Hospital. O'Shea had completed his Economics Degree part-time, and with a Masters in Healthcare Economics, had joined the Department of Health as an Executive Officer.

He quickly rose through the ranks and, with the politics that he had learned within the cut and thrust of the Hospitals, ended up as Permanent Under-Secretary to the Minister. He had been introduced to Brennan six years previous, on a rare family holiday to Spain. They were away on a holiday with his brother and family. His brother had a slightly shady past. He worked in some sort of insurance company owned by Brennan. His brother had bought a villa in Tenerife with an insurance salesman's salary, this mystified O'Shea. After several large scotches one evening, O'Shea had boasted about his control of the Department, Brennan had contacted him back in Dublin and made him an offer he couldn't refuse. Brennan was involved in an insurance company who were quite interested in a piece of the Treatment Purchase Fund business. If O'Shea could grease the wheels within the system and ensure that a decent proportion of this business could find its way onto the books of a certain Lighthouse Insurance Services, he would receive a significant bonus for each group of patients who found their way to the Lighthouse. This bonus was significantly more than his Higher Executive Officer's salary, and he had gotten to depend on it, a lot. Part of his whinge was the fact that he had a handicapped daughter, and he, more than anyone, knew the measly financial help that was available from the Department of Health for necessary conversions to his house. Christ, the specialist stuff was so expensive.

Maintaining the Funds' existence became his raison d'etre. Quietly, he enlisted the help of one or two junior clerks. The promise of a speedy promotional pathway and as much overtime as they could handle was all it took for them to keep up the effort required to pull the figures together. This would convince the Minister to keep it rolling. The Minister, however felt it was his idea, and was getting all the kudos. "Minister, the savings alone with the Fund would shut the lobby groups up. Shall I have them published?" This was his favorite threat. He knew if the details of how deeply insurance companies were involved in the running of the fund were leaked too early, the Minister would be very quickly buried in the shit from opposition and every lobby group in the country shouting for something or other from his office. Timing was everything with this delicate matter. Fitzpatrick looked up quickly, loosening his tie spoke with some resignation, "No, Bobby, lets get some more figures together first. We'll take a good look at them, get the best spin people onto them and then re-evaluate."

O'Shea smiled to himself. He wanted to keep this under wraps for as long as possible. His time would come. He knew that what Fitzpatrick didn't want out in the open was the massive breaks by way of special Corporation tax rates that were being afforded to the insurance companies who were involved in partially underwriting the fund. This was the secret, but also diametrically opposed to the delicate partnership talks that were underway just up the hall in Finance between the Government and the Unions. No, keep it shut was the best plan.

"Let's take a look at the latest figures then," he held out his hand towards O'Ceallaigh. Pearse opened up his manila folder. He had spreadsheets and columns of figures set out in a way that only he could understand. Fitzpatrick looked at the rows of figures. He was naturally an impatient man and he thrust the papers back at the nervous young civil servant, "Just give me a synopsis."

O'Ceallaigh started, "Minister, €34 million spent since inception of the Fund. 15,000 patients treated so far. The waiting list for hip replacement is down to two weeks, same for Ear, Nose and Throat lists in the Childrens' Hospitals."

This is what the Minister wanted to hear, "What about Cardiac Surgery?" he barked with impatience.

"972 extra patients operated on so far, at a cost of €14 million," O'Ceallaigh offered.

Fitzpatrick rubbed his chin. He had been on the road since 6am and he felt like he could do with another shave. "What is the waiting list like now?" he asked with a thoughtful frown.

"A couple of weeks in places where there are bed problems, but generally it's under control." Pearse nervously pressed ahead. He had been told by O'Shea that it was very important to him to keep the Fund rolling. He had his own interest in the system. He had been promised a speedy career path within the Department if his research was up to scratch. And also he had carte blanche on any overtime that was incurred in the processing of the figures.

"Minister, the relative figures are the most impressive," Pearse offered.

"What do you mean?" Fitzpatrick asked with a curious look on his face.

"Sir, I dug up some figures from the partnership talks down the hall," Pearse pressed on.

"What have those talks got to do with this?" Fitzpatrick asked with obvious impatience.

O'Shea was getting nervous now; this jumped up junior clerk was stepping into the unknown. This was his first real test. "Sir, I found some figures, compiled by accountants within the Health services branches of the Unions, that showed that it would cost around €10 million a year in overtime and extra costs to clear the Heart Surgery waiting list over a three year period." He paused for effect.

The Minister seemed confused, "Get to the point son" he barked.

"Sir, the Fund has cleared the waiting list at less than half the cost that the unions predicted that it would." Fitzpatrick looked incredulous. "Also, Minister, it's costing less per week to keep the waiting list at bay than ICTU's accountants warned. They forecasted that it would cost €150,000 per week extra to cover any extra cases. The Private Hospitals carrying out the work are charging a much lower premium per patient. It's costing less than €60,000." Pearse paused looking nervously between the Minister and O'Shea.

Fitzpatrick's eyes widened and he became animated, "Brilliant...what's your name son?"

"O'Ceallaig, Pearse, Sir," he stuttered with a smile.

"Brilliant work son. Dig up some more of those figures and put them into some sort of presentation. The whingers can't ignore these figures." He looked up at O'Shea, "This is a winner, we can keep the fund rolling until the election, what do you think Bobby?"

O'Shea looked nonchalantly out the window and thought

to himself, "The shagging Fund will continue for as long as I say it will." Finally he sighed, "I suppose it's a good idea." Fitzpatrick wasn't listening. He was already halfway down the corridor towards the Dail restaurant, and a lunch of Beef Wellington, helped along by a bottle of Bellingham Pinotage.

27

I SET THE TIMING on the Intra Aortic Balloon pump on the patient in Intensive Care. This is the balloon that is placed outside the heart in the aorta, giving the heart a piggyback ride. The timing of its operation is critical and I spent twenty minutes or so with the Intensive Care Nurse explaining the settings to her. There had been four procedures that day and the third one had encountered some problems after the Heart/ Lung was switched off. The Balloon Pump was inserted a few minutes later, following the usual cocktail of drugs. The patient stabilized and was transferred back to the Intensive Care Unit. I was covering the call and I always gave the ICU a final check before heading home. I gave the other patients my own quick check, looking for "grey hue" clues. I confirmed with the senior resident that all was well with the rest of the days patients and headed towards the changing room. As I approached the door, the security beep sounded, followed by a click as the door opened. Prof. O'Riada emerged from the changing room. We exchanged pleasantries while I held the door with my foot. He rambled on for a minute or two about the state of the greens in the golf club. After a minute or so of complete waffle, he left. I pushed the door open and entered the changing area. The door closed quietly behind me. The changing room was divided into three separate areas, divided up by walls of lockers. I found my locker and fished my key out from my scrubs pocket. I was thinking of when George might be back in contact when I became aware of a voice I recognised in the changing room. Reddy was talking on a mobile, and by the sounds of it, he was under pressure. "The surgery is scheduled for Friday, I told you...I can't reschedule, the lists are full until then..." The only patient scheduled for Cardiac surgery on Friday was Mulligan, and hearing this gave me a jolt.

His voice was raised quite a bit. He obviously hadn't heard me come in and thought he was alone. "I can only reschedule if there's a real problem or emergency...Jesus! I can't just call it an emergency...I'm taking enough risks as it is with this crap ...Don't threaten me like that...I don't care what Brennan says..."

The mention of Brennan hit me like an electric shock. Tracksuit boy was insistent on bringing me to see a Mr. Brennan. Who was this Brennan? Johnny B. he called him. Reddy sounded mightily pissed. What the fuck was going on here? As Reddy closed his phone, I ducked quickly in behind the shower curtain. I heard a locker door slam and the exit door opening. The door almost lifted off its hinges as it was slammed shut. I waited a minute or two before climbing out of the shower. Shit, was Reddy involved in this too? Something stank to high heavens. Then the name Brennan came to mind again. I had come across that name before. My subconscious was shouting it at me, but I couldn't quite place it. Like chasing smoke, the harder I thought of what that name meant to me, the further it slipped away. I decided to leave it and let it come back to me. I finished changing and exited the changing room. As I headed towards the stairs, I remembered I had left my MP3 player in my office. I quickly doubled back towards the back entrance of the Operating Theatre and on into my office. I retrieved my MP3 player. As I switched it on and scrolled through to something to suit my mood, a chart sitting on the desk caught my eye. It was closed but some of the letters and sheets were visible from the way it was lying. It was from the last patient of the day. I stopped for a second. My subconscious was screaming at me. I opened the chart and firstly checked the patient label: EI-TP. I looked in the section inside the front cover where the admission notes were normally kept. I didn't know exactly what I was searching for, but I let my hands do the walking. Surgical Patient evaluation, Pre-admission work-up, Nursing Care plan, Insurance details...I ran my eyes up and down the form. Treatment Purchase Fund-External Insurer ... transferred from LUH to SWC. Nothing grabbed me. I went back to the admission sheet. Financial details...EI-TP, then in hand writing, Reddys hand...LIS with a number beside it. LIS...LIS...I lifted the letter out of the chart and straightaway I felt something. A business card stapled to the back of the letter. I folded the letter back and looked at the card. It hit me like a bolt of lightning. The colorful logo of Lighthouse Insurance Ltd shouted at me from the card. Shit! Brennan, the name Brennan was on the list of directors in the small print at the bottom of the letter that I had come across the previous day, alongside Reddy's. My heart hammered against the inside of my chest, it had to be! I threw down the letter and grabbed a handful of the under copies of the Heart/Lung Machine data sheets. I was trying to find the name of the patient in whose chart I had seen the letter from Lighthouse to Reddy. After a minute or two of frantic searching, I found the three patients from the day on which I had found the letter. Of the three patients operated on that day, two of them were EI-TP patients. This made life a little easier. It was only two days ago, so the patients were still going to be in the main post-surgical ward. I noted both the names and headed towards the ward. I was in such a frenzy to get to the ward, I forgot that I had already changed back into civvies. Not that this was a problem, but I didn't feel that Nike tracksuit pants, dirty trainers and a rain jacket were an appropriate uniform to be rummaging through patients' charts. I looked at my watch, it was twenty to seven. I was going to be late home again, but I had to get this information. There had to be a connection. I dumped my bag and helmet in the office and charged back to the changing room. The anonymous uniform of theatre scrubs and a white laboratory coat would guarantee that I wouldn't be disturbed. I threw on fresh theatre scrubs and my laboratory coat and ran to the stairs. I took them two at a time. The first thing I noticed was the extra plain clothes detectives hovering around one of the private rooms.

Waiting for two minutes for my breath to come back, I walked slowly towards the reception desk. A pretty Nigerian receptionist looked at me and asked, "Can I help you Doctor?" A mouthful of snowy white pearls contrasted with her chocolate brown skin with black pools for eyes. I didn't correct her on her assumption that I was a Doctor, I didn't want to shatter her illusions and besides, if it helped me get what I wanted quicker, she could call me Professor if she wanted to.

I nodded towards the detectives outside the room, "What's the presence for?"

The receptionist looked around and lowering her voice said, "Mr. Mulligan is in there, after that shooting the other night, more police arrived. Sister is very cross with them."

I was momentarily taken aback, I was here investigating some skullduggery, or so I thought and there were armed detectives less than ten metres from me. Although it was completely irrational, I became a little nervous. "I'm looking for two charts; I need to check some billing details."

The mention of billing details always got a reaction from administration staff, and it worked again. She jumped to her feet, "No problem, Doctor, give me the names and I'll fetch the charts for you."

"Thanks a million...Letitia" I read from her name tag and handed her the slip of paper with the two names on it.

She moved gracefully and I was left standing at the reception desk watching her walk across the carpeted hall with the elegance of a supermodel. From the corner of my eye, I noticed somebody standing quite close to me. I turned to see an elderly gentleman in expensive looking pyjamas under a silk dressing gown. He was in his seventies, and I could just make out the start of the median sternotomy scar, beginning just above the neckline of his pyjamas. He was staring after Letitia and as I looked across at him, he caught my eye. A grin spread across his face, "Don't tell Mr. Reddy you saw me eying up the staff" he laughed.

I smiled back at him. "As long as you don't tell my wife, and we'll keep it from Sister," I nodded in the direction of the Ward Sister marching up the corridor.

He lowered his voice and said in a mutter, "She'd give Hattie Jakes a run for her money." I burst out laughing and for my trouble, received a glare from sister. "Back to your room now Colonel," she ordered the silver-haired man, "tea's on the way."

He smiled, "Served in the Congo, Middle-east and Burma, never came across a sergeant Major like her."

She laughed, "You're on my turf now sir, you'll do as ordered."

He nodded in my direction and headed towards his room. "Are you being looked after?" she eyed me suspiciously. I could see her reading my name badge on the lapel of my lab coat.

"Yes, I'm OK, Letitia is getting some charts for me; I need to check some billing details on two patients before the charts disappear." She seemed satisfied and sat down behind her desk.

After a minute, supermodel returned with two charts. "Here you are Doctor." She loaded me up with the charts and I looked around for somewhere to lay them down, "I'll only be a minute or two, is there somewhere I can use to read these?" I asked hopefully.

Sister looked impatiently up over her glasses, "Use the storeroom there." She indicated behind the reception area.

"Thanks Sister, I'll only be five minutes. Thanks for your help Letitia," I gave her a big smile and got one in return that would light up a room. "No problem Doctor."

As quickly as I could, I moved into the storeroom There were shelves with various packages, drip packs, fluids and a white metal press with a red light on the outside of the door. This was the Dangerous Drugs cupboard. It was open and the red light was on. This corresponded with a red light and low pitched alarm that was sounding on the panel on the reception desk outside. A thought had crossed my mind of looking for Succamethonium in the press, but the red light and alarm sounding put me right off. I took the first chart and flicked through the main body, nothing there. I went to the plastic pouch inside the cover. There were a few documents there, admission notes, booking forms and financial details, but no sign of the letter. I closed the chart and started on the other one. I pulled the sheaf of notes out from the inside cover and flicked through them. I came across the form from finance, and then my heart leapt, there it was; Lighthouse Insurance services. I looked straight at the bottom where the small print was. There it was, J. Brennan, among the list of directors, next to P Reddy. Suddenly I felt like a burglar. I was torn between stuffing the letter into my pocket, and walking out of the ward, and asking Letita to photocopy it for me. A group of nurses arrived back from their break and the noise level at the desk went up a notch or two. I became a felon, I removed the letter and after checking that no-one was watching, I rolled it up and placed it loosely in the back trouser pocket of my scrubs. I resolved to return it by stealth at the next available opportunity. I walked back out to the reception area. Two or three of the Nurses looked at me but no-one was interested in an anonymous theatre lackey. I placed the charts back on the desk in front of Letitia's chair. It was empty. I decided to play the Doctor card again so I gave my full attention to the blank notepaper that I had brought in with me for the purposes of writing down any clues. I walked without looking back at the Nurses station. I grunted an unintelligible "thanks." I had pulled a fresh Theatre cap low over my eyes, and that was exactly what I wanted, anonymity. I could have been any of the Medical or Surgical residents, and there were about twenty of them in the hospital.

I made my way back to my office. I felt like a criminal with a hot diamond necklace in my back pocket. Trying to decide what the best thing to do with this was, I decided to make an electronic copy of it. I passed some secretaries offices which were empty. The doors were open, obviously waiting on the cleaners. I saw an opportunity and took it. I walked deliberately into the office. There were no signs of anybody about. The desk was tidied for the night and the computer was switched off. I closed the door over about half way and checked the fax machine. I hoped that the standard dial 9 would get me an outside line. I used a free internet based fax carrier called eFax. If I faxed a document to a UK number, it would appear as a scanned item in my email box. Giving one more quick check, I placed the letter on the tray. I dialed 9, followed by the fax number. I held my breath for a minute. Holding my breath, I gave a small "Yessss" as the number connected and the paper started slowly feeding into the body of the fax machine. I looked at my watch, quarter past seven; Victoria would be on the phone now looking for me. It seemed to take an eternity for the fax to go through. Eventually the paper disappeared through the machine. I grabbed it from the tray and, after quickly checking that I hadn't disturbed anything, I slipped out of the office. Two minutes later I was at the computer in my own office. Using Google, I performed a quick search. I found the website of Lighthouse Insurance Services. It was pretty basic. There was no significant information given out, other than the address and contact details. Their business portfolio included health, motor, life insurance and pensions and everything in between. A link at the bottom entitled "Life

& Pensions" brought me to another page that, among others, offered Health Insurance. I followed this link to another page which sported the logos of four or five of the large multinational insurance companies. Beside each one was a synopsis of two or three of their more popular plans. A quick search of the Companies Registry Office webpage revealed two companies with the term Lighthouse in the title. The second one was the insurance company, and with the list of directors that I had read on the letter, the company was still trading. The address of the company was Upper Oriel Street. I was vaguely familiar with the area and I knew that calling Upper Oriel Street part of the Financial Services district was really stretching the truth. A badly run down part of town, and if my geography was correct, pretty close to the bar where I met Joey Cassin to pay my gambling debt. I pulled the name, address and telephone numbers across to a blank Word document, titled and saved it to a folder. Logging out of Explorer, I didn't bother closing down the computer. I charged to the changing room, threw on my tracksuit and ran for the basement.

28

WHEN HE WAS SURE that the office was empty, Marty slipped into the Perfusion services office. He had heard the inner door slam shut and the changing room door bang, so he was confident he had a few minutes. Checking the computer screen again, he was in luck; the PC was still switched on. But this time however, the Internet Explorer window was closed. He had also been lucky a few days previous while delivering a new computer to the library. An Indian Doctor had come into the library had looked a bit lost, trying to log on to the internet. Marty seized the opportunity and offered to help. He was charming and helpful and helped the Doctor log on and find the medical research sites that he was looking for. A few days later, although he couldn't remember the Doctor's full name, he could clearly remember his username and password to access the internet. In the Perfusion office, Marty opened Explorer. It opened to the Google home page. Because the program had been closed, clicking the back key was useless. He clicked the History button and it showed that today, there had been visits to the home page of Lighthouse Insurance and a couple of visits to the Companies Registry Office. Although he couldn't access the searches on the CRO, he was willing to bet money that the details of Lighthouse were the subject of the search. This was all the information he required. He closed down the Explorer program and had to stop for a moment to try to remember if the PC was on or off when he came into the office. He decided to leave it on. One last check, he repositioned the chair and slipped out of the office. It had taken less than five minutes.

Ten minutes later, I was on the bike pounding through the car park. As I raced out of the service entrance at the back of the hospital, I hardly noticed Marty sitting on the low wall at the back gate. He looked up and saluted as I passed. He was tapping out a text on his mobile. "Lucky bugger," I thought to myself, "probably texting one of his recent conquests for a night on the razz and whatever else." I pumped my legs like pistons and hared along the canal towards home. I had the original letter tucked in the back of a folder that I carried in my bag. I made it to Sandymount in record time and I was glad that my phone hadn't rang in my ear. I rounded the corner to my road and freewheeled into the garden. I noticed that Victoria's car was missing. She must have nipped out for a message. I pulled my bike into the garage and entered the house through the utility room at the back of the kitchen. The radio was still playing and a pot of pasta was simmering on the hob. The smell of a rich, garlicky tomato sauce reminded me of how hungry I was. It was late for Victoria to be out with the kids, particularly so since they obviously hadn't eaten. "Something must've come up," I thought to myself as I threw my bag into the cloakroom. I headed back to the kitchen, noticing from the clock on the oven, that it was just eight o clock.

After the punishing cycle home, I was ravenous with hunger, so I grabbed a plate from the press. Lifting a large forkful of fettuccini from the pot, I spooned a generous helping of tomato sauce and meatballs over the pasta. I grabbed a beer from the fridge but, remembering that I was covering the call, I opted for a glass of iced water and I headed to the living room. I fell into a chair and wolfed down half the pasta and meatballs. I had downed half the water and a large portion of my plateful before I paused for breath. I jumped channels on the TV for a minute or two and settled down to watch a news program. This was a rare luxury, sitting in the armchair, enjoying my food without a running commentary or constant chattering and questions from the kids. I thought I noticed the smell of maple syrup again. Was I losing the plot? That was the third time I had gotten that smell in as many weeks. I ignored the smell and enjoyed the solitude for a few more minutes. I finished the water in the glass and stood up to head to the kitchen for a refill. I noticed, or rather my subconscious noticed something amiss. It took a few moments to work out what was wrong. There was normally a picture of Victoria and the kids in the centre of the mantelpiece, one taken on holidays in Florida two years previous. It was gone. In its place was a small Polaroid, the type that comes from an instamatic camera. It was a picture of somebody whose face was obscured by a baseball cap pulled low. He was standing in the middle of our living room; I could clearly see the armchair with the cushion and TV remote in the position that I had picked it up twenty minutes earlier. He was holding a newspaper, and with his free hand was pointing to the headline. It was that day's late edition of the Post. This picture was taken in the last hour or so. A sickening feeling rose in my stomach and I had to grip the mantelpiece to stop me stumbling. "They couldn't have taken Victoria and the kids, Jesus...no, Christ no, not the kids..." I started panicking. What am I going to do now? Think...think think! I tried to stay calm. There were no signs of a struggle: that was a good thing, or was it? I was in shitstate. I picked up the house phone and called Victoria's mobile. It seemed to take an eternity to connect. Then it rang. After twenty endless seconds, I became aware of a phone ringing in the house somewhere. I ignored it for a second, until I realized it was coming from the cloakroom. I ran to the hall with the house phone still to my ear, ringing. It took me another ten seconds to realize that the ringing phone in the cloakroom was in fact Victoria's mobile. She hadn't taken it with her, and it was still in the pocket of her leather jacket hanging under the stairs. By this stage, I was shaking with fear and dread. "What the hell am I going to do now?" I went back to the living room and fell into an armchair.

Would I call the police? Would I call the latest mobile number I had for Brennan and his cohorts? Jesus! I had no idea what to do. Would calling the police do anything, or would it worsen the situation? Then I thought of George, and the meeting we had the other day. I could call him on his mobile and get some help. I dug out my mobile from my jacket pocket. Scrolling through the numbers, I came across the number that George had sent me. I lifted the house phone and dialed. Being ex-directory, the house number wouldn't display on the recipient's handset. I dialed George's number. It rang three or four times, and then the ringing stopped as if it had been cut off. "Strange, must be a bad signal," I thought to myself. I tried again, same thing. A sense of panic engulfed me again. One more time I dialed the number. Just as I was about to hit the dial button, a thought crossed my mind. I cancelled the number and went back to my mobile. With George's number on the screen, I pressed the dial button on the mobile.

After two rings George's voice came on the line, "Robbie, that you?" I almost collapsed with relief. "Was that you ringing the last two times? Sorry about the cutoff, I never answer calls I can't identify," he explained. "What's the problem?"

I launched off at a hundred miles an hour, "Shit George, I think something's happened Victoria and the kids. I arrived home..."

"Slow down, slow down Robbie, take it easy, what's the problem?" George said. I stopped for a minute, took a breath and, as slowly as I could, relayed the events to him. He was quiet as he listened. "Where are you now?" he asked.

"At home," I answered.

"OK," his calm demeanor was very helpful. "Have you spoken to these scumbags recently?" he asked.

"Yes, a couple of days ago," I tried to remember. I related

the call I had made to them demanding that we be left alone to research the job, and that I would be useless to them if Victoria or the kids were harmed.

"Good move Robbie," George went on, "I don't think harming your family is in their interest. Let's give this an hour or two and see if they get in contact. I have a suspicion about something. I'll be in touch later, OK?" He was as businesslike as ever.

"Thanks George," I said.

"By the way Robbie, switch all the lights on in the house and look like you're panicking big time. I think your house is being watched," he instructed me.

I managed a laugh, "That won't be difficult, I'm planking." I hung up and headed into the hall. Switching on all the lights, I headed upstairs and into our bedroom. Before I lit the room up, in the darkness, I peered out the window up and down the road. There were no signs of anyone watching the house. I drew the blinds and switched on the light. I sat on the bed for a few minutes nearly crying with despair, what was I going to do about this whole mess? I walked from room to room, pulling blinds and switching on lights as instructed.

After an hour of nailbiting and pacing, I became aware of a tapping at the back of the house. I froze in fear, what's going on now? A gentle tapping at the back door, "Robbie, Robbie" in a hoarse whisper. "Who the fuck is that?" I picked up a golf club from my underused set in the utility room and crept into the kitchen.

"Robbie, for fuck sake, let me in its George." I nearly burst out laughing. "Knock off the kitchen light and unlock the door."

I did as instructed and two seconds later George was sitting on the floor in the kitchen with his back to the dishwasher, in darkness. He was all business, "Go out into the hall where you can be seen, leave the kitchen light off and close the door over." Again I did as instructed. "I was right, the house is being watched. There's two boyos across the road in a garden watching the house. I checked with the local station, there's been very little activity about tonight. I don't think your family has been taken. I think those two were watching and, when they saw an opportunity, took it to scare you." He was speaking, still on the floor in the kitchen, while I was standing in the hall. He guessed what I was thinking, "I think they wanted to see what you would do. I don't want to let them see me here, hence the backdoor approach." I felt a little better with George's explanation, but I was still desperately worried about Victoria and the kids. Again, he read my thoughts, "Have you called about to see where they might be?" he asked.

"No, not yet" I answered.

"Try a few places where she might be, but use your mobile." I retrieved my mobile and thought for a moment or two. Firstly, I dialed the number of Victoria's parents. Her father answered, "Hi Grandad," I said. "Oh hello Robert," he answered in a sleepy voice, "I was dozing on the chair, how're you?"

"Good," I lied, "are Victoria and the kids with you?" I paused for a second, I didn't want to alarm an old couple in their eighties, so I gave a sparse explanation. "They were gone out when I got home from work, I was wondering if she wants me to make supper for the kids, you know, mobile phones work better when you take them with you."

He laughed, "No they're not here. They were here earlier; Victoria seemed a bit upset, kept checking on mother. She worries about us too much, that girl. Anyway, they left about twenty minutes ago." He rambled on about the kids for a minute or two, but I wasn't listening. I was trying to keep my voice from breaking with relief.

I turned towards George, who was still sitting in the dark in the kitchen. "Victoria's dad says that they were there and they're on their way home." I felt a bit stupid having panicked and called George. Here he was sitting on the cold tile floor in my kitchen in the dark, having responded to a panic call from me which turned out to be a false alarm. He seemed to read my thoughts exactly. "That's a relief," he said with no hint of being pissed off with me, "I'll stay until she returns and slip away quietly."

"George, you don't know how much this means to me," I started to grovel.

"Don't sweat it a bit Robbie, you must be under awful pressure."

As he spoke, I heard the revving of a car engine and the hall turned red from the rear lights as she reversed into the driveway. I was almost overcome with relief. George started getting up, "Robbie, set up a meeting with these boyos, and I'll try to get a look at them, give us an idea who we're dealing with. Call or text me the time and place, OK?" He opened the back door and slipped out into the night.

"Cheers George thanks again," I called after him. I opened the hall door and saw immediately that Victoria was quite upset. I gave her a hug and she buried her head into my shoulder. "What's up pet?" I asked her with concern.

She lifted her head, and I saw that her eyes were red with tears. "I got a horrible phone call," she said, trying to stop her voice from breaking, "some bastard rang the house and told me that mammy had a stroke and the ambulance was at the house."

I felt like I had been hit by a shovel. "Bastards" was all I could manage. Victoria stopped for a second as she shepherded the kids up the stairs to bed. "OK kids, pajamas on now, it's very late." Alice and Nick grudgingly stomped up the stairs. When they were out of earshot she went on, "I tried to call Daddy, but there was no answer. I panicked and bundled the kids into the car and drove around to them. They're fine. Daddy was in the shed and Mammy was in with the neighbors. That's why the phone didn't answer." She broke down crying again for a moment or two but quickly got control of herself again.

"Did you get a number?" I asked.

"No, the number was withheld. What sort of sick bastards do things like that?" she ranted for a second, "I'm going to the police tomorrow."

The mention of the police gave me a jolt. Shit, the photograph, I had forgotten about the photograph that I found on the mantelpiece when I came in. The last thing I wanted was Victoria visiting the police with that photograph, at least while this Mulligan thing was hanging over my head. I nonchalantly strolled towards the living room. Victoria paused to remove her jacket and I seized the opportunity. I grabbed the picture which was lying face down on the mantelpiece, and stuffed it in my pocket. Brennan and his cronies had sent a very loud and clear message again—we can get you or your family whenever, wherever we want. The manner in which the message was delivered was as if they were toying with me, to see what I would do under pressure and it scared the shit out of me.

Now I needed to set up a meet with Brennan and his gang. I thought of an excuse to call them and thought of the research I had come up with on Succinylcholine and some other stuff I had on the use of potassium. I decided that I would call them and tell them I had two or three ideas that I wanted to discuss with them and needed to meet them.

I followed Victoria up to the kids' bedroom and helped her get them ready for bed. "Why don't you take a bath when the kids are asleep, I'll bring you up a glass of wine, might help you relax," I offered.

She looked at me with gratitude. "That'd be lovely."

This would give me an opportunity to slip out and call Brennan's boys. An hour later, Victoria was lounging in a hot bath, scented with lavender aromatic bubbles sipping cold chardonnay. I put my head around the door and said, "Just nipping out to the shops, need anything love?" I got an incoherent mutter in reply, she was half asleep. I took that as my cue and slipped out. Remembering to bring the latest number I had, I headed out of the house and climbed into my car. I drove around the corner towards the local shop and stopped the car. I dug out the number and dialled. After three rings, a voice I didn't recognise answered "Yeah?"

"Robbie Valentine here, I need to speak to someone now!" I was rough and insistent hoping that this would give a result.

"Who do you think you're talking to?" said the voice.

"Just fucking get me someone in charge, now!" Anger was driving me on, and it seemed to be working. The phone went silent and I could hear background noises like in a bar.

After about a minute and a half, a more confident voice came on. "Who is this?" it asked with a surprisingly well spoken accent.

"Robbie Valentine here, I need to talk to Brennan," I demanded again.

"I'm Mr. Brennan's associate, what can I do for you?"

I was a bit taken aback by the fact that he didn't seem to recognise me. "It's about...that Doctor's appointment on Friday."

"I know what it's about, what do you want?"

This took me completely by surprise. "I need to meet with someone as soon as possible," I said with some resignation in my voice.

"OK, I'll set it up and get back to you," came the reply. I started calling out my mobile number but after a second or two, I realised that the phone was gone dead. They had control again. There was nothing I could do but wait. I drove on to the shops and bought some chocolates. Arriving home, I found Victoria curled up on the couch talking on the phone to a friend. I made two cups of coffee and brought one into Victoria along with a bar of chocolate. She had brightened up considerably and was talking animatedly with her friend. I flicked the channels on the TV while Victoria chatted. I had my mind on my mobile waiting on a call or text from Brennan for the meeting. At about eleven, we headed to bed. Around midnight, I was lying awake when I heard my mobile phone beeping, announcing the receipt of a text message. I retrieved my phone from my jeans pocket and, under the covers opened the message, "2pm tomorrow. Bar, Wynns Hotel" was all it said. I needed to let George know and looking at the time, I wondered would he be really pissed if I texted him now. Debating it, I decided there was more to gain than lose. I forwarded on the text, with an addition explaining that I had just received it. Within five minutes I received a reply, "Good. Just go along, I'll contact you afterwards."

29

THE NETWORK ADMINISTRATOR was at his desk carrying out random checks of the use of the internet in the hospital. As network administrator, one of his jobs was to randomly check the use, watching sites visited regularly and also watching certain computers in various locations around the hospital. Tonight however, as well as his own standard procedure for locations and types of sites that he would run a check on, he had been given a list of three more computers in the hospital that he was told to check. He normally was left alone to run his department, and took suggestions with a pinch of salt, but this request had come from the top. He wondered as he checked the matrix of webpages visited. He set up a file and copied the list of web pages visited on the three specific computer locations. The logon passwords were at the start of each list so he was able to identify the person who logged on to the specific sites. The usual low fares airline sites, medical searches. One computer showed Google searches for Lighthouse Insurance Services, subsequent visits to websites of a company of that name. The history file showed searches for the use of Anesthetics as a weapon. Interesting, some of these Docs carried out some strange research. He listed the departments and computer locations and the lists of websites, pasted them into an email document and sent them to the Clinical Services Manager, and an outside email as instructed.

30

THE NEXT DAY, after running the first case of the day, I headed for the basement and climbed onto my bike. By twenty to two I had locked my bike to a rack down the side road alongside the GPO. I strolled out onto O'Connell Street and headed down towards the Liffey. Using some of the hints that George had told me, I soon spotted what I thought were two tails. One was wearing a tracksuit top over jeans with Doc Martin boots and the other sported a Chelsea top over tracksuit bottoms with filthy trainers. Crossing over O'Connell Street I entered a chemist shop. Chelsea boy followed me in. I wasn't sure yet but when I strode confidently into the Ann Summers sex shop, and he reluctantly followed, his cover was blown. Tracksuit took up the tail, and when I went from a secondhand book store in Abbey Street straight into a religious book shop he stood out like a pimple on a baby's bottom. As two o'clock approached, I made my way towards Wynns Hotel. Traditionally, this is where the clergy would normally meet for lunch, and true to form, there in the bar were three or four priests at different tables having lunch. I approached the bar and called for a coffee. I looked about for anyone I recognised but saw no-one. There was no sign of George either, and I felt a little vulnerable. A pretty polish barmaid served my coffee and as soon as I turned to retrieve it, a man appeared at my right shoulder. "Robbie, how are you?"

I turned quickly. I didn't recognise him immediately but after he spoke, I realized it was the one who called himself Tom in Molloys bar. "I believe you want to talk to us Robbie," he said with undisguised impatience in his voice.

"Yes, I want to let you know what I am going to use, and let you know of the possible effects." I had been rehearsing what to say.

He looked at me with irritation, "You're the scientist Robbie, I don't need to know the details."

I pressed on, "Yeah, but didn't you say at some stage that you didn't want him dead, just...incapacitated." As inconspicuously as I could, I looked around for some sign of George, nothing.

He shot me a dagger look putting his finger to his lips and nodded his head in the direction of a booth in the corner. He carried a drink and I brought my coffee towards the booth. A large waiter with glasses immediately was over at our side. He tried to take the drink from Tom, "Pleese sir, I carry for yuh, theese way pleese."

"It's all right, I can carry it myself." Tom pulled it back from him.

The waiter wasn't for turning, "I carry sir, I carry." Tom started to lose it.

"I said I'll carry it myself" he almost shouted at the waiter. He got the message and left abruptly. "Bloody Romanians," Tom snorted as he sat down in the chair facing the window.

"You or your boss said that you would prefer if he wasn't dead, just incapacitated. That makes a big difference to me if I am to do the dirty work." I kept my voice low and steady, "The drug I told your boss about repeatedly stimulates and finally paralyses, respiratory muscles. This causes respiratory failure and death. The usual dose in surgery is 20 mg but changing the amount and timing of the dose could render someone comatose indefinitely if hypoxic brain damage occurred from the respiratory arrest." He was staring out the window as if not listening to me. He was silent for a moment. I went on "I need to know what level of incapacity you want." He looked at me.

"Speak English for fuck sake," he barked at me.

"The drug will cause him to stop breathing. When and for how long this happens will determine how much brain damage will occur. So I need to know exactly what you want from this."

He looked back at me and said in a low voice, "We don't want this fucker to wake up, but we don't want him dead." His coldness was palpable.

"What's the difference?" I asked quietly. He looked at me with a chilling look and his eyes looked like he was trying to decide if I deserved an answer or not. Eventually he said quietly, "So long as he's out of the picture but alive, he won't be replaced."

So that was the plan. Incapacitate the boss; put your own people in place, so they are positioned to strike when the time comes. "I get the picture now," I said.

He stood up, "We'll be in touch." He went to leave.

I suddenly remembered Victoria and the phone call, "By the way, I wasn't happy with that stunt you pulled yesterday."

He looked down at me, "That was two of the lads trying to be funny. Mr. Brennan isn't happy about that. It won't happen again." And with that he was gone. I let out a loud sigh. Draining my coffee, I waited until he had disappeared from sight before leaving. By three o'clock I was back in my office, sitting by the phone. I couldn't concentrate on anything, so I packed up and decided to head to the library. I shouldered my bag and strolled towards the stairs. I noticed a uniformed guard standing outside a fire exit to the emergency stairs. Since the shooting of one of Mulligan's lieutenants, the police presence in the hospital had been upped to the level that it had been just after his admission. Whatever about having a big time criminal as a patient, having somebody shot while a patient was unthinkable. Suddenly the reality of the situation hit me. There were armed detectives guarding a patient from a possible attempt on his life, and here I was working out a way of killing or maiming him using standard medicines and medical equipment. As I strolled along the corridor, I spotted Mick, our oversized porter from the operating theatre. He waved to me as he pushed a trolley full of sterile instruments towards the sterile storage area of the operating theatre. I remembered the night some weeks ago when I went for a few pints with Mick. I had met some interesting characters that night. I wondered if that was where it all began. Mick had known the lads we met and I vaguely remembered some inference that Mick had probably done some time, or at the very least know some of those ex-cons quite well. I was snatched from my dreaming by my mobile phone beeping. It was George. My heart leapt into my mouth. Instinctively, I looked around. God knows what for; I guess I was being paranoid thinking that everyone knew what I was involved in. I ducked in behind a portable X-ray machine that was parked by the wall of the corridor. I opened the message, "*got some info 4U. Call me 2 meet. G.*" Reading the text, I felt like a child on Christmas who had just received a present, but couldn't open it until later. I was overwhelmed with the urge to call George. I felt that at last, I was on the verge of getting some information that could help me.

31

"NURSE, NURSE...for fuck's sake...nurse...I'm fuckin dying here!" Mulligan was frantically pressing the call bell that was attached to the shelf above his bed. The call bell was connected to an alarm panel outside on the desk at the central Nurse's Station. The buzzer was sounding and the red light was on, but there was no-one at the desk to hear or respond. The armed detective posted outside Mulligan's room had slipped off to the hospital restaurant for a coffee. It had been mind numbingly quiet for the past twenty four hours and he was bored senseless. Although he had been ordered never to leave Mulligan unattended, the past eight hours of watching old men and women shuffle from bed to the toilet, or being wheeled in and out of the lift was finally taking its toll. He had decided to nip down for a quick cigarette and coffee. At the time Mulligan was cursing the nurses, Detective Moroney was sitting in the shelter behind the service entrance of the hospital enjoying a coffee and a smoke.

After five more minutes of frenzied button pushing and shouting, Mulligan climbed out of bed and staggered towards the door. A crushing chest pain had started in his mid-chest an hour ago and was moving into his left shoulder and down his arm. The pain was quite nasty now and he was beginning to find it difficult to breath, "Jaysus, nurse...help me...for fuck's sake get me a shaggin Doctor." He half staggered, half fell out the door into the arms of a passing ward attendant.

"Mr. Mulligan, what's wrong?" asked the attendant as he manhandled Mulligan back towards his bed.

"I'm fuckin dying here," Mulligan said in a half whisper, "I've a poxy pain in me chest for the past hour and there's no-one answering the bell. I could be fuckin dead."

The attendant helped Mulligan back to bed, "I'll get someone straight away, sir," he said as he disappeared out the door. He was only an attendant, with no medical or nursing training, but he recognised an acute angina attack when he saw one. That, plus Mulligan's position as a high profile patient, instilled some urgency into his step. He picked up the phone outside the room and dialed the code to summon the Medical resident. Then he paged the Ward Sister to come to the room straight away. Two minutes later, the Ward Sister came marching down the corridor with a face like thunder. "This better be good," she announced. She marched straight into Mulligan's room. She'd had enough of his abuse and particularly the commotion that the police presence was causing to her ward. "What is it now Mr. Mulligan?" she demanded with undisguised irritation. However she was momentarily taken aback when she saw the condition of Mulligan. He was very pale but sweating and lying back on his pillow, he was obviously finding it hard to breathe. Her twenty five years of experience told her immediately that this was most likely an acute ischemic attack, or angina. She called to the attendant, "Joseph, get me a GTN sublingual spray quickly and a nasal oxygen mask." Joseph, the Latvian ward attendant ran towards the storeroom. Maureen, the ward sister sat Mulligan upright, fixing his pillows and despite her initial irritation, very quickly became the motherly nurse again, "There now Thomas," she clucked like a mother hen, "I'm getting you something for the pain and I've paged the Doctor."

Joseph burst into the room and handed the small red canister and green tubing to Maureen. She broke the seal on the lid of the canister and after quickly checking the dose and expiry date, she administered the spray to Mulligan. "Open your mouth now Thomas," she ordered. Like an obedient child he complied. "Lift up your tongue." Knowing the drill, Mulligan obeyed. Maureen gave two sharp puffs of the spray under Mulligan's tongue. He closed his mouth and let his head drop back onto the pillow.

Maureen unwrapped the green tubing and threaded it around the back of his head with the two open ends under Mulligan's nose. She hooked up the other end to the oxygen flowmeter and turned the flow to twelve litres of oxygen. The gentle hiss of the gas was barely audible, but very quickly a more normal colour returned to Mulligan's face. "Is the pain easing Thomas?" Maureen asked gently. Mulligan gave a slow nod. She turned to Joseph, "Will you page the Medical reg on-call." He nodded. "Done already Sister," he proudly announced.

Just then an Indian Medical Resident appeared into the room, "What seems to be the problem here, Sister?" he asked in his Bombay accent.

"Mr. Mulligan has had a nasty angina attack, Raj. I've given him sublingual GTN," Maureen replied. She turned to Joseph, "Will you fetch Mr. Mulligan's chart, please." He left the room.

Raj turned to Mulligan who was still propped up on two pillows with his eyes closed. "Is the pain gone now Sir?" he asked. Mulligan nodded without opening his eyes. "Could you give ten milligrams of Midazolam please and if you could run an ECG and some cardiac enzymes, that would be great." Raj gave his orders while reading the chart. "I'll call Mr. Reddy's team to see if he wants to transfer him to ITU." He walked out of the room, leaving Maureen to organize the tests.

The Electrocardiogram would show if the attack was just an angina attack or if it was more serious. This information, along with the levels of the enzymes in the blood would determine the best course of action to be taken. This could include pushing the surgery forward. Raj sat at the nurse's desk and dialed the surgical resident on call. Habib answered immediately. They discussed the situation for a few minutes. Habib thanked Raj for his treatment and assured him that the surgical team would take over the case now. Raj scribbled a note in the chart, closed it up and headed back to the residents room to hopefully have a few hours rest, he could be in for a busy night.

32

I REPLIED TO GEORGE'S TEXT setting up a meeting for the following day at two o'clock in a small bagel bar off South King Street. I got an "OK" in return. I trotted down the back stairs and out towards the car park. As I strolled with a considerably lighter step, I noticed the tall dark figure of Habib heading towards the door that led back in to the hospital. "Hi Habib, forget something?" I smiled. "I had just left when the medical registrar called me. That chap for Friday has become unstable. We may need to operate tonight." My first reaction was "tough break Habib, I'm not on call" with a grin. Then it hit me like a bolt of electricity, the only patient scheduled for Friday was Mulligan. I felt weak for a second. Christ, if Mulligan's surgery was pushed forward, then I was in deep, deep shit. The ante had been upped big time now and I had no idea what to do or how to do it. I swallowed hard, "Hope he doesn't need surgery tonight." Habib politely bid me goodnight and disappeared through the door. I was now flapping good style. What was I going to do? Use a large dose of Pavulon a similar drug to Succinylcholine but used much more frequently in surgery. I didn't want to kill or maim anyone, but in my panicking state, I thought that I could come up with some method of keeping Mulligan asleep much longer than he would normally be after surgery. This could, if I told Brennan and had it confirmed by say, a leak to the press, buy me some time. A large dose of

Fentanyl, a narcotic anaesthetic, or thiopentone or one of the benzodiazepams. The trouble was I had no idea how much to give or what the effects of giving a large dose would be. This was getting ridiculous. I was rambling like a maniac. Then I thought of George, maybe he could help.

I called George's number. He answered after two rings, "George, there's been a development," I launched, "Mulligan has gotten worse, and I'm afraid if they go ahead and operate..."

George butted in, "Hold on Robbie, not on the phone... meet me in one hour." He paused, "Tomorrow's place. Check your tail, OK?"

I felt better immediately, "OK George, I appreciate this, see you in an hour." The phone went dead. I decided to head directly into town to give me time to identify and shake any tails. The last thing I wanted to do was to lose my only ally. As I climbed onto my bike, I thought that I'd better call home to buy some time. I called Victoria, "Hi sweetie, I need to stay here..." She interrupted, "What time will I see you?" She was well used to these sudden calls to stay at work. I hated lying, but I felt I had no choice. "I thought that Bruce was on call," she said before hanging up. "Yeah, he was but he had to play a rugby game." I said the first thing that came to mind, "He's gonna cover one night next weekend for me, we can go out." I tried to soften the blow.

"On call, on call..." I thought to myself, "Oh shit, Bruce's on call!" If there was a worsening of Mulligan's condition and he was brought to surgery, Bruce would be called and the surgery would go ahead as normal. "This isn't what Brennan wants," I thought to myself. Would they be pissed off enough to harm Victoria and the kids like they threatened? I couldn't take that chance. I looked at my watch, five twenty, fifty minutes to meet George. I charged up the stairs again towards ITU and stuck my head in the back door. I caught the eye of one of the Nurses, "Ange, will you put my name on call for tonight, there may be a case coming up from the ward." She waved her acknowledgement and I slipped back towards the stairs. On the way I met one of the Theatre nurses walking up the stairs with a plate of chips and a cake on a tray. The sight if the food made me realise how hungry I was. I gave her the same instruction. She gave me a guilty look as I greedily eyed the chips. I made a mental note to buy a bar of chocolate or something.

I haired back down the stairs had a thought. I had been tailed by kids on BMX bikes and large motorbikes and hadn't picked up anyone of them. I decided to take the LUAS across town. By twenty five past, I was running hard across the street towards the LUAS stop. I just missed the one that was pulling out and I waited with a dozen office workers from nearby office buildings. I noticed a County Meath GAA jersey at the end of the concrete platform. He was sweating profusely; looking like the last thing he should be wearing should be a football jersey. He was eyeing me closely, and when I caught his eye, he looked away quickly, taking a sudden interest in the LUAS timetable.

There were no other characters about who looked like they were interested in me. I kept my head down while watching Navan man out of the corner of my eye. His gaze bounced between the timetable, the surrounding billboards and me. After about three and a half minutes the office workers started to gather up their newspapers and stand up. The distinct rumble of the LUAS announced its arrival. I almost forgot to buy a ticket and just in time, threw a two euro coin into the ticket machine. The doors of the tram opened and there was a rush for the best seats. I stood near the door and gazed out the window. Navan man was standing on the other side of the tram trying to show an interest in the small advertising boards inside the doors. I was staring out the opposite window but the reflection gave me a clear view of my GAA all star. The tram trundled along for ten minutes or so, I had figured out that I would get off two stops from Connolly and tab it as fast as I could to my meet with George. This would give me more scope to lose my tail if my plan didn't work out. I checked the map over the door and worked out the stop I needed to be ready for. Looking down, I spotted one of those free newspapers that are given out in the mornings to passengers getting on and off public transport. I picked up the news rag and studied it intently. Occasionally I looked at the map, and then out the window, changing my focus to see if Navan man was still interested in me. He was. I checked our position; the next stop was Abbey Street, where I was going to make my move. The tram rolled in alongside the platform and ground to a halt. I had my head buried in the newspaper but with my peripheral vision, I was looking at my colleague and then at the doors that were opened beside me. I tensed my body, and struggled to keep my position by the door. He seemed to be half interested in me but was content to stay leaning against the opposite door. There were now about six people between us.

At last, I heard the sound I was waiting on, the hiss of the hydraulics signalling the imminent closing of the doors. Without moving my head, I focused on the doors. They quivered slightly, and then slowly started to close. At the last possible moment, I dived out through the doors and jumped behind the metal and glass shelter. My sudden movement had caused a ripple of excitement but the tram carried on. The last thing I saw was a Meath Jersey slamming his fist against the window as the LUAS disappeared on around the corner towards Busaras. Mightily pleased with myself, I checked my watch, ten minutes to go. I set off at a trot, taking a roundabout route towards the bagel bar and my rendezvous with George.

I reached the café at eight minutes past. George was sitting outside. As soon as he saw me, he stood up and walked alongside me. Two or three turns up and down various streets and a dozen rotations per minute of his head, and we were in a small internet café, down a side street close to Stephens Green. I picked up two lattes from a bored looking Asian behind the counter. Finding a quiet table in the corner, we sat down.

"What's the problem now Robbie?" George asked. As much as he tried, he couldn't disguise the slight patronizing tone in his voice.

"Mulligan has gotten worse," I explained, "this means that the surgery could be pushed ahead at any time." I paused for a second, "George, I'm terrified what they'll do if things don't go their way. If the surgery is called for tonight, I have no idea what to do. I don't want to harm him but if the surgery proceeds as normal…"

George looked at me and read the terror in my voice and expression. "What did they say they wanted?" George asked quietly.

"Incapacitated, preferably not dead," I recounted.

He put his head down as if in deep thought. Suddenly he lifted his head, "Anyway, I have some names." His change snapped me back to reality. He took out an old style wirebound notebook from his jacket pocket, opened it and searched through the pages.

"I thought they were binned since the Pulse system was introduced," I indicated his notebook.

"Oh no sir, the notebook is a vital tool in the collection of evidence," he said in an exaggerated Kerry accent. "I got some pictures of the man you met. His name is William O'Shay. He has no record, although his name does appear in some fraud cases, usually as a footnote."

"How did you get the pictures?" I asked curiously.

Taking the coffees from me, George looked at me with a smile, "Pleese sir, I carry for yuh, theese way pleese," he put on an Eastern European accent.

I burst out laughing. "That was you!" I almost shouted.

"Yeah" he acknowledged.

"I'm well impressed," I smiled.

"Anyway," George went on, "apparently he works for an insurance company."

My eyebrows disappeared under my hairline. "Wouldn't be Lighthouse Insurances by any chance, would it?" I asked tentatively.

"Yes, spot on, you know them?" George looked surprised.

"I've come across the name on some finance forms. They are brokers and I think they would handle some of the bigger multinationals who underwrite some of the patients we get into the clinic..." My voice trailed off as I began to see a pattern emerge. Reddy's name appearing beside a Brennan and a McCarthy as directors of Lighthouse Insurance services. "George, I may have inadvertently stumbled onto something. Did you find anything else out about Lighthouse?" I wished I had brought the letter that I had lifted from the chart.

"No, I hadn't time," George answered with a sigh.

"I'd like to get some more information on this company, I think they may be the link in this whole business," I thought out loud.

33

MICKEY FITZGERALD settled into the large Buxton chair. He was attending the Genetic Clinic at the Holy Trinity University hospital. He had been born with a rare metabolic condition known as Maple Syrup Urine Disease. This is a hereditary condition that gets its name from the distinctive sweet smell of the urine and sweat. It is caused by abnormal metabolism of certain amino acids and enzymes. He had been born to a poor family in a sprawling inner city flat complex. His mother always knew that there was something wrong with Mickey. Somehow, she had managed to keep him to a reasonably healthy diet which basically kept him alive and just about out of the realms of mental retardation. With seven other children and a useless husband who, when he wasn't in the pub, was inside on remand.

Mickey had suffered dreadfully in school. He was given a variety of nicknames in school, all pertaining to the smell that came from him. Sweetie, Maple Mickey, that one stuck, and other such labels that other kids give any child that doesn't fit the norm. He had suffered poor development as a child, not doing terribly well in school and it wasn't until a district nurse visited the school when he was six that he was referred for investigation. Waiting in the communal hall on the district nurse to examine the boys, Mickey was very nervous and this naturally made him sweat. A smart community nurse had gotten the smell and immediately was suspicious. Having spent a couple of years in a large Renal Unit in New York, she had come across the condition on a number of occasions. She referred him for investigations and a mild form of the condition of Maple Syrup Urine Disease was made. He visited the Biochemical Geneticist every year and with a specially controlled diet, he had developed normally. However, as a result of the hard time that he got from in school from the other boys, he didn't so well, and left school barely able to read and write.

Naturally he ended up in crime and became a popular assistant on midnight "mooching" sessions with some of the more successful criminals. Owing to his underdeveloped size, he could slip in through windows and openings that were impossible for a larger kid of the same age, and he could open doors for the rest of the crew. He had fallen off the wagon with his diet and it took a good bollicking from both the nurse and Doctor and the threat of a liver transplant to make him promise to behave himself and stay on his specialist diet. At eighteen years of age, he still was embarrassed at the smell that exuded from him whenever he got stressed. Problem was, working for a criminal such as Brennan, meant that he had to do as he was told. He had been ordered to perform some strange tasks recently. These included breaking into a car in Sandymount and placing a sticker on the steering wheel, and he had just been ordered to break into the house where the car was and to take a photograph and leave it on the mantelpiece.

He sat back and looked at the pictures in The Sun, slowly and painfully picking out the letters, trying at least to read the headlines. Something about Roy Keane's crucial...Crusheeat... ligament...lega...what the fuck was that? Some type of new car?

The pretty young student nurse approached smiling, "how are you today, Michael?"

Folding up the paper with the practiced skill that made it look like he had no problem reading, he sat up grinning. He had met this nurse at last year's visit and was flattered that she remembered his name. Maybe he might try for a date later, you never know. She lifted his jacket from the seat and escorted him into the phlebotomist for his annual blood tests.

34

THE IRISH INDEPENDENT:

Irish man questioned in Amsterdam over drug seizure.

An Irish man was being questioned last night by Dutch Authorities concerning the recent seizure of over €10 million worth of drugs in Dublin. The man, named as Gus Power, with addresses in Drimnagh and Alicante was arrested at Schipol Airport where a security check of his hand luggage showed him to be carrying over €200,000 in cash and stolen travellers cheques. Gardai from the drugs unit were tonight on their way to Amsterdam to question Mr. Power who they believe has connections to the criminal gang led by John Brennan. The gang, believed to be based in the south inner city have being making strides to increase their position in the lucrative drugs market but Brennan has so far evaded police attention. A Garda source said today, they hoped that stupid mistakes by mules like Power could enable the Garda to break open gangs such as Brennan's.

AFTER MAINLY A SLEEPLESS NIGHT, I arrived in work the next morning at 7.30. Two members of the team were already in and setting up leaving me free to carry out management duties. The first thing I did was head out to Intensive Care. Mulligan wasn't in ITU. That was good, he obviously hadn't worsened. I continued on out into the ward. As discretely as I could, I checked on Mulligan's condition. He had stabilized and although his medication had been increased, the urgency of his surgery hadn't changed. This was a relief. This still left me with three days to the scheduled surgery. Returning to my office, I switched on my computer. Opening Outlook, I checked my email messages. No new ones from Brennan's group. There were the standard hospital communications including one from the Clinical services manager. The one from my manager was directly to me and not a general all users mail. I opened the mail. It was requesting a meeting with me as soon as was practical.

I called the Clinical manager's office. His secretary answered. "Hi, Robbie Valentine from Theatre here, I got an email saying that Nathan wants to see me?" I asked.

"Oh yes, Robert, hold on, I'll put you straight through to him."

I was a little taken aback. "Robert, can you pop up and see me please?" Nathan came on immediately.

"Yes no problem, I'll make an appointment with your secretary," I answered.

"Can you come up now?" he asked.

I was now a little anxious, "Em...yes...let me check how the list is going. I'll try to come straight up. If I can't, I'll call you, OK?"

He signed off. I sat thinking what was so important it couldn't wait for an appointment. Normally it took a week or ten days to get an appointment to see him. I thought about it for a moment or two racking my brains. Coming up with nothing, I decided to head up. I checked with the other lads on the team. The day's work was proceeding well. The first and second patients were underway and my team were on top of things. "I need to nip upstairs to talk to Clinical Services, OK?" I said to Bruce.

"Sure, no worries boss," he answered.

I threw on my lab coat over my scrubs and took the back stairs up to the administration floor. I knocked gently on the door and stuck my head around the door, "Come in Robbie," the secretary said, "go straight in." I went on through to

Nathan's office. He was on the phone with what sounded like a heavy duty conversation. I gave a gesture of, "I'm sorry, I'll wait outside" but he waved me in and pointed to the vacant chair. I sat down and tried to look as if I wasn't listening to his conversation. After three long and uncomfortable minutes, he hung up. "Sorry about that Robert, Hospital Lawyers, you know how lawyers are, they're paid to talk."

I smiled. "What's the problem?" I blurted out. I was quite anxious about this unscheduled meeting.

"How's everything going?" he asked benignly.

I wasn't convinced that this was the primary reason for summoning me here. "Good," I replied, "Numbers are up, overtime is down and the natives are happy," I tried to lighten my mood.

"Good," he replied. He placed both of his elbows on the desk and lowered his head dropping the tone and volume of his voice. "Last week when you were giving me your report... you...em...mentioned some figures that...were...Let's say outstanding."

He seemed extremely uncomfortable talking to me. I was by now more than a little anxious. I thought for a few minutes, "Oh yes, the treatment purchase fund patients with the different codes," I remembered out loud.

"Yes...yes!" he almost shouted.

I was now thoroughly intrigued. "Why, what's the problem?" I asked.

He stood up and walked to the door of his office. He made a show of checking that it was closed and then he strolled to the inner door that led to the ante-room where his secretary was ensconced. Again he made a show of closing the door. "Robbie," he began, "there are certain...things that...em...you shouldn't concern yourself with."

I left a silence while my mind worked a thousand different scenarios that could be causing him so much grief. "What are you trying to say Nathan, did I do something wrong?" I couldn't think of anything and he was beating around the bush big time.

"Look Robbie," he burst out, "you are not to go digging in areas such as...that Insurance company."

"Lighthouse!" I said louder than I needed to. This caused him to turn a light shade of purple. "Why, is there a problem?" I asked.

He stuttered again, and after carefully considering his answer, finally came out with, "Actually, there are arrangements with companies like Lighthouse...that, lets say, the competition would be very interested in. Private Medicine is becoming more and more competitive. We need the edge all the time." He suddenly got into his stride, and nodded to himself, "Yes, you are not to go digging into issues such as that. I'm no businessman, but I know that any unnecessary digging might interfere with ongoing...contracts." He relaxed with his own explanation. "Do you get the picture Robert?"

Desperately trying to put some sense onto what he was saying, I tried to explain "I was only trying to square away the figures, you know me, I'm a scientist, so I need completion on things like figures."

He walked around the desk towards me. He became my best mate, "You're very good at your job Robert. Let's let the accountants take care of the figures. They have...arrangements with various insurers...and we don't need to know the details. I don't need my P45 yet," he laughed at his own joke, "OK?"

I got the strong fetid stench of a coverup. "Sure," I said without much conviction, "consider it forgotten about."

"Good man," he said with relief on his face

I left the administration floor and took the stairs back down to the operating theatre. All the way back, in my head, I went over the meeting with Nathan. I was, in no uncertain terms being told to stop looking into Lighthouse. Although the P45 reference was a joke, it was a thinly veiled threat. I began to ask myself if the hospital management were involved in this mess. Surely a modern 21st Century, state-of-the-art Private Hospital wasn't involved with a criminal gang trying to wipe out the competition. Jesus, what the fuck was going on here. The whole thing was beginning to stink to high heaven. Thinking about it for a second, there was no way that the hospital could be involved. I wouldn't have been surprised to learn that there were deals in place that were a little less than 100% above board, after all business was business and one man's interpretation of illegal was another man's opportunity. I decided to dig as much as I could into Lighthouse, but do it as covertly as possible. Also I began to think about Reddy's involvement in this. Some information about the extent of Reddys private referrals and the link to Lighthouse would be very useful, the problem was that I was seriously up against it with time.

If Mulligan stayed stable, I had about sixty hours until the scheduled surgery. I took the back stairs down towards the theatre and my office. As I exited the stairwell onto the corridor, I met Mick the porter. Suddenly I had a thought, "How's it going Mick?" I stepped up alongside him.

He was pushing a trolley, he had just dropped off a patient in theatre and he wasn't rushing. "How are you Robbie?" he asked with a smile.

"Good," I was thinking fast. "Any more big wins?" I asked.

"I wish!" he rolled his eyes, "I could do with a little injection at the moment."

"Must get out for a pint, with some of the lads," I tentatively suggested.

"Sounds like a plan," he grinned.

I pressed on, "Remember that bar we went to a couple of weeks ago, super pint, great place?"

He looked to heaven for a second, then, "O'Learys?"

"That's the place," I piped up. "Nice bunch of lads," I tried to push the right buttons.

He laughed out loud, "Bunch of tossers, harmless though."

I decided to fish a little, "What was that chap's name, McCaffery, the chap who came in late, seemed to know you well?"

Mick's eyes darkened a little, "Macker, Terry McCarthy, yeah, I met him a few years ago when I was a little," he paused, "wayward." He laughed.

"Ever hear of a chap called Brennan?" I pushed it a little further.

"Shit, you don't wanna go near that looney," he shot me a glance. "Why, do you know him?" he asked.

"No, I came across him during a business deal," I tried to keep as quiet as I could.

"He runs a security company, Terry McCarthy works for him." Mick assumed a serious tone.

"I remember him saying that," I tried to get him to elaborate. "Is he into insurance as well?" I fished a little further.

"Could be," Mick shrugged, "he worked as a porter in the College of Surgeons for years. Also he spent a year or two in Holy Trinity University Hospital as a morgue attendant. Strange bloke, into everything. He always thought of himself as a businessman. When he was in the College, he had all sorts of scams running."

I was intrigued. "Really?" I asked.

Mick got into his stride, "Yeah, everything from photocopying library books and selling the copies to running a personal chauffer service for the foreign students at serious rip-off rates" He laughed out loud, "I heard half the Consultants here were caught by some of his scams."

My eyes were like saucers and this was giving Mick all the encouragement he needed, "I heard Reddy was in his debt at one stage." I was desperately trying to file this away in my brain. Lights were going on inside my head like a Christmas tree. "What's his first name?" I asked.

"John, I think," Mick thought hard.

I seemed to remember that the name on the Lighthouse letter was an M Brennan. "Does he have a brother or someone else that looks after his business?" I was still walking and talking and conscious of the fact that Mick hadn't a clue why I was asking all these questions.

"I think he has a brother, but I think he is retarded, Downs Syndrome or something like that. I think he lives in a nursing home down the country somewhere. Why'd you ask?" he inquired curiously.

I thought that not giving him some explanation or some flimsy story would probably insult or at least piss him off. "Ah, I heard of a business deal, and I was wondering if it was OK to get involved, something about life and health insurance. Brennan's name was mentioned. But it was an M Brennan on the letter." I kept the story as plausible as possible.

"That's probably Michael, the brother. Uses him as a legitimate front name on some of his business deals. Crafty bastard is our Brennan." Mick seemed to be quite familiar with Brennan and his business.

"What was Reddy into him for?" I finally asked, overcome with curiosity.

"Don't know exactly, but I know that as a student, Reddy was quite good at chemistry," Mick winked at me and sniffed loudly, "and apparently, used quite a bit of it himself, to help himself keep up the studying, as well as work. Brennan was the chief supplier and I heard that Reddy got into him for quite a bit over the years in college." This was gold dust. "I still have a mate over there, Ronnie O'Dwyer, he knew both Brennan and Reddy. Think he's still there, anatomy department I think."

"I might drop over when I'm there, say hello," I suggested.

"Yeah do that, he might have more stuff on Brennan that might help you make up your mind." Mick turned down towards the Day Surgery unit and I headed on towards theatre,

"Cheers Mick, talk again," I saluted and disappeared on down the corridor. The urge to run out the door and straight over to the College was overwhelming. At last, some clear information that could help dig me out of this hole. Checking in with theatre, I saw that the first case was well under way and the second had started. They were both being looked after by the other members of my crew and, having completed the spurious duties, I was effectively free. I went back to my office and sat in front of the computer. I clicked on Internet Explorer. I wanted to search for some news articles on Brennan. I typed my username and password and hit "OK." Immediately a message came back telling me that the password or username was incorrect. Trying again, I got the same result.

Bruce came wandering into the office. "Any trouble getting onto the net this morning?" I asked. The computer in the office was heavily used and sometimes acted up. "No Boss, worked fine when I used it." I shrugged my shoulders and tried again. Same result. "Bloody useless thing," I said out loud to myself as I picked up the telephone to call the computer department.

One of the computer techs answered. "Hi, Robbie Valentine from Theatre here…" I explained that I was having problems logging on to the Internet.

"Hold on a second Robbie," he said, "I'll check it from here." I could hear him clicking away on the keyboard. All the passwords and usernames were filed on the server. He clicked away for a few more seconds and then was silent. "Robbie, did you get any emails from the network administrator?" He sounded uncomfortable talking to me.

"About what?" I asked, getting concerned.

He came back sounding apologetic and embarrassed, "It says here that your internet privileges have been suspended, and that if you…contact us, we are to notify the network administrator"

I was shocked and embarrassed at the same time. "Does it give any reason?" I asked incredulously.

"It just says inappropriate sites visited." The meeting with Nathan had obviously been about more than my nosing into some outstanding financial abbreviations. Now I was worried that the hospital management were involved in something that they didn't want anyone digging into. I really needed to find out what was going on. I couldn't leave it so long as there was a threat hanging over Victoria and the kids. I was now more determined than ever to find out anything that I could. I decided to do some more digging before I would start screaming and shouting. I sought out Bruce and Mike, "I'm heading over to the College Library to dig up some research. I'll be back around lunchtime and one of you can head away early." "No problem boss," both of them said. I strolled to the changing room and then remembered that I had driven to work this morning. That meant I would have to suffer the hassle of parking or walk. I chose the latter. Taking the back stairs two at a time, I met Marty coming in the opposite direction, "You're in a hurry," he said. "Oh, just heading to the college library. Need to do a bit of research." He smiled. "You're a devil for punishment," he remarked. But I was gone.

Marty stopped on the stairs and removed his mobile from his pocket. 'RCSI Library. He's on the way' Pressing send, the text message entered cyberspace and a second later was received and passed on to three other mobiles in various parts of the city.

35

AFTER CHANGING, I left the theatre area and strolled towards the main entrance of the hospital. As I passed the admissions office, I thought of the various finance forms that I had come across in the charts, including the letter I had lifted from the chart. It was still tucked away in my folder. I resolved to replace it in the chart at some stage this afternoon. Exiting the hospital, I ran the few blocks to the LUAS. Standing waiting on the tram, I noticed an oversize tracksuited, shaven headed man appear from behind the shelter. He stared at me for just a fraction too long. I caught his eye as he looked away quickly. Was this my tail for today? This was getting wearisome; annoying because of being followed and scary that they were paying so much attention to me. After three or four minutes, the LUAS appeared. The half dozen passengers boarded and the tram made the fifteen minute or so journey to St Stephens Green. I racked my brains thinking of a way to shake today's shadow. The tram pulled into St Stephens Green station and I was ready. I pushed my way and was first off and hared off down Grafton Street as quickly as I could. It took my shadow by surprise and he almost fell over an old couple as he leapt clear of the tram doors in his attempt to tail me. No doubt he was under strict instructions not to loose me. I half ran, half power walked down Grafton and quickly turned left by Weirs Jewellers. I ducked into the doorway of an expensive hat shop. I stayed there for a minute or two. Within a minute, tracksuit man appeared on Grafton Street and stopped. He was frantically looking around. I was hidden in the doorway, no more than thirty feet from him and I held my breath. He started walking down the side street towards me, still looking around frantically. He stopped no more than twenty feet from me. I was tempted to duck into the shop, but I was terrified to move. He took out his mobile phone and tapped out a number. I couldn't hear what he was saying, but I could guess. About twenty seconds later another tracksuit jogged from the direction of Grafton Street and joined him. Two or three barked orders from number one tracky, and number two took up a position covering the entrance to Brown Thomas's, Weirs and the side street. Number one tracky ran off down Grafton towards the statue of Molly Malone. I waited and watched number two. I recognised him from somewhere. Tall, shaven head with protruding teeth, he was all nervous and twitching. His head darted about like a small bird's, and he seemed to be taking everything in. Shit, if he was staying there, I was buggered. I looked into the hat shop where I was standing and some large women were packing there latest Phillip Treacy creations into bags and making ready to leave. By the look of them, I would have to step out into the street to let them out, and then I would be twigged. Frantically, I glanced back at tracky. He was leaning out to look up Grafton. I grabbed the opportunity. Taking a deep breath and fighting the urge to run, I walked straight across the street towards Brown Thomas. In my peripheral vision, I could see that he was still looking up Grafton. I raised my hand to push the door into the fashion department of BTs. I had almost made it except for two elderly ladies who arrived on the inside of the door at exactly the wrong moment. I cursed the Christian Brothers for my instinct, which was to step back and hold the door for the two ladies. Just as I stepped back, tracky twigged me. He immediately ran towards the door. I ducked inside and tried to disappear into the shoe section. No luck, I was spotted. He strolled into the shoe section and took an extremely high level of interest in a pair of suede ankle boots that would guarantee a kicking and his rapid expulsion from the local bar. His eyes darted from the boots to me and back. I strolled out of the shoe section and on into the make up department. He followed me at a discrete distance. I passed a large make up stand with a full length mirror. As I passed, I watched him behind me in the mirror. He was talking on his mobile, probably calling tracky number one to watch the exit.

I took the stairs to the gent's clothes section. I was still carrying my shoulder bag, and as I saw my reflection in the wall mirror as the escalator moved briskly upstairs, I realized that the blue shoulder bag was as good a visual distinguishing mark as I could give to any tails. I glanced sideways and saw Tracky two, about fifteen or twenty steps down the escalator, still talking on his mobile. I ducked and dived through various departments but this tail was like Velcro. This was a toughy, and was going to get tougher if he was calling up the reserves. There was no point in hiding in the changing rooms and hoping that they would go away. There was bound to be someone watching the doors. In my shoulder bag was my rain jacket, a small folder and my MP3 player. As I entered the gent's clothes department, I walked past a stand of leather wallets. I suddenly had an idea. As covertly as I could, I glanced around and spotted Tracky boy hovering behind a rack of expensive trousers. I strolled over to a shelf full of jeans. I took two or three styles and tucked them under my arm. I picked up a stripy YSL short sleeve shirt and headed towards the changing room. I paused by the stand of wallets and made a show of fixing the bundle of clothes under my arm. Under the jeans, I grabbed two wallets and kept them hidden there. I strolled into the changing room, chose one as far from the entrance as possible and unloaded onto the small seat. I closed the curtain, ensuring that I couldn't be seen through the sides. I opened my bag and put on the jacket placing the MP3 player into the pocket. I shoved the folder into the inside pocket, it was a bit of a struggle, but in it went. I stuffed the shirt and the two wallets into the shoulder bag. I was a bit nostalgic about losing the bag, but hey! Desperate times called for desperate measures. I took the jeans off the hangers, to make sure it looked like I had tried them on. Finally, I checked the bag, it looked the same shape and no different to when I came into the changing room. I shouldered the bag, gathered up the jeans and left the changing room.

Tracksuit was half hiding among a rack of long coats. As soon as I exited the changing area, he was onto me. Apparently without noticing him, I left the jeans back on the shelf and meandered over to a shelf of sport shirts. Placing the bag on the floor, I picked up various shirts, Tommy Hilfiger, Ellesse and other pricey tops. I put them back and moved down a row or two to tracksuit legs. Making sure to keep Trackyboy in sight, I deliberately left the shoulder bag on the ground. I moved around different sportswear, moving gradually away from the bag. After about five minutes, I noted that Velcro boy was still tailing me. He was three rows away but still directly in my line of sight. The text message alert tone of someone else's mobile phone sounded very close. Great, a perfect cue! I made a scene of taking my phone out of my pocket and reading a text. I replaced my phone and headed straight for Velcro boy. He ducked down to look at kids trainers on the bottom shelf, but I saw what I needed to, the strap of my shoulder bag sticking out from under his tracksuit top. He had taken the bait.

I kept walking but slowed up so he would be reasonably close to me when I made my move. I approached the main doors onto Grafton and spotted tracky number one standing outside McDonalds directly across the street. The traditional doorman with the top hat and coat was busy holding the door for some American tourists. Scanning as I walked, I stayed in the store and walked parallel to the line of doors. Then I spotted what I wanted, a side door, with a security guard. I made straight for that one. Hoping it was far enough away that tracky one wouldn't be watching. I nodded to the tall black security guard. Glancing in a make-up mirror, I noticed that Velcro boy was about twenty steps behind me. I stopped for a second, patted my jacket as if looking for something and then made my move. I passed through the alarm detectors and walked straight out the door. I held my breath and counted. I turned back down the side street and walked slowly. Eight, nine, ten…Suddenly I heard the beautiful sound of the shop security alarm go off. The sound of running feet followed by a loud voice with a heavy African accent, "hey, you stop there!" I paused and looked around. Velcro boy was looking around for me, but he didn't realize that the security guard was shouting at him.

He eyeballed me and started after me but not before the Security guard grabbed him and manhandled him back into the shop. He had fallen into the trap. The security tags on the shirt and wallets I had stuffed into the shoulder bag had ensured that he wouldn't leave the shop unhindered. As he fought with the guard, I checked that Tracky hadn't copped on. I couldn't see him so I didn't think twice and hared off down the side street. I quickly turned left on to South William Street and half ran, half walked, dodging van drivers carrying armfuls of clothes into the many clothes wholesalers. I ducked left down alongside the Powerscourt Townhouse centre on to Clarendon Street. I hoped that Tracksuit one hadn't seen me, but I was taking no chances. I turned right on to Clarendon Street and on up towards the College of Music. The sound of a string quartet mingled with the lunchtime smell of Indian cooking and coffee from the various restaurants and coffee shops made me realize that the rest of the world was having a life. A surge of anger overwhelmed me for a second and I fought the urge both to cry and scream. I needed to sort this mess out. I turned right, passing under the windows of the Music College and back towards South William Street. Pausing on the corner, I checked down both South William and Clarendon. There was no sign of Tracksuit one or two. I waited in the doorway of a coffee shop for a few minutes, and after satisfying myself that I had lost any tails, I trotted across the road, past Mercers Medical centre, and on up towards the College of Surgeons.

36

THE IRISH TIMES:

Decorated Detective convicted on drugs charges.

A decorated Detective with over fifteen years experience was convicted in court yesterday for possession and distribution of narcotics. Denis O'Gorman, who was based in the serious Crime division of the Combe Central station and has had citations for bravery, had been charged with fifteen counts of possession of Narcotics and twelve counts of intimidation. In court yesterday, he pleaded guilty to eight sample charges of possession and distribution of Heroin and Marijuana, and two counts of harassment. Detective O'Gorman was described as a loner and a "loose cannon" by former colleagues. One former colleague said that O'Gorman lived in a fantasy world, where he patrolled the streets as a Hollywood style Supercop. Justice Jeffery Guinness said that he had cultivated relationships with major criminals in the city for his own ends and described him as the worst type of white collar criminal, who abused his position of trust to enrich himself. Sentence was adjourned until the fourteenth of December. Detective O'Gorman will be remanded in Cloverhill prison until sentencing.

APPROACHING THE COLLEGE from York Street, I checked behind me again and took the steps into the foyer two at a time. I remembered to fish my College ID card from my wallet before I approached the door. I didn't want to be standing in the doorway for more than a few seconds. I had recently finished a course there and the ID card entitled me to use all the College facilities for the remainder of the year. I flashed the card at the security guard sitting at the desk and was quickly swallowed up by the sea of faces exiting the college for lunch. Groups of Arab, Malaysian, Indian and African students showed the cultural diversity of the college. I got a courteous nod from the Security guard as I passed him. He was a burly, middle aged man in a standard blue uniform. With graying hair and gold rim glasses, he was unremarkable. But something struck me about him. I couldn't put my finger on it, but again my subconscious was screaming at me. The electronic notice board showed that the College was busy today; there were exams for the Emergency Medical Technicians in the main hall, a nursing seminar on the third floor and a meeting of General Practitioners in the Board room.

I headed down the main corridor and downstairs to the bowels of the building towards the anatomy department. The anatomy department of the College of Surgeons is where students first encounter the subject of gross anatomy. It is also where those who donate their bodies to science end up and it is a typical sight to see classes of students standing around eight or ten partially autopsied cadavers. It is a grisly sight but a vital part of a Doctor or Surgeon's training. There was an eerie calm after the hustle and bustle of the main foyer. The anatomy laboratories were deserted, the students having left for lunch. I peered into the first laboratory. Four tables displayed four bodies, all opened with the classic "Y" autopsy incision. The large skin flaps folded neatly down over the sides of the two men and two women. My eyes were automatically drawn to the open wounds. I was still peering around the open door and at least thirty feet away from the tables, but some voyeuristic instinct made me strain to look. "Remember what you're here for" I mentally scolded myself. I looked around the room for any signs of life. No sign of any staff. I tried the next room. I thought I spotted some movement at the back of the room. I reluctantly entered. Passing the open thorax of an old woman, my eyes were drawn inside. Twenty years of Heart Surgery, and I have seen just about everything there is to be seen, but an open corpse still gave me the serious willies. I trotted on past the PM tables and put my head around the door of a small office. A young man in a porter's uniform was sitting reading a custom car magazine. He looked up with a shocked face when he noticed me. "Jaysus, don't do that to me!" he exclaimed.

"Sorry to startle you, this place gives me the willies as well," I flashed my student card, "I'm a postgrad student, I'm looking for Ronnie O Dwyer?"

He looked at his watch, "Ronnie's gone on lunch, he's probably still in the restaurant."

"Great, thanks, I'll find him." I turned on my heel and, tying not to look at a gutted granny, left the anatomy lab.

I took the stairs to the second floor and strolled along the corridor. The walls were decorated with pictures of classes graduating. The numbers of Irish students seemed to diminish evenly with the passing years. Passing the entrance to one of the lecture rooms, I noticed a lecturer in full flight with a PowerPoint presentation full of impressive looking figures. The lecture hall was about half full with bored looking students, suitably pissed off that lunchtime had well and truly started and this lecture wasn't over yet. I turned left, past various administration offices and immediately heard unmistakable restaurant sounds. The restaurant was heaving with students and staff. I didn't know what Ronnie looked like, but at a table at the back of the room, I spotted three porters uniforms. "Bingo," I said to myself, "they'll know where he is." I poured myself a glass of water from the water dispenser, and sauntered down towards the table at the back of the room. There were three porters sitting at the table. Two of them were in their twenties and one was obviously the senior man. He was holding court, explaining something or other about submitting a sick note directly to salaries was better than going via the social welfare. He seemed to have all the angles. "I'm looking for Ronnie O'Dwyer," I asked as politely as I could.

"Who's asking?" the senior man asked with a suspicious look.

"Robbie Valentine," I offered my hand. "Mick Delaney in The Southwestern Clinic told me to talk to you."

His face broke into a grin, "How's the big fella?" he asked.

"He's great," I said. "He said you were here a while, and knew all the characters."

His chest puffed out a little. "Twenty four years" he said looking at the two juniors. "Trying to teach these lads a thing or two to survive in this place." He stood up and stacked his tray, "I'm heading out for a smoke, if you want to join me."

I was delighted; I didn't want to discuss anything sensitive in front of these two juniors. "Yeah, sure," I said with a smile.

He asserted his authority for my benefit, "Youse two, finish up and be back in the lab by two." They both looked up and answered in unison, "Yes Boss." Ronnie rolled his eyes, "Cheeky pups."

We strolled out towards the door and out into the covered smoking area at the back of the college. "So, what can I do for you?" he asked with more than a little self importance.

"I heard of a business deal, and it's possibly quite lucrative," I began. I wanted to appeal to most people's natural sense of greed. "Trouble is, when I mentioned the name of one of the blokes involved to Mick, he warned me off, said you knew him better and would give me the low down. I need the money though." I tried to sound as sincere and desperate as possible.

Ronnie looked thoughtful. Obviously, this appealed to his sense of importance, "What's the chap's name?" he inquired.

"Brennan, John Brennan. Mick said he worked here for a spell," I said, gauging his reaction.

He looked at me with wide eyes, "Brennan, I think Mick was right. I wouldn't get involved with him if I were you." He was adamant.

"Jesus, he must be some character," I said. We reached the shelter. Apart from two eastern European cleaners, there was no one else there.

"Brennan basically ran the place here," Ronnie said as he lit up his cigarette.

I tried to hit the spots, "Did he work for you?" I asked.

He looked a bit uncomfortable for a minute, "I was his senior, but he did what he wanted." He picked an imaginary bit of tobacco from his lips and went on, "He ran scams on everything. He took the foreign students to the cleaners, finding accommodation for them was a favorite of his. He'd make a few calls and carpet bag the best accommodation from the noticeboard or the Herald, then he would put the word out among the students and basically dutch auction the apartments. Made a killing every September, even had his own headed paper." He studied the lit end of his cigarette as he talked.

"Mick said he was into...dealing a bit?" I asked tentatively.

"Yeah, but he managed to keep it low key. He only dealt in speed, E, that sort of shit He had a quite a few on his books." He dropped his cigarette butt on to the concrete and made a big deal of squashing it out. He gave the impression that he was thinking about what to say next.

"Mick mentioned that there were some guys who are consultants now who were involved with him," I was careful not to push him too far, but this sort of information could prove to be so valuable.

"Yeah, one or two," he looked around. "You know that heart surgeon Reddy, spends a lot of time here in the college?"

My attention level went up a couple of notches straight away, "Yeah, I know of him," I answered, playing it down.

Ronnie tapped his cigarette packet on his fist in an American detective way of getting a fresh cigarette out. He pulled a lighter from his pocket and in a dramatic gesture, cupped his hands around the cigarette and lit up. He paused for a second, as if wondering how much to tell me. "He was a character here. He studied and worked twenty four seven. The only way he could keep it up was amphetamines. Brennan was his supplier. Reddy was caught once trying to lift some chemicals from the Chemistry lab, his own recipe for speed, I heard. He was brought before the President of the College, and was on the way out the door. I heard Brennan intervened and the case was dismissed. He got away with a warning."

I was agog. My mouth was open like a goldfish. A lot was beginning to make sense now. Reddy in Brennan's debt from college. Brennan uses Reddy as a professional reference on his company and this enables him to get plenty of business. Still, it sounded strange why a major criminal was into life and health insurance. I didn't think that the profits would be anywhere near big-time drug dealing. The germ of an idea began to form in my head.

"So you think you'll take up this business offer with Brennan?"

I looked at Ronnie. He was staring at me waiting for an answer. "What business?" I had been miles away mulling over the story that I had just been told.

He looked at me with a frown, "Your business deal with Brennan."

I was snapped back to reality, "Oh...oh...yeah, sorry I was doing some calculations in my head," I stuttered, "sounds like I should steer clear of him. I was wondering how he can get legitimate business, with a name and reputation like he has."

Ronnie fixed his tie and made like he was heading back to work. "He has powerful contacts. I heard that one of his salesmen has a brother who works in the Department of Health. He pops in here occasionally, one of his other companies has the security contract for the college."

Then it hit me like a shovel, the security guard at the main entrance. It wasn't him that I had seen before, the logo on his hat, it was Lighthouse's logo. "He has the security contract for here?" I asked incredulously.

"Yeah, and it wouldn't surprise me if he has plenty of other big ones, with his contacts."

We walked back towards the college building. I was conscious of how much information he had given me and I didn't want to push things too far. I looked at my watch, "I better go and do the research I came here for." I pointed to the sign on the wall for the library. "Thanks for your time Ronnie, you've been a great help."

We shook hands. "Anytime mate, tell Mick to come and see us here, catch up on the news."

I turned and headed towards the stairs and the main foyer. The library of the College is located across the street in the old Mercers hospital building. As I passed the security guard, I slowed and studied the logo on his hat. Luckily his hat was on the desk so I wasn't staring at him directly. It was definitely the same logo. There was a triangular plastic identification gadget on the desk. After the couple of episodes of being tailed, I didn't stop beside it but tried to take a mental photograph as I passed. Lighthouse security services, 10 Canon Lillis Avenue. I didn't bother with the phone number, I could get that later. I continued on out onto the street and turned right.

I paused and put my MP3 player headphones on. I used the opportunity to scan for any new tails. Nothing, well at least I couldn't see any. While looking around for any tails, I noticed a small sign on the railings of the college, "*This building is protected by Lighthouse Security Services*" it boasted. I crossed the street towards The Mercers building turned up the side lane and entered the foyer of the library. Another Lighthouse security guard sat at a desk. I flashed my card at him and he waved me on. A little ironic, I thought, an employee of the company whose boss was trying to nail me, was checking my security credentials. I strolled into the main section of the library and headed upstairs to the computer room. There were private booths where I could do some research without fear of interruption. I had to wait for five minutes until one became free. A young black man gathered up his bag and stood up to go. The booth was facing the glass wall and door that led out to the main body of the journal section of the library. The great thing about using the college computers was that the net was logged on all the time and no password was needed. I pulled up the Companies registration office again and searched for lighthouse again. This time I saw the second entry, Lighthouse Security. The address was Canon Lillis Avenue. I had no idea where this was, but four clicks later, using Google Maps, I saw that it was very close to the address of the other Lighthouse, at Upper Oriel Street. "Where to go from here...where to go from here?"

I mused for a couple of minutes. I had been given a lot of information by both Mick and Ronnie. Ronnie had been particularly generous with his information but I needed to figure out what to do with this information. I was looking around thinking, when the security guard from downstairs strolled through the journal section, outside the window. He appeared to be looking for someone. He paused every few paces and stared around. Passing close to the section where I was seated, he stared hard in through the window. I looked back at the screen, trying to think of an angle. Movement in my peripheral vision caused me to raise my head. The security guard had his hands cupped and his face pressed up against the window. I was sure that he was staring directly at me. "Shit, he is staring at me!" I thought. I slipped as low in the chair as I could, bringing the computer screen between the Guard and my face. After a minute or two he was gone. I was really paranoid now, everyone was either a tail or a potential mugger. I shook off the feeling; I had lost the tail from earlier and checked my back leaving the college. I gave myself a mental bollicking. I thought about some of the stuff Ronnie had spoken about; Reddy in Brennan's debt from college, Brennan using Reddy as a professional reference on his company, this and his contacts enables him to get plenty of business. Contacts...contacts...

what was it Ronnie said? One of Brennan's salesman had a brother in the Department of Health. I racked my brain how I could use this information. I wondered if a visit to this Lighthouse insurance company would be useful, and more to the point, would it be safe? I searched the internet for a while longer, trying to come up with some more information on Lighthouse and Brennan. There were a few articles, but not a whole lot that I could use. One of the articles that came up, but not connected to Brennan or Lighthouse, was an article about the Criminal Assets Bureau. They were investigating various high profile criminals.

The germ of an idea that had flickered while talking to Ronnie re-emerged. Assets...Reddy drove a spectacular Kompressor Mercedes. I wondered, if Reddy was connected to Lighthouse and Brennan, and would such thing as a company car give a lead. George, he could find out fairly quickly. I decided to head towards the part of town where the Lighthouse group were located. Now, with my level of paranoia having been raised, I deleted the contents of the history folder, closed down the internet window and left.

Approaching the security desk at the exit, I noticed a tall Addidas tracksuit with his back to me. His head was close shaven, with red fuzzy stubble remaining. Despite the no-smoking sign in the hall, he was puffing on a cigarette. He chatted animatedly with the security guard who took no notice of the cigarette smoke. I moved to the far right door, as far away from the pair as possible, just to be sure. As I passed through the door and walked diagonally away from them, I could feel two pairs of eyes burning into the side of my head. The main pedestrian traffic turned left and out on to Mercer Street. As I exited, a bunch of Arab students approached the door. I deliberately walked into the centre of them as they came against me towards the door. I moved across the lane among the group and quickly did an about turn. I ducked my head and made like I was looking in my jacket pocket. I was now at the back of the group on the outside. As they pushed through the doors into the library, I ducked back and headed on past the door up the lane in the opposite direction from Mercer Street. I trotted up the lane and ducked into a doorway. It was a service entrance or fire exit from the library. I held my breath for a minute. A couple passed from the right, I felt ridiculous but I folded my arms and put my head down assuming the position and demeanor of one of those hundreds of anonymous homeless we pass everyday but fail to notice. It worked. After a few more seconds I peeped out and back towards the library exit. A single female exited and then the Addidas tracksuit stepped out. He looked down the street towards Mercer Street. He turned his head back up the lane. I pulled my head back quickly, banging it on the door as I did. I held my breath and tried not to move a muscle. Next thing I heard was the sound of running feet off down the lane towards Mercer and the main street. I waited for another few minutes and, when I was sure that he wasn't going to appear back up the lane, I stepped out and headed out of the lane. A thought struck me, I about turned and headed up the lane in the opposite direction. The lane brought me out on to Aungier Street, so I tabbed it down on to Dame Street and along towards College Green.

Watching my back and carefully studying any tracksuits, I turned down towards the Adelphi Cinema. The pedestrian traffic was much lighter, with lunchtime finished and taking the sidestreets made it easier to make good time. While walking, I decided to call George and see what he could dig up. He answered on the second ring, "Robbie, how's it going?" he sounded upbeat.

"Good George," I answered, "I've got some info, if you could confirm it in some way, I could have something that we...sorry...I...could use to get out of this mess. Problem is, I only have until Friday."

George went straight down to business, "Give it to me."

I explained what Ronnie had told me about Brennan.

The Security Company with the contract for the College of Surgeons, the alleged brother of O'Shea in the Department of Health and my theory of Reddy's Mercedes. "I'm heading over to the Lighthouse Office now to see if I can come up with anything."

George was silent for a moment, it sounded like he was taking notes. "Robbie," he said in a serious voice, "be careful, these scumbags don't take prisoners. By the way, did you read about your mate O'Gorman."

It took me a minute to remember detective Elvis's real name. "No, what's the story with him?" I asked.

"Gone down for seven years on four counts of possession and distribution."

Not for the first time, I felt like I was hit with a shovel. "How did I pick the most bent guard in the force to look for help?" I said out loud.

George laughed, "He's not the only one, don't worry. I'll dig as much as I can and get back to you."

"Great, talk to you later." I hung up and continued across Butt Bridge and on towards Connolly station and the Financial Services Centre where the Lighthouse Corporation's addresses were located. The busy early afternoon traffic petered out as I turned off Amiens Street up towards the back of the Financial Services Centre and kept checking the street names. Remembering the map, I turned left onto Commons Street. I was now traveling away from the river. I reached a junction and saw a sign for Upper Oriel Street. Bingo! The area was a mix of warehouses and lockups. There were more than a few burnt-out cars and the odd bunch of kids, but otherwise the place was deserted. I reached another crossroads and searched the numbers on the doors for the number of Lighthouse. Between the graffiti and the posters for concerts, it was difficult to find the numbers. There were plenty of custom clearance offices and a few clothes wholesalers but no insurance offices. I kept on walking and crossed a crossroads onto lower Oriel Street. I was beginning to think of abandoning my search when I came upon another turn, Canon Lillis Avenue. I turned back onto Oriel and then nearly dropped with shock. Outside a rundown office building on the opposite side of the street, was a gunmetal grey Mercedes Kompressor, 320CLK. I couldn't swear it but I was certain it was Reddy's. I ducked into a doorway and almost fainted with the smell of urine. I positioned myself to see the car and waited. It wasn't there long as I had just passed that section of building a few minutes ago and it wasn't there. I hoped if it was Reddy, then he would be in and out of the office as quickly as possible. I couldn't see him spending any longer than was absolutely necessary. I waited.

After a few minutes, my phone rang in my pocket. I retrieved it and saw that it was Victoria. "Hi Vic," I said with as much enthusiasm as my position would allow.

"Are you nearly finished?" she asked.

I had started on an early shift and was due home about now. "Yeah, I had to go over to the college library for some research, I'll be home in about an hour." I hoped that I could get some info and get home in the hour, I seriously doubted it, but it would keep home off my back. I would get the DART straight to Sandymount from Connolly. I hung up and went to put the phone away. I had a photograph of the kids as a screensaver and I looked at it for a second. I looked up at the Mercedes again and after a moment or two, a sharp blip sounded and the indicator lights flashed twice. Here we go! After about twenty seconds, a figure emerged from a doorway in one of the buildings. I moved myself to get a better view, and there he was, the unmistakable figure of Mr. Peter Reddy. I quickly switched my mobile phone to camera mode and held the phone up. Using the screen as a viewfinder, I took three or four pictures of Reddy emerging from the building with his car in the foreground, him climbing into the car and the car driving away from the building. Now I had something, although a picture of Reddy leaving an anonymous building

273

wasn't exactly what you could call incriminating evidence, I felt like I had cracked the DaVinci Code. I waited for a few minutes more and after a debate in my head, I decided to head into the office. I felt I was on a roll and it was worth the risk. I checked up and down the street, and ran across towards the building that Reddy had just left.

37

THROUGH THE WINDOW, Reddy checked his Mercedes for the twentieth time since he had entered the Lighthouse office. He declined the invitation to sit and at that moment was standing, staring out the window at his car, hoping that the bunch of kids playing football that he had passed up the street, wouldn't suddenly take an interest in the alloy wheels, or the whole car itself. "What the fuck d'ya mean, you want out?" Brennan was shouting. Reddy remained calm and unflappable. His involvement with this company had taken on a new facet. He had been asked to sign medical certificates for insurance claims that were beyond the realms of suspect, and into the vicinity of downright fraud. He could justify his involvement as far as the NTPF patients went, as that was right up his avenue of thinking with regards to medical funding. Insurance fraud was a totally different matter. Also, he was getting distinctly nervous about this Mulligan patient. He had mentioned the names to a detective friend of his and what he heard, he hadn't liked. Apparently Mulligan and Brennan were sworn enemies. Recent gangland murder victims were alleged members of both gangs and their murders attributed to the other gang. He felt that he was being dragged into the final act of a macabre game. He was sure that something was going to happen to Mulligan during his stay in the Clinic. His Chief Perfusionist Robert approaching him with some story of him being approached about the surgery had rattled him. That was when he asked his detective friend to check out the two names. He had never mentioned that he knew anything about Lighthouse Insurance. He wondered if Robert had had any more contacts with Brennan. Being a typical Surgeon, a "hot house flower" student, straight A's all the way, he had cruised through medical school. With a little help from Amphetamines, he had managed to hold down a couple of jobs as well as putting in a punishing study routine. Unfortunately, as a result of his isolated existence in college, he was the type of man who couldn't deal very well with something he wasn't in control of. He couldn't bring himself to speak to Robert and he was beginning to worry more and more about this Mulligan case. "I'm not happy where the business is going." He tried to remain calm. Inside he was quite nervous. Brennan was an intimidating character at the best of times, and when he was in a foul mood, he was terrifying. Calling him during his "business lunch" in the bar wasn't the cleverest of moves and he was now paying the price for that. He tried another tack, "What we've gotten into here is illegal. I could have my medical licence revoked. Where would you be then?"

Brennan exploded laughing, "Sudden attack of conscience, is it Doctor?" He became serious suddenly, "Listen here you. You're as guilty as the rest of us here. So don't go giving us one of your fuckin lectures." He pointed his finger menacingly at Reddy, "You do very well out of us. Don't fuckin forget where that flashy Merc came from, or the lovely fat fees you receive come from." He stepped closer to Reddy. Close enough for Reddy to smell his breath, "You're going fuckin nowhere, Doctor. You're out when I fuckin say you're out, OK?"

Reddy turned on his heels and walked quickly out of the office. He hit the button on the remote. Turning up the music, he gunned the car in a U turn and sped away down towards the River and civilization. Cursing himself for not standing up to Brennan, he swore that he would find a way to extricate himself from Lighthouse and the slimy grip of Brennan. As his Mercedes sprayed up gravel, he didn't notice the figure half-hidden in a doorway across the road checking the picture that had just been taken of him on a camera phone.

38

As I approached the door, I noticed the steel cladding that was part of the security. The Lighthouse logo was on a brass plaque beside the door, decorated with graffiti from a black marker. There was an old staircase leading up to a half landing. The carpet was virtually threadbare and the building smelt of must and urine. Looking around for any signs of life, I didn't want to be surprised by anyone exiting the office or any homeless bodies sleeping in the stairwell. The stairs creaked loudly as I took them two at a time. I paused on the landing. There were another dozen or so more steps to the main landing where there were three doors. One of them had a brass plaque with the Lighthouse logo stuck to the outside. Debating whether to continue on any further, my mind was soon made up for me when the door opened and a man in a dark suit came out. His back appeared first, and he was still talking to whoever was inside. "Get those numbers to Mick as soon as you can, and I'll see you for a pint later, OK." The hoarsy Dublin accent made me freeze in fear. I turned on my heels and, fighting the urge to run, I took a piece of paper from my pocket. I walked slowly down the stairs waiting to be challenged. "Ah howya son, you allright there?" It definitely was Brennan. Now the question was, had he seen me before, and would he recognize me.

I paused, turned my head slightly towards him and in my best north Dublin inner city accent asked, "Is this Sherlocks clothing wholesalers?" At the last second, I remembered the name of one of the clothing wholesalers that I passed a few blocks back.

"Ah no son, you're a bit lost," he said, while fishing a cigarette out of his jacket, "Tommy Sherlock's place is down the road a bit." He started down the stairs after me.

"Thanks mate, bleedin hangin today," I muttered in my Skobie accent. I heard Brennan laugh behind me. I was sweating heavily and I thought Brennan must be able to hear my heart pounding. Here I was, within touching distance of the scumbag responsible for my dilemma and he was laughing and joking. I had to make a ferocious effort to control myself. After three recent episodes of muggings and, particularly where I had gotten the better of my attackers with the simple self defence techniques, I had to fight an overwhelming urge to smash his face in there and then. Instead, I exited the building, paused and looked firstly at the slip of paper in my hand and then up and down the street.

Brennan exited behind me. He pointed to the left, "see that building with the sign?" He pointed to a three storey building on the opposite side of the street, blackened from fires lit against the wall, with heavy grills on every window.

"Cheers bud," I managed. He passed me, heading back towards town. I stopped and made a meal of folding the paper and replacing it in my jacket pocket. Then I turned and walked slowly in the direction of Sherlocks, my alleged destination. I passed a doorway that was open and glanced over my shoulder. Brennan was walking quickly back towards the city. He was staring straight ahead, away from me so I ducked quickly inside. I had to hold my breath, the smell of urine was so strong. I waited about five minutes. Carefully I peered around the door and looked in the direction where Brennan had gone. I could make him out still walking quickly and turning back on to the main drag back out towards the river. I hoped that he wouldn't suddenly remember something and high tail it back to his office, but this was a chance I had to take. I exited my stinking hiding place and immediately felt better with the fresh air. I crossed the street back towards Lighthouse. Entering the building again, I paused listening for a second. I made my way up the stairs. Slowly enough to be aware of anyone moving in or out of an office, but quickly enough that someone entering the door behind me wouldn't get suspicious of my movements. I turned the corner at the half landing and paused. Go or leave, go or leave. I had a moment of terror as I thought of the ruthlessness of some of these bastards. I pushed the thoughts of Victoria and the kids into my mind and a surge of anger drove me on.

I walked brazenly up to the door that Brennan had exited some ten minutes earlier. I could hear talking on the other side of the door. A surge of panic rose in my throat and I fought the urge to run. When I realized that whoever was in the office was alone and just talking on the telephone, I relaxed a bit. I knocked gently and waited. After a pause, I heard "Yeah." I pushed the door open and stuck my head around the door. A morbidly obese man sat behind a very untidy desk. The first thought through my head was relief that he didn't recognize me and I had no idea who he was. He was sweating profusely, despite the window being open. His comb over was blowing like a flag, giving him the appearance of a punk rocker from the eighties. He had two or three chins and large sweat stains under the arms of a white shirt that looked like it hadn't seen the inside of a washing machine since taken out of the wrapper. While talking on the phone, he gestured me to come in.

He pointed to a chair opposite his at the desk. I stood beside the chair and looked about the room. It could badly do with a lick of paint and a makeover. There was old marble effect lino on the floor and the walls were painted a puce colour. A three drawer filing cabinet was straining under the weight of folders and papers and a computer on a desk in the corner was switched off. The keyboard was placed on top of the monitor with the cables wrapped around it. The office smelt of stale smoke and must. "I know, Bobby I know. Let's have the list and I'll see if I can figure it out. I'll get back to you, and before you say it, I know...don't use the main number...I know. Good luck!" he hung up abruptly. He looked up at me and pointed to the computer desk, "There it is there, fuckin heap of shite. You can tell your boss if that isn't sorted bloody quick, I'll never buy so much as a floppy disk from him again, OK?"

I held my palms up with a questioning look on my face. The second thought that leapt to mind was that if I had been quick enough, I could have used the opportunity to apologise and take the computer off his hands. But I was neither a computer expert nor had I any means of transport with me. Besides, I hadn't the first clue about how to search a hard drive.

"Oh are you not here for the computer?" he asked.

"Sorry, no," I said apologetically.

"Sorry about that, fucking useless piece of junk. What can I do for you?" He suddenly turned back into the businessman.

Putting on the Dublin accent again, I rolled the dice; "A mate of mine told me you do some good deals in the insurance." I was as vague as possible.

"Yeah we do exactly as it says on the tin," he laughed at his own comment. "What area are you looking for?"

I was trying to gain as much information as possible for as little output as I could manage. "The bird's due a baby next month and I was thinking about Health Insurance, that might, ya know...get her a decent bed in a private room or something like that, know what I mean?" I made it sound like "nowharroimeen."

His face immediately lit up, followed by a businesslike frown as he started off explaining, "Well, it's a bit late to get cover for this confinement, but I can give you details of Health cover that could, in a couple of months give full cover for mother and child. There are standard waiting times for most of the plans..." He launched off into his sales pitch. It sounded like the pitch didn't get as much of an outing as he would have liked and he was using this opportunity to brush up on his sales technique.

I played dumb and egged him on, "What do you mean, will she be covered when the baby comes?"

He moved around the desk and sat on the edge, "You see..." he paused, "sorry, I didn't get your name."

I thought for a second, "Richard...Sherlock." The name was still in my head from the clothes wholesalers.

"Eamon Fitzpatrick." He held out his hand. I shook it "Who did you say told you about us?" he asked with a little frown. I quickly felt that I needed some credibility or he would get suspicious straight away. Trying to remember one of the names that George had given me, I thought quickly, and mumbled some incoherent first name but gave "O'Shea" as a surname. He immediately lost the suspicion in his voice and said, "Willy?" I nodded my head, "Yeah, Willy was telling me about some of your plans. But you know, I couldn't understand what he was talking about." I played the Dublin accent and the slightly dumb act as much as I could. I thought he felt he had a piece of putty here and he changed his demeanor. "Listen, Willy's a great guy, but he couldn't sell skag to a junky."

He started to explain the finer points of health insurance and all the wonderful benefits that it would confer to me and my partner and child's life. I listened for a second and tried to work out a strategy that would get me information that was useful. He was in full flight and I hadn't heard most of it when I asked, "Say eh...me or the bird, or the kid needed some big operation or something like a heart operation. One of me mate's kid needed a heart operation it took bleedin months, how would that work, would we have to wait like he did?"

He paused, thinking for a second, and then launched, "Well there was a time when the waiting list meant that you could be months or even years on the waiting list. But thanks to insurance companies like us, you won't have to wait any longer than a few weeks." I was getting somewhere now. "The Doctor who operated on me mate's kid was brilliant; could we pick our own Doctor if we needed to?" I started trying to direct the conversation towards the result I wanted.

He was still on form and went on, "In the main yes, but there may be extra fees payable over and above the insurance policy but we do have named participating Consultants who have direct contracts with the insurance companies and if you are referred to one of these, the policy will cover everything, including the Consultants fees."

I didn't want to ask directly about Reddy, so I used another angle. "Could you give me some details and prices?" I asked.

He walked over to the filing cabinet and pulled a pre-packed information package. It looked quite old but I browsed through it as he explained. "This package should give you all the information you need to make up your mind." He looked up to heaven as he explained that he always made it his business never to press a client into a decision, but he was confident that I would be back. "I never push too hard," he explained, "a lot of salesmen make that mistake. Just give clear information and let them come back to you." He sounded like he was giving me his resume.

I flicked through the package, trying to make it look casual but I was desperately trying to find the list of participating hospitals and Consultants. I came across a list and doing my best to speed read, I spotted the name Reddy near the end of a short list. I snapped the package shut and stood up, "Listen, you've been great. The bird will be thrilled. If I could, I'd sign right here, but y'know she organizes that sort of stuff."

He went to escort me to the door and gave me an understanding look. "Don't worry, you can promise her peace of mind. And you'll get the brownie points." He stopped for a second, searching for something. "Give me your number, just in case. I'll tell Willy I looked after you."

A jolt of adrenaline surged through me. I hadn't thought

of that and not giving him a phone number would be very suspicious. I also started to panic, I couldn't remember the first name I had given him. I had plucked it out of the air. He helped me there, "Richard Sherlock you said," he wrote down on a post-it note.

I racked my brains for a number that wouldn't sound made up. At the last second, I remembered an old alarm code. Long since changed, but the number was still fresh in my mind. I gave a mobile prefix and then rattled off the number. He was satisfied and opened the door. As he was finishing off his sales pitch, I became conscious of somebody coming up the stairs. I was shaking hands with Fitzpatrick when a red head with a freshly shaven scalp approached the door. He was wearing a football jersey over a pair of jeans. He stared at me for a minute and a very suspicious look spread over his face. I noticed this and as quickly as I could, made my way past both of them and on down the stairs. I could feel his eyes burning into the back of my neck and I could hear a low muttering, followed by "oh just a new customer." I heard the door shutting and the conversation continuing. I slowed down and strained my ears. I heard the new voice talking on a phone, "Were you supposed to be following that bloke Valentine today. Yeah...yeah...what was he wearing...yeah?...yeah?...oh shit!"

I heard feet stomping towards the door so I upped and hightailed it out the door as fast as I could. The obvious route was left back towards the city, so I turned right and ran as fast as I could. I turned right down another street and ducked into the first open doorway I came across. I looked across the street and saw a sign on the corner declaring it to be Canon Lillis Avenue. "Out of the frying pan," I thought. This was the street where Lighthouse Security Services was located. I stopped and listened for a few moments. There was a lot of barking, as if there was a dog pound close by. I wondered if Lighthouse had a large dog security department. I heard the sound of running and shouting. It got closer and closer. I looked around and saw a stairwell. I moved to the back of the hall and hid under the stairwell. The sound of feet pounding along the pavement got dangerously close and, through the bannisters, I saw a character running past the door, in the direction of the insurance office. I ducked back in under the stairs as the sound of the running disappeared down towards the main drag. I waited for about ten minutes and slowly stuck my nose around the door. There was nobody about. From my memory, Canon Lillis Avenue was a cul-de-sac as was the part of Oriel Street where Lighthouse Insurance was. This meant that in order to get back to civilization, I would have to pass Lighthouse's office. After being pinged by the football jersey, I thought this was a dangerous move, especially as it had sounded like the troops had been called up from the security company. I had to find another way back towards the Financial Centre. Checking once again that the area was clear, I trotted back towards the corner of Oriel and Canon Lillis Avenue. I looked around the corner and down towards Lighthouse's office. Two cars that weren't there before were pulled up outside the building. Definitely, it would be foolish to pass in view of the windows. Looking at my watch, I noticed that it was two-twenty. I needed to start making tracks home. But how would I get there without passing the doors of Lighthouse. In the distance, I could hear the sounds of traffic and normal life. Then came the clatter of the Dart. It sounded quite close. I looked through the gap in the buildings and saw the bright green of the Dart heading diagonally to my left, about a kilometer away. I wondered if I headed behind the buildings and towards the train line, would I come across some access to the station. I looked towards the offices again and when I was satisfied, I walked fast across the road towards the gap between the two buildings. I was very tempted to run, but I guessed that running would probably attract more attention than walking. Expecting to hear a shout challenging me any second, I made it without any challenges. I made my way up the lane between the buildings. Stepping over old cardboard boxes and crates, I ended up in a lane that ran behind the rows of old warehouses and buildings. Looking up and down, I saw that the lane ran parallel to the street. I wondered if it ran all the way onto the main road that I crossed. If it did, I would end up halfway back towards the Dart Station without passing in view of the offices. On one side of the lane was a wall about eight feet high. There was wicked looking barbed wire attached to the top of it, and sections where bits of broken bottles were fixed into the cement along the top. But I could already see plenty of gaps in the wire and broken glass. I decided it was worth the gamble. If the lane ended abruptly, I could climb the wall and make my way over the waste ground towards the train line. I started along the lane. There were piles of beer cans, used condoms and syringes piled at intervals along the walls. At the gaps between the buildings, I double checked and ran across the gap. I tried to count the buildings to where Lighthouse's offices were. I didn't recognize the only building visible where I guessed their block was. I kept walking as fast as the rubbish and broken pathway would allow.

I was concentrating hard on watching my footing, watching the gaps in the buildings and watching in front and behind me that I nearly jumped with fright when my mobile phone rang. Expecting it to be Victoria, I looked at my watch. I saw that the number was blocked and my stomach tightened. I pressed the answer button. "Yes," I said tentatively.

"Robbie, George here."

I exhaled heavily with relief.

"You sound under pressure," he said with concern.

"I went over to Lighthouse's office, I got some information. Reddy definitely has some deal with them. I spotted him there."

He blew out loudly, "I hope you were careful, are you still there?" he asked.

"No, I'm on my way home, but I'm still in the area."

He sounded concerned, "Be careful, I dug up some stuff on

your mates. Very interesting portfolio." He started explaining what he had found. "Firstly, Reddy's Merc is registered to Lighthouse Insurance, and the insurance policy is held by the company also. O'Shea, that bloke you met in Wynns, he works for Lighthouse, but get this, he has a brother who is some heavyweight in the Department of Health, Minister's office no less."

Now I blew out loudly. "No shit," I exclaimed.

"It doesn't stop there. There is a sister company called Lighthouse Security." I remembered the logo on the security guard's hat in the College of Surgeons and the alarm box outside on the wall. "Well, they have some seriously heavy contracts on some of the larger hospitals, a lot of the Health Centres in the suburbs and would you believe it, they even have the security contract guarding the e-voting machines."

I was amazed. "They obviously have contacts high up," I said.

George was laughing. "I doubt if any heads will roll, but there is probably enough information here to hang a few juniors."

I was thinking as fast as I could. "George, do you have anything in writing that could confirm any of this?" I asked in an almost pleading voice.

"I can confirm Reddy's car details, but not a whole lot more," he replied, "only quotations and copies of tender documents but a clever journalist could very easily follow the paper trail and it would lead to, Christ...all the way to the Wizard of Oz!"

I was instantly disappointed but I managed, "Send me anything you have, thanks a million George." I gave him my efax number and hung up. The sound of traffic announced that I was nearing the end of the lane and about to hit the main drag. I stopped and slowly put my head around the corner onto Seville place. Looking up and down, I saw nobody who aroused suspicion. I would have had to cross the street and walk down Oriel Street to get to Amiens Street and the Dart station. I felt that having gotten this far undetected, this was an unnecessary risk. I saw diagonally across the street a broken wall that was effectively an entrance to a building site. This site seemed to stretch as far as the railway line. I took a gamble on it having some way out either onto the main street further along or out into the back of the Financial Services Centre. Taking a last look up and down, I fast walked across the street and ducked in behind the broken wall. A quick look around revealed a large crater populated with steel rods standing erect in a sea of freshly poured concrete. Immediately a scene from The Sopranos came to mind. A sea of fresh concrete that would soon, no doubt support a few hundred apartments or offices would be an ideal place to dispose of a body, with an almost cast iron guarantee of never being discovered. This thought prompted me to check around for anyone who could be following me. I skirted the crater, and moved alongside standard wooden hoardings. The traffic noise from the other side led me to believe that I was running parallel to the main street and the increasing volume strongly suggested that I was approaching Amiens Street. I spotted a gap in the hoardings and made for it. A worker in a yellow hat was lifting a section of wire fencing to block up the gap. I shouted and ran towards him. He looked at me with a frown and I slipped between the fencing he was manhandling and the gap in the hoarding. He shouted something at me in broken English. I gave him a half salute and shouted "lost." I lowered my head and joined in the pedestrian traffic into the Financial Services Centre. Crossing the road, I recognized where I was. I was at the back of Connolly station in the Financial District. An alley under a four storey glass building brought me under Connolly station. Signs for the Dart pointed out onto the street. I upped my pace and by five to three, I was on the Dart heading for Sandymount and home.

39

Consultants Slam Decision not to Review Contracts

Representatives of Consultants today slammed the decision of the Ministers for Finance and Health and Children to defer the establishment of a steering committee to review the Contracts of Hospital Consultants. Prof. Geary went on to say that the Minister has apparently decided to defer a pay review which is contractually provided for in the Consultants' Common Contract until agreements on accesability to private patients has been reached. Consultants however feel that they will have no input into any new contract negotiations. The Government insists that it is seeking discussions with the IMO on any proposed new Consultant's Contract. Prof. Geary told the Times today that given that the Department of Health and Children has consistently refused to give a written undertaking to the IMO that there will be no further attempts to change the Consultants Contract, and in spite of a request direotod through the Labour Relations Commission to this effect, the Departments of Finance and Health and Children have apparently decided to tear up the rule book on industrial relations and have fatally damaged the prospect of such contract negotiations resuming in the near future. The IMO are advising any prospective new applicants not to accept any contract offered until this dispute is resolved.

I ARRIVED HOME by three thirty, and had some normal family time. I was very distracted and Victoria gave me what for, after I let a pot of vegetables burn. I apologized, telling her that I was under a lot of pressure in work. I spun some half-truth about being called to the clinical services manager's office, and being told off about some report I made a month or so earlier about the insurance classifications. "I've told you before to keep your mouth shut," she told me.

One of my problems is that if I see something wrong or unjust, I will usually say it out loud to somebody. I had on previous occasions been told to keep my mouth shut when I pointed out something to the wrong people. That seemed to satisfy her, but I desperately wanted to tell her everything. I promised I would after this whole mess, Christ...would it ever be over? The familiar lurching of my stomach returned.

Eventually, after dinner and putting the kids to bed, we relaxed with a glass of wine and some Robbie Williams. I was still very preoccupied with the Mulligan/Brennan situation and it wasn't until Victoria pinched me, did I realize how quiet and preoccupied I was. "What's wrong with you lately?" she asked with irritation.

I was on the verge of spilling everything, but I held back. I reiterated the story of being under pressure in work and started dreaming about "giving it all up and doing something else completely different." We shot the breeze about this notion for a while and eventually headed off to bed.

About three o'clock, I was awoken by my mobile phone ringing. I was only dozing, and, recognizing the number as Intensive Care, I answered it quickly.

"Robbie," it was one of the ITU nurses. She had her 'middle of the night phone call' voice on. "Habib wants to put an Intra Aortic balloon into the second patient from today."

I hadn't been around for most of the list, while climbing out of bed I asked "Who's the Consultant?"

"Professor O'Riada, but Habib will go ahead and put it

in" she answered. Leaving something like this to a Registrar as experienced as Habib was normal, besides, Habib was probably there already and we would only be a short while, as there would be no waiting around.

I whispered to the prone form of Victoria, "Gotta go in for an hour or so, won't be long" she muttered something about Bruce supposed to be on call and promptly fell back asleep.

I grabbed a sweatshirt, and a pair of jeans. Finding my shoes proved a little tricky in the dark and I ended up with a pair of good black leather shoes that I had worn to a wedding some weeks before, and with the old jeans I threw on, I wouldn't win any fashion awards. Grabbing my phone and keys, I tiptoed out the door and remembered to reset the alarm as I exited the house. Other than the standard population of taxis, there was no traffic and I made it to the hospital in ten minutes. I parked on the street opposite the main entrance and after locking the car, ran across the shiny black tar to the main doors. It had been raining and without the usual mayhem, the streets had that freshly washed feel. I trotted across the street.

The main door was locked but I hit a buzzer on the side. Almost immediately a voice came back, "Yeah, can I help you?" I identified myself and was a bit miffed when the voice asked me to hold my ID card up to the camera. This wasn't normal but, then again, there was a special patient still here. Luckily, the jeans I had picked in the dark were the ones with my wallet in the back pocket. I fished my ID card from my wallet and was rewarded by the sound of the door being unlocked remotely. I passed the security desk ten seconds later.

Jimmy, a middle aged man who normally worked the night shift was sitting at the desk reading the paper. He looked at me and grinned, "Sorry about that Robbie, don't know who might be wanting to visit the Suit."

I smiled and added, "can't be too careful."

He rolled his eyes, "orders from upstairs, y'know the story."

I nodded and headed towards the stairs towards Intensive care.

Habib had, not only started the insertion of the Balloon Pump, he was almost finished. All that remained to do was to connect the catheter coming from the patient's femoral artery to the computerized pump and we were finished. I retrieved the pump from the operating theatre, and within ten minutes of arriving, we were finished. Normally, I would be in for at least an hour and a half, but fair play to Habib, he didn't hang about.

While fine tuning the settings and handing over to the Nurse on duty, I noticed something that switched a little light on in my head. After the patient has been taken off the Heart/Lung bypass machine, all the blood remaining in the tubes, reservoir and artificial lung is normally pumped into blood bags and reinfused given back to the patient. This is called pump fluid. It is moderately diluted blood and, if the patient has normal kidney function, they will pass any extra water and concentrate the blood. This can very often push the Hemoglobin levels back up to close to normal levels and negate the need for blood transfusions. This means that a very high percentage of patients who undergo heart surgery, do not need a blood transfusion at all, even though they have had their chest split open, and very often their leg opened from ankle to thigh. This bagged blood is normally given back over the few hours immediately following the surgery.

What struck me was that now, fourteen hours after the surgery, the patients blood from the machine, was still being infused slowly into the patient. The Perfusionist ultimately controlled this blood. An idea dawned on me. During the surgery, the anesthetist would prepare and give various anesthetic drugs to the Perfusionist to administer via the Heart/ Lung machine. I thought, if things went to and beyond the surgery, and I hadn't sorted anything out, if I added a full dose of normal anesthetic drugs to the pump fluid that Mulligan would receive back after the surgery, he would be kept asleep far beyond the normal time. This fact, could if given a little push invariably leak out to Brennan's crew. This could buy me some more time. There would be no harm done to Mulligan as he would metabolise the drugs normally and wake up eventually. This, I hoped could go undetected and also give me some wriggle room if required. I shuddered at the thought of deliberately doing something like this, but it was temporary and, hopefully if I got the dose correct, no permanent harm would be done. It was common enough for an Anesthetic resident to draw up the drugs for an operation only to find that the Consultant anesthetist had already drawn up whatever was required. It wasn't unusual to have two or three syringes of drugs left over after the operation was complete, or it could easily be arranged.

I strolled over to the central monitoring station. Habib was writing notes in the patient's chart. He looked at me, "No point in debating for an hour whether to insert the balloon or not."

I smiled. "Couldn't agree more Habib, just get on with it."

He explained the history of the last few hours following the surgery. The patient had gotten progressively worse, and increasing the amounts of cardiac support drugs had only served to compound the problem. Habib had weighed up the situation and decided, relatively early in the proceedings, to insert an Intra Aortic Balloon pump. A lot of Doctors would wait a lot longer to insert one of these gadgets, and this could mean that you had a much sicker patient on your hands.

Habib finished his notes and walked over to the X-ray viewing bank. The X-Ray technician had just returned with a film taken immediately after Habib put in the last stitch and Habib studied the film. I came up behind him and noted that the radio-opaque tip of the balloon catheter was perfectly positioned at the second rib space. "Might be a bit high," I teased.

Habib turned to me with wide eyes, "You think so?" He turned his gaze back to the film and studied it carefully.

"Only messing," I laughed, "you happy if I head home?"

"Oh yes Robert, and thank you very much for your help."

He was as courteous as ever. The only thing I had done was to connect the tube to the machine. I checked that the duty nurse was happy with the operation of the machine. These machines effectively look after themselves, and so long as they're set up properly, there are rarely problems. "Night all," I saluted and left the Intensive care unit.

Although Habib had called Professor O'Riada, I noticed that he hadn't made an appearance, nothing new there. Having a Resident as experienced as Habib about, had its benefits. Then I began to think, Consultants not about? Other than sleeping patients and night nursing staff, the hospital corridors were virtually deserted. I wondered if the Consultants rooms, or suites as they liked them to be called, were open. If they were, this was as good an opportunity as I was ever likely to get to see if I could find anything in Reddy's rooms that I could use.

I was halfway down the stairs towards the reception area where the security desk was. I hadn't turned the final corner yet so Jimmy, the security guard most likely hadn't seen me. I doubled back towards the first landing and slipped back onto the corridor. I walked purposefully along the corridor past the Intensive Care Unit and on around to the back corridor where there was a lift to the administration block where the Consultants rooms were located.

I was just about to hit the call button for the lift when a thought struck me. I snapped my hand back, although I was on call and perfectly entitled to be in the hospital at this hour, it was a different thing to be snooping around Consultants rooms. Calling the lift and traveling to the administration floor would definitely noted by security and, I reminded myself, that there was a police presence in the hospital. I turned and headed into the stairwell and started climbing the four or five floors to the floor where the Consultants rooms were. "The rooms are bound to be locked," I thought to myself, but I hadn't thought that far ahead. I would cross that bridge when I came to it.

I was breathless when I reached the administration floor.

Pausing and checking up and down the corridor, the last thing I wanted was to bump into Jimmy's partner for the night on his routine security rounds. After checking that everything was clear, I exited the stairway and onto the main corridor. The main lights were off and there was only a dim, security light on at twenty or thirty metre intervals. I couldn't remember which room Reddy occupied, so I looked for the lowest number, intending to work my way up.

After a few minutes, I was more confused than ever. The suite numbers seemed to go in random order, nine was next to sixteen. I turned a corner, and came across number one. I spotted Professor O'Riada's room. Next to it was a room with a photocopier and a scanner with a coffee maker. Ten more minutes of searching and I finally found Reddy's room. Holding my breath, I tried the door. I pushed it gently, it didn't move. My heart sank and in frustration, I pushed harder. It opened. I was thrilled. It was the thick pile shag carpet that was holding the door closed. I held the open door in my hand, waiting for an alarm to go off. Nothing did, I slipped inside leaving the door open. I was about to switch on the light when I noticed that the curtains weren't drawn. The hospital building was shaped like a rectangular box standing like a skyscraper. The corridors ran around the outside and the hollow in the centre overlooked a garden. However, as the administration floors were on the opposite side of the rectangle to the reception, you could look up from reception, across the garden and up at the administration and Consultants offices. If I put on the light here, it would be the only light on in that section of the building that was supposed to be completely empty now. I stayed with the light off, letting my eyes adjust to the darkness. I couldn't see much, let alone read anything. From the glow of the security lights in the corridor, I could make out the writing on the drawers. Desperately trying not to waste the opportunity, I went down on my hunkers to try and read the names on the drawers. It was a struggle. I shuffled a little and went to move my mobile phone from one pocket to another. "Mobile phone, that's it," I almost shouted to myself. The kids bought me this phone for Christmas the previous year. It was a Nokia, with a camera, radio and guess what? A torch. Taking it out of my pocket, I tried to remember how to switch it on. Then I remembered press and hold 9 and a mini torch came on. It was powerful enough to read by, but not so powerful that a beam dancing around an unoccupied office would draw any attention.

I moved the beam around the different filing cabinets in the room. Nothing jumped out at me. Then I began to think, if this was as potentially explosive as it was suggesting, keeping files that were connected to this case in a general office, was foolhardy to say the least. The Consulting rooms were divided in three sections, an office where the secretary was housed, and an ante-room where the Doctor discussed the illness with the patient and an examination room where the patient was examined.

I ventured into the ante room. Sure enough, there were two large filing cabinets in the corner of the room. I was just about to pull one of the filing cabinet drawers open when Mr. Paranoid made me check for any security devices. There were no alarms and, by the light if my torch/phone, I was able to read the title of each manila folder in the drawers. There were various surnames, drug titles I recognized that were still undergoing studies and different operative references. Nothing leapt out at me. I was getting frustrated now and was about to close the door, when something caught my attention. All the folder titles had something written that was relevant to a busy Cardiac Surgical practice. One jumped out at me. There was a full folder with no label on it. I looked at it for a minute, until something told me to take it out. It was a file of copies of the letter I had found in the patients chart that had started me digging into lighthouse. Obviously, he kept copies to ensure that he got paid. The secretary probably followed up on the letters to the NTPF, but no doubt, Reddy followed up Lighthouse Insurance to ensure that the money was forthcoming. I lifted the folder from the drawer and set it down on the desk. I opened it slowly. It was a stack of all of the same letters, one of which had made its way inadvertently into the chart I found the other day. These letters linked Reddy to Lighthouse. However, this in itself wasn't a crime as he probably did business with lots of other insurance companies.

As I scanned the stack of letters, they were in order of date of admission. I began to wonder. If Mulligan was an NTPF patient, was there any chance that he came in under the Lighthouse umbrella. The fact that those who were demanding that I sabotage the operation were also the directors of Lighthouse was too coincidental to ignore. I ran my mind back to the day ten days...no nine, when Mulligan had been admitted to ITU and a balloon inserted. I checked the calendar on my phone and looked for any letters with that date on it. After a few minutes searching, I hit paydirt. A letter from Lighthouse thanking Reddy for accepting a Mr. T Mulligan for Coronary Artery Bypass Surgery, under the terms of the National Treatment Purchase Fund-External Insurers section. I had a piece of information that directly linked Reddy to Lighthouse and Mulligan's planned surgery. Now I needed to decide what to do with this information. Go to the police? George? The Hospital Authorities? I remembered the veiled warning off looking into Lighthouse that I had been given. Other than George, I hadn't been very lucky with my choice of confidants so far.

I took Mulligan's letter out, lifted the entire folder and after checking that the corridor was clear, I ran towards the utility room I had seen earlier. I prayed that the photocopier was switched on. They can take an eternity to warm up, sometimes they're left on so I could be lucky. The room was dark, but immediately I could see that the lights on the copier were out. I double-checked, no luck, both the copier and scanner were powered down. I was beginning to despair when my eyes fell on a large phone/fax machine. I immediately thought of my efax number. It was taking a major chance, but time was something I was desperately short of. The phone number stuck to the machine gave me a boost, it was a direct line. This meant that it wasn't connected via the switchboard. I had no idea if any lights would show at the reception desk if I called from a regular phone, but at least now I didn't have to worry about that. I gathered about ten of the sheets together with Mulligan's on the top. This way, tomorrow I would have an email with an attachment of all these letters scanned. I picked up the receiver to check that there was a normal dial tone.

Yessss! I dialled my eFax number. The machine whined to life and slowly started to eat the pages, one by one. I watched with satisfaction until a noise outside gave me a jolt. I ducked behind a large filing cabinet and peered out beyond the door. A security guard was strolling along the corridors, checking into each room. He was still about twenty metres away so I took a major gamble. The door was closed when I got here, but I had left it open. This was a dead giveaway as he probably did rounds every hour or so. Staying low, I stretched my leg out and gave the door a gentle nudge. It moved about a foot. There was no change in the sounds of the movement outside. I tried it again. The door closed all the way over but didn't click closed. Finally, I leaned over and, as gently as I could, I closed it over fully. A gentle click announced that it was fully shut.

The fax machine was still busily pulling the paper through, but there was nothing I could do about that. I was committed now. I looked around for a place to hide. The best I could do was under the desk. I curled up in the tight space and waited. After about three minutes, I heard the door opening. I began to breathe through my mouth, as this was quieter. After a minute or two, I began to drool out the sides of my mouth. The fax machine seemed extremely noisy but that was probably because of the silence of the small hours of the morning. The glowing hands of my watch showed it to be ten past four. I had been in the hospital less than an hour, but it seemed like a lifetime.

I saw the beam of the Security Guard's torch sweep the room and stop on the fax machine. I hoped that the Guard wouldn't get nosy and want to read the fax. I hoped he would make the assumption that it was an incoming fax, and not somebody sending an illicit one. After what seemed like an hour, I heard the click of the switch on the torch as it went out and the door close. I waited for about fifteen minutes, or until the cramp in my leg was unbearable before I climbed out. Shaking the cramp out of my leg, I retrieved the letters from the fax tray and put them back in as good an order as I could. I replaced the folder in the filing cabinet drawer and, slowly, re-entered the corridor. Taking the stairs again, I decided to use the service entrance at the back of the hospital. Habib, the X-Ray tech and the Nurse on call would all have gone home by now and I didn't want to arouse suspicion by passing the reception desk later than everybody else. I took the back stairs down to the service area at the back of the hospital. Despite the sign stating that "This door must remain locked at all times," the door to the service area was wedged open with a bag of dirty linen. I strolled out into the cool damp night air.

"You're here late," a voice broke the silence.

I spun my head around searching for the location of its owner. Marty was leaning against a large linen bin smoking. "Oh hi Marty. Just finished an emergency in Intensive Care. Pain in the ass, this on call lark."

He stamped his cigarette end out, "Yeah, I saw the Surgeon and nurse leave about a half hour ago."

I thought I detected a hint of suspicion in his voice. I shook off the feeling; I was really getting paranoid now. However, I still covered my tracks, "Yeah, every time we attach one of those machines to a patient, I get stung for a twenty minute explanation to the nurse on duty."

He nodded, "Always the last to leave. Oh, did you check the

results, that second horse, *Chinese takeaway* won, hope you had a couple of quid on it."

I pulled my keys from my pocket and remembered the twenty euro I'd put on it. A familiar rush came over me. I fought to contain it. "I can't remember if I did or not, I'll have a look in my wallet, anyway I'm going home to bed, cheers."

I exited the back gates and then remembered that my car was parked at the front of the hospital. I walked around the corner, following the railings towards the front entrance. My mind was working a mile a minute. I was starting to gather a lot of information that showed, at the very least a conspiracy that involved a criminal gang fronted by an Insurance company, a Cardiac Surgeon who was involved with the company and by default the gang, contacts inside the Minister of Health's office and a plot to effectively knock off the head of a rival criminal gang. It sounded like the script of a Hollywood movie. I began to wonder if anyone would believe me if I started shouting about this. Now, with forty eight hours to go to the scheduled surgery, I had to decide what to do. I decided to ring George first thing in the morning and let him know what I had discovered.

On top of this, the last thing I needed was a resurgence of my old gambling habits. Focusing on my mental exercises that the hypnotherapist who helped me kick the habit. A momentary lapse was bad enough, but the fact that both the horses had won was a major danger to my staying off the gambling. Pushing it out of my mind, I reached my car and ten minutes later, I was cruising along the canal towards home.

40

TWO AND A HALF HOURS LATER, I was back in the car, heading to work for a seven o'clock start. I parked the car in the staff area of the multi-storey, and headed towards my office. I had lain awake for the two hours I was back home after the visit to ITU and Reddy's office and the bones of a plan had formed in my head. Reaching my office, I firstly checked the operating list. It showed only two operations. I was mindful of the fact that I was very preoccupied with my own problems and was hardly contributing to the work of the department. I was first in this morning and having checked that the first procedure was coronary artery bypass grafts, I set up a Heart/Lung machine and primed it so it was ready for the first patient. The first patient was due in at eight o'clock and at ten past seven, the machines were set up and ready. I switched on the computer and having let it boot up, opened Outlook. The first thing I saw was three email messages announcing that I had fax messages. I closed the outer door and opened the first fax message. It was a copy of the single letter from Lighthouse to Reddy that I had found in the patients chart some days before. I closed and opened the second one. A cover letter appeared first. It was from George: "Hope this helps, be in touch" was written in George's unmistakable handwriting. I remembered him being the English teacher's favorite as his writing was always impeccable. I scrolled on down the fax message and came across a page that showed a blown up picture of what looked like an identity card. It bore the name Robert O'Shea followed by a staff number, and he apparently was a Higher Executive Officer in the Minister's office. There was an identity picture but the photocopying effect of the fax made it very difficult to recognize the face. He had the same curly hair as the chap, who called himself Tom that I met in Wynns Hotel and previously in Molloys bar. I thought I detected a resemblance but that could have been because of the suggestion that George had made.

I scrolled on down and came across a page that looked like it had been printed from the Internet and photocopied. It bore the eTenders Public Procurement logo at the top. It showed a list of tenders, a reference number, the Department where the tender originated, the date when the tender was published and the company to whom the contract was awarded. The page started with a tender for the "Supply & Installation of a telephone system" from the Department of Justice, Equality and Law Reform. The contract had been awarded to a company called Digital Electronic Communications Ltd. About one quarter of the way down, there was notice of a tender from the Health Service Executive. It requested the "Brokering and/or underwriting for the provision of Healthcare Insurance to the National Treatment Purchase Fund" There was a reference number and then the diamond.

The contract had been awarded to none other than Lighthouse Insurance Services Ltd. I stared at this for a minute or two. This really was a gold nugget of information. The question was how to use it to the maximum effect. I had the outline of an idea that could get me off the hook in the short term, but the problem was how to get these goons off my back for good. I scrolled on down the page and came to another tender document. "Provision of Security Services" It came from the Department of Health and the contract was awarded to Lighthouse Security Services. I began to get excited now. I scrolled on further. The eTenders document ended and the next page was from the City Council's Registration of Motor Vehicles. It listed a Grey Mercedes, SLK 320, with an 05 D registration. The registered owner was a Lighthouse Insurance Company Ltd. I felt now that I had some really useful information.

Looking at my watch, I saw that it was twenty to eight. I went to close the email and a thought struck me. I checked that I had my flash disk in my pocket. I plugged it into the computer and saved the faxes to the flash memory. I closed down Outlook and headed to the operating theatre. I wheeled the Heart/Lung machine into the operating room as a friendly "G'day mate" broke the silence of the room. Bruce appeared and helped me push the pump into the room. "Can you look after number one here Bruce?" I asked, "It's primed and ready."

"No problem," he smiled. "I can have my breakfast now." I left him to fine-tune the system and headed for the coffee room. After a feed of tea and toast, I checked the time. It was quarter to nine. I had a call to make but I needed to find a quiet place and wait until after nine. I spent a few minutes checking that the faxes I had received had transferred to the flash disc. If I was going to use them, I needed to make sure that they were intact and available to view and print. I then deleted the messages from the email box and closed down Outlook.

I strolled out into the corridor and headed to the back storage area of the operating theatre. There was a telephone mounted on the wall just inside the door. The good thing was, early in the day, the storage area was usually empty of people. At five past nine, I closed the storage area door, pushed a large plastic sack of dirty linen partially across in front the door and picked up the phone. I had looked up the number of the Department of Health's central office and through that had tracked down the Minister's office. I used the line that I had previously used during my thesis when I was researching the possibility of upgrading local health centres to be used as outlying Cardiac and stroke clinics. During this research, I had called over a hundred Health centres and spoken to as many nurses and managers. My opening line, introducing myself and my research, usually got me straight through and after a minute or two, I had always managed to strike up a useful conversation that got me the information that I could use in my research.

The phone rang six or seven times and was answered by a young sounding girl with an accent that I couldn't quite place. It was Polish or Czech, but she had flawless English. Debating whether to use my real name or not, I though that whoever answered could easily check my *bona fides* and establish that there was or wasn't a postgraduate student of that name. I hoped that that was as far as any checking would go. I used my real name explaining that I was a postgraduate student in the College of Surgeons, and as part of my thesis for a PhD in Healthcare Management, I was researching the nature of the funding of the Health Service. I was particularly interested in the success of the National Treatment Purchase Fund. She was bright and courteous and had no problems helping me to track down the most appropriate person to talk to. "Putting you though now," she signed off and I was left with the ringing tone again.

After five rings, a man answered. "Minister's office, research section—Pearse O'Ceallaig speaking" was the complicated greeting.

I had just began to groan, thinking that I had been put through to an answering machine, when I realized that there was silence and Mr. Pearse O'Ceallaig was waiting for my reply. I repeated my opening story and he was immediately interested in talking to me. He seemed to be very proud of the fund and was extremely knowledgeable of the figures. He started quoting figures, left right and centre, all extolling the virtues of the fund. I reiterated that I was interested in how the fund was financed. He paused for a second and mused that he thought that the money came from a fund set aside specifically for the purpose of tackling the waiting lists. I agreed, "but didn't the Minister recently announce that the Fund was being extended even though the original money had run out?"

He seemed stumped. "Oh...oh...yeah," he seemed to be searching for an answer, "but the insurance companies...are still...em...involved. So there is still cash available." Suddenly his demeanour changed to someone who was struggling as if he had run out of information and was desperately trying to find an acceptable answer.

I seized the moment. "So there are insurance companies financing the fund?" I pressed.

"I...I...I, there are one or two...I think..." He was struggling big time now. I was taken back a little. Why was this clerk, or whoever he was stuttering and stammering so much when I mentioned the insurance companies. I guessed that he knew more than he was saying but he clammed up. "I don't know anything about the insurance companies involved or the financing."

I backpedalled a bit and with a little contrition in my voice explained, "Sorry to hassle you, but my research supervisor is putting wicked pressure to have this section of the research in by the end of the month."

He calmed down a bit. "Sorry, but the financial information is kept under wraps, as you can imagine." I agreed with him in an understanding voice. He suddenly became my best friend again, "If you need to get some more information, I could have Mr. O'Shea call you back, he is the undersecretary with primary responsibility for the fund. He's the one to talk to."

The mention of the name was like an electric shock, I paraphrased him out loud. "O'Shea controls the fund?" I asked with more than a hint of incredulity in my voice.

He replied, "You know Mr. O'Shea?" I suddenly realized what I had said.

"No...no, it's just I thought that...the...em...Minister would control that sort of money." I was thinking fast and furiously. He laughed, "We all know that the senior civil servants really run the Departments."

I joined in, "Oh yeah…"

"Give me your number and I'll have Mr. O'Shea call you back."

This time I was struggling, "Em…listen, I'm in surgery… all day. I'll call again, thanks a mill, bye." I dropped the phone like a hot potato and cursed my stupidity.

If this O'Ceallaig chap mentioned my call and the fact that I had mentioned surgery to O'Shea, and he in turn to his brother, I was rightly buggered. Anyway, I had confirmed that an O'Shea worked in the Minister's office as a Higher Executive Officer and not only that, he controlled the fund. A contact like that was worth a fortune to a company like Lighthouse. Also, the security contracts that Lighthouse enjoyed were obviously a result of the contacts snaking out from somebody like O'Shea. I now had information that unequivocally linked Reddy to Lighthouse Insurance, that linked a very senior civil servant to the same company and a string of documents that showed that there was a steady stream of patients that came from the National Treatment Purchase Fund and were being routed through this company with whom it appeared had an unhealthy relationship with both the senior civil servant and the Surgeon who would ultimately be operating on these patients. My simple plan was to confront somebody, I wasn't quite sure who yet, with this information, and hopefully, the documents would be incriminating enough to put a stop to this whole mess.

Looking at my watch, I noted that it was half past nine. I headed back to the operating theatres and my office. The operating list was well under way and the lads had everything under control. I decided to head to the ward to investigate how Mulligan was doing. There hadn't been any calls from the ward or ITU about him, so I assumed that he had stabilized. I took the lift to the ward and stepped off on the floor where Mulligan's room was located. The ward was a hive of activity at this hour in the day. Patients were coming and going to different departments, X-ray, blood testing, Electrocardiograms and the like. I strolled along the corridor towards where the patients' rooms were. About twenty metres ahead, I noticed a bored looking detective sitting outside a room where I guessed Mulligan was in residence.

As I passed the first room, my mobile phone rang. The noise took me by surprise and I scrambled to pull the phone from my pocket. I received dagger looks from a nurse leaving one of the rooms. I was in such a hurry to answer it that I didn't look at the number displayed. "Robbie son, howya," came the familiar throaty voice. My blood ran cold and I almost started shaking. I immediately turned on my heels and out into an emergency stairs exit.

"Yeah," I was as curt as possible, I couldn't trust myself not to start shouting or my voice shaking so I spoke as little as possible.

"Robbie, I thought I told you not to act the bollix, and just do what we told you?" He had undisguised menace in his voice and it was chilling.

I stuttered and stammered for a second, "What...what are you talking about? I didn't...speak...go..." I was stumped.

He interrupted again, "Robbie, we told you not to speak to anybody about this..."

I was panicking now, and thinking that they had twigged to George, I pressed ahead, "I haven't spoken to the police about this, I've worked out exactly what I'm going to use and when and how I'll give the drugs." He was silent for a second. I pressed on. "I'm going to wait until the surgery is over and lace the recycled blood with anesthetic drugs that will do the job." I was conscious of my voice echoing around the stairwell, anybody coming up or down the stairs would be able to hear me, but at this stage, I couldn't have given a damn.

"We are going to have to take some insurance to make sure that you co-operate." This threat was delivered with no change in tone and scared the living shit out of me, it was so calculated. "Someone's been digging and nosing about in things that don't concern them...you wouldn't know anything about that, I suppose, would you?"

"Please, don't do anything to..." I started begging and the sound of my pathetic grovelling made me sick.

He interrupted me again, "I want you to come and see me today, one or two of my lads will bring you, it seems you're a bit slippery."

The thought of the chases through town came to mind. I was both amused and scared at the same time. "I haven't got the time to come see you," I began, but after a second or two, I realized that I was talking to a blank phone line, he had hung up. I leaned against the wall and racked my brains for a way to get long term relief from these scumbags. I wanted to bang my head against the wall when his threat of taking some insurance to ensure my co-operation came to mind. I immediately thought of Victoria and the kids. I made a decision. I dialed Victoria's number and she answered after three rings. "What's up?" she said with a giggle. It sounded like she was in coffee shop.

"Victoria, listen love. Something's come up," I was as serious as I could be.

"What's new?" she came back with a groan.

"No this is serious." I was reaching for some explanation that would get the message across without alarming her. "You know that we are due to operate on a high profile criminal tomorrow?" I paused for a moment.

"Yes, I read something about that in the paper," she said and it sounded that her attention had gone up a notch or two.

"Where are you now?" I asked.

"Having coffee in the shopping centre," she said. The background noise died down as if she had left the shop. "Security has told us that there have been threats from his gang, and..." I paused to put this as credibly as possible, "and to members of the surgical team."

"Oh Jesus!" was all she could manage. I seized the moment and pressed on, "Security has told us to put our families on alert and to look out for any suspicious activity." I stopped finally. I hated lying to Victoria, but this was a version of the truth and I was desperate to get Victoria out of the firing line, especially now after Brennan's latest threat.

"They called the police, didn't they?" she sounded a little panicky.

"Of course, there are armed detectives in the hospital here." I was happy to be able to give her some truth. "Security just want us to make sure that there are no threats to any member of staff or their families."

She was quite serious now. "What do you want me to do?" she asked.

"The surgery is scheduled for tomorrow, so..." I paused, "why don't you take the kids to your sister in Galway for the weekend?"

She blurted out, "But the kids are in school tomorrow."

I pushed a bit further, "Victoria, love, this is important, these people are dangerous, and I would prefer if you were out of any danger."

There was a silence, "Rob, you're frightening me now." She sounded scared.

"I don't want to scare you but, there's a strange atmosphere around here at the moment. Can you do this for me? If the surgery goes well, he'll be out of ITU by Sunday, and on the way home by the middle of next week."

She was silent for a second, "OK, I'll go home and pack now. I'll wait until you're home to leave. The kids will wonder why you aren't coming."

I was relieved and it sounded in my voice. "One more thing Vic," I needed to up her level of awareness of any possible threats, "security also told us to look out for any suspicious activity, like someone following us."

She laughed, "You and your spy books! Talk to you later."

She hung up. I hoped that I hadn't sounded paranoid but equally I hoped that she took me seriously. She was unlikely to meet anyone from the hospital that she knew and was likely to discuss this with, so I was reasonably confident, if she got packed and picked up the kids, she would be out of town and the line of fire by tea-time.

I went back to my office to think. Sitting in front of the computer, I reviewed the documents that George had faxed me and thought about the information that they contained. Three or four times I had to quickly close down the window as people came and went from the office. I wondered if there was enough information there to make any impression on Brennan. Would the fact that I was in possession of this information scare him, or would his arrogance and apparent Teflon skin allow him to slip away. Connecting Reddy to Brennan should mean trouble for Reddy, and I felt that his ego was big enough that he wouldn't like his name to be smeared. I needed to think of some way of using this information, and fast.

I was deep in thought when the phone startled me. With all the phone calls from Brennan, I was getting jumpy when phones rang. I lifted the receiver. It was one of the ITU nurses. "Robbie, Brigid in ITU here," I relaxed a little, "the Intra Aortic Balloon in bed six is not working properly..." She started to explain that the pacemaker on the patient was causing problems with the timing of the balloon.

"I'll be over in five minutes Brigid," I cut her short, "is the patient stable?"

She seemed a bit miffed that I had stopped her in full flight. "Yes, he's fine," she answered, "thanks a million Robbie" and she hung up. I sat watching the computer screen for a minute or two looking for inspiration. Nothing came so I closed down the windows, logged out of Outlook and headed for ITU. I made an educated guess as to what the problem would be with the Balloon Pump. I was strolling across the link corridor when my mobile phone in my scrubs pocket started ringing. I stopped and pulled it from my pocket. My jaw tensed as I lifted the phone to read the screen. "Number unavailable" was flashing in time to the ringing. I slowly brought the phone to my ear while pressing the answer key. I held my breath, "Hello?"

"Robbie, George here."

I sighed with relief. "How are you George?" He seemed in a hurry. "Good, how are you doing?" he asked with genuine concern.

"Hanging in there I guess," I answered with as much enthusiasm as I could manage.

"Listen, good and bad news. I did a little PI work there yesterday. Got some very clear pictures of your friend Reddy and our mate Brennan. Reddy seemed to be under severe pressure from Brennan."

My mood lifted significantly. "Could I use them?" I asked desperately searching for something I could use as leverage.

"Probably, but their impact would depend on how you used the other information." I was a bit deflated. He was kicking the ball back to me. "Bad news is that I have been sent on a course for the weekend, leaving tonight. Would you believe it, insurance fraud!" he stifled a laugh.

I was gutted and it sounded in my voice, "Christ, the surgery is tomorrow."

He came back immediately, "I know, Robbie, and if I could get out of it, I would. Anyway listen, I'll give you the number of the hotel where the seminar is on. You can call and leave a message, I'll get back to you as soon as possible." He started calling out a number.

"Hold on George, I don't have a pen," I was searching in my pockets for a pen while walking. As I turned towards the Intensive Care Unit, Marty exited the double doors. He saw me struggling with the phone cradled under my chin. He reached into his pocket and produced a pen. I mouthed thanks.

"Go ahead George." I wrote the number on the the leg of my scrub suit and signed off. I lifted my head and Marty was still standing in front of me. "Thanks Marty, coming to my rescue again," I held the pen up and looked at without really seeing it, "amazing all the technology, computers and the like, but you're buggered without a pen when you need one." He lifted his hand to take the pen and I turned it slightly.

It was one of those thousands of pens that are handed out by sales reps with the name, phone number and logo of the company emblazoned on the side. I noticed a multi-coloured design with some small writing printed on the side of the pen beside it was a small icon of a Lighthouse. Without looking closely, I could see the name and address of Lighthouse Security Services as clear as if I had a magnifying glass. I stared at it for a fraction too long. I raised my head and caught Marty's eyes. We stared at each other for a few seconds. I knew in an instant that it was him who was following me around the hospital. The amount of times we had 'accidentally' met, his friendly disarming manner had ensured that I had told him more than I should have several times. Christ!

After the mugging, he even knew Victoria's name without me ever telling him. He looked away immediately and, muttering something, he turned on his heels and was gone. I was shaken. Marty, someone with whom I had become quite friendly, another trustee down the toilet. Having a Lighthouse pen suddenly became worse a crime than pedophilia. Shit! Marty involved in Lighthouse! He had definitely noticed my hesitation and looking at the pen. His manner had changed immediately and he disappeared quickly without his usual banter. Now as well as me knowing his involvement, I had to assume that he knew I knew. Jesus! How long was he watching me? I was now in shit state worrying.

I entered ITU and Brigid, the nurse that had called me caught my eye. I walked over to her at the patient's bedside and she started giving me a long winded story if what was happening to the patient. "Robbie, every couple of minutes the Balloon Pump stops working and the patient's blood pressure drops." I was miles away and I had to ask her to repeat herself. I glanced at the monitor above the bed and saw the problem immediately. I should have explained to Brigid, but the problem was a little complicated and I wasn't in the mood for a long winded lecture of the finer points of the algorithms of pacemaker analysis by the computer in the balloon pump. I gave a brief, half-hearted explanation and changed the settings on the computer. The problem went away almost immediately. I walked away without acknowledging Brigid. She called after me, "Robbie, what will I tell Professor?" I stopped and turned. My mind was totally preoccupied and I turned with a blank look on my face, "Tell Professor about what?"

Brigid stared at me. "Where are you Robbie? What will I tell Reddy that you did to the balloon pump settings?"

I awoke from my trance. "Sorry Brigid, miles away today. I'll explain to Habib, he can tell him, OK?"

She rolled her eyes and laughed, "OK, no problem." I turned and left the ITU. Immediately, my mind returned to Brennan and Mulligan's surgery for the next day. I decided in an instant to head to the ward where Mulligan was to see if I would be inspired. I took the stairs and entered the ward from the back entrance. The first thing I was aware of was an overweight Detective with a grey crew cut arguing with a young man about half his size, dressed in a Celtic jersey and jeans. It looked like the young man was trying to visit Mulligan, but the Detective was having none of it. There was a lot of shouting and the ward sister was standing to the side with a red face, looking mightily pissed off.

After a minute, Celtic boy gave up the fight and sulked off in my direction. He caught my eye and scowled at me. I got a rush of blood to my head and stopped him. "Do you work for Mulligan?" I asked. He was in his early twenties and had that permanent "everything is shite" look.

"Who wants to know?" he snarled back at me. He obviously had had his belly full of authority and another white coat telling him what to do was the last thing he needed.

"I do," I said, standing in his way. "Who's running the show with Mulligan in hospital?" I demanded with as much authority and with my Oscar winning Dublin accent.

He stared at me for a second, and sizing me up answered, "Spider is…was…now Mick is, why, who the fuck are you?" He pulled himself up to his full height, and squared up to me. I sensed the anger, so I moved to diffuse it. I looked over in the direction of the Detective, looked around and nodded towards the emergency stairs. I stopped talking and walked through the heavy fire door. He glanced about and followed me. The voices echoed around the corridor.

"Story man?" he asked me as the door closed slowly behind him.

I decided to go for it. "I need to know who's running the show with Mulligan out of action," I said again. He looked at me with suspicion. I decided to give a little more. "Listen," I said lowering my voice and adapting my Oscar winning Dublin accent again, "I'm on the operating team, and I need to talk to your boss urgently, it's about the surgery tomorrow."

He looked at me for a second or two, "Mr. Mulligan's wife is downstairs in the restaurant, you could talk to her if there's a problem." He was smarter than I had guessed.

"The thing is, see, that this is a business problem, not a medical one," I paused to see if he would catch on, "I need to see whoever is running the business" I left it at that, and hopefully his suspicious mind would push him into contacting somebody. I handed him a piece of card with my name and mobile number on the back. "This is very urgent, have him call me." I walked slowly towards the door. I looked out carefully, making a show of being cautious. I pulled back quickly as the Detective outside the room stood up to take off his jacket. I then made a motion as if the corridor was too risky and headed down the stairs. This was all for show, but I felt if he saw me act suspiciously, he was more inclined to act. I disappeared down the stairs and back towards my office.

One floor above where I stood talking to Celtic boy, Marty stood slightly back from the banisters out of sight of anyone looking up the stairwell but listening to the slightly distorted voices of Robbie talking to one of Mulligan's goons. The echo gave the voices a strange sound, as if you were listening to them through a tube, but they were perfectly coherent. He heard every word. When the voices had stopped, Marty slipped quietly back on to the corridor of the ward above Mulligan's. He headed towards the lift and down to the basement and service area where he could use his mobile phone without hassle and in private.

41

I ARRIVED BACK at my office seven minutes later. The clock in the bottom corner of the computer showed that it was half ten. I was surprised as I thought it was much later, probably because so much had happened. I opened my personal file on the computer and browsed the faxes that George had sent me. I hit the print key and printed out two copies of everything. I also connected my phone to the computer and uploaded the picture that I had taken of Reddy's car outside Lighthouse's office. I was delighted when I saw the quality of the image. Checking back to my email box, I noticed another new email with George's address. It was an attachment of a photograph. I opened the attachment and clicked on the image icon. It was a photograph of Reddy talking to a man in a grey suit. I recognised the other man as the man I had met the other day while in Lighthouse's office, Brennan I presumed. The jacket was several sizes too small for his large frame. He had graying black hair and plenty of it. It looked like it was wet or gelled across his head. The sweat stains under his arms were evident and were in marked contrast to the highly polished suave image of Reddy in his sharp cut, perfectly fitted navy jacket over grey slacks.

I printed the image and saved it to my personal folder and also to my flash drive. Thinking about it, I printed both images again and ended up with two sets of documents and photos.

Placing the bundle behind some stock sheets on a clipboard, I walked to the Theatre secretary's office. There was no-one there, coffee break I presumed. Searching around the desk, I soon found a box of large A4 envelopes. I removed two, and then changed my mind and took a handful. Back in my office, I placed the bundle of documents and photos in one envelope and placed the remaining envelopes in a stationary drawer. Sealing up the filled one, I sauntered to the changing room. I opened my locker and shoved a load of junk to the back, razors, old pay slips, pens and other miscellaneous junk that had built up all were pushed unceremoniously to the rear of the locker. As I did my hand hit the sharp points of the electrodes of the Tazer Stun gun. I stared at it for a minute and threw some papers over it. I placed the filled envelope in the locker along the sides and covered it with some papers that had built up. I closed the locker and turned to leave the changing room just as my mobile phone rang. Snatching it quickly from my scrubs pocket, I looked at the number that was flashing on the screen. I didn't recognize it and my stomach tightened up at the sound. Letting it ring on, I quickly left the changing room and slipped into a back corridor which was deserted. Luckily there was no-one there. Closing the fire doors behind me, I hit the answer button and with a dry mouth answered, "Hello?"

A nondescript Dublin accent came on the line, "Robert Valentine?"

"Yeah, speaking," I said, while trying desperately to moisten my mouth so I could speak clearer.

"I work for Mr. Mulligan. One of our lads said you wanted to see us." He spoke with the accent of someone who had grown up in a rough area and seen hard times but had been educated.

I took a deep breath and went for it, "I work on the operating team that will be operating on your boss tomorrow."

He immediately interrupted, "What do you do, you a Doctor or something?"

I quickly answered, "I'm one of the technicians. I look after the life support machines that will be used during the operation."

He sounded very suspicious. "Why do you need to talk to us?" he asked with an increasing degree of irritation in his voice, "the quacks are looking after everything."

I pressed on, "I need to talk to whoever is running the show, and I need to do it now." I put as much authority as I could into my voice, but in reality, I was shaking and my mouth was bone dry.

"Tell me what you know, and I'll decide who you can speak to," he answered with thinly disguised anger.

I thought about it for a second. I needed to get to the top of Mulligan's organisation in order to start flexing the only muscle I had, the documents that George had sent me. I didn't want to prematurely reveal any cards until I had spoken to someone very high up. However, this guard dog was doing his job well, and I wasn't going to get any further until I gave something that would cut through the bullshit. "Listen," I said, "I have information and proof that something heavy is going to go down during the surgery tomorrow. I need to get the information to the top as a matter of urgency."

There was a silence, with the sound of heavy breathing. After about ten seconds he came back, "I'll need more than that if I'm to organize a meeting. How do I know you're not some nutcase looking for a slice of the action?" he asked.

I needed to gain some ground and some credibility here quickly. "I know it sounds crazy, I'm not looking for anything. I just need to be sure that this information is passed on to the best person who can do something about it." He came back straight away, "Yeah but..." I interrupted, "Listen, set it up for as soon as possible, anywhere in the city, I don't give a shit. That way you can control the meeting, and if you don't believe what you hear...well, I'll leave that up to you."

The thought of what they might do to me if they decided

that they didn't believe me nearly caused me to lose control of my bowels. I pushed all unpleasant thoughts firmly aside and focused on Victoria and the kids.

42

AFTER THE NORMAL MADNESS of getting the kids out the door, Victoria had dropped Alice to school, Nick at his Montessori school and headed for a coffee with two of the other mothers from the school run. They were relaxing in Starbucks in the shopping centre when Robbie rang. He had sounded a little strange, going on about security risks and people following members of staff's families. But there had been lots of press coverage about that Mulligan chap having surgery in the Southwestern Clinic on the back of the NTPF. God knows there was endless radio airplay about it, so it wasn't beyond the realms of possibility that there would be security problems. But taking the kids from school and leaving her home to go to her sisters for the weekend, that was pushing it a bit. She decided to pick up the kids from school at the normal time and head to her parents. If he was still going on about it by bed time, she would head off tomorrow morning. After saying goodbye to the girls, she picked up a few bits and pieces in Tescos in the centre and headed towards the car. She put her groceries in the back of the car and drove out from the car-park. Robbie had mentioned checking if people were following her, and she had laughed it off blaming his addiction to spy books, but she looked around just in case. There were no suspicious looking cars or people about, only a black motorbike with a rider with his helmet still on and he was sending a text message. She sat in the car and, after pulling on her seatbelt, negotiated the Opel Vectra out of the car park. Pulling out onto the Merrion Road, Victoria cruised towards home while listening to James Blunt on the CD player and with the morning traffic easing into the window before the lunchtime rush started; she was home in a matter of minutes. She pulled into the garden and switched off the engine. She placed the key of the house between her teeth and lifted the two small bags of shopping from the boot of the car. Reaching the hall door, she struggled to shift the bags to one hand while trying to take the key and open the hall door. The bag started to slip from her grip. Just as the bag was about to fall, a tanned hand grabbed the bag by the handle and rescued the shopping. "Let me help you there," he said with an educated accent with a slight foreign tilt.

She looked up and her eyes met a tall dark, Spanish looking man. He had a mop of black curls and the deepest black/blue eyes she had ever seen. Immediately she felt herself blushing. He was, as the girls would say, "DDG, drop dead gorgeous." He gently lifted the bags from her and said, "I saw you struggling with those."

He was about ten or twelve years younger than her, but she felt she was in quite good shape and she blushed again as thoughts that would embarrass a sailor entered her head. She regained her composure and opened the door. Turning to her rescuer, she leaned to retrieve the bags. "Thanks for your help, you are a gentleman. I didn't think there were any left," she smiled and went to lift the bags.

"Actually, I'm looking for someone who lives on this road, Valentine, Robert Valentine," he looked at her with his Spanish eyes.

Victoria's eyes opened wide, "I'm Victoria, Robbie's wife."

Marty stood to his full six feet two and looked down at her, "Well he didn't tell me about you, and I can see why."

Victoria blushed again. "Robbie's at work, probably be home at four or fiveish," she said.

"Oh, I'm sorry to disturb you then," he looked at her with

puppy dog eyes, "I just wanted to collect something from him, I'm on my way to work, I work with Robbie. I'll call later. Ciao."

He turned to walk away. Victoria thought for a second, "Hold on...sorry what's your name again?"

He turned and held out his hand, "DeSouza, Martin DeSouza." She took it and heard herself say, "Victoria Valentine." She paused, "Aren't you the chap that rescued Robbie when he was mugged?"

Now it was his turn to blush, "Only helping a mate." He seemed embarrassed.

"That's not what Robbie told me. He said you were like a professional. Kickboxing is it?"

He shuffled from foot to foot, "Yes, Mugendo."

She thought he held her hand for a little too long but she shook off the feeling, "Why don't you come in for a coffee and I'll call Robbie, see if I can find whatever you need." She surprised herself with her forwardness.

"If it's no trouble," he smiled.

She opened the door wider and gestured for him to come in, "Robbie will be pleased to hear that the man who rescued him is now protecting me."

Marty walked slowly into the hall, and looking about said, "Protecting, you don't need protecting."

"But isn't there a security alert with that criminal in the hospital. Robbie told me that security had told everyone to be on the lookout for suspicious activity around families of staff. Something about threats to members of the surgical team and his gang also." She was busily putting the few groceries away into the cupboards. Marty was still standing in the door of the kitchen. "What was Robbie up to?" he thought to himself. Victoria answered that one for him, "Robbie wants me to take the kids and leave town for the weekend. Did you ever hear the like?" she laughed quietly. "He reads too many spy books," she said over her shoulder.

Marty though about it for a second, "Oh yeah, security are giving everybody a hard time in the hospital." He was as non-committal as possible.

She filled and switched on the kettle, "Tea or coffee?" she asked.

"Coffee's good," he answered and sat down. Victoria fussed about the kitchen gathering cups, milk and sugar. She spooned coffee into two cups and poured boiling water into the cups and pushed one across towards Marty. "Where do you work in the Clinic?" she asked.

He switched into his famous chat up mode and within five minutes she was eating out of his hand. "So where are you heading for the weekend?" he asked.

"Oh, Robbie went on about heading to my sister in Galway."

He went with that. "I love the west," he said, "where is her place?"

After a couple of minutes, he had all the details of where Victoria was taking the kids for the weekend.

A flush of guilt came over Victoria as she realized that she was sitting in her own kitchen, flirting like mad with a hunk with the body of Adonis and the looks and charm of George Clooney. She stood up, "I better call Robbie before the neighbors start talking." Walking towards the phone in its cradle on the wall, she noticed that it was after twelve. She was shocked. She had been sitting talking non-stop for over an hour. That was the effect that Marty had on her. He seemed genuinely interested in her and anything she spoke about. She had rambled on about the kids, school and other mindnumbingly boring stuff to most people, but he had sat and listened politely. He laughed at her silly stories about the kids and gave some stories of his own about his childhood days in Spain with his grandparents. She lifted the phone from the cradle and dialed Robbie's office number.

Marty sat in the kitchen watching Victoria fussing about like a mother hen. He had to admit it, his charm was irresistible. Pity that he couldn't spend a bit more time here, especially that she had said that she wasn't expecting Robbie home until four or five-ish. He began to undress her in his mind. Normally he wouldn't go for older women, but she was gorgeous, and he had detected more than a little flirting on her behalf. She obviously kept herself in shape and it showed. Maybe he would turn up the heat a little, enjoy a little reward for the past few weeks of boredom shadowing her husband. "No!" he slapped himself back to reality.

He had passed on the message that Robbie had contacted Mulligan's people. Marty still wasn't quite sure what was going on. He had guessed that Brennan would make a move on Mulligan and it became clear that his position as a porter in the Southwestern Clinic would serve that end. Robbie had obviously been dragged into this and Brennan obviously had Robbie by the balls, otherwise, why would he co-operate? Marty still couldn't quite work out what they expected Robbie to do, and how. Brennan's instruction after hearing of the contact with Mulligan was to visit Robbie's home and find out what information he had and to get it from him by using his wife as leverage. Robbie was smart, he seemed to have figured out quite a lot already. The question was, what would he do with the information? Marty had been sent to Robbie's house to ensure that he did absolutely nothing with it. "Well," thought Marty, "there's more than one way to skin a cat." Instead of using the sledgehammer approach as so many of Brennan's crew had on many occasions, he had simply charmed her and had gotten much more information than any of the goons would have. When he accidentally gave Robbie the loan of a Lighthouse pen, he had given himself a bollicking. He had blown his cover as one of the good guys, and he was sure that Robbie now knew that he was working for Brennan. Now Victoria was about to call Robbie and he would have to make some move then. The genie would surely be released then. Pity, he was beginning to like Robbie. He was smart and likeable, especially now that he had met Victoria. Could have been the beginning of a beautiful friendship.

The phone in Robbie's office rang out and onto the answering machine. Victoria hung up without leaving a message. "He's not in his office, I'll call his mobile," she announced over her shoulder. She had enjoyed the coffee and the small interlude from her routine, but now it was heading for lunchtime and she would have to make tracks to pick up Nick from Montessori school. Marty didn't seem to be in a hurry to leave and she didn't want to be rude. She decided that if she couldn't contact Robbie on his mobile, to find out what it was that Marty was looking for, she would offer to drop him to a Dart station. She hit the speed dial button for Robbie's mobile and after two rings the phone answered.

43

AFTER HANGING UP the phone from Mulligan's people I leaned against the wall for a couple of minutes thinking. I had set something in motion now and I had to let it play out. I pushed the door open and headed back towards my office. As I approached the door, I could hear the phone ringing. I hurried towards my office and as I opened the door, the ringing stopped. The message light didn't come on so there was no point in looking for a message. I sat down at my desk and put my head in my hands. "Lord, where was this going to end," I let out a heavy sigh.

After two minutes, I felt a vibration in my pocket. I jumped when I realized that it was my mobile. I nervously retrieved it from my scrubs pocket. "Home" was flashing in time to the vibration. I noticed that the battery indicator had only two bars left. I plugged the phone into the charger that was permanently on my desk and hit the answer key. "Hi babes," I said in an upbeat tone. No point in sharing my misery.

"Hi Rob," she sounded in good form, "how're things going there?"

I needed to free myself up for a few extra hours to do what I had to. I had spun a few yarns to Victoria recently and was feeling guilty as hell. However, on I went again. "Great, nearly finished," I started, "but I need to go over to the college library. I've been asked to put together some lectures for the new batch of Nurses," again, I was surprised how easily the lies came, "shouldn't be much later than four."

She replied in a bubbly voice, "I have a friend of yours from work here. He's keeping me company for a bit."

My stomach tightened a notch. Shit, had she been talking to someone about the security situation? If so, then she would cop on that what I had told her was fifty percent bullshit and then it would really hit the fan. "Who is it?" I asked tentatively.

"The chap who rescued you from that mugging a few weeks ago." My stomach immediately did a somersault, "Marty?" I asked quietly. "Yeah, quite a guy," she sounded impressed. I had to physically swallow the bile that was rising in my throat.

"What's he doing there?" I managed to ask without my voice breaking.

"He said he dropped by to pick up something from you?" Without saying another word, I knew what he wanted. He was the one who was shadowing me in the hospital. He must have checked my computer and found out that I was investigating Lighthouse and he was now sitting in my house with my wife. There was only one reason he was there and that was that he had realized that I had spotted the Lighthouse pen and now knew that he was involved. Visiting my house was ensuring that I would still co-operate. Victoria was in good form, I hope this meant that he was keeping his mouth shut and threatening me with his presence instead of actually doing anything. The image of him punching the bloke who was involved in mugging me sent shivers up my spine and a fresh round of nausea into my stomach as I realized what he could possibly do to Victoria and the kids. Shit! The kids! I looked at my watch, ten past twelve. Victoria would need to pick up the kids. She would need to leave soon to pick up Nick. Marty wasn't going to let her go if he was looking for something from me. "Put him on," the phone went silent for a second.

"Robbie, how're you doing today?" Marty's voice came on

the line. A surge of anger rose inside me and I fought to regain control, "What the fuck are you doing in my house?" I spat out with venom.

He replied as if he wasn't listening, and he didn't want Victoria to hear the exchange between us. "Yeah, great Robbie, just dropped over to pick up that research stuff you were doing the other day on Succamethonium, oh and if you have those insurance details you found on the net, I'd appreciate it."

If I wasn't sitting, I would have fallen down. My knees nearly buckled. He obviously had searched my computer and found out that I was researching Lighthouse. Now I knew what he wanted, anything I had dug up on Lighthouse. I was speechless, "If you lay a finger on Victoria, or any of my kids, I'll..."

He interrupted me as if I wasn't there. "Hey Robbie, Victoria was telling me that security were giving you grief as well about this Mulligan case," he spoke as if he was having a perfectly normal conversation, "yeah, they told me that it was very important to follow their instructions and if we suspected anything, to go to the head of the security company and he would liaise with the police...strange isn't it...you work for ages in a place and you think you know what's going on. Anyway, if you could get that stuff to me, everything will be fine. I'll be in the area for a bit, I'll keep an eye out for Victoria and if she gets scared, I'll be close. Don't worry about a thing. Ciao, see you later."

I just managed to spurt out, "Put Victoria on...please." Victoria's voice came back on the line. "You OK babes?" I said quietly. "Yeah sure, why, everything OK there?"

I couldn't think of anything to say that wouldn't arouse Marty's suspicion. Also Victoria was in good spirits and, I felt that keeping her there would be better when she picked up the kids so I said, "Take care love. I'll finish up here as quick as I can and get home, OK pet?"

The anger and frustration was boiling over inside me now and I had to take a few deep breaths to calm myself down. I weighed up the situation. Marty had told me loud and clear what he wanted: all the information I had on Lighthouse. He had also sent me the most powerful message yet, he was inside my house, and he could get there with relative impunity. Time was running out fast, and this latest twist put a new urgency into things. He had only mentioned the internet stuff and not the emails or faxes. I wondered if I could assume that they were safe.

I ran to the changing room and my locker. As I was unlocking it, I remembered from the books I had read, the relatively simple task of marking a door or drawer so as you could tell if it had been interfered with. It involved placing a small marker like a piece of paper in some hidden location inside the door fitting or some place that would be disturbed if the door was breached. It would fall out and upon your return; you could tell immediately if the door or whatever had been interfered with. I heaved a sigh of relief when I saw the A4 envelope still standing to the side of the locker. However I kicked myself for not marking the locker so I could tell if it had been disturbed or not. I removed the full A4 envelope, rolled it up and placed it into the back pocket of my scrubs. Before I closed the locker, I looked around for a piece of paper. I found a scrap of paper in the pocket of my lab coat. I folded it over two or three times and placed it under the door of the locker and closed over the door holding the piece of paper so it was hidden between the door and the base of the locker. It couldn't be seen unless you bent down and peered in through the gap between the door and base. Testing my "marker" I opened the locker. The piece of paper fell out onto the floor. This was what I wanted to happen. If anyone opened the locker, I would know if the piece of paper was missing. Heading back to my office, I thought hard about what I could do now. I hoped that Victoria would be OK. I felt that they wouldn't attempt anything until after the surgery was complete and they were sure that they had or hadn't got what they wanted. Marty had said that he would be "in the area" and not with her. But I had to assume that he knew her plans and would be closely watching, especially considering his remarks during the one way conversation. I decided to change and leave the hospital. If I needed to get anywhere fast, at least I would be ready. I closed down the computer and walked towards the changing room.

As I entered the changing area, my mobile started vibrating again. Pulling it quickly from my lab coat, I didn't recognize the number. Looking around for a suitable place, I ducked into a storeroom and pressed the answer button. "Robbie Valentine?" said a gruff voice. "Yeah, who's this?" I answered back as assertively as I could. "None of your fucking business who I am. The question is what the fuck are you talking about, something heavy going down during the surgery tomorrow?"

He was quite obviously up for a fight but I wasn't going to reveal anything until I was sure I was talking to someone high up the food chain. "Listen," I pushed on with as much sincerity as I could put into my voice, "no disrespect, but I need to know that I am talking to someone quite senior. The information I possess is, let's say...quite explosive. It needs to get to the top, soonest."

There was a silence, and it sounded like he had his hand over the phone and was consulting with a colleague. There was a minute or two of further muttering. I began to sweat about the battery in my mobile now on top of everything else. The last thing I needed now was my battery dying just at a crucial moment. A different voice came on, "Mick Holland here. You can talk to me. What the fuck's going on?"

He sounded older and more in control and I hoped that this was the same Mick that Celtic boy had said was running the show. I desperately wanted to spill all, but I needed to be very sure and set up a safe meeting somewhere. I decided to half tell. "I know for a fact that there is a plan to sabotage the surgery tomorrow," I blurted out.

"What the fuck?" was the inevitable reply. "You heard me,

and I have proof of who's behind it." I waited for a minute. "Who's involved in this? Get that information to me fucking now!" he raised his voice.

I lowered my voice and it had the effect of calming him down, "I need to talk face to face to you or whoever is in charge straight away."

He paused for a second and then asked, "Where are you now? I'll send someone to pick you up."

The last thing I wanted was a member of Mulligan's crew coming to pick me up under the noses of Brennan's goons while Marty was within spitting distance of Victoria and the kids. "No, I'll come to you. Tell me where, anywhere within reason, I'm not driving."

He was silent for a second, "There's an amusement arcade beside the music centre on Vicar Street. You know it?" I said I did, at least I remembered one that I noticed two years earlier at a gig in Vicar Street. "There's a snooker hall above it. Be there at two, OK?"

I looked at my watch, twelve twenty. That gave me over an hour and a half to do what I had to. "OK, see you there," I pressed the call end button and checked the battery, three bars. The short boost had pushed it up a notch. I left the storeroom and re-entered the changing room. Opening the locker, my marker piece of paper fell out, at least that was working. I changed quickly and as I was repositioning my marker, I had a thought. I opened the locker again and, after first checking that there was nobody about, I fished the stun gun out from the back of the locker. I placed it in the inside pocket of my rain jacket and put the A4 envelope over it. I had no other means of protection and I hoped to God that I didn't need to use it, shit, I didn't even know if it would work, but it made me feel a little better. I slipped back into my office and took a fresh battery from the store cupboard. Using a fifty cent piece, I clicked open the Tazer and fitted the fresh nine-volt battery. Snapping it shut, I placed it in the outside pocket of my jacket.

I thought it was ironic that the batteries we used in temporary pacemakers fitted the stun gun. I hoped I wouldn't have to put it to the test. I checked the envelope that was inside my jacket. Thinking about it for a second, I took out the copy of the Lighthouse letter to Reddy underwriting Mulligan's surgery. Also the photo of Reddy talking to the character I assumed was Brennan. I put them in a separate smaller envelope and closed it over without sealing it. Placing it in the inside pocket, I looked around for somewhere to put the A4. I had decided not to bring any more information with me, hoping that the letter and pictures would be enough to get what I needed. I slipped it behind a filing cabinet and left the office.

I took the lift to the ground floor. In the lift, standing opposite me was a patient in a dressing gown. He was reading the Irish Times. I glanced over towards him and read the headlines. Casually looking over the front page as he held it open to read the inner pages, I saw an article about the crime journalist, William Livingston. He was being threatened with charges of contempt of court for not revealing a source. It was in connection with a gangland murder and he had been subpoenaed as a witness for the prosecution as apparently one of the gang involved in the murder had told Livingston the whole story. He had staunchly defended his right to protect his source, and the murder trial was being delayed as a result of his refusal to co-operate. NUJ spokesman, Eamon O'Leary had come out in support of Livingston and gave a long statement. As I strained to read it, the door opened and the patient closed up his paper and stepped out into the lobby. The story made me think if I was about to do the right thing. Perhaps I would rethink some aspects of my crude plan. I strolled across the lobby and past two uniformed Gardai. I exited the hospital into the late autumn sunshine. It was sunny but cool and I zipped up my jacket. I knew I needed to be extra vigilant for tails. Me visiting Mulligan's crew could be suicide or cause one of Brennan's goons to do something to Victoria or the kids. The thought of

Marty sitting in my kitchen chatting with Victoria sent a fresh burst of anger through me and I walked with renewed vigour. As I walked away from the hospital, I immediately noticed two men appear from a doorway and falling into step behind me. "Here we go," I thought to myself.

One, a short wiry, dirty looking character with a filthy woolly jumper full of holes over a pair of dirty grey trousers and his mate, an older clean shaven man with eyebrow, nose and both ears pierced. As I was crossing the road, I glanced at them. They made no attempt to hide the fact that they were following me. This was strange, normally they would have looked anywhere except at me, while trying to look like they were interested in everything and anything except what I was doing or where I was going. They stared at me and kept walking.

I upped my pace slightly heading towards the LUAS station. There were about twenty five or thirty people waiting at the station. I approached a group of people and stood beside them. My two mates shaped up and stood about ten feet from me. They menacing presence was making me nervous and they made no attempt to disguise the fact that they were watching me. After a minute or two, they moved closer to me. The crowd I had initially approached looked at the two lads and moved away. Scruffy jumper moved next to me as Mr. Piercings took up a sentry style guard in front of me facing outwards.

"Mr. Brennan wants to see you," Scruffy said.

I ignored him, while trying to control my fear and focus on a pebble on the ground in front of me.

"Hey, Valentine, I'm fucking talking to you," he persisted.

I continued to ignore him. I had my hands in my pockets and I wrapped my hands around the Tazer. He started to get agitated and shuffle from foot to foot. He moved closer to me and repeated his order, "You're fuckin coming with us now to see Mr. Brennan," he said through bared teeth. He was on my left side and the Tazer was in my right jacket pocket. I needed to get him on my right side if I was going to use the stun gun. I had played with the Tazer after I acquired it and, with a small bit of internet searching, I figured out the basic operation of the gadget. There was a two point switch. Switching to the first point charged and primed the device. The second point released the charge. When the device was charging, it let out a high pitched whine. Just like the flash on a camera charging. If you knew what it sounded like, it would be a dead giveaway. I had acquired it from one of these goons so I assumed that all of them knew what it would sound like and knew how to use one. "See an opportunity and take it," one of the mantras of the SAS came to mind. A truck carrying building waste passed slowly grinding its gears as it tried to get purchase on the road to overcome the inertia of its load as it slowly built up speed. I immediately pressed the switch to the charge position. The bone crunching grinding of the trucks gears blew any chance of the high pitched whine being overheard. I was aware that I was taking a huge gamble as there was no way I could check if the charge light was on and the noise of the truck had drowned out any sound. So I didn't know if the thing was going to fire if required. I looked up at Scruffy, and turned towards him. "What'd you say?" I said, trying to look stupid and as small a threat as possible.

He rolled his shoulders as if squaring up for a fight and stepped so close to me, I could smell his rancid breath and the overpowering whiff of Lynx body spray barely covering his wicked BO. He leaned in towards me so our faces were almost touching, "I fuckin said you're fuckin coming with us to see Brennan."

I stepped away and slightly to my left. He stepped in closer to me and our bodies touched. "I'm going nowhere mate," I muttered.

He pushed me with his left side and, inside my pocket I raised my hand with the Tazer. I pushed it out into the lining of my jacket and into his arm as hard as I could. He took this as a challenge and met my push with a counter push. When you press a stun gun against an assailant and activate the trigger, the charge passes into the attacker's body. Since it has a fairly high voltage, the charge will pass through skin and, I hoped I had read this right, heavy clothing. Mr. Piercings was still in his sentry mode and wasn't aware of any of this. Something like a red light flashed in my head, and it was screaming, "opportunity!!" I took a deep breath and fired the Tazer. The batteries supplied electricity to the circuit consisting of various electrical components. The circuitry included multiple 56 transformers, which boosted the voltage in the circuit, from a harmless nine volt battery to a stunning 50,000 volts. In less than a second this was dumped into Scruffy's nervous system. The charge from the Tazer became mixed with the normal electrical signals in his muscles and nerves. This made it very difficult for his brain to decipher any messages. I felt him twitch. Removing my left hand from my other pocket, I felt a small sting. The type you would get from a car if you were wearing nylon and you touched one of the doors after a long drive. I suddenly realised that my eyes were closed. I opened them and saw Scruffy shaking like he was having an epileptic fit. My eyes were like saucers watching him shake uncontrollably. I looked him up and down and noticed a large wet stain spread out around his groin area, he had pissed himself. He crumpled to the ground.

His mate turned and looked at us. His expression changed immediately when he saw his partner in a crumpled heap on the ground. "What the fuck?" he exclaimed.

"Don't know, I think he's had a fit," I said and without hesitating I went to run. Deep furrows appeared in his brow as he realised that something was wrong. He blocked my way and went to place his hand into his pocket. "Oh Jesus," I thought, "he's got a gun." He was about six feet from me and starting to move. Instinct took over; I raised my right elbow up so as it was out in front of me at shoulder level and I started to run towards him. The red mist descended. I wasn't fully aware what I was doing. He was still watching his mate on the ground and I wasn't sure what he was going to withdraw from his jacket pocket.

I charged towards him and gripping my right wrist with my left hand, I put my full seventy eight kilos behind the charge. My right elbow smashed into the right side of his face. He fell backwards and hit the ground like a sack of shit. I looked back at Scruffy, he was starting to come around. His mate was rolling around the ground clutching his face. I came back to reality and without hesitation, I ran as fast as I could away from the LUAS station. I hared towards town, parallel to the tram lines. After about two or three hundred yards, I slowed and looked back. Scruffy was being helped to his feet by his mate who was still clutching his face and looking decidedly wobbly on his feet. I turned and kept running. Looking to my right, I bolted across the tracks and the street narrowly missing a taxi and ran up a side street. Turning left, I ran parallel to the main street and the tram tracks.

After about ten minutes running, I stopped for breath. Ducking into a newsagent, I bought a large bottle of water. I used the time to rehydrate myself and check that I had made it away from my two latest fans. There seemed to be no-one following me. I tried to cool myself down by opening my jacket. My hand bumped against the Tazer. I had no idea how many shots you could get out of a new battery, so after leaving the shop. I stood in the hall of one of those houses that has offices or usually a hairdresser upstairs. The hallways fitted the same design pattern, dirty lino, drab magnolia paint and filthy curtains. I was becoming quite the expert now, I quickly opened the Tazer and fitted a new battery. After snapping it shut, I placed it back inside my jacket pocket. I was still quite warm so I left my jacket off and carried it draped over my arm. I left the hallway and strolled back on to the street. Checking every few metres, I headed in the direction of Suir Road. After a few hundred metres, I came upon Suir Road LUAS station.

There was no-one waiting there so I checked the timetable. Checking my watch, it was ten to one. I had just missed a tram so I decided to keep walking. Standing alone at a station was a dead giveaway if anyone was checking the LUAS route. I crossed to the pavement and continued on a zig-zag route towards Rialto.

After about ten minutes, walking along Tyrconnell road, I passed the large imposing building of the Oblates Church. Once a magnificent building, it was suffering from the indignity of large wrought iron gates welded between the gothic pillars at its entrance. These gates were locked as soon as mass was over. The car park surrounding the church was permanent home to two or three burnt out cars. The broken glass strewn about was vivid testimony to the hard times that the area had undergone. The Celtic tiger had all but missed this area. Today the car-park was packed with mourners. As I passed the church yard, a funeral service seemed to be finished and the mourners were gathering in groups engaging in the great Irish tradition of sympathising with the family. There was a serious amount of bling about. Gold and silver glittered on black leather and silk. Whoever this was, he was popular and important, or else it was important to be seen there. Groups stood smoking and chatting as a chain gang of funeral directors carried wreaths of flowers from inside the church and placed them on top of the coffin. There was a small fortune in flowers. One of the more striking floral displays was a six letter display. Each letter was made entirely of flowers and spelt out the word, "SPIDER." In a different time I would have laughed. Suddenly my memory tugged at me. Something was trying to get out from my memory. I also noticed a young dark man whom I recognised. I couldn't quite place him but I knew I knew him. He was talking to a group of men while holding a notebook and occasionally jotting notes in it, standing to the side of the church, he seemed slightly out of place but strangely at home with the group of men. Then, like a bolt of lightning, I remembered both the dark man and the "SPIDER" reference. It was the funeral of Spider Sheehan, the senior trustee of Mulligan, and the dark chap was Livingston, the crime correspondent of the times. "Jesus, how coincidental is this?" I asked myself. Then I began to think and the scene in front of me gave me, possibly the best idea I had had since this whole mess began.

I had to contain myself from running over to talk to Livingston but it was neither the time nor the place. I rejoined the LUAS line on Suir road and heard the bell of the tram coming behind me. I double timed it to the tram station and leapt aboard without buying a ticket. There were six or seven other passengers on the tram and I studied them all closely. After ten minutes, the LUAS pulled into the grounds of Holy Trinity University Hospital, my old stomping ground. I decided to exit the tram and walk the rest of the way. It would give me a chance to check for tails and also time to get my thoughts together. I fought my way through the oncoming crowd, all fighting to board the tram. Eventually I was able to walk freely along the concourse area of the hospital and out towards Thomas Street. As I passed the front entrance of the hospital, I noticed the security desk. I had worked there and passed that desk hundreds of times over the years I worked there. Today however, I noticed something that I had missed every time I had passed the security man; his Lighthouse Security Services uniform.

I walked a roundabout way down St. James Street, down past the old Dr. Steevens hospital. Checking behind me all the time, I strolled along by the Liffey, I turned right up Watlin Street and back onto Thomas Street. Fifteen minutes later, I approached Vicar Street. As I turned onto the street, I could see a sign for the snooker hall three blocks beyond the concert venue. There were two or three characters standing outside smoking. I paused and put my jacket back on, feeling the Tazer inside my jacket, a sudden panic came over me, what if they search me? I paused and stared at the list of upcoming concerts. After a minute, appearing satisfied I turned and headed back onto Thomas Street. I walked about a hundred metres towards Christchurch and stopped at a Dublin City Council bin. Waiting until there was a gap in the pedestrian traffic, I quickly removed the Tazer and stuffed it into the bin, out of sight. I felt a mix of relief and fear. I had lost my only weapon, but I had been terrified for the entire time I carried it.

I turned back and walked back towards Vicar Street. The group had dispersed and I approached the entrance to the snooker "emporium." Stepping inside the dark hall, I noticed a flight of stairs heading up. There were no other doors or routes, so I slowly walked up towards, oblivion, annihilation, salvation? I didn't know what. The stairs ended abruptly on a landing where there was a door which was locked. An intercom was positioned to the left of the door. I pressed the call button and waited. "Members only today," a rough voice barked.

"Robbie Valentine here," I answered, and not knowing what to say next, I came out with, "I have an appointment." As soon as I said it, I regretted it.

"What for, a fuckin perm? This is a snooker club," was the response with audible laughter behind the voice.

Anger starting rising again and I raised my voice, "Tell Mick Holland Valentine is here, right!" There was a silence and after about thirty seconds, a beep and a loud click sounded. The door opened about an inch. I pushed the door inwards and the first thing to greet me was a cloud of smoke. No smoking bans in operation here. My eyes slowly adjusted to the semi darkness.

There were about ten full size snooker tables spread out in the large rectangular room. Two tables were lit up with games under way but the rest of the tables were just black shapes in the semi darkness. There was a badly constructed counter/bar at one end with an office behind it. A large ugly shape leaned on the counter counting out a mountain of one and two euro coins. I stopped and looked at him. Without raising his head from his task, he nodded in the direction of the office behind him. I raised a section of counter top and walked inside. I entered "the office." It was a room with a desk and chair. The desk sported a computer. On one side of the room was a kitchen sink and cupboards with the standard kettle, bag of sugar and litre of milk.

A morbidly obese, bald man with a pencil moustache sat behind the desk punching keys on the computer keyboard. A second man appeared from behind the door where I saw the other end of the intercom was. I tried to gain control from the outset, "Which one of you is Holland?" I announced.

The fat man looked up at me over reading glasses and arched his eyebrows. His expression quickly changed to a scowl and he answered, "I am, why, what's the problem?" His mate, a well dressed man in his late thirties wearing an expensive shirt over beige chinos moved towards me and sat on the edge of the desk.

"I'm Robbie Valentine. I spoke with you earlier."

Fatboy closed whatever he was working on and looked up. "What's this all about?" he asked.

"I know that something heavy is planned for tomorrow during Mr. Mulligan's operation," I started. I was very unsure about how to proceed so I treaded carefully.

"What do you mean something heavy?" asked Chinos.

I paused, trying to find the most efficient way of explaining things, "There's a plan to sabotage the operation."

Chino snorted, "How can you fuckin sabotage an operation?" He was silenced by a wave of Fatboy's hand. "Have you told anybody about this?" he asked.

"No," I lied, "who'd fucking believe me?"

Fatboy sat up, "Good, now what information do you have that proves your theory?" He became all businesslike.

"Someone is in a position to cause problems during the surgery tomorrow that could mean that Mr. Mulligan will never wake up again." I relaxed a tad, having lightened my load a little.

"You certain about this?" Fatboy asked.

"Oh yeah, quite sure," I answered.

"And do you know who's behind it?" Fatboy inquired again. Chino went to say something, but Fatboy's hand did the trick again.

"Let's say, I know who's responsible for giving the order, and also who's going to do the business," I said as vaguely as possible.

He paused for a minute looking thoughtful. "Have you proof of this?" he asked eventually.

"I have some proof, yes that could make life very difficult for the...organisers." I struggled to find terms that were generic enough.

Again he looked thoughtful, "Do you have it with you?"

I patted the side of my jacket, "Yes, right here."

"What have you got?" he asked.

His lack of urgency concerned me a bit. "I know that someone was able to organise that Mr. Mulligan would have his heart operation in the specific hospital on a specific day by a specific surgeon. He has also organized that a member of the team be placed to sabotage the procedure...operation so as Mr. Mulligan will most probably be brain damaged after and never wake up...remain in a coma."

Chino's eyes were like saucers. "What the fuck? How the fuck could he organize that?...Who's the bastar..." He was silenced by Fatboy's hand again.

"I know for a fact and have proof that John Brennan is behind this, and the Surgeon is working with him." Fatboy closed his eyes and shook his head. Chino stood up and clenched his fists. "Bastard!" he shouted, "Let me take a bunch of the lads and teach that prick a lesson." He was gunning for action. "Sit the fuck down!" Fatboy ordered. Chino looked at him questioningly and put his ass back on the desk. "Story Boss?" Chino asked in a shaky voice.

Fatboy looked at me, "Do you have this proof with you, and

can I assume that you are the staff member who is supposed to carry out the task?"

I shrank physically, "Yeah, it's me. I'm supposed to do it."

He rubbed his chin. Chino straightened up and glared at me. Fatboy asked, "What has Brennan got on you?"

I felt like crying. "A serious gambling debt and he can get to my wife and kids anytime." He was silent for a minute or two. Chino looked from me to Fatboy and back a dozen times. I was sure he would have taken me out the back and shot me with the slightest nod from his boss. I went to reach inside my jacket to take out the envelope but immediately Chino leapt to his feet, "Hey, slow down there." I froze, and realized that he didn't want me putting my hands out of sight and retrieving God knows what. He reached over and put his hand into my inside pocket and brought out the envelope. I was glad that I had dumped the Tazer.

He handed the envelope to Fatboy who opened and took out the photograph and the copy of the letter from Lighthouse. "The chap in the navy blazer is the surgeon. I think the other man is Brennan."

Fatboy nodded. "I presume this isn't the only copy," was all that he said.

I was a bit puzzled now. He didn't seem at all surprised by the information, and wondering about the only copy worried me. "I copied the information to a floppy disc and deleted it from my computer," I embellished the truth. Something was screaming at me that all wasn't as it seemed.

Chino was getting very impatient by now. "What're we gonna do about it Boss?" he asked. I almost added, "Yeah what are you going to do about it?" I was anxious to hear what Fatboy's next move was going to be. "Nothing, we're going to do nothing right now," Fatboy said with authority. I felt as surprised as Chino looked. "What're you talking about boss?" Chino exclaimed. He was verbalizing exactly what I was thinking. "I'll go and talk to a few people and find out what's going on," Fatboy explained.

"But...but, the surgery is tomorrow," I stuttered in a panic now. I was hoping that confronting Mulligan's crew with this information would bring a swift result. I was wrong. There was definitely something amiss here.

The sound of the counter section slamming back down made all three of us look up. "Ah Mickey...story Sweetie?" two or three voices said one after another. A very young looking chap entered the room. He addressed Fatboy first, "Mick, story Bud?"

Fatboy gave an uncomfortable "Oh Mickey, how're you?" The young chap looked strange. He looked very underdeveloped. He was underweight and quite obviously undersized for his age. He also looked sick, as if he had kidney or liver disease. Chino looked at him and nodded, "Mickey, how'd the hospital go?"

Mickey looked up and said, "The usual shite, don't do this, don't do that, all that bollix." He stared at me for a moment and nodded a greeting. He strolled over to the kitchen area and lifted up the kettle.

There was an awkward silence for a moment or two. I had a niggling feeling that I had seen Mickey somewhere before, but I couldn't place it. Fatboy started talking again, "I'm gonna look into this now and find out what the fuck is going on, OK. I don't want to start a war on the streets by rushing into anything."

I was only half hearing him. What had caught my attention was the very strong smell of maple syrup that had drifted around the room. The sense of smell is many times more powerful at evoking memories than any of the other senses. My subconscious memory was screaming and slowly I began to realize what was going on. Mickey had put the kettle down and was turning to look at me. The smell of maple syrup had been in my house after Victoria had received that rogue phone call, in my car after the sticker on the steering wheel incident and I had definitely seen this Mickey chap before.

As Fatboy rambled on, the scientific, analytical part of

my brain was working overtime. I remembered a lecture I was at years before on genetic conditions. The lecturer gave extreme examples of different conditions: *"an inherited error in the metabolism of leucine, isoleucine and valine...branched chain ketoacid dehydrogenase...Deficiency of this enzyme system causes the sweet odour of maple syrup in body fluids, especially urine and sweat...Maple Syrup Urine Disease is an extremely rare inherited metabolic disorder characterized by a distinctive sweet odour of the urine and sweat."* I was staring at Mickey. A light slowly came on in my head, probably at the same time as it was flickering in Fatboy's. Had he just realised that I had copped on? Fatboy was working with Brennan to get rid of Mulligan...Sweet Jesus! I was screwed now.

44

FATBOY WAS LOOKING from Mickey to me and back. He dismissed Mickey and Chino with a wave of his hand, "Eddie, Mickey, give us a minute here and close the door." I don't know if I was more nervous with or without the two of them present. He had a look of intense concentration on his face. I didn't know if I was being carried away with paranoia but I thought I read in his face that he realized I was now switched on. Mickey was obviously the go-between. Chinos' demeanour and reaction to Fatboy's suggestions all reinforced my conclusion. Chino was gunning for a big showdown; Fatboy was having none of it. Now the playing field had changed. If Fatboy was Mulligan's deputy and was in league with Brennan, then the only explanation was that there was a coup attempt underway. Brennan and Fatboy were in bed together. If Fatboy knew that I was switched on to this, then one phone call is all it would take and Marty would be told to make a move on Victoria. I nearly got weak when I thought of her and the kids. I needed to get out of there fast and do something. Now I was fighting on two fronts.

Fighting to stay calm I looked at my watch, "I need to check on my wife and kids." I patted my pockets looking for my mobile. Looking at Fatboy, his expression was a mix of puzzlement and concern. He was wondering if I had twigged to what was going on, and was concerned if I did, what was I was going to do. "Will you make some calls please?" I asked in a pleading voice, "The surgery is scheduled for tomorrow. I don't want to have to do anything, but I will if I have to protect my family..." I paused and watched his expression. He visibly relaxed and his voice became softer.

"Listen Robbie," he said, "the last thing I want to do is cause all out war on the streets, Christ there's been enough deaths lately." Watching his body language closely, I nodded as sincerely as I could. "I'll make a few calls and get to the bottom of this and get back to you." He seemed to be having trouble keeping eye contact with me and his eyes were darting all around the room. I guessed that this was a sign that he was lying.

"Will you get back to me as quick as you can, please? I just want to protect my family," I put as much emotion as I could into my voice. I wanted to convince him that I would go ahead with the scheme if I had to.

"Don't worry Robbie," he stood up, "it'll all be over soon" He went to shake hands with me. Something in his expression convinced me that he was lying. I still wasn't happy that he was convinced that I wasn't wise to the arrangement. I couldn't start explaining to him how I could put his boss into a coma as easily as emptying a syringe. If I was right, and he was involved, that's exactly what he would have wanted and if he displayed this, then he was revealing his hand. On the other hand, if I convinced him that I wasn't going to do anything, and he was involved, one phone call is all it would take and Victoria and the kids were in real danger. I had to tread very carefully. I rolled my last dice. He opened the door for me. I closed it over for a second and lowering my voice whispered, "Actually, I have a plan. I can make sure that Mulligan stays asleep for a lot longer than normal so it looks like he is in a coma." I paused.

"Go on," Fatboy's forehead creased up in concentration.

"If I need to, I can do this. There's huge risk. But I think I can manage it if I get the dose right."

He looked down and appeared to be in deep thought for a moment. He looked up at me and said, "Don't worry, we'll sort it."

I stared at him, looking deep into his eyes. I was trying to see into his soul. He held my gaze for a couple of seconds and looked away quickly. "Help me out here please," I pleaded and left the office. I walked out of the snooker without looking back and had to shield my eyes against the daylight. As my eyes adjusted to the brightness, I noticed Chino talking to Mickey. They were standing in the entrance to the concert venue. Eddie was smoking and appeared to be ranting and raving. He was waving his hands about, probably boasting about what he was going to do to me when he was given the go ahead. Mickey looked in my direction. I turned my head quickly and walked back on to Thomas Street. I was desperate to get back to the hospital. I had no doubt that Fatboy would ring Brennan and they would tighten their noose around Victoria and me. More than likely, there were a bunch of goons looking for me now, probably on the way over here right now.

Without thinking I hailed a taxi. A large wine coloured Volkswagon seven-seater stopped in front of me. Looking around me, I checked that there was no-one who looked like they were following me. I climbed into the back seat, "Southwestern Clinic, please. Bit of a hurry, if you can." I sat back and instinctively shrunk down in the seat.

"No problem bud," the driver said. "Bit of bad news, whah?" he attempted to engage me in conversation. I ignored him and took out my mobile and dialed Victoria's number. She answered immediately. "How're you love?" I asked tentatively.

"Good," she answered. I let out a sigh of relief. "The kids are thrilled that they're going to their cousins for the weekend." I relaxed when I heard her talking like this. Tensing up, I asked "What'd you think of Marty?" I wanted to hear that he was gone hours.

"Mmmh, nice guy," she said teasingly, "he didn't stay for long.

He said you're to drop that stuff to him as soon as you can."

At least he wasn't camped out in our house. I knew it wouldn't take long for word to percolate down to the troops that I needed to be watched carefully. "Will you be home soon?" she asked in a voice that made me want to cry.

"I'm on my way back from the college," I said, "should be home by five." I hated this; I had no idea when I would be in a position to get home. I could only hope that some breakthrough would happen soon.

45

MARTY WAS BORED. After having left Robbie's house, he had been contacted again by one of Brennan's goons. He was told to meet two other men in a bar in Ringsend and return to the house. This time, he was told to sit tight in the house until he received further instructions. "How long will I be there?" he had asked.

"Just fuckin sit tight, OK?" was the repeated instruction.

"What the fuck am I going to do there for a couple of hours?" he asked, "Especially with two monkeys in tow."

The voice had laughed, "That's up to you. Just do as you're told, there's a good lad Marty."

The phone went dead. Groaning to himself, he headed to the Seven Bells bar in Ringsend. He half recognised two lads sitting in the bar watching an early afternoon race meeting from somewhere in the UK. One wore a denim jacket over a football strip and the other sported a hoody top. The two freshly shaven heads looked up at Marty. "You Marty?" hoody asked. "I suppose you're my team for the day?" Marty sighed. "Come on, let's move." The trio left the bar and walked through Ringsend, out onto the seafront and along Strand Road. Twenty minutes later they approached the front of Robbie's house and rang the doorbell.

46

THE TAXI PULLED AROUND in front of the main entrance. The usual throngs of patients were shuttling between taxis and ambulances and the main door. Half a dozen or so ambulances were parked in the ambulance bay with teams of drivers and Emergency Medical Technicians standing in groups smoking and drinking cans of Coke. Great advertisement for modern medicine, I thought. "Twelve euro please, bud," the driver announced. Pulling cash from my pocket, I almost let my flash drive fall to the floor of the cab. I'd forgotten that I had it in my pocket. I would've been rightly screwed if I had lost that. Just as I was about to pay him, I noticed two characters standing to the side of the main crowd. They appeared to be scanning the groups coming and going. One with red fuzz for hair turned towards the taxi I was in. His county Meath GAA jersey gave him away. He had followed me onto the LUAS some days earlier. His partner was a bald chap with protruding teeth. He was wearing a tracksuit and I recognized him from town.

I panicked for a second, and then sat back in the seat. "Actually, can you drive around to the service entrance, I'm knackered today," I said to the driver. He shrugged and putting the car in gear again negotiated his way back into the flow of traffic. He was mumbling something as he fought the traffic and got into the right hand turning lane that would bring him around to the back of the hospital. I looked out the rear window and saw tracksuit man still looking into the crowd. The taxi stopped at the service entrance at the back. I gave the driver fifteen euro. "Keep the change, bud," I said and stepped out of the car. Just as the taxi drove away, I turned to head into the service entrance. "Hey, Valentine, prick, don't fuckin move," I looked up and saw Scruffy, the poor bastard who had been on the receiving end of the Tazer, running towards me. He had changed his dirty grey trousers into a pair of blue tracksuit legs. He was running, shouting and trying to text dial his mobile at the same time. Behind him, just rounding the corner was his mate with the multiple piercings. He had a vicious bruise and lump on the side of his face. I stood frozen with fear for a second staring at the two of them. My mobile phone rang, snapping me back to reality. I turned and ran into the service yard. Praying that the security door was open, I ran between a truck delivering linen and a cardboard bailing machine towards the security door. Someone had just come out through the door and it was slowly closing over. "Hold the door!" I screamed.

The Russian cleaner who had just exited, looked at me with wide eyes and turned back catching the door just in time. I dived inside and slammed the door. I ran along the corridor and into the stores area. I became aware that my mobile was still ringing. I stood behind a trolley full of boxes of syringes and retrieved the phone from my pocket. Looking at the number, I saw it was a hospital extension. I guessed it was the ITU, probably looking for something small done to the balloon pump. I hit the answer button. "Hello, Robert?" came a voice I recognised, but couldn't place, "Elaine Mulready here." It was Nathan Richards, my boss's secretary. "Hi Elaine. How're you?"

She seemed uncomfortable. "Good thanks Robert," she got straight to the point, "Nathan wants to see you as soon as possible."

My stomach launched off into its latest favourite sport,

turning somersaults. "I'll make an appointment to see him," I said.

"Actually Robert," she was very serious, "can you come to see him straight away?"

I was taken off guard. "Oh ...em...yeah...sure," I stuttered. "Any idea what it's about?" I inquired.

She avoided the question, "He'll talk to you when you get here, half an hour OK?"

Again I was surprised at the urgency of the order, "Sure, see you then." I headed straight to my office. I closed the door and sat down in front of the computer. Internet privileges pulled, told to stop digging into the EI-TP codes, what the fuck was going on? I became decidedly nervous about the meeting with Nathan. Checking that there was no-one about, I retrieved my flash drive from my pocket. I plugged it in and opened the files that George had faxed me. I browsed them for a second and made a snap decision. I'd had enough of this mess and all the bullshit that was accompanying it. I printed off six copies of everything I had. The letters of referral from Lighthouse to Reddy, Letters on Southwestern Clinic headed paper from accounts outlining the cover, Mulligan's referral letter signed by Reddy, the pictures of Reddy meeting Brennan. All of the documents, including the eTender documents that showed the numbers and types of contracts that Lighthouse were getting. I had to reload the printer at one stage. At five minutes to go to the meeting with Nathan, I stopped the printer, closed the files and removed the flash drive. Gathering up all the printed sheets, I piled them all into an envelope and slid it down behind the filing cabinet. Taking the back stairs up to the administration floor, I knocked on the secretary's door. She opened it immediately and without making eye contact said "Go straight in, Robert." She seemed embarrassed. I was now thoroughly shitting myself. Normally she would engage in small talk, but today, she avoided my eyes like the plague. I went on in to Nathan's office. He was on the phone, talking in a low voice. I couldn't make out what he was saying. I could have sworn I heard him say, "yes, he's here now" but that was probably my paranoia which had gone into overdrive lately. He stood up. He was wearing a lilac Ralph Lauren shirt and a purple tie which was opened at the neck. With his hair unkempt, he looked like a man under extreme pressure. "Robert, sit down," he mimed the words and pointed to a vacant chair in front of his desk. Waiting on him to finish on the phone, I looked around the office. I knew that he spent extraordinary hours here, and the only clue that he had a life outside here was a golfing magazine thrown on to a windowsill. He finished his conversation on the phone and gave me his attention. "Robert..." he began in a very serious voice.

He was deep in thought as if he was working out in his mind how to phrase something, "I spoke to you a couple of days ago about...em...digging into areas of the business side of this hospital that really don't concern you."

I had been half expecting this, and immediately leapt to my defence, "I know, and I stopped digging." He nodded so I pushed on, "I appreciate that there are areas that are, let's say sensitive so I'm...off the case."

He smiled with the phrase. "It appears that you're on a quest to find something that doesn't exist."

I frowned, "What do you mean?"

He interlaced his fingers and placed his hands under his chin, "It seems that you were doing a bit of digging where you shouldn't have been and some people aren't happy about it." He assumed the demeanor of a school head master.

"I was only trying to find out about a bunch of patients who came from the same insurer that accounts hadn't heard of," I stuttered and stammered to defend myself.

He seemed to seize on my discomfort, "Robert, I told you a few days ago that you were to leave that go." He moved his hands down so they covered his mouth, the classic 'speak no evil' monkey position, he was very uncomfortable giving this lecture. "Lighthouse Insurance is none of your business," he blurted out.

"I...I...was only..."I started to try to qualify my defence.

He had been avoiding eye contact with me, but gaining confidence, he looked up at me and changed tack, "There is a strict Internet usage policy here." He seemed to be searching for some foothold.

I was now completely confused. "How can visiting a medical insurance company's website be against Internet usage policy?"

He looked at me over his reading glasses and opened a drawer in his desk. He pulled an A4 sheet of paper with some spreadsheets on it. "I was hoping not to have to do this, but..." He slid the sheet of paper over towards me.

I read the first few rows of the spreadsheet. In the first column was a list of websites, and the second showed times and dates. I recognized the sites, Lighthouse Insurance Services, Companies Registry Office, eTenders. My eyes scanned down the list and stopped suddenly. My head began to swim; listed among the sites visited were about ten pornographic sites. If the titles were anything to go by, the sites were seriously hardcore. All of the pornographic site addresses were highlighted in yellow, and had obviously been checked. "I never went near these sites," I almost shouted, "I'm being set up here!"

He stood up and walked around his desk so he was very close to me. "Robert," he dropped his voice to little more than a whisper, "I know you've been under pressure lately, and we are all human and can easily succumb to temptation..."

I was seething with rage. "I fucking didn't visit those sites," I said through bared teeth.

"Robert," he tried to calm me down, "they were all visited using your username and password, and at times when you were in the hospital, I checked."

I looked back at the list. I noticed 03.22 am, 05.12am. I was well and truly being framed here and it seemed that there was bugger all I could do about it.

Nathan took off his glasses and spoke slowly, "There have been several dismissals in the NHS over this type of conduct."

I looked up incredulously, "What are you saying, am I being sacked?" I asked. My voice began to crack. The first thing I thought of was that if I wasn't in work, Brennan would do... Christ knows what to Victoria and the kids, apart from losing my job, which seemed trivial.

"Robert, whatever you think you've found on Lighthouse and whatever else you think you have, lose it...fast, and maybe...we can overlook this." He raised the A4. My head was spinning and working at a rate of knots. I was being framed here. Someone had definitely hacked into my internet account and set me up with those visits that were all logged to me, someone who knew when I was in at emergencies. I was now rightly buggered. I was in danger of losing my job and reputation as well as everything else. Without acknowledging him any further, I stood up and walked out of his office. All I wanted to do was scream. I had now been told twice by my boss to drop any investigation into Lighthouse. I was being watched and monitored. "What the fuck am I going to do now?" I stopped and placing my head against a wall nearly wept with despair.

46

WALKING ALONG the administration corridor, my head down watching the floor, I made my way back to my office. Passing some of the other senior admin offices, I noticed today's Irish Times folded neatly outside the door of the Finance Manager's office. This meant that he wasn't in today and his paper had been left there. All senior management received a complementary copy of the Times placed outside their office every morning. I remembered the article on William Livingston that I had read in the lift earlier that morning. I looked around and, seeing nobody, I lifted the paper. I read the full article. Refusal to reveal a source! I began to think. My rudimentary plan resurfaced. Pocketing the paper, I ran all the way down the back stairs to my office. If the information that I had put together was so explosive, then it better be handled with extreme care. Using it to get out of the Mulligan plot was obviously going to cause me a river of shit, and probably cost me my job. Not using it and going along with Brennan's plan could put me in jail, not to mention Victoria and the kids. I had to do something.

I burst into my office giving Habib and Nasser a fright. They were reading some angiogram films on the computer. "Oh sorry to disturb you," I said.

Habib stood up, "We are finished here Robert."

I moved to the screen and sat in the seat vacated by Nasser. They left the office, leaving me alone. I think they left out of politeness. Habib left his rain jacket hanging over the chair and his briefcase under the desk.

Firstly I retrieved the envelope from behind the filing cabinet. Opening it, I took out all the copies I had made. I scanned through them all and made a small file containing one copy of each. Plugging in my flash drive again, I checked that I had printed everything that I had received, along with the information I had taken off the Internet from eTenders and the Companies Registries Office. When I had six piles of documents, I put each pile into its own A4 envelope. Opening Word on the computer, I wrote a short letter, giving a brief synopsis of the events so far and after printing six copies, I signed and dated it. A copy went into each envelope. I sealed each envelope and signed and dated the seal. Now I hand wrote a name and address on each envelope. I had received a parcel some weeks earlier with some lecture material. It had come in a large jiffy bag, bigger than an A4 envelope. Being a bit of a magpie, the jiffy bag was still in a drawer. After a few minutes of searching, I found it. Placing the six envelopes inside the jiffy bag, I sealed it with tape and signed and dated the seal. I felt I had just primed a bomb. Now I needed to deliver it to where it would have the greatest effect.

47

VICTORIA WAS MAKING LUNCH for the kids. They were inside watching afternoon kid's television programs. She had finally gotten rid of that Marty chap. He was a looker all right, but he seemed quite happy to sit there until Robbie came home from work. Eventually he left after promising to make Robbie bring whatever package he had belonging to Marty. She had headed to Nick's Montessori and then on to collect Alice. "Who'd like to go to see their cousins in the country this weekend?" had been greeted with shouting and screaming and a million questions about what toys to bring, could they go swimming in the sea, could they milk the cows. She fielded all the questions, as she hadn't called her sister yet.

Cutting Alice's ham sandwiches into triangles and Nick's peanut buttered bread into soldiers, she organized their lunch. She placed a handful of crisps onto the plates and poured Ribena into two cups. Placing the plates and drinks onto a tray, she walked carefully towards the living room. Lunch time after school was a treat and one of the only times in the week when they were allowed eat in front of the television. Just as she crossed the doorway into the hall, the doorbell rang. "Just a minute," she called. Placing the food in front of the kids, she closed the living room door and walked to the halldoor. Seeing three shapes through the frosted glass, she expected it to be freelance gardeners. They tended to call around this time offering major garden renovations at knockdown prices. "Oh," she said, "hi, did you forget something?"

The smiling face of Marty gave her a shock. There were two rather unsavoury characters standing behind him. One wore a hoody top and was smoking; the other had a denim jacket and was paying a little too much attention to the inside of her car.

"Victoria," he said with what sounded like false sincerity, "I spoke to Robbie, and he told us to wait here with you until he got home." A confused look came over her face. Marty placed his foot inside the door and stepped closer. The look of confusion became one of panic,

"I…I don't think…"

Marty looked at her, "Sorry about this Victoria, but we need to wait here till Robbie gets home. It's important. He has some important information for us." He stepped into the hall followed quickly by Hoody and Denim boy. Marty closed the hall door. "We won't get in your way. You just work away as if we weren't here, OK?"

She was so stunned and overcome that she nodded silently. Hoody walked on in towards the living room. Staring at Marty, she was aware of the living room door open and Alice's voice. "Hello, who are you?" Alice asked innocently. This snapped Victoria out of her trance. She walked quickly in towards Alice and sat down on the sofa beside the kids. She was nervous and confused but managed to say, "These men work with Daddy. They are waiting on Daddy to come home from work to talk to collect something." That seemed to satisfy the kids. They went back to watching the TV.

Marty started talking to the kids and in five minutes had them laughing. Victoria relaxed a little. The other two were a little menacing and kept her on edge. She felt a little strange. She decided to try and take an opportunity to call Robbie and see what this was about. She would wait until she was alone in the kitchen. "Anyone want tea?" she asked as bravely as she could.

"Coffee please," Marty answered. "Milk, no sugar." Hoody piped up. "Black and sweet, like me women!" Denim boy came out with before exploding laughing at his own joke. Victoria stood up and headed to the kitchen. No-one followed her so she quickly closed the door and hit the speed dial. The phone rang for an eternity but eventually Robbie answered. "Robbie," she said, sighing with relief. Just as she was about to spill, the chap in the hooded tracksuit walked into the kitchen. Quickly she changed her tone to chatting about the kids.

48

I WAS STILL REELING from the meeting with Nathan when I felt my mobile buzz in my pocket. I answered immediately. It was Victoria. My mind immediately returned to home and the kids. It was ten to four, later than I had expected, but I hoped that I might be on the home stretch. "Robbie," she sounded relieved. "Are you coming home soon?" she pleaded.

"Is everything OK?" I asked with alarm in my voice. "Fine, fine everything's good here," she said unconvincingly. I could hear her walking. She chatted nonsensically for a few seconds about Alice's day at school. "Robbie, Marty's back with two of his mates, and they they're acting strange."

I was flapping now. "What do you mean strange?" I asked. My mouth had dried up.

"They called about a half hour ago and said that you were to bring them something. They said they'd wait here until you got home. They said you knew what they wanted and that you told them to come to the house and wait. Robbie I'm scared." She suddenly started talking a mile a minute about Nick's Montessori school. Somebody had obviously come in to where she was standing.

"Victoria, listen," I tried to sound as in control as possible, "there's something going on and it's something to do with that operation that's scheduled for tomorrow. I'm on the way home, but I need to make a stop on route. It's got to do with your friends there." She was very quiet on the other end and I guessed that she wasn't alone. "I promise everything will be OK and sorted out by the time I get home. OK love?" She gave a weak frightened "OK, see you later." I hung up the phone and shouted "Bastards," punching the wall.

Stuffing the jiffy bag inside my jacket, I checked the battery on my mobile, three bars; it was going to have to do. I knew I was going to have some company as soon as I left the hospital. No doubt Fatboy had contacted Brennan and I was due to be hauled in to be dressed down by Brennan. I had planned to visit Brennan to put a stop to this business, but I was damn sure that I would do it when I was good and ready. So another round or two of lose the tail was going to be called for. I left my office and nipped into the changing room to use the toilet. The stress of the past few hours was telling on my bladder. I used the toilet. Standing washing my hands, I looked in the mirror. I could see dark circles forming under my eyes. I could've done with a shave. Anyway, I was going to meet these scumbags with a view to sorting my life out, not to date them. I looked at my reflection. I was a sorry sight, in my navy blue golf rain jacket. Suddenly an idea hit me. I ran back to my office and was glad to see that Habib hadn't collected his rain jacket. I pulled my own jacket off and lifted Habib's red sporty Kappa jacket off the chair. It was heavy with keys, change and wallet. I took all these out of the pockets and put them in a neat pile. I scribbled a short note to Habib explaining that I borrowed his jacket for a short while. The jacket was a bit on the long side, but it did the job. My fans outside were looking for blue jacket, this red one might give me a head start. Habib's jacket had an inside pocket that my jiffy bomb fitted neatly into. I stepped out onto the corridor and with a renewed sense of purpose, was ready to do battle.

Peter Reddy was at the Cardiology/Surgical angiogram review conference in the University Hospital. This is where all the patients' angiogram films for the previous week were reviewed by a rotating group of the duty cardiologists and surgeons. There were two other surgeons present with Reddy as well as two Cardiologists and a dozen or so junior Doctors. Dr. Martin McDaid was chairing the session. He hit the return key on his laptop. The conference was being held in the lecture room of the Postgraduate research centre of the University Hospital. A state of the art facility, it had been built with funds from a grant from a consortium of medical insurance companies. It had been opened three years earlier by the Minister for Health and Children. The lecture room had a state of the art computer system with monitiors at every seat. This meant that every image projected up onto the main viewing screen was also displayed on the small screen at every seat. This made these types of conferences relatively painless compared to previous ones. It also meant that Reddy could with very little effort take details of the patients who were likely to come his way. The grant from the Insurance was heralded as a new era in Public/private partnerships that was going to bring about major reforms to the ailing health services. Ironically, one of the benefactors to the research fund was Lighthouse Insurance Services. The irony wasn't lost on Reddy.

"*Sixty two year old, male, Short history of Dyspnoea and chest pain on mild exertion. Angio shows sixty per cent left anterior descending block, OM one completely blocked, OM two, seventy per cent, Right looks reasonable, good left ventricular function.*"

Martin McDaid read out the report from his speaker notes. "The blockage in the LAD is too far down to safely attempt Angioplasty," he thought out loud. He was notoriously conservative with his patients and much to the annoyance of a lot of his colleagues he referred a significant number for surgery. Some of the newer Cardiologists he felt were way too gung ho with their enthusiasm to shove catheters inside patients' hearts. In a lot of cases, they ended up going for surgery anyway, so why put off the inevitable. Naturally his unpopularity was more than made up for by the esteem with which the surgeons held him in. He directed his comments at Reddy, "Most likely a Surgical candidate, your list Peter?"

Reddy looked up to where McDaid was sitting two rows ahead. Reddy was busy sending a text message to his secretary, "Oh...Yes...no problem." He hit "send" on his mobile and thrust the phone back into his pocket. He had informed his secretary not to accept any more patients from Lighthouse, having informed her to start reducing the list accordingly. As he was talking to McDaid, his phone gave a gentle bleep indicating that he had an incoming message. McDaid moved on to the next angiogram. "*Forty two year old, normal coronaries. Trans-oesophegal echo shows a Myxomatous mitral valve. Could do well with mitral repair...*" McDaid directed the referral to one of the other surgeons.

Reddy took his phone from his pocket and opened the text message. It was from his secretary. *File with another 20 patients arrived from LH. I called them to say you didn't want anymore. Reply was unrepeatable. A Mr. Brennan said you are to call him.*

Reddy's stomach churned as he read the message. He needed to get away from Brennan and his group. The trouble was that the only way he could see of doing that and staying in Cardiac Surgery didn't appeal to him at all. There were ongoing negotiations between the Department of Health and the various Consultants groups on new types of contracts. One of the contracts on offer was a public only contract. This effectivelly doubled the standard public salary, but meant signing away your rights to private practice during public hours. He had mused long and hard over this and was beginning to think that the only way to dump Brennan and Co. was to accept the new contract on offer. With his present contractual and private arrangements, he was pulling nearly a million a year. Trouble was, he spent frivolously and often and had gotten quite used to the lifestyle. Dropping down to a quarter of that would hurt big time. He groaned to himself and tried to focus on the angiogram on the screen in front of him. It was difficult, "*Reply was unrepeatable,*" sounded in his head. He ran his hands through his hair and sighed heavily, where was he going from here? The conference wrapped up and the Surgeons went their separate ways. The Cardiologists always hung about after and discussed various items. Reddy gave a few monosyllabic responses to greetings from some of the group. He wasn't in the mood for small talk. Having no operating list today, he decided to head home and probably hit a few balls on the driving range: try to clear his head. He strolled out of the lecture hall and headed for the multistory car park. The sight of his Mercedes calmed him. The thought of the major drop in income made him shudder as it could mean that he would have to surrender his precious car.

Sitting in the virtually soundproof cabin, he ran his hands along the walnut dashboard, onto the beige leather of the seats and then, almost sensually, he gently touched the leather sports steering wheel. Flicking on the stereo, the gentle sounds of La Boheme filled the cabin. Relaxing into the soft bucket seats, he pulled the car out onto the street and into the early afternoon traffic. Turning towards Rialto, he drove over the bridge and turned left down alongside the Canal. The traffic was light enough but starting to build. He decided to spin by his private rooms to check a few things out before heading to the golf club. Along the canal, out through Inchicore and, following the tracks of the LUAS, he soon spotted the impressive glass and concrete façade of the luxurious southwestern clinic. The building always impressed him. In his mind it represented what modern medicine should be all about; investment, private/public partnerships that encouraged people to invest in their own healthcare. The NTPF arrangements worked superbly well and an efficient American style health service was going to be the result. His contribution had made a significant impact on the public waiting list. Lighthouse insurance returned to his mind. Surely there was another way of dealing with this. Staring at the modern, state-of-the-art private hospital, the thought of abandoning all this unnerved him. "No," he said to himself out loud, "I'll talk to Brennan. I'll find another partner company. There's plenty more fish in the sea." Luciano Pavarotti's voice rose to the final chorus of 'Nessun Dorma' as Reddy turned the car towards the rear entrance where the underground car park was located. "Vincero, vincero..." The orchestra lifted to a crescendo as Pavarotti pronounced Victory. The music lifted his mood and he felt better. He'd deal with these Lighthouse boyos and continue his practice as it was. With almost no effort, he steered the Mercedes around the corner towards the back of the hospital. Out of the corner of his eye he noticed a large, heavy-set bald man crossing the road. He looked vaguely familiar. Turning to check for traffic, the afternoon sun glinted off three or four metal studs in his eyebrow, nose and ears. Reddy got a shock, he recognized him, having seen him a number of times in the Lighthouse offices. As Reddy rounded the final corner, he spotted a man in a red sports jacket running towards the hospital. "That's Habib," Reddy said to himself. Then he looked again, no, too pale. Behind the runner, looking like they were in hot pursuit were two, no three men. Reddy looked back at the runner, it wasn't Habib, although he recognized the Dubai Desert Classic logo on the jacket, it was Robert. He was looking over his shoulder while running. Reddy was distracted but driving slowly as Robbie ran towards him. Turning his head forward and stepping into Reddy's path at the same time, Reddy had to slam on his brakes to avoid hitting him. Time stood still for a second. Standing in front of the sleek Gunmetal Bonnet, Robbie squinted to see beyond the tinted glass. Their eyes met for the briefest of seconds. Reddy looked behind Robbie and saw the three pursuers. He recognized a second one. These were Brennan's goons and, by the looks of things, Robert was in for it. From somewhere in his brain, a sense of team loyalty emerged. Robert was a damn good member of the team. He didn't deserve this. He knew Robert had been dragged into this Mulligan affair, but he wasn't quite sure how. He hit the central locking button on the dashboard and a dull *thunk* announced that the car was fully unlocked. Looking back and meeting Robert's stare again, he nodded towards the passenger door.

With seconds to spare, Robert dived into the passenger seat. Reddy gunned the Mercedes forward and the momentum caused the passenger door to slam shut.

49

TAKING THE STAIRS, I intended to use the service entrance. However as I passed the ground floor, I looked into the lobby and saw that there was a continuous throng of patients and staff moving in and out of the main door. I thought that there was a much greater chance of using the crowd to slip past anyone looking out for me. Turning back from the stairs I approached the hospital lobby. Keeping close to the wall so it would be more difficult for anyone outside looking in for me, I positioned myself behind the security desk so I could see as much of the area surrounding the entrance as possible. I picked out Scruffy standing to the left of an ambulance. Opposite a small landscaped area with a fountain, a red fuzzy haired chap in a County Meath GAA jersey stood smoking and talking on a mobile phone. I couldn't see any more potential tails. Coming across the central area of the lobby, Mick the porter was pushing a wheelchair with a blue rinsed elderly lady sitting up looking like the queen mother. A small group, consisting of a silver haired gent, about the same age, a stunning looking tall blonde clutching several bunches of flowers escorted the chair. Two young children, about the same ages as Alice and Nick trotted alongside. The little boy was clutching his Grandfather's hand. The little girl had a firm grip on a bunch of get well cards. The top card was obviously drawn by either herself or her brother. A nurse took up the rear, carrying the old lady's vanity case and a smaller bunch of flowers. A large black Chevrolet Grand Cheroke pulled up quite close to the door. Seeing an opportunity, I fell in behind the queen mum's procession. Mick steered the chair out of the doors and down the wheelchair ramp towards the Chevrolet. Walking close to the group, I got as close to the car as I could and spotting an ambulance crew coming towards the entrance. I ducked out from the royal entourage and disappeared into the ambulance crew. With the combination of jumping from group to group and Habib's red jacket, I made it beyond both scruffy and GAA man. The crowd thinned out and fighting the urge to run, I walked away from the hospital.

Just when I started to relax, a heavy set man rounded the corner coming towards me. I looked up and spotted, as well as the car, nose and eyebrow piercings, the purple swelling of a fresh bruise on the side of his face. His eyes opened wide and he raised his hand as if he was going to wave to me. I must have been about a half second ahead of him. I turned and ran straight across the street, heading diagonally away from the hospital. He shouted loudly behind him and another tall lanky teenager with protruding teeth appeared around behind Mr. Piercings. "There's the fucker," he shouted. Goofy sprinted after me and within a few seconds, Scruffy and GAA man were in on the chase. "How'd he get past you, ya blind fucker?" I heard Piercings scream at Scruffy.

Panicking, I slowed and looked around. Scruffy, GAA man and Goofy were approaching me from three sides. Piercing was on his mobile phone. With my back to the wall, I ran back towards the hospital entrance. As I went to cross the road, I nearly fell over the bonnet of a large dark grey Mercedes which had pulled up abruptly in front of me. I looked up into the windshield and was greeted by the angry stare of Peter Reddy. He averted his gaze to look behind me and I noticed a glimmer of recognition in his eyes. Turning back to me, he pointed to the passenger door as if he was stabbing somebody. I looked quickly to my left and right. Goofy and GAA man were bearing down on me. Without thinking twice, I yanked the passenger door open and jumped in. My ass had barely touched the seat and Reddy had floored the accelerator. The momentum pushed me back into the seat and I struggled to put my seatbelt on as the slick grey missile rounded the cornered as if on rails and we were gone.

Looking over my shoulder, I spotted Goofy, Scruffy and GAA man staring after the car. The one with the piercings was ranting into his mobile phone, gesticulating wildly and pointing in our direction. Reddy was silent and had a look of intense concentration on his face. After the initial shock of the chase and narrow escape, there was a minute or two of a very awkward silence. It was a moment of realization that, "You're involved, I'm involved. We both know that now, so what are we going to talk about?" He broke the silence trying to lighten the mood, "Like the jacket, I hope Habib has another one. He promised me one for the Golf Club." He forced a laugh at his own comment. I shifted uncomfortably in the seat. I felt the large bundle of the jiffy bag full of A4 envelopes inside the jacket. This grounded me. "What the hell's going on Peter?" I asked with emotion in my voice.

"What do you mean, who were those lads chasing you?" he asked in what I detected was a false tone.

"Don't give me that BS," I raised my voice, "I saw you recognizing one of them."

His grip tightened on the steering wheel and the car seemed to speed up. I stared at the side of his face and could clearly see the muscles in his jaws tighten and slacken rhythmically. He always did that in surgery when things got very tense. He was silent for a long time, "what has Brennan asked you to do?" he eventually asked in a low voice.

"I'm being blackmailed into sabotaging the operation," I said. I decided that I wasn't just going to answer questions; I was going to get some answers as well. "How long are you involved with these scumbags in Lighthouse?" I asked.

He took his eyes off the road for a second, giving me daggers. "Mind your own fucking business," is what his eyes said. "I thought you were told to keep your nose out of business that doesn't concern you," he said bringing his gaze back on the road.

It became clear to me now who had reported me to Nathan. Reddy didn't want his dirty little secrets hung out for public airing. He had a very good working relationship with the management of the hospital, this however took the biscuit. I had been framed into stopping my digging into the insurance antics of this company. It made me think that I had unearthed a serious can of worms. I started to panic a little. "Listen," I said in desperation, "I'm don't give a damn where your patients come from, or what arrangements the hospital have with insurance companies. I got a little curious and fell onto something "

He looked like he was contemplating his next sentence. "You don't need to be involved here at all," he began, "I know that Brennan's methods can be a little difficult. I think if I speak to him we can square this whole thing away."

I sensed a chink of light. Maybe Reddy could be the key. It was possible he could either postpone the surgery, or speak to Brennan, and get me off the hook. I didn't care what happened afterwards. "Problem is Peter, I am involved," I pushed, looking for the weak spot. "Brennan's crew are holding my wife and kids," I didn't know if this was technically correct. "I just want them safe. Could you speak to Brennan?" I pleaded.

He nodded. "I'll speak to Brennan. Trouble is he doesn't see the big picture. I don't want to touch this scumbag Mulligan as much as you. Brennan has me over a barrel as well though. All due respect, I've a lot more to lose than you."

I raised my eyebrows, my anger rising. He was happy to let my family suffer or see me possibly go to jail to protect his career and his private practice. "He doesn't have your family with a gun to your head," I began to raise my voice.

He seemed to be ignoring me. "The situation here is quite

delicate. We've...I've made a huge hole in the national waiting list with this arrangement. The minister himself endorses this type of arrangement. Five years ago, there was nearly a two year waiting time for heart surgery. I've turned that around..." He looked at himself in the mirror while he was giving me this party political broadcast.

"Jesus," I said to myself, "he's giving me his sales pitch." I felt that the speech was as much for his own benefit as mine.

"Of course there's going to be small problems in a scheme such as this. Not everyone believes in such a system. But I persisted and look where it's got us. The waiting list is virtually gone. No-one waits more than a couple of weeks now for a heart operation. Christian Bernard, Denton Cooley, Magdi Yacoub, all great visionaries, they had a plan and went for it. They became legendary in Cardiac Surgery all because they took risks." He was justifying his actions to himself. I was shaking with rage. I swore that I would bring this fucker down. "I'd hate to lose you from the team; there are always casualties when this sort of thing goes astray," he went on.

"As long as it isn't you?" I added with venom. I couldn't hold it in any more, "Either I ensure that Mulligan ends up as a vegetable or I go down and my family suffer?" My voice broke. "You're a selfish, vindictive bastard, you know that?"

He either was ignoring my ranting or he couldn't hear me in his own little world. Looking out the window, I noticed that we were approaching Rathgar. I had lost track of where we were going. "We'll go and see Brennan now and give him the information that you have. It'll be over in a flash," he said. I was silent for a minute. My plan was to send all the evidence I had collected to various people, journalists, politicians, the police, among others. I hoped that confronting Brennan and telling him what I had done would force him to call the whole thing off. I was so livid now, I wanted to stop now and mail the envelopes I had inside the jiffy bag. As we drove through Rathmines village, on the way to town, I was suddenly overcome with an overwhelming sense of claustrophobia. I had to get out if the car. I banged on the dashboard, "Stop... stop the fucking car." My sudden outburst shocked him and he brought the Mercedes to an abrupt halt in a gateway. "I'll see you in theatre tomorrow, this isn't over yet," I said probably to myself more than him. He gave me a frightened look as I slammed the door over and walked away.

50

VICTORIA was getting more and more frustrated. Marty and his two monkeys showed no signs of moving. She had already crossed swords with one of the boys when he had started to light up a cigarette. "Hey, don't smoke in here," she shouted at one of them.

"Fuck off," was his reply as he continued to light up. Marty walked back from the toilet and one look was all it took. "Sorry," he mumbled as he put his pack and lighter away.

The kids were still watching television. A major treat, as it was normally switched off as soon as lunch was finished. The two boys were bored and walked around the living room and kitchen making nuisances of themselves. They made no secret of the fact that they were bored. Marty tried to remain polite, but his patience was wearing thin. He was told that this would take an hour or two at most, but there was no sign of Robbie. He was probably up to something. Marty shivered at that thought. He would probably receive a call from Brennan's office, instructing him to do something nasty to Victoria or one of the kids. He kept pushing that thought to the back of his mind. Robbie wasn't that stupid, he'd co-operate. He'd better, time was running out. Brennan wanted whatever information Robbie had.

"What has Robbie got that's so important?" Victoria asked at one point when Laurel and Hardy were out of the room.

Marty was taken aback. He didn't know exactly what was in the information but he knew it was something to do with Brennan's insurance company. "Don't know exactly," he answered, "probably something to do with that chap having surgery."

Victoria looked surprised. "I hope he isn't revealing any confidential patient details, he could get fired for that."

Marty shifted uncomfortably. "Hope that doesn't happen. He needs to pay back his gambling debts," he said with concern.

Victoria's eyes opened wide, "What gambling debts?"

Marty looked surprised. "Christ, she knows nothing about this" he thought to himself. "Eh...eh...anyway if he brings us the information, it'll all be ok?" he lied hopefully. Victoria's face flushed red. Marty watched her. "Hate to be in Robbie's shoes," Marty thought. He immediately felt sorry for Robbie. As a result of an old gambling debt, he had been dragged into this. "Come on Robbie, get your ass home and we can get out of here," he willed Robbie on. The last thing he wanted to do was hurt Victoria or the kids, but orders were orders, you don't fuck around with Brennan.

51

REDDY DROVE ACROSS THE CITY. Fifteen minutes after
Robert had abruptly left the car in Rathmines, he was driving
across Butt Bridge and turning left down the quays towards the
streets behind the Financial Services Centre. Robert's tantrum
had been out of character and Reddy was a little worried about
Robert having a knee jerk reaction and doing something stupid.
He was a smart chap and hopefully the Clinic's management
had put the fear of God into him. They'd better have, if they
wanted to maintain the steady flow of patients, paid for by
the NTPF. He drove up Upper Oriel Street, slowly to avoid
the kids playing football, and stopped outside the Lighthouse
Insurance office. Killing the engine, he sat in silence gathering
his thoughts. This was it; he was going in to resign from
Lighthouse Insurances. They were getting too hot to handle.
He would find another insurance brokerage firm and continue
his mission to change the nature of the funding of Cardiac
Surgery in Ireland.

   He thought of all the pioneers, Debakey, Lilliehi, Gibbon.
They all had their problems but they persisted. Yes, he was doing
the right thing. He exited the car, pausing to hit the remote.
The solid *thunk* followed by the flash of lights announced that
the car was locked and alarm activated. Taking a deep breath,
he entered the lion's den.

   "He fuckin got away again? What sort of wasters are youse?"

Brennan was sitting in his office ranting on the phone, "I want that little bollix over here now. And I want any information he might have with him. Make sure he has it with him, no fuckin excuses, try his mobile again."

Next to Brennan, a tall young chap straddled a metal chair backwards. He had his legs spread and he was leaning onto the back of the chair. He had a high forehead with jet black greased hair falling loosely above his shoulders. He wore a pencil moustache and a black leather jacket. He was an evil looking bastard, Reddy thought. Brennan looked up as Reddy walked in. "Ah Doctor, me auld flower," he said in his raspy Dublin accent, "we were only talking about you, have you spoken to that little bollix Valentine today?" He looked up at his colleague, "This is Macker, one of me associates"

Reddy nodded. "I need to talk to you John," he said

Brennan ignored him and immediately asked, "Everything all set for tomorrow?"

Reddy stopped, "That's one of the things I want to talk to you about." He waited, expecting Brennan to finish with this Macker chap and escort him out, but Macker remained where he was, straddling the chair, lounging back smoking. Brennan made no effort to ask him to leave. "Can I talk to you about a client, John...a patient...confidentially," he paused hoping that Brennan would get the message. Patient confidentiality hadn't really entered his head in this case, but it seemed a reasonable excuse to get the stranger out of the room.

"Ah Jaysus, don't mind Macker here, sure he's part of the company as well," Brennan laughed.

"Shit," thought Reddy, "I think we need to be very careful about the outcome of tomorrow's operation..."

He went to continue but Brennan interrupted him, "Have you spoken to that bollix Valentine?" he asked with a frown.

Reddy was silent for a moment, "He told me that he was being blackmailed into sabotaging the operation."

Brennan stood up and walked over to check that the door

was closed, "You only concern yourself with operating on Mulligan. You don't need to see the whole picture."

He was still standing. Reddy steeled himself and went for it, "Any negative outcome would adversely affect my practice. In fact, a poor result could bring this whole arrangement crashing down…"

Brennan laughed, "Getting cold feet now Doctor are we?" he asked with a snarl, "let me look after the…what's your lovely saying…post-op care?" He laughed out loud and it turned into a fit of phlegm rattling coughing. Macker was laughing out loud too. This annoyed Reddy, he pressed forward, "In fact, this will be the last Lighthouse patient that I operate on…" He paused for effect.

Brennan suddenly stopped laughing and coughing. He stared hard at Reddy, a stare that sent a shiver down Reddy's spine, "You'll do no such fuckin thing…Doctor" each word was punctuated with a pointing of his index finger, "you'll do as you're fuckin told. You are in till I say you are, and you're finished when we are finished with you."

Reddy was shaking inside, but he drew a deep breath and tried to retaliate, "How dare you speak to me in that manner, I'm a Consultant Cardiac Surgeon in good standing…"

Brennan silenced him with a look, "Mister Reddy, you are in this up to your fuckin neck. You'll go back to your office in your flash Mercedes, ride your fancy secretary, take those chemical fuckin smarties that you were so fond of in college and wait until we send you the next batch of patients. And you'll spend the fees that we send you for each one of them and you won't say another fuckin word about this, right?"

Reddy's face turned white, both with rage and fright. Macker was staring at him and he seemed to be staring into his very soul. Turning on his heels, Reddy left the building as quickly as he could. Pressing the remote before he had reached the bottom stair, the *thunk* welcomed him. Aggressively pushing the stick into drive, he gunned the 3.8 litre engine sending a spray of gravel in his wake as he got away from the offices as fast as he could.

Brennan turned to Macker, "Dangerous fucker, that. Watch him, I think we might need to dismiss him and find a replacement...what do they call them...a locum?" Macker nodded, understanding the unsaid instruction.

"Leave it until after the operation," Brennan said as he watched the dark grey sky bear down on the city. It matched his mood. "And find that little fucker Valentine, he needs to be reined in quickly, as a matter of fact, does your contact give discounts for doing two at the same time," he laughed out loud, "sort of do one, get one free?" He laughed out loud and broke down coughing

"No problem Boss, I'm on to it," Macker answered as he fished in his pocket for his mobile to see if his contacts still had the number of Gerry Murphy. Looks like he'd be calling him soon.

51

STANDING WATCHING the early evening traffic, the normal activities of normal people going on with their normal lives, an overwhelming sense of despair overcame me. I thought of Victoria and the kids. A cold, nauseous sensation overcame me thinking of Marty sitting in the house with Victoria and the kids. I had promised to be home by now with the whole thing solved. Now, after being chased by Brennan's goons, listening to Reddy pontificate about solving the entire waiting list problem and going down as a legend in medical history, I was nowhere nearer to solving my situation. I stood outside the impressive building of the church in Rathmines. Listening to the bell sound for five o'clock mass, I barely heard my mobile ring. Pulling it out from my pocket, I didn't recognise the number. I stared at it for a few seconds collecting my thoughts before answering.

"Robbie, George here." I nearly melted with relief. "How are you doing? I've just got out from the conference, how are things?" he asked with genuine concern.

"Not good George," I explained the situation.

"What are you going to do with the information?" he asked me.

"I've no idea," I answered despondently. "I was going to send copies to a string of people, journalists, the Minister's office, the cops and various others"

He laughed, "That ought to piss them off big time" He was silent for a second.

"Trouble is George, the hospital is threatening me as well." I told him about the meetings with Nathan, and that Marty was sitting with Victoria as we spoke. "I don't think he'll hurt her or the kids, but I can't go home until I've figured out what to do."

"Jesus," he whispered, "damned if you do and damned if you don't." After a minute he said, "It sounds to me that you have a lot of the rope now. Last thing you want to do is hang yourself. Maybe the best way of using this information is not to use it."

It was my turn to be silent. "What do you mean George?" I asked with a frown.

"Once you've sent that information out, you've played your trump card, after that you've no cards left to play. I think the threat of using that information keeps you in control of the game. The best thing you can do is..." Two beeps told me that battery was depleted. The phone went dead in my ear.

Swearing, I looked at the screen. It had gone blank. I tried to switch it back on, "Battery empty" flashed and the phone wouldn't power up. "Ah Christ, that's all I need," I groaned stuffing the phone back into my pocket. My hand felt the jiffy bag. George's words replayed in my head. I walked on up Rathmines road towards the bustling village.

Rathmines, traditionally, the student quarter of the city, a large proportion of its occupants were students up from the country studying in the various colleges and universities of the capital. The main street into Rathmines village consists of large three or four storey Georgian houses. Many, if not all of these houses had been converted into flats. Some very creative landlords had in some cases managed to convert their houses into impressive numbers of bedsits. Even the smallest of bedrooms were converted into student accommodation, and charged handsomely for the privilege of an eight foot square room that was bedroom, lounge and kitchen. Sharing a bathroom with up to twelve or fifteen others was part of the privilege. The few houses that managed to escape were, in the main, used as offices.

One of these offices was occupied by the company of Garvin & Gleeson Solicitors & Commissioner for Oaths. I had used the good offices of Garvin & Gleeson a number of times in recent years when we bought our first house and subsequently moved to Sandymount. I knew the senior partner, Oliver Garvin reasonably well. His wife had worked with me in a previous lifetime, and we had kept in touch. The great thing about Oliver was that he didn't speak legalese with clients, he spoke English. And, it seemed that nothing surprised him. He always kept the same pragmatic attitude whether it was a traffic violation he was handling or a court appearance for major tax fraud.

As I passed the office, George's suggestion replayed itself in my head *"the best way to use that information is not to use it."* One of the hardest things to learn about my job, in fact, a lot of jobs in Medicine and Surgery, is knowing when to do nothing. A very senior Surgeon, while talking about heart surgery once told me, "you spend the first five years of your career learning all about the operations. The next five years learning how and when to do the various operations, and the rest of your career learning when to do nothing." Oftentimes, the hardest thing to do is nothing. I thought about that for a minute and stopped in my tracks. I turned and headed straight back to the offices of Garvin & Gallagher Solicitors and Commissioners for Oaths.

Marty was getting irritated now. Pinky and Perky, his two 'assistants' were really getting on his tits now. They were playing with the kids toys and making both of the children cry. Victoria was putting on a brave face, trying to pacify the kids without screaming at the two low IQ morons that were camped out in her house waiting for her husband to come home. Marty realized now that Victoria was wise to the fact that Robbie was mixed up in something a little unsavoury. She had adapted a "couldn't give a monkey's" attitude since Marty had let slip something about a gambling debt. But the slamming of kitchen presses, the shortening of her temper gave it away. Marty moved the curtain back an inch or two to survey the road. Just as he lifted the curtain, a large motorbike that appeared to be parked on the opposite side of the quiet suburban street, started up and moved away. Marty looked after it. "Nice machine," he said to himself, Yamaha XJ600, he guessed. Red tank and fairings, four stroke, 598cc, double overhead cam, classic bike, lovely machine. He envied the rider, in his black one piece and black helmet. He was off, free. Not like me, stuck here with Pinky and Perky, a stuck-up bitch and two screaming kids. "Oh where the fuck are you Robbie?" Marty silently prayed to himself.

51

GERRY MURPHY/Maguire/Maloney/McGrath, whatever his name was today was performing a service on a red and white Yamaha XJ600. Although it was nearly ten years old, the bike was in immaculate condition. Gerry performed a full service, including a change of brake shoes. Normally after fitting new brakes, the bike required a decent run-in with some heavy breaking.

Gerrys phone alerted him to an incoming call. "Number unavailable" usually meant it was a business call, and not the business of fixing motorbikes. Whenever Gerry needed to make a business call, he used a low cost phone card. Not for economic reasons, but because calls routed via international computers, were much harder to trace, and "number unavailable" was usually the only identity that appeared on the recipient's phone.

"Gerry?" came the rough Dublin accent. "Yeah?"

"That business you checked out last week...by the coast, yeah?"

"Which one, North or Southside?"

"Both, the boss wants you to prepare both those jobs, yeah?"

"For when?"

"As soon as you get the nod, but get ready as soon as you can, yeah?"

"G'luck," the phone went dead.

"A spin from Sandymount to Howth was just what this bike

needs," Gerry said to himself. He shouted to the boss of the garage, "Taking this Kwaker for a spin. I need to open her up, I might be gone about an hour." The boss acknowledged with a wave. Gerry pulled on his black leather jump suit and helmet and pushed the bike out into the lane in a back street in Ballybough. Three minutes later, he was cruising along Fairview strand and out the coast road towards the affluent village of Howth, and to check and time the route to the targets house.

As he passed the junction of the Alfie Byrne Road, with his left hand, he set the tripometer on the speedometer clock to zero. On the way back, he would take that turn towards the Eastlink bridge and on towards Sandymount. He didn't mind using the Eastlink during jobs. Unlike the Westlink Toll bridge, the Eastlink didn't charge motorbikes. Again not for monetary reasons but stopping for change increased the likelihood of being pegged. Also, as bikes weren't charged, the company who managed the toll booths didn't see fit to have a camera pointed directly at the lane that motorbikes used.

Gerry had already logged the target's movements, and knew that at this time, he would be somewhere between the Southwestern clinic and the Golf Club. He cruised through the picturesque village of Howth, turned right up past the Abbey Tavern and on out towards the Summit. He turned off the main road and down a small gravel track. Stopping momentarily, he fished out a plastic vest which went over his black leather jumpsuit. It bore the logo of *Speedway Couriers*, and sported a picture of a motorcyclist holding a letter as if it were made of pure gold, while racing to get the mail to its destination. Anyone curious enough to dial the number would reach an answering machine which would announce that all the operators were busy and a message would be responded to immediately. Amazing what an old mobile phone number could do for your credibility. The vest immediately gave him a reason for being on the private road, and any nosy neighbours would only see a standard motorbike courier looking for a house. As there were many professionals living in the area, a courier delivering a letter was normal.

He drove slowly past the large wooden gates, noting the position of a security camera long before he came into its field of vision. He carefully skirted the cameras arc and also noted an intercom mounted on the left pillar as you entered. He slowly cruised on down the gravel pathway, coming across the only other house on the private road. The road ended abruptly in a dead end, beyond which there was scrubland leading on out towards cliffs and the sea. The view from the end of the road was spectacular. You could see right across to the Southside of the bay, Dun Laoghaire, Killiney. The HSS super ferry was heading out to sea and there were about a dozen more boats, commercial and private, visible in the autumn afternoon. Squinting slightly, he could clearly make out the Martello tower in Sandymount in the distance, a stone's throw from the second target's house. After mentally recording everything in and around the gates of the target's house, he decided on his plan of attack. Because the road was a dead end, he would approach from the Sutton side of the head. He would leave his courier RD350 hidden from view in a small bushy undergrowth that he had noticed just off the road about 1500 metres from the turn off to the private road. He would tab it on foot, and as soon as an opportunity presented itself, he would leave the pathway for the scrubland at the back of the houses. Approaching the house from the back, he would gain entry to the garden, find a laying up point inside the garden and wait for the target to arrive. As soon as the target was inside and the gates had closed, he would hit the target, and escape back across the scrublands towards his bike. He had noted that the driveway to the house, inside the gate was a few hundred metres long; this meant that it would probably take quite a while to notice that the target hadn't arrived from the car to the house. By that time, Gerry would probably be over the East link and in Sandymount and on to his next 'job.' Being conscious of the time, he didn't want to spend more time than was necessary that would alert suspicion; also he needed to get across the city to Sandymount to recce his second target.

An idea came into his head and he smiled at the idea. One of the more famous residents of the Howth peninsula was Gay Byrne, the retired broadcaster and housewives' favourite on the radio for decades. He lived quite near the target's house. He had, in a highly publicised show, received a Harley Davidson touring bike from the members of the supergroup U2 as a present for his contribution to the entertainment industry. It would be a nice touch if he could organise for Uncle Gaybo's Harley to be stolen and used as the decoy bike. He wondered to himself, which would receive more media attention and Garda time, a dead Heart Surgeon or Gay Byrne's stolen motorbike. He made a mental note to work on that one.

Ten minutes later, Gerry was cruising along through Sutton cross and on out towards the city. He carefully noted the position of the traffic lights and anywhere there might be police check points. The problem with the Howth peninsula, is exactly as the name suggests, it is a peninsula with one road on and off. If there were any problems or police check points thrown up, anyone on the peninsula either had to take their chances with a roadblock, or stay in the area until the road blocks were lifted. He cruised past the turns for Baldoyle, Kilbarrack and passed St Anne's Estate public park, the former estate of the Guinness family, now a beautiful public park spread over a few hundred acres in the heartland of Clontarf and Raheny.

Checking his speed, he passed the police station after the Yacht bar and as he turned left onto the Alfie Byrne Road, he noted the numbers on the tripometer. Three minutes later, an anonymous motorcycle courier slipped along the outside lane for motorbikes on the East Link Bridge. Double checking that there were still no cameras pointing at the motorbike lane, he cruised on through without slowing down. Twenty three minutes after leaving Howth head, he was passing the Martello Tower in Sandymount. He turned right at the tower and entered the maze of streets.

He came to the one where the second target lived. Stopping up the road slightly, he removed a map from his inside packet. To the casual observer, a courier was consulting his schedule for the day and probably confirming an address. Gerry was checking the level of activity on the quiet suburban street.

Using the dark shade on his helmet as a cover, he studied the houses along the street either side of the target's. He noted the high wooden gates and the Opel Vectra parked in the driveway. There was no sign of the blue Megane that was there the last time. He noted the alarm box high up on the outer wall. Slowly, he maneuvered the Kawsaki on down the street towards the house, without looking directly at the house. He stopped briefly on the opposite side of the road. He was still using his peripheral vision to garner as much information about the layout of the driveway as possible. He hadn't made a decision yet on how this one was going to work. Planning, careful planning was the key to his success. Over twenty 'hits' and never as much as a questioning by the police. Planning, that was the secret.

As he scanned the front of the house, he noticed the curtains in the front room move. He thought he saw a figure of a man, a dark, Spanish or Mediterranean look out for a brief second. He stared directly at the bike for a moment. Because of the dark helmet visor and the anonymity of the bike, there was no danger of anyone recognizing him, however, Gerry made a show of talking on his mobile, pointing to the sheet of paper from his pocket and appearing to search for a particular house. Then he moved swiftly away.

Pulling into the early evening traffic, he checked the choice of routes, left onto Strand Road and either left towards Ringsend and the city, or right towards Blackrock, or even back through Sandymount village and on into the city passing St. Vincents

Hospital. No problems with escape routes on this side of the city. He cruised through Ringsend, over the Canal Bridge and back towards the North side of the city.

53

I STOOD IN THE HALL of the offices of Garvin & Gallagher weighing up my options. George's advice kept ringing in my ear. I had decided to try one last ditch effort. I retrieved my mobile from my, well Habib's, inside pocket. I pressed the power button and it fired up. No sooner had it finished its powering up, when the sound of an incoming text sounded, *"you have four new voice messages."* I dialed the messaging service number and was rewarded with the sound of a rough Dublin accent. The first two sounded like whoever was calling either didn't want to or didn't know how to leave a coherent message. However the third said it all, *"Valentine, Mr. Brennan wants to see you, straight fuckin away, no actin the bollix. We're watchin your wife and kid. Get your arse over to Molloys bar on Grand Canal Street, fuckin sharpish. By the way, Sasquatch and Knacker can't fuckin wait to see you, Sasquatch's face is a fuckin mess and Knacker pissed his pants. They're not happy."* An explosion of laughter ended the message. I didn't feel like laughing, but I managed a smile thinking of the pair. One who received the full blast from the business end of the Tazer stun gun and the other who had a short sharp introduction to my elbow. The time was well and truly here to end this thing. I had run out of options and places to run to. Looking at my watch, it was five to five. I hoped that Oliver Garvin was still in the office. I remembered that he had a voracious appetite for work and rarely left the office before seven. I hoped that this hadn't changed since I met him last.

I knocked timidly on the office door. "Come in," a female voice answered. A young pretty secretary looked like she was closing down the office for the day.

My hopes were fading fast. "Is Oliver here?" I asked with desperation in my voice.

She was leaning over the desk shutting down the computer and she looked up at me. "Yes, he hasn't left yet, but his appointments are all finished for the day, can I help you?" She looked pissed that a client had arrived with five minutes to leaving time.

"Is it at all possible to speak with him for five minutes, old friend and client?" I gave her my puppy eyes. More like pissholes-in-the-snow eyes after the week I had just put in, but I gave it my best.

She thought for a second and, much to my relief, said, "Hold on, I'll check if he has time." She walked towards another door. Opening it, she looked back at me, "What's your name?"

"Robert Valentine," I answered.

She disappeared inside the inner office. I looked around the office. Heavy oak antique furniture mixed with IKEA style office furniture. There were mountains of files precariously balanced on the arms of chairs, on modern desks and stacked up on the window sills. I could hear voices inside and I strained to make out what was being said. A minute later, the secretary emerged. She looked at me and, smiling inclined her head over her right shoulder. She was followed by the large bulky figure of Oliver Garvin. He hadn't changed much since I saw him last, lost a bit more hair, gained a bit more weight but still had that infectious smile that was instantly disarming. He had a shock of grey hair that waved like a crinkle cut crisp and a pair of half circle reading glasses perched on the end of his nose which made him look ten years older than his forty eight years or so. "Robbie, how are you?" he pumped my hand.

I relaxed immediately, "Good Oliver, everything well with you?"

He laughed waving his hand in the direction of a mountain of files. "You know me," he laughed, "this won't take long, will it?"

He had his jacket in his hand. He was obviously making ready to leave, "If I'm not gone by ten past, you can call security," I smiled.

He looked at the secretary, "You head off Paula, I'll lock up." he dismissed the secretary. She was out the door like a shot from a gun. He turned back towards the office, "Come on in. You can talk while I'm shutting down. What can I do for you?" I followed him into his office. I had to step over boxes of files and lift some folders off a chair to sit down. "What's the problem?" he said, as he was pushing papers into his briefcase.

"I'm in a spot of bother Oliver, in fact quite a large spot," I said in a resigned tone. He stopped packing his case and looked at me directly. "What sort of trouble?" he asked. I started to give him a very brief synopsis of the situation. He sat down and held up his hand, "Whoa, hold on a second. Give it to me from the start." He assumed his business demeanor.

I began with the emails I had received and gave him as much of the story as I could remember. He asked me the same question that George, and ironically, Fatboy had asked me, "Why didn't you go straight to the police?" I told him about the gambling debt and Officer Elvis. He blew out slowly, "What do you want me to do? I'm not a criminal lawyer."

I looked at my watch. It was half past five. "You'd better call security," I said smiling. He laughed. "Sounds like you need more than security," he seemed a little nervous. "What do you want me to do?" he said again. I outlined my plan.

Twenty minutes later, I was sitting in a taxi heading towards Molloys bar on Grand Canal Street. As the taxi traversed the back streets of Rathgar, heading towards Ballsbridge, my phone rang. Without thinking, I answered, "Robbie, me auld flower," came the dreaded hoarse voice. "I've been trying to get hold of you all day. You're one slippery bastard."

I cringed. "What do you want?" I played the dumb card.

"You know very well what I fuckin want. You're a nosy little bollix as well. I want any information that you dug up, right." The phone emitted a blip warning me that the battery was low. "Listen, Valentine, the only fuckin reason your wife and brats aren't history is because I need you in that operating theatre tomorrow. Now you'll get your arse over here now if you know what's fuckin good for you and your kids."

The line went dead without him saying anything else. I checked the screen on the phone. Still one block on the battery indicator. The taxi was approaching Donnybrook, about five minutes from Grand canal street. I dialed Victoria's mobile. She answered immediately, "Robbie, thank God. Where the hell are you?" she blurted out.

"My battery is very low Vic, listen please. Is Marty still there?" I asked.

"Yeah, and those two goons," she added.

"Are you and the kids OK?" I inquired with some urgency. "Yeah, but the kids are getting bored and irritated. Robbie, what's going on? Marty said something about a gambling debt."

I groaned inwardly. The cat was out of the bag now. "Victoria," I said with sincerity, "I've been dragged into something and I'm on my way to sort it out, I promise, it'll all be over soon" I had to fight hard to control the emotion in my voice.

Victoria lowered her voice, "Robbie, tell me what's going on."

The taxi turned onto Beggars Bush and headed towards Grand Canal street. I spotted the sign outside Molloys Bar. "Victoria, I'll be home very soon, I swear, I'll tell you everything. I've gotta go now. Will you put Marty on for a second?"

She handed the phone without saying anything else. Marty's

voice came on, "Robbie?" He tried to sound like my best friend. I was having none of it. "I'm outside Molloys now. I have that information with me. I'm going inside to talk to Brennan now. Get out of my house right now."

He was quiet for a second, "Robbie, I'll leave when Brennan tells me. OK? I have orders to..." The two beeps came again as the phone died a second time. We had stopped outside the Bar. The taxi driver waited patiently while I spoke on the phone. He must have got the gist of the conversation and he was very quiet. I paid the fare and left the cab.

Standing outside the door of Molloys, I noticed four or five men standing outside smoking. I immediately noticed the man with the piercings and now, a wicked purple bruise on his face. He looked directly at me and elbowed another chap whom I recognized as scruffy. The two of them looked at me with venom and started towards me. I ducked inside quickly. Whatever they had in mind for me would have to wait. My eyes adjusted to the semi-darkness as I looked around. I didn't recognize anyone. A hand on my shoulder startled me. I turned to meet the metal and bruised face of Mr. Piercings. I couldn't help it, "Sasquatch I presume," I said. He was obviously fuming and waiting for the word to exact revenge for the redecoration of his face. He put his forehead right up to mine and his closed fist up to my chin. Through bared teeth he said, "When Mr. Brennan's finished with you, you're mine...fucker! Now get the fuck in there, he wants to see you."

He propelled me forward with a shove towards the back of the lounge. The barman looked up at me from the racing pages of a red top and pointed to a section of the bar that was hinged open. I walked uncertainly through the opening and saw that a small arch led to the other side and out into a small snug type bar. Two men were sitting in a small booth. Both of them were smoking. The snug measured about twenty feet by twenty feet. There was a door to the outside, but it was closed and locked. The older of the two looked up at me, "Ah Robbie, me auld flower. You're one slippery fucker." I shrugged my shoulders, "Maybe your crew need to go to Specsavers." He exploded laughing and coughing, "Good one...good one. Anyway, I believe you have something for me."

The second chap was texting on a mobile phone and didn't lift his head for a moment. When he did, and looked at me, I took a second to remember him; long, jet black hair, emerging from a high forehead and hanging just above his shoulders. He had dark eyebrows which almost met. Fredo from the Godfather came to mind, along with the last time and place that I had met this chap. It was Terry "Macker" McCarthy. My jaw dropped open and my eyes widened as I remembered spilling out my guts to this man in O'Learys bar near the hospital some weeks previous. He was the start of it all. My confession and explanation of what I did for a living had obviously given him the idea to use me as the weapon. I felt like the secrets of the universe had just been revealed to me, and I didn't like what I had learned.

"You know Macker?" Brennan asked without surprise.

"We've met," I said, shaking my head.

Macker stood up, "Sorry about all the crap Robbie, but you know the way it is in business?" he held out his hand to shake mine, "No hard feelings Bud?"

I looked at him with wide eyes, "I didn't come here to make friends," I said. I was fuming with rage inside and I was making a desperate effort to think clearly. I had had a long conversation with Oliver Garvin, and had come up with the closest thing to an exit strategy that we could manage. Faced with these scumbags, it was difficult to think clearly. I focused on a beer mat on the table in front of Brennan.

"I hear you've been doing a bit of detective work," Brennan said with a snarl, "pretty nifty on the computer as well, I understand." He grinned at Macker who looked at me and shaping his hand like he was gripping something, he moved his hand up and down in front of his groin. There was no mistaking what he was indicating, they had somebody, Marty perhaps, hack into my computer and visit those pornographic web sites that Nathan had shown me on the record sheet of the history of sites visited. "Bastards!" I lunged forward at Macker. He closed his fists and squared up to me. Brenann stepped up and between us, "Now now lads, lets sort this out like gentlemen." I took a few deep breaths, trying to calm myself down.

"Tony," Brennan called, "get's a couple of pints in here, like a good lad."

The barman appeared instantly, "No problem Mr. Brennan" he said. I looked at the barman, "Nothing for me thanks." He gave me a strange stare that said, "He didn't mean you." I felt a bit stupid.

Brennan sat back down and started the ritual of lighting up a cigarette. As the plume of blue smoke rose over him, he broke into a fit of coughing. His face nearly turned blue as he fought for breath. At last, he sat back and laughed. "I know, I know, I should give them up, but they're me only vice," he laughed waving his hand in a dismissive gesture. "Anyway, Robbie me auld flower, I know what your game is, can't say I blame you though, I'd probably try do the same." Brennan seemed to be reveling in my situation. Macker sat back and looked like he was enjoying watching me suffer. "All the information in the world is fuck all use to you. Some of me boys are watching your darling wife and kids and your boss is none too pleased with your mooching around. You'll be looking for a new job if you're not careful, so as the man says, we have you by the bollix." I focused on a picture of a vintage advertisement for Guinness on the wall. I studied the picture of the cart being pulled by a huge farmer. The horse was sitting in the back of the cart with a grin on his face. *Guinness is good for you* announced the picture.

Brennan stopped talking and looked at me. "This is just business Robbie son," he said, "the trouble with you is, you're taking this too personally."

I snorted in disgust, "Your goons are holding my family. My job is on the line and if I do as you ask, I'll be basically attempting murder. I think I'm entitled to take it fucking personally."

Macker looked up at me, "Careful with your language Valentine." Brennan laughed to himself, "So, did you find anything interesting about me while you were digging?" He stopped talking and sat back in the chair as Tony the barman placed two creamy pints on the table in front of Brennan and Macker. Tony disappeared quickly behind the bar and off into the main bar. "There isn't a whole lot about me in the papers. Let's say, I keep a low profile." He was boasting now and he picked up the pint. "You can't have anything worthwhile on me," he said before he picked up the pint, studied it for a second and downed a third of it.

"Yeah," I said, "but I found some interesting stuff on your companies. You've been very successful with government contracts, especially in health."

He placed the pint back down on the table, "I've always been interested in the health services y'know. All those tablets..." He looked at Macker and grinned. Macker laughed back, "Yeah, lots of sick people." I caught the exchange between them remembered some newspaper articles about drug seizures and Brennan's name being mentioned. I wasn't surprised with the reference. The insurance and security companies were a perfect front for money laundering.

"I must say," I said, "the medical insurance company is a stroke of genius."

He looked surprised, and his chest puffed out slightly, "Yeah, it's good innit?"

When I arrived here, I had an overwhelming urge to hear the whole story from Brennan, now, I just wanted to get out of there as fast as I could and home to Victoria and the kids. "I just want this to be over" I said in a resigned voice.

"I know son, I know" Brennan said, just give me whatever

you have, do your job tomorrow and we'll be out of your way, except of course the small matter of your account."

The mention of the gambling debt made me wince. I was under no illusion that after the operation on Mulligan, Brennan wouldn't just up and leave me alone. I had worked out this contingency. "The trouble is Mr. Brennan, I love my job, I like what I do for a living and I want to carry on doing it. I respect the confidentiality of patients and I have a moral duty to do what is right, regardless of who they are. I would be the same if it was you on the table and the situation was reversed."

He shifted uneasily in the seat, "Don't give me a fuckin sob story Robbie, just give me the information you have and let's all go fuckin home"

I reached into my inside pocket and brought out an expensive buff coloured envelope. "You see Mr. Brennan, although I couldn't find anything on you, I did come up with quite a bit on your companies. There's a lot of juicy stuff there that could set journalists, or worse still someone like the Criminal Assets Bureau digging. Probably even start another tribunal, Payments to Surgeons Tribunal or something like that. I did find quite a bit of stuff."

A deep frown appeared on his forehead. "What did you do with this information?" he asked.

"Oh, don't worry," I said, "everything you need to know is there." I handed him the envelope.

"Is this it, all of it?" he looked uncertain.

"It's all there," I said. This was it, my final card played, now I was all out of cards, I couldn't bluff any longer. Now it was time to start calling the players, "Now call the goons off my family please."

Brennan waved me silent with a gesture of his hand. He opened the envelope. It contained a single typewritten page on the headed notepaper of Garvin & Gallagher, Solicitor and Commissioner for Oaths. "What's this, a fucking solicitor's letter?" He shook it like a rag with a smile of complete disbelief,

"Can you believe this Macker?" "What are you going to do, fuckin sue us for hurtin your feelings?" Macker laughed out loud.

"Read the fuckin letter," I raised my voice in panic and frustration. I hoped my exit strategy wasn't coming apart before it had started. Brennan, still laughing, patted his pockets looking for his reading glasses,"Fuck it, where's me specs?" He thrust the letter at Macker, "Here Macker, read it, give us a fuckin laugh." Macker straightened the page out and started reading:

To Whom It Concerns:

I represent the client, Mr. Robert Valentine.

Mr.Valentine visited me today, the 22nd October 2001 and related certain events that had occurred over the past three weeks. He had in his possession, various documents, photographs and copies of official government documents, all referring to certain Lighthouse Insurance Services and Lighthouse Security Services Ltd. as well as information pertaining to a certain Mr. Peter Reddy FRCSI, Consultant Cardiothoracic Surgeon.

This information has been viewed by me, but under normal legal representative/client confidentiality privilege, I am forbidden from revealing the details of either the conversation or the documents to anybody, including the authorities. He has instructed me, however, that in the event of any unforeseen or unexplained event befalling him or any member of his family, that copies of all the documents be circulated to various parties.

According to newspaper reports, Mr. Thomas Mulligan is scheduled to shortly undergo Cardiac Bypass Surgery. My client has also instructed that in the event of the outcome of this surgery being less than favorable, that I follow the same instructions.

I have been instructed not to wait on direct instructions

from Mr. Valentine but upon confirmation from independent sources of any problems with Mr. Mulligan's recovery from the surgery, to send the documents. Likewise, I have put a scheme in place that will quickly confirm any incident that may befall my client or his family.

The list of contacts who will receive copies of the documents is as follows:

The Garda Commissioner.
The Criminal Assets Bureau.
The offices of The Taoiseach and Ministers of Health & Children and Justice.
Mr. William Livingston, Chief Crime Reporter, Irish Times.
Chief News Reporter, RTE.
The Medical Council.
The Health Insurance regulator

So long as Mr. Mulligan's surgery proceeds uneventfully and no harm comes to my client or his family, the documents will remain in total confidence. The documents have been transferred to a safety deposit box in a bank of my choosing; where they will be held until such time that they may be required to be circulated.

Yours sincerely,

Oliver P. Garvin, LLB.

Brennan stared at me with a look of complete confusion, "What the fuck is this about? That's a load of shite." Macker was reading the letter closely with a look of intense concentration on his face. "Macker, what's this about?" Brennan was losing his cool now.

"Mr. Brennan," I said calmly, "I dug up enough information on you and your companies to have the authorities all over you like a rash. Mulligan will have his surgery tomorrow, and everything will proceed normally. The letter simply says that if Mulligan doesn't wake up, or doesn't do well after the surgery, everything I've dug up will be sent to the people on the list." Brennan turned to Macker who nodded slowly. I pressed on to play the advantage, "Also, if anything happens me or my family, that can't be explained, same drill."

Macker looked at me with a cold hard stare that seemed to penetrate into my soul, "Why didn't you just send the information to the cops?"

I thought about that for a second, "You're in the insurance business, you figure it out," I said. "I don't give a shit where the patients or funding come from, in fact I think there's beautiful irony that your dirty money is helping to fund the health service. I just want to get on with my life."

Macker shook his head slowly. He mouthed the word, "fuck" to himself.

Feeling a little more confident, I decided to push a little further, "There's another few things as well."

Brennan was looking from me to Macker and back. He started to stand up, "You little bollix." Macker pushed him down and he fell back in the seat. Brennan began to rub the centre of his chest.

"You're not looking terribly well Mr. Brennan," I said with overdramatic emphasis, "pain in your chest, is it? You really should give up those cigarettes and lose a bit of weight." I let that sit for a second as Brennan started perspiring heavily. "I do a lot of on-call at the Clinic," I said, "I'd hate to meet you professionally, know what I mean? I assume you have medical insurance and you'd like the best heart surgeon to look after you if you needed, say, a heart operation." Brennan's eyes widened even further, "Don't worry, I'd make sure that you were well taken care of." Brennan seemed to physically shrink. "One last thing," I added. Brennan looked up at me with the eyes of a scolded child. "It's about that gambling debt," I said.

Macker slowly looked up at me. "Don't push it Valentine," he said. I took my wallet from my jeans pocket. Rummaging in the back, I came across the betting slip that I had placed the double that Marty had told me about. I flicked it across at the two of them, it landed on the table in front of Brennan "That should cover it. Now call the goons off my family and let me get on with my life."

Brennan caught Macker's eye and gave a sharp nod. "Watch yourself Valentine, fuckin watch yourself..." Brennan said with venom in his voice.

"Don't think that I'll ever look at some bloke standing on the street in quite the same way ever again," I said, "every time my phone rings, I'll be wondering, who the fuck is this? So yeah, of course I'll watch myself. It's gonna be hard fuckin time for me as well, and before you say anything, I'm not gonna tell anyone about this sordid little mess, it's not in my interest." I turned to leave.

"Just fuckin watch yourself Valentine," Macker said again.

I paused, feeling that I needed to get the last word in. "You take care of yourself Mr. Brennan," I said while rubbing the centre of my chest. I wanted to remind him that he could as easily end up on the operating table, with me at the controls of the Heart/Lung machine. I especially hoped that if that scenario were ever to unfold, that that would be the last thought that would cross Brennan's mind as he drifted into unconsciousness. My last image was of Brennan reading the letter from Oliver again. He looked like a child reading a particularly difficult school book and Macker tapping furiously on his mobile phone, "Gerry, do nothing about those two jobs, North and Southside, yeah? Forget about them for the moment, yeah? G'luck." Leaving the snug area, I wondered who Gerry was, and what was he into Brennan for.

I turned and left the bar, negotiating my way through the group of lads who were still gathered outside the bar. Sasquatch stared me down as I walked through the group. He seemed surprised that he hadn't been given the go ahead to rough me up. I left the group staring in my wake and walked as fast but as casually as I could down the street and away from the bar. I turned the first corner I came across. Not to head anywhere in particular but just to get out of the line of sight of the monkeys. Once I was around the corner, I stopped. An overwhelming sense of, I don't know what came over me. It was like I had just survived a horrific crash where everybody else had been killed. Fear, relief, nausea, the urge to scream and cry, all came at me at the same time. My head started to spin and I had to grip a railing to stop myself from falling. I had no idea if playing my last card as I had done would really work. I only had the faxes that George had sent me and some general information on Brennan and Mulligan's gang's activities that I had dug up from the internet. However, with the tenacity of some of these journalists, I hoped that my extra little titbits would point them in the right direction if required and send the big boys running for cover. I hadn't included the Clinic's management in my little mail-merge list but I was confident that the message would quickly filter through to the appropriate authorities that what I had was potentially damaging to the hospital's reputation but wouldn't be used unless something untoward happened to either Mulligan or myself. I could only do so much; the rest was out of my hands.

I checked my phone and tried calling home. Victoria answered immediately; "Robbie, they've gone," is all she said before bursting into tears. "Robbie, what's going on?" she sobbed. A beep reminded me that the battery was critically low.

"Victoria, I'm on my way home. I promise I'll explain everything." I turned and walked towards Dame Street and looked for a taxi home. An overwhelming sense of relief came over me, but I couldn't relax yet. There was the small matter of Mulligan's surgery to worry about. Everything hinged on him coming through the surgery unscathed and, after all, he was a very sick man.

53

23RD OCTOBER, 6.45AM
Main Operating Theatre, Southwestern Clinic.

AS QUIETLY BUT AS CONFIDENTLY as he could, a dark figure in theatre scrubs slipped unnoticed into the anaesthetic storeroom. Using a large bunch of keys, he quickly found one that opened the Dangerous Drugs or DDA Cupboard. He pulled a small piece of paper from the scrubs pocket. Searching along the alphabetic list, he looked for the names of three or four specific drugs that were named on the piece of paper. A couple of hours spent on the Internet had given him the commonly used Anaesthetic drugs. Unfortunately, he hadn't taken into account the fact that American brand names are very often quite different from European ones, and the fact that on labelling drugs, a lot of staff use the chemical name for the drug instead of the branded or generic title. He cursed loudly when no drug label in the cabinet resembled any from his handwritten list. "What are you doing there?" came a stern voice that lifted him out of his skin with fright. "Doing a Pharmacy stock check," was his rehearsed reply. "Oh...OK," the Nurse Manager sounded confused. The dark figure picked up a clipboard and started walking towards the door. "Wait there please, I want to check with Security." She turned and reached for the phone on the wall behind her. "What's your name please?" she asked, turning slowly. But he was gone. She dropped the phone as one of the night security men answered. Running towards the exit door, she tripped and almost fell over a theatre scrub top and pants that had been discarded loosely on the ground beside the door to the emergency stairs that was now closing slowly as if someone had just opened it and let it close behind them. The pockets in the discarded scrub suit showed later to contain four ampoules of Succsamethonium, two of Fentanyl or Sublimaze, two of Diprivan or Propofol and five, two millilitre ampoules of pancuronium bromide or Pavulon. What was unusual about the find, was that all drug counts and invoices for that morning were correct. It was as if someone was trying to plant drugs in the DDA cabinet so that they would be used in place of regular stock. The contents of the ampoules weren't analysed as no crime, other than trespassing, had been committed. So the show went on.

54

MULLIGAN WAS WHEELED into the anaesthetic room. This is an ante-room, outside the main operating theatre, where the patients are anaesthetised and various drips are placed in different arteries and veins, and the patients are put asleep in preparation for the surgery. He had been given a dose of Ativan, a strong Valium. Ativan is used as a pre-medication, usually about two hours before surgery. This helps relax the patient and also, Ativan has a strong amnesic effect, which can be useful with very nervous patients. It also has the effect, sometimes of completely taking away any inhibitions that a person might have. This was the case with Mulligan. He had turned into a leering, lecherous monster, probably not a whole lot different from normal, but now he wasn't making any attempt to hide his lust. After several attempts at pinching whatever piece of flesh was within reach and gazing openly at the nurses' chests and behinds, Dr. Sapsford decided very quickly to change the order of the anaesthetic procedure. Normally before inducing full anaesthesia, that is putting the patient asleep, he would have the patient curl up into foetal position to facilitate the introduction of a spinal/epidural drip in the back for pain relief after the surgery. Then he would have inserted a number of drips into the patient's neck and, finally after various other small chores had been completed, he would have put Mr. Mulligan asleep. This morning, after ten minutes of watching the Nurses suffer the indignity of Mulligan's lecherous attempts, Dr. Sapsford opted to put him asleep immediately, and after a few seconds of mumbling about how "those bleeding drugs don't affect me" Muligan fell silent and slipped into drug induced oblivion, much to the relief of the two Philipino floor nurses in the anaesthetic room.

After a sleepless night, as a result of giving Victoria the explanation she deserved, not quite the one she wanted, but the truth, nonetheless, or at least an economic version of same, I had arrived at work at six thirty. Over an hour before the scheduled surgery time, not because of any renewed commitment to the Clinic, but I was completely paranoid that Brennan might try something and pin it on me. I had no idea what I was expecting, sabotage, ambush, God knows what, but my imagination was working overtime. I carefully checked the Heart/Lung machine from top to bottom. Other than the volatile anaesthetic Vapouriser needing filling up, there was no sign that anything had been interfered with. Discarding the sterile set that was already on the machine for emergency use, (we would normally use that one on the first procedure of the day) I opted for a sealed, unopened one from the stores department in the basement. I was determined to make this a flawless Cardiopulmonary Bypass run. The last thing I needed was any problems for Mulligan because of anything I had overlooked. Forty minutes after being wheeled into the anaesthetic room, Mulligan was lying, naked and yellow, having been painted from head to toe with antiseptic paint, in the middle of Operating Room eight, with a tube in his throat and a catheter in his bladder. He was covered completely with sterile green drapes and Nasser, the Saudi Resident Surgeon, started opening Mulligan's left wrist to expose his radial artery. This would be used as one of the four bypass grafts that Mulligan was due to receive today to relieve the symptoms of his Ischaemic Heart Disease. Five minutes later, as I was pushing the Heart/Lung machine to its operating position beside the patient, Habib appeared in sterile scrubs ready to split Mulligan's chest open to expose his heart. I positioned the Heart/Lung machine alongside the operating table. Using standard sterile technique, I handed the sterile tubes to the scrub nurse and double and triple checked that they were bubble free and intact before switching the pump to standby mode and clamping the tubes. Having double checked with me that the tubes were intact and clear, the scrub nurse clamped the tubes and positioned the connectors and cannulae, ready for the primary surgeon to place them in the heart.

Normally all this would take place as the first assistant was opening the patient's chest, but today, it was all completed before Habib had scrubbed to the table. As Nasser was performing an Allens test on the radial artery, that is ensuring that the patient's wrist had two working arteries, radius and ulnar, before removing one of them. Mulligan's hand passed the test and Nasser started stripping out the Radial artery. Habib approached the chest, and after a polite "good morning" to everybody, and checking with Dr. Sapsford, he started the chest incision.

There was no sign of Reddy yet. It was still a bit early, but given that Habib and Nasser were setting the pace, it was prudent to get as prepared as possible, especially considering the VIP on the table. I went about my primary setup procedure, checking and double checking, and today, I triple checked everything. Nasser was busily taking out Mulligan's radial artery while Habib repositioned the operating table and the special rib-spreader so as he could access the internal mammery artery and dig it out of the inter-costal, the chest muscles. This would be used as a bypass graft to the Left Anterior descending Coronary artery, one of the main arteries supplying the left side of the heart. I cross-checked the sterile tubes with the Phillipino Nurse that was scrubbed with Habib and had them ready well in advance of the required time.

I started musing about the previous day's events. My exit

strategy, I hoped would be enough to keep Brennan and his associates off my back. I had dug up enough information, and combined with the stuff that George had set me could if required, make life very difficult for people like Reddy, Brennan, a few senior civil servants and not least, the management of the Southwestern Clinic. Oliver, my lawyer, had eventually agreed, contrary to his legal instincts with George's comment about the best way to use the information to protect myself was not to use it. Together we had come up with a scheme that, rather like a sawn-off shotgun, would yield the best results, that is total mayhem, for the least effort. The lynchpin was now Mulligan coming through his surgery as smoothly as possible. So far everything was going smoothly. I was especially paranoid about checking things this morning. I had no idea if Brennan would try anything else. I just hoped Mulligan would do his bit for me and make it through to Intensive Care in one piece.

Checking over the drug dosages for the fifth time, I became aware of the sensation that I was being watched. I looked around me and caught the eye of Reddy standing outside the operating theatre in the scrub-up area. The doors into the operating theatres had small windows, about eighteen inches square through which you could observe without entering the room. Reddy was staring at me with the strangest look I have ever seen. I had no doubt that he had heard about my exit strategy by now. It could affect him gravely if invoked and I wondered what was going through his mind right now. Catching his eye, he held my gaze with; I don't know what, contempt, disgust, hatred. Whatever it was, this wasn't going to be the easiest Heart/Lung bypass I had ever managed. He seemed to be in some sort of a trance, he held my gaze for so long. I broke eye contact and tried to fix my mind on the 'now.' My only concern was managing a safe bypass. Nothing else mattered.

I guessed that I had about twenty minutes or so before being called so I nipped out to grab a quick coffee and use the toilet.

Before I left, I arranged the vials for the different drugs that I would use during the operation. The monkey tapped me on the shoulder again and I placed the vials in a certain order. I lined up the letters on the vials of Magnesium Sulphate and Lignocaine with the calibration marks of the pumpheads. This wasn't obsessive compulsive disorder, but I did it so when I returned, I could tell if the drugs had been interfered with.

After a quick coffee and pit-stop, I left the changing-room and made a slight detour to my office to pick up something. One of the floor nurses pushed through the theatre door out into the corridor with a concerned look on her face. I didn't stop to ask what the problem was and pushed my way into the operating theatre.

The sight sent a cold icy finger of fear down my spine. Habib was standing, staring intently at Mulligan's heart with the two spoon shaped electrical defibrillator paddles in his hands. I looked from Habib to the main monitor to Dr. Sapsford and back to the operating table. The blood pressure displayed on the monitor was critically low. The Electrocardiogram was indicating that Mulligan's heart was not doing well at all at this point. Dr. Sapsford was busily injecting various concoctions of drugs in an attempt to kick start Mulligan's heart.

"Will somebody call Peter please," he said, gently, but with unusual firmness. The floor nurse had already sent a runner to find him and she said so. He looked at me, "Robert, he doesn't like this. His oxygen saturations are dropping, and his ST segments are elevated."

"Did he arrest?" I asked

"No, just extreme bradycardia," Habib answered. This was where the heart had slowed down to a dangerous level.

This was exactly the news I didn't want. Mulligan was struggling now, quite early in the operation and this didn't bode well for the rest of the procedure, or for my future.

The door burst open and Reddy appeared. He looked pale and gaunt with red eyes, like he had been up all night.

"What's the problem?" he barked.

Habib explained the situation.

"Are you finished taking the Mammary down?" Reddy snapped.

"Yes," Habib answered, looking surprised at Reddy's gruff manner.

"Move along, I'll be in in a minute." He disappeared out the door to scrub up for the procedure.

All the relief I had experienced in the past twelve hours evaporated and the familiar knot of tension returned. I felt like I had hit the extra long snake that sits waiting near the finish line in a game of snakes and ladders. Had I come this far to be knackered this close to the finish?

"Heparin please, Doctor Sapsford?" Habib asked politely.

"Twenty five thousand units gone in Robert," Dr. Sapsford informed me.

"Thank you," I acknowledged and started the clock.

Two minutes later, I withdrew a blood sample from the line in Mulligan's arm and injected it into a glass test-tube. I placed this into a machine that would start counting how long it took for the blood to clot. I had already taken a sample earlier and I knew that Mulligan's baseline activated clotting time was one hundred and seventy two seconds. This was quite a high baseline, but given the fact that he had been on the ward for over a week now and had been given quite a few doses of drugs to slow down his blood clotting, this was acceptable.

Habib skilfully and swiftly positioned the heart and placed the special suture lines in the aorta and heart to place the tubes that would connect Mulligan to the Heart/Lung machine. I was watching the monitor slowly spell out Mulligan's vital statistics. His heart rate had slowed down considerably and the pattern of his Electrocardiogram showed that his heart was suffering badly. Habib was working steadily and I was also watching the Activated Clotting Timer slowly count up the seconds that it took for the blood sample to clot. The magic number was four hundred and eighty seconds. This is the shortest time that it should take the blood to clot after having been given the drug to slow down the clotting. Any less and there was danger of clots forming in the tubes of the circuit and causing strokes.

"What's the ACT?" Habib asked.

"Two fifty and rising," I answered.

Normally the surgeon would wait until he got the nod from the Perfusionist before placing any tubes in the heart. But one look at the monitor was all it took to start moving, and if needs be, use skill and experience to take shortcuts. Today was one of those days. The blood pressure had bottomed out in the twenties, critically low. Something needed to be done fast. I had no doubt that Dr. Sapsford had given the full dose of the drug and going on experience, I told Habib to go ahead and place the tubes in the heart. I expected the clock to reach the magic number before we would have to start the Heart/Lung machine.

"Go for it Habib." I made the call.

Habib looked around briefly, presumably to check if Reddy had entered the room. No sign, so in seconds he had placed the main tube in Mulligan's aorta and connected it to the Heart/Lung machine. A minute later Habib had muttered a barely imperceptible grunt, this was followed quickly by a shrill alarm announcing that Mulligan's heart had stopped completely.

"De-fib please, quickly," Nasser announced. The scrub nurse handed across the two spoon shaped paddles which when held up to the heart, would send an electric shock across the heart muscle, causing it to momentarily stop and start again in a normal rhythm.

"No, let's get on bypass," Habib overruled.

I looked at the Activated Clotting Timer, still less than three hundred seconds. In anticipation of the next instruction, I drew up another fifty milligrams of Heparin, the anti-clotting drug and injected it directly into the Heart/Lung machine. This was probably overkill, but I wasn't taking any chances. Habib placed the venous tube in and called, "On bypass please."

"ACT is two eighty, OK?"

"Are you happy to go on?" he asked me. He was leaving the call up to me.

"I've a hundred in the prime," I replied. He held my gaze without saying a word as the clock approached three hundred.

"OK, let's go." I released the venous clamps and started the arterial pump. Establishing oxygen and blood flow, Mulligan's blood pressure started rising under the influence of the Bypass machine. This took about ten seconds. A high pitched beep announced that the activated clotting counter had detected a clot and the test was over. Looking at the number I inhaled sharply, the clock had stopped at three hundred and four seconds, nearly two hundred seconds short of the mark. I had anticipated this and given a supplementary dose, but it still gave me a shock. I immediately withdrew a sample of blood from the pump and repeated the test. I hoped that the extra dose I had given would carry the result over the line. There was nothing else I could do now except settle the patient down and wait. Normally ACT results are ambiguous at best, as there are teams who work with much lower numbers with no ill effects to the patients. I just hoped that the low result from a full dose of the drug didn't indicate an underlying problem. Six minutes later the result sounded, three hundred and seventy seconds: still short. I threw another hundred milligrams in and hoped that Mulligan wasn't going to have clotting problems after the surgery. God knows, I needed a good result from this surgery for Mulligan.

After five minutes on the bypass machine, I noticed that Reddy still hadn't scrubbed to the table. Habib had started to size and clean up the veins and piece of artery that would be used as bypass grafts. A minute or so later, Reddy entered the room. Habib carefully placed the veins and artery back into the galley pot and stepped back to move to the left hand side of the table, the traditional position for the first assistant. Reddy held his hand up and moved to the assistant's position.

"Actually Habib, I'm not feeling well. Can you do the grafts? I'll assist," Reddy said in quite a low voice. My stomach lurched. What was this about? Reddy had definitely heard about my escape strategy and was rattled by it.

"Are you sure sir?" Habib asked politely, stepping back to the primary surgeon's position.

"Yes, stomach bug or something," Reddy nodded. I thought I detected a slight inclination of his head in my direction, but that was probably paranoia. At least now I wouldn't have to look Reddy in the face for the duration of the operation as the first assistant always had his back to me.

"LAD, Circ, OM1 and right?" Habib proffered, referring to the various arteries that were due to have grafted, Left Anterior Descending, Circumflex, Obtuse Marginal and Right, four bypass grafts or to Joe Public, a quadruple bypass. Five minutes later Habib put his head down and started placing the grafts on Mulligan's paralysed and motionless heart.

With Habib now at the helm, the operation proceded with calm efficiency. There was a minimum of conversation other than the instructions to the scrub nurse for sutures, instruments or time, pressure or flow details from myself to Habib.

The Heart/Lung machine ran smoothly except for a constant struggle to keep the clotting time as long as possible. I knew Mulligan was a heavy drinker and this sometimes explains why it takes a lot more of a drug to have the same effect on a moderate or non-drinker. Constant heavy drinking puts your liver into overdrive. This means that certain drugs are burned up quicker. The other reason could have been that for his week or so stay in the hospital, Mulligan would have been receiving a drug to slow down the clotting of his blood, typically Heparin. It is not uncommon for somebody to become almost immune to a drug such as Heparin. All very interesting, but the problem was that I wasn't sure if Mulligan's clotting was under enough control. I was shovelling vial after vial of Heparin into the Bypass circuit to keep the numbers above the minimum required to run a safe bypass, or so say all the books. Being paranoid at the moment, this all ran through my head. Would Mulligan develop a coagulapathy, or major blood clotting problems during or after the surgery? This could result in a stroke, and Mulligan not waking up after the surgery. Exactly what Brennan ordered, and worse still, after I had pissed him off with my exit strategy.

Forty seven minutes after starting the grafting procedure, Habib removed the clamp that was isolating the heart from the rest of Mulligan's circulation. I was expecting a very sluggish response from the heart but was surprised when Mulligan's heart responded immediately by contracting vigorously.

Reddy, who up to this point had remained silent throughout the whole procedure, looked up at Habib.

"Can you finish up here?" he asked with uncharacteristic politeness.

"No problem sir," Habib answered. Reddy left the operating table as if he had been burned. He disappeared out the door of the operating theatre without a word.

Following instructions from Habib and having confirmed that the lungs were operating normally, I weaned Mulligan from the Heart/Lung machine. After five minutes of operating under his own steam, the numbers on the monitor were high enough for Habib to remove the tubes. I pumped the remaining blood into a re-infusion bag and handed it to Dr. Sapsford. I looked at the full re-infusion bag and thought that I could as easily be handing a loaded weapon to the Anaesthestist to administer to Mulligan. 'How quickly things change,' I thought. On another day, this bag of blood might have been laced with Succemethonium or Puncuronium Bromide, or some other lethal cocktail that I had come up with. Now, I hoped and prayed that my escape strategy was enough that this wasn't necessary and I could get on with my own life.

Leaving everything setup and intact, I slipped out to the coffee room for a quick caffeine shot. I scanned the papers in the coffee room. Half expecting some glaring headline exposing Brennan and his antics, I was almost disappointed to read about sixteen US soldiers killed in a booby trap bomb in Iraq, and a Fianna Fail junior minister photographed leaving a gay night club in London. After fifteen minutes or so, I headed back to the operating theatre. Habib and Nasser would most likely be on the final closure now and I could drain any remaining blood in the tubes into a reinfusion bag to give back to Mulligan.

Habib and Nasser were working in perfect tandem putting in the final layers of sutures to close the wound in Mulligan's chest. Reddy had disappeared and I heard Dr. Sapsford mutter to Habib, "I wonder if Peter's ok." Habib gave a look that said, 'don't ask me.'

Having drained and binned all the tubes, I pulled the Heart/Lung machine out into the storage bay to have it cleaned. The scrub and floor nurses pulled the drapes from Mulligan and got him ready to be transferred back to the Intensive Care Unit. Mick the porter wheeled the bed into the operating theatre and positioned it alongside the operating table. The theatre technician attached the monitoring equipment to a portable monitor that was fastened to a pole on the bed and with well practiced co-ordination, ten seconds later Mulligan was lying in bed covered with a fresh white sheet and blankets. He looked asleep and the gentle hiss of the oxygen entering the endothraceal tube into his lungs gave away the fact that he wasn't just having a nap. Why did I therefore detect a 'grey hue?' The numbers were good, no excess blood in the chest drains, all was well. I gave myself a mental slap and walked towards the ITU behind the bed that Mick was steering towards the double doors that led into the corridor that led into the Unit. Dr. Sapsford was briefing the young Polish anaesthetic resident about this case and was looking at the notes as he gently squeezed the ambu-bag that was pushing oxygen into Mulligan's lungs.

A slow rhythmic beep was emitted by the monitor as if it was calling out the walking pace as we made our way the thirty or so metres from the operating theatre to the Intensive Care Unit. As we entered the ITU double doors, business started in earnest. Two Indian Nurses were standing as a reception committee in the bed space where Mulligan's bed would be parked. One was programming in the settings for the ventilator that Dr. Sapsford was calling out as we crossed the open floor space from the double doors to the vacant bedspace.

There were the normal sounds of a busy intensive care unit: beeps, hisses and alarms. Alarms were a normal part of the soundscape. ECG alarms sounded for many reasons, a patient moving, a nurse changing a lead position. ECG alarms...I looked at Mulligan's face as Mick steered the bed across the floor. Grey hue...no mistake. Dr. Sapsford was chatting animatedly to the Polish resident who was concentrating on understanding the instructions from Dr. Sapsford. The scrub nurse was giving a verbal report on the case to the Intensive Care Nurse. I moved quickly to the head of the bed and checked the monitor. Instead of showing a nice rhythmic pulse, like you see as an advertisement for health products, the ECG was displaying a wild squiggle, like something a child would draw... Shit, Ventricular Fibrillation. The blood pressure was gone.

"He's fibrillating," I called pulling the blanket back.

"Oh dear!" Dr. Sapsford exclaimed.

I pulled the bed the last few feet into its position as one of the ITU nurses grabbed the crash trolley. Two gel pads were quickly placed on Mulligan's chest.

"Charge to two hundred...Everybody clear?...shoot!" Dr. Sapsford placed the paddles on the gel pads and fired the two hundred joules of energy across Mulligan's chest to try and restart his heart. Everybody looked at the monitor, still the uncontrolled quiver.

"Charge to three hundred please...everybody clear?... shoot."

Mulligan jerked violently in the bed as three hundred watts of electricity was blasted across his chest in one second.

The blood started to drain from my face as I realised what was happening. I charged back to the operating theatre to get a Heart/Lung machine ready. I was immediately heartened to see that one of my crew had already set one up for the second patient of the day who hadn't arrived yet. I manhandled the machine out into the corridor and performed an emergency prime. The machine was ready to use in seconds. I ran back to the Intensive Care Unit to see Habib standing over Mulligan holding the defibrillator paddles up in the air and staring intently at the monitor.

I began to sweat as I realised what was happening before my eyes. Mulligan, despite our best efforts, was slipping away before our eyes. If things didn't get better, I was looking at my escape strategy being rolled out later that day. God knows what Brennan would do when my package landed on the desks of various law enforcement officers, journalists and poilitical offices and the excreta hit the air conditioning.

I had to fight to keep calm as I watched Habib and Dr. Sapsford, now assisted by the Cardiac arrest team work furiously to save Mulligan's life. The portable monitor that was used during the transfer had been disconnected and Mulligan was connected to the main bedside monitor. The portable monitor had been abandoned on a shelf. To pass the time, I took the portable monitor and studied it for a few moments. I wondered why the alarm hadn't sounded when Mulligan's heart stopped during the transfer. The monitor was left switched on. I flicked through the menu pages and quickly discovered that although the main alarms were switched on, the alarm volume was set to zero. This was very unusual. In order to change the setting to this level, you had to scroll through three of four menu pages. It would be almost impossible to 'accidently' do this. Whoever had changed this setting had known exactly what they were doing. Something was stinking to high heaven.

I looked up towards the action at Mulligan's bed. The defibrillator paddles had been put back in their positions on the crash trolley and Habib had his arms folded. Some semblance of peace had descended on the place. I tentivaely crossed the floor towards the bed.

"What's happening Habib?" I asked with trepidation.

"He's back in Sinus Rhythm now," he told me.

"You taking him back to theatre?" I asked.

"No, I don't think so," he said.

Just then the Nurse who was looking after Mulligan handed Habib a blood gas result. He scanned it and I noticed his eyebrows rise.

"What was the potassium running at during the bypass Robert?" he asked me.

I opened the chart and pulled the bypass data record out.

"Four point three to five, we came off bypass at four point eight, why?" I answered. These numbers were perfectly normal.

"His serum potassium is nine point six now," Habib said

"Oh Jesus," I whispered.

Something was stinking now and no mistake. Mulligan had been weaned from the Heart/Lung bypass machine with a normal potassium level and now it was nearly twice the normal level. High serum Potassium causes abnormal heart rhythms. The only logical way that someones Potassium level could rise from Four point eight to nine point six in such a short time was a deliberate overdose, and the alarm volume deliberately set to zero.

"Run a dextrose and insulin drip straightaway," Habib ordered.

I began to try to backtrack in my head and time how long Mulligan was on the portable monitor. The time from moving onto the bed to the time I noticed the abnormal rhythm was about six minutes. It was highly unlikely that Mulligan's heart was stopped for that full six minutes, but even two or three could result in irreversible brain damage. I desperately wanted Habib to check the pupils, this would give an indication if there was brain damage, but I was also afraid to draw attention to myself. Dr. Sapsford had left the Intensive Care Unit and I didn't want to start asking him if he knew how long Mulligan was fibrillating. A few awkward questions would raise suspicions immediately. I decided that the only thing to do was to wait for the normal length of time to pass in which Mulligan would be expected to recover and wake up and then check. "Another sleepless night," I sighed to myself. I double checked with Habib that he was happy.

"We'll check the Potassium every twenty minutes and keep the defib close and take it from there," he said. There was nothing more I could do except wait and pray! I headed back to my office to find something that might occupy my mind for as long as possible.

52

We were in the lounge of a bar I knew well. I didn't know the name but I had been there a few times before. The whole operating team was there, Reddy, Habib Dr. Sapsford, Prof O'Riada and about a dozen of the Philipino Scrub Nurses. Reddy was operating on Mulligan and he was connected to the Heart/Lung bypass machine. My whole family was sitting in the lounge area watching the operation as well as Brennan and his crew. Half of them were smoking. I tried to tell them that you couldn't smoke during an operation. But they kept pointing to the sign on the wall that said that the smoking ban wasn't coming into operation for another three weeks. I looked and tried to read the sign. The lights were out in the bar and it was difficult to see. I looked back at the Heart/Lung machine and got a shock when I saw that all the blood from the tubed had leaked out onto the floor. The pump was still turning. I was pumping nothing but air to Mulligan's brain. I looked at Reddy, he hadn't noticed. I tried to reprime the system without alerting Reddy. I was panicking inside but tried to stay calm so Reddy wouldn't know that I was in trouble with the bypass machine. I looked back at my family. They were all staring at me, willing me to do something. I needed to try to prime the circuit without stopping the pump, but this is impossible. I didn't know how long the pump was turning before I looked at it. How much air had been pumped into

Mulligan? I was certain he was going to be brain damaged. Two policemen entered the bar, they led Victoria and the children away out the door. I wanted to shout to follow them. But shouting would alert the rest of the operating team that I had a major problem with the bypass. I felt glued to my seat. The bubble alarm started to sound as the tubes became full of air. I tried to silence it. The alarm kept sounding. Reddy still hadn't heard it. The alarm kept sounding.

The alarm on my mobile phone was ringing. I looked at my watch in the darkness. The hands glowed six thirty. It was Saturday and I wasn't due in work. I hadn't slept much the night before after Mulligan's surgery and the cardiac arrest episode in Intensive Care Unit after. I had lain awake most of the night staring at the ceiling. I desperately wanted to know how Mulligan was, but I was terrified what I would hear. I felt that calling so early would arouse suspicion but sleep was gone. The kids were asleep and normally a late sleep on Saturday was a rare treat. Fishing my mobile from my jeans, I tiptoed downstairs. Flicking on the kettle, I grabbed a mug and threw a spoonful of instant coffee in. I sat watching the eastern sky slowly turn from charcoal to stone grey and gradually to a dull slate colour as I sippped my coffee. Ironically, today the kids were sound asleep long after when there would normally be movement. I was missing a rare lie-in. I glanced at my watch, seven twenty. The Intensive Care Nurses would be changing their shift now. They normally had a hand-over meeting where the details of every patient were discussed. It was probably as good a time as I was going to get to call. I tentatatively dialled the direct dial number.

"Hello, Intensive Care, Nurse Bintu speaking."

"Hi, Robert Valentine here, Perfusionist on-call. All well there?" I opened as benignly as possible.

"Hello sir," Bintu said. "Did someone call you?"

"No," I said, trying to avoid a long winded explanation. "I'm on call and I want to check how everything is, I want to take my children swimming." I tried to remain calm, but my stomach was turning somersaults. Was Mulligan brain damaged? Had he been without circulation for any length of time during the transfer when the monitor alarms were disabled? Had he suffered any more cardiac arrests with the abnormally high potassium readings? Was his potassium reading still off the scale?

I was highly suspicious that there had been some foul play with the monitor and the potassium. It would have been easy to slip some potassium into the cocktail of drugs that Mulligan had received as part of his anaesthetic regime.

"Hold on please sir, I'll get someone to talk to you. I've just come on duty," Bintu said. I desperately wanted to scream at her, *I just wanna know how Mulligan is fucking doing!!!* but I held my breath. Two agonisingly long minutes later a voice came back.'

"Brigid here, how can I help you?"

As casually as I could I explained that I was on call for the weekend and I wanted to know if everything was OK. I wanted to bring the kids swimming, I would be away from the phone for about forty minutes or so. My mouth was dry and I felt like I was guilty of some horrendous crime and was trying to explain myself.

"Oh, no problem Robert. Hang on a sec and I'll talk to whoever's looking after him." She put the phone down on the desk and disappeared. Another two endless minutes passed. I heard the phone being lifted up.

"Robert, I don't know what you did to him in theatre..." I suddenly felt dizzy and had to sit down,

"Why...what's the problem?" I managed to get out through a bone dry mouth.

"He's fine, in fact he's giving the staff a lot of grief...He's already asked two of the Philipino Nurses to marry him. Go on and enjoy your swim." She was talking to an empty phone. I had dropped the phone and collapsed into a chair with relief.

Epilogue

THE IRISH TIMES, ONE WEEK LATER.

Minister announces scaling down of NTPF.

In an unexpected reversal of policy, yesterday in the Dail, the Minister of Health and Children announced that funding for the National Treatment Purchase Fund was to be gradually reduced over the next year. An increase in funding had been announced recently which was met with mixed reactions from the opposition. The minister explained that a recent trawling of records had shown that overall waiting lists had been dramatically cut to the point where threre was effectively no real waiting time for most types of major surgery. He praised the work done by the Medical and Nursing staff on the patients who benefitted from the fund and called the program a 'runaway success.' The opposition spokesman for Health attacked the Minister for his 'childlike indecision' in policy making and this about turn being in true Fianna Fail fashion.

Heart Surgeon accepts controversial new contract.

At a press conference of the Health Services Employment Agency yesterday evening the Minister of Health and Children congratulated Heart Surgeon Mr. Peter Reddy on becoming one of the first Consultants to accept the controversial new contract. In return for a substantial increase in his public salary, Mr. Reddy will be one of the first Doctors to provide 24hr in-house Consultant Cover;